THE BLASPHEMY LAW

Salman Shami

For Aliya, my free-spirited and freedom-loving wife.

I would like to thank everyone who gave so much of their time and love to make this book possible. In no particular order, they include Aliya, my wife and editor-in-chief, my friends who were my beta readers, my daughter, Nadia, who helped me with proof-reading and with the lingo used by people of her generation, my son, Haroon, for valuable insights into some characters, and my friend Graeme Cameron for his in-depth technical advice.

I would also like to thank members of the Australian Fiction Writers Facebook page for their amazing support and advice throughout the whole learning experience. Special thanks also to Ding! Author Services for a great cover that has resonated so well with readers.

For more information:
https://www.facebook.com/TheBlasphemyLaw/

Glossary:
Please check out the glossary at the end of the book for an explanation of the Urdu words

BEFORE

His mind reeled as he read and then reread the geologist's report. He had always been rich, but this was wealth beyond measure. It could make him the richest man in Asia, maybe the world. That kind of money meant unimaginable godlike power. He double-checked the map. All that gold, easy and cheap to extract, but it started where his lands ended.

INADVERTENTLY

Shakar Parian, Thursday 24 November, 5:00am

It was five in the morning and still dark, the most beautiful time to wake. Jane breathed in the earthy smells of freshly tilled fields, cow dung fires and boiling *chai*. The chirping of birds mixed with the gentle hubbub of early risers, people conversing in quiet, polite tones. Women were making flatbread and churning *lassi* for workers heading out into the fields. The village was gently waking from its peaceful slumber.

The air on her bare shoulders was pleasantly nippy. Two weeks ago, it had still been quite warm. A gentle breeze wafted into the small room through the open window and the cracks around the crudely made door.

She shivered ever so slightly, pleasantly aware of the warmth under her light blanket. A bird twittered nearby. One had made a nest in the thatched roof of her hut. Outside, close by, some hens clucked. A rooster crowed. In the distance, cows lowed.

She pulled up her blanket and fell asleep again. It was the sweetest time to sleep.

She shifted languorously. A smile came to her lips. A delicious shiver ran through her. A gasp of pleasure escaped her lips as he entered, filling her deep. Her hands caressed his muscular back and felt him quiver under her touch. A warm tongue, not his, licked around her ear and traced a path along her cheek towards her mouth. She moaned and turned her face sideways to meet it, hungrily feeling for that sweetness. Long dark hair curtained her face. Their lips came together. She sucked on the tongue. Now there were four hands on her.

A different hand was on her shoulder. Although still soft, the touch was no longer sensuous. Instead, it was urgent. Jane opened her eyes. Sunlight streamed into the room. She must have overslept. Clara stood next to her. She had just spoken, but the words had not registered.

'Hi, Clara.' Jane rubbed the sleep from her eyes. Are you OK?' Her Fitbit showed it was 7:21. The *charpoy* creaked as she sat up, holding the blanket to cover her bare shoulders. Any visible skin made the villagers uncomfortable.

'*Mem Sahib*, they are back again,' Clara said in a strained voice.

All sleep dropped away. Anger rose inside her. 'OK, I'll come, give me a minute.'

Clara left and closed the door behind her. Jane stood up, feeling dizzy. Oversleeping always made her feel somewhat heavy headed. Her clothes, freshly washed and ironed were lying in a neatly folded pile on her chair. She pulled on a pair of jeans and a long saffron yellow *kameez*, embroidered in red, green and blue thread, and ran her fingers through her shoulder-length blonde hair. The always efficient and hardworking Clara had been busy last night. Two new water bottles lay on a second pile of washed and carefully folded towels. What a woman she was. She never seemed to sleep yet always looked fresh and cheerful, except today. Come to think of it she had never seen Clara look worried before.

Jane poured some water from one of the bottles on a small towel and wiped her face. It immediately refreshed her. She took a few sips and walked out. Clara was waiting along with Allah Boota, the village headman. He bowed his head and touched his forehead in greeting. 'Good Morning, *Mem Sahib*.'

'Good Morning Allah Boota,' she said with a smile. He did not smile back. Allah Boota was always good-natured and friendly and went out of his way to make her feel welcome. Today, however, his brow was furrowed with worry.

All the villagers were lovely people, warm, and open. She was blonde, with grey-green eyes and an almost milky complexion. She spoke a different language and belonged to a different culture, but that did not seem to matter to them. Even though most of them did not speak any English, their friendly smiles made her feel at home, like she belonged in the village.

She was going to miss Shakar Parian, but she always ended up falling in love with wherever she went. Such was life; one could only ever be in one place at a time.

In spite of how pleasant the last two months had been, she was dying to go home, to Razane and Sergei, the centre of her universe.

Jane followed Clara and Allah Boota who led her over a dirt path through a cluster of nicely made but simple mud huts, set among a grove of magnificent old banyan trees.

The day had well and truly started for the village folk. People were going about their chores; some women were sweeping out their houses, while others were dressing their young children. Majeed, the old cobbler, with his glasses held together with baling wire and tape, was setting up his rudimentary tools in the shade of a wall, where he always sat. The village teacher, and postman, was straightening the mats in the outdoor classroom in preparation for his students.

This was life in its most basic form, barely changed over the last hundreds and maybe thousands of years. The village folk did not shun modernity, but they also were not rushing to embrace it. Why should they? People here had next to nothing to their names, but they ate well and slept even better. They lived happy and healthy lives with next to no crime or violence.

Of course, not all who were born here stayed. Desire,

greed, and restlessness were wired into the human DNA. The glamour of faraway cities and the near magic of modern technology seduced many. They traded their simple but idyllic existence for life in big cities. It affected the young more than the old which was a shame because it would eventually undermine the fabric of village society. Hopefully, her project would help to reverse that. If the villagers could get free electricity from the sun and have access to the Internet, they would be able to share in opportunities available to city folk. Then, maybe, fewer of them would move away from home.

They crossed over a ditch and through a gap in a low mud wall. The wall and the ditch ran all around the village. Their primary purpose was to channel rainwater away from the huts during the monsoon. It was also a psychological boundary. It marked their collective home and represented safety and security.

It was mustard growing season and the fields surrounding the village were in full bloom. The rich golden yellow flowers formed a carpet in all directions, as far as the eye could see. The path continued for a few more minutes and ended in the village parking lot. Her Toyota Landcruiser stood in its usual spot. Mr Ali, her driver, waited beside it. Seeing her, he raised his hand in greeting. She greeted him back.

Jane opened the door in the back for Clara and motioned for Allah Boota to climb in as well. She sat next to Mr Ali in the front and told him where to go.

They drove out of the car park and turned left onto a narrow road. Its surface had not been maintained, and only a few small patches of bitumen remained in what had become a bumpy and rutted dirt track.

Her stomach rumbled; she was ready for breakfast, but she would deal with this problem first. Hopefully, this was the last time.

The Landcruiser rounded a bend in the road and slowed to enter a small gravelled parking lot, through a break in the ditch running on the left side of the road. They parked next to a chain-link fence that enclosed a large paddock. It contained what she had been working on for the last two months, a rectangular array of two hundred and twenty large solar panels. They were mounted on motorised frames, that would pivot to follow the path of the sun. The frames were on legs that were attached to solid concrete blocks, embedded in the ground.

It was her baby, her best work so far. She and her team were going through the final stages of testing, and last-minute adjustments before the project was handed over to the villagers. Tomorrow was the completion party.

Jane jumped out as soon as the Landcruiser came to a halt, slamming the door angrily behind her. The object of her ire was a group of men, inside the fence. They were all dressed identically in white *shalwar kameez* and white skull caps. Most of them had long bushy beards. They were religious zealots and had been there a week before.

Last time they had entered the enclosure and had pasted large posters on her panels. The posters depicted drones dropping bombs and killing children. Emblazoned in large red letters were the words, "Death to America".

She had called the police. By the time they came, the glue holding the posters had dried. It had taken her team a whole day to get the sticky residue off. The police had warned the men of dire consequences if they returned. The fact that they had, meant they were not afraid, which was a problem.

Today they were at it again. Rooted to the spot, Jane's mind spun in a turmoil of frustration and indecision. She watched in disbelief as two groups of two worked away with one man applying glue out of a bucket with a roller and a second man holding and then placing the poster on the panel. Why would they come out here in the middle of nowhere and disrupt her work like this? It made no sense at all.

Their leader was an older man with a round weather-beaten face. His beard was scraggly but long. He had an irregular scar on his left cheek that looked like he had stitched it together himself. He carried a rifle slung on his back and wore a wide ammunition belt diagonally over his shoulder and hip. He appeared ready to go to war.

Anger and frustration welled up in her. She needed to finish the work today. Her flight back to Melbourne left in two days. These people were stuffing everything up.

In a red haze of fury, she walked over to where one of the men had just finished aligning a poster. Standing on tiptoes, she reached up, grabbed hold of it and pulled it down. The glue made a squelching sound as the poster peeled away. Jane tore it up, ignoring the streaks of putrid smelling glue, which came off on her hands. She grabbed another one and ripped it up as well. Bits of glue flew through the air, a blob landing on her left cheek, but she didn't care. No one was going to stop her work, never mind what guns they carried, or how many people they were.

She became aware everyone had stopped what they were doing. The men were no longer pasting new posters up. The old man had taken out his phone and was recording her.

Jane continued pulling them down. As she yanked off the last one and ripped it to pieces, she shouted, 'don't you come back here with your filthy posters, ever again!'

The old man was still recording. Jane felt like ripping the phone out of his hands and smashing it on the ground, but controlled her impulse.

What was happening here? Why were they suddenly behaving so oddly? Her head began to hurt, and she felt light-headed. She flung the last scrunched up poster on the ground and turned to Clara and Allah Boota.

'Please get some water and wash this glue off while it's still wet,' she said.

Allah Boota and Clara did not move, not even as much as a muscle. They just looked at her, their faces frozen in horror.

Their unexplained reluctance made her even angrier. She turned to the old man. 'How dare you bastards come back here and put up your filthy posters? I'm going to call the police again and have you locked up this time.'

The old man said nothing. He put the phone in his pocket and said something to his men. He looked at Jane with a malevolence that immediately unsettled her. As he turned away, she had the weirdest feeling he was smiling inside, as if he had just played a cruel trick on her, or won some big victory.

He unexpectedly turned back and stabbed a calloused finger in her face, so close she could see his long and ugly fingernails. 'You call *pulis*. I call *pulis*.' With that, he turned and motioned to his men.

They picked up their things and climbed into the back of their white Toyota van. He walked to the vehicle with a limp and hoisted himself into the front passenger seat. As soon as he slammed the door shut, the van reversed out of the open gate, its front wheels spinning, showering them with gravel.

What had just happened? She shook with anger and relief, and hunger. The three still stood in the same spot. Clara was weeping. Allah Boota looked like he wanted to. Mr Ali was flicking little stones off the Landcruiser and looking the other way, trying hard to avoid eye contact.

'What's wrong with you people?' Jane said in an exasperated tone as she tried rubbing the glue off her hands.

The old man waited till they were on the main road and his phone had a signal. He dialled a number. 'It is done.'

'Well done *Maulana Sahib*, well done.' The voice on the other end of the line sounded pleased.

DIRTY GAMES

Islamabad, Thursday 24 November, 10:00am

The pain began in his sternum and grew stronger. His breath came in short bursts. His hands became clammy. The room became darker. He was having an anxiety attack. He had to pull himself together. The CEO of Carbonon could not go to water like this. He breathed in deeply. For a brief moment, his sternum hurt even more but then it settled down. He was re-establishing control.

'Mr Kucic. Are you OK?'

'Ahh, yes... Yes, I am. I think I just had a small heart attack,' Simon replied with a mirthless smile, the deep breathing made him cough, 'I thought I heard you say, we should temporarily suspend the project.'

'Yes, that is what I was saying. We need to put it on hold temporarily,' the minister said.

Simon fought the urge to punch the man in the face. Temporarily suspend it when they were one day from handover. Yes, he'd do as this fucking bastard wanted, when hell froze over. He managed a smile. 'Surely not. Why? For how long?'

'That I cannot say.' The minister balanced his letter opener on one finger.

'You are Pakistan's Minister for Agriculture, a very powerful man. Who's higher than you?' Simon kept his voice even. 'If you can't say then who can?'

The shock that had numbed his mind was beginning to recede, in its place, white-hot anger. His hands shook with rage.

He had to keep breathing, manage that temper of his, like his psychologist, had counselled him. He so badly wanted to pick up the tractor-shaped glass paperweight on the large desk and smash it into the minister's smug looking face.

'Look I need to confirm this is not going to cause power issues in the province.' The minister made as if to get up. 'I have another--'

Who was pulling this corrupt fucker's strings? He was going to have a real heart attack right in this bastard's office.

'But this is a stand-alone project. It's not connected to any grid and doesn't cost the government anything. You're getting it for free.'

'Yes, and other villages will want it as well, and that could be a … problem. Now I really must ask you to leave.'

So, he wasn't talking about electrical, but political power. Just what he'd thought. This fucker was so bloody full of himself he didn't even care to hide his motives.

'OK, but surely… Look, Carbonon will be happy to accommodate them one by one; after all, it's what we do.'

'Mr Kucic, it is not that simple.' He was standing up now.

Someone was pulling this man's strings. He'd been warned about doing business in Pakistan when they were doing feasibility studies eighteen months ago, but back then Khalid Mahmud was the minister. He was a visionary and supportive of the project. He had even helped identify the village that could receive the pilot installation.

Khalid Mahmud had suddenly retired, due to ill health. The new minister had quickly developed a reputation for being as slippery and corrupt as his predecessor had been straight and honest. Simon could now understand why. How was he going to save the situation?

Jane had completed the UNDP, United Nations Development Program, project two days ahead of schedule. They were going to hand over to the villagers tomorrow. Simon needed signatures from the Pakistani government departments involved in the project so the UNDP would release the final payment to his company.

If Carbonon didn't get paid he'd have to cut staff. It would limit the number of new projects they could bid for. Worst case, they'd struggle to stay afloat. At the very least any plans for expansion would have to be put on hold, indefinitely.

But he was getting ahead of himself. He knew a few people at the UNDP. Surely, they'd be aware of the corruption in Pakistan. Maybe they'd understand this situation. There could be a workaround for him to get his money.

Fuck this minister. He was going to turn on the power whether he liked it or not. Whether he signed or not. Simon stood up as well. He was about to turn to leave when his better judgement asserted itself. He'd try one last time to rescue the situation.

'Can we please discuss this over dinner?' Simon's voice had become calm, almost friendly and cajoling. This man was not all powerful. He could not stop him turning on the power, but there was no reason to break ties. 'I heard La Maison is really great. You could let me know how I can help you in other ways.' He picked up his briefcase. 'Maybe we can work something out.' He hoped that had sounded like he wanted it to. It was called greasing the wheel.

If he could convince Tajammul it would save a lot of time. Maybe the minister just wanted something small. It would still be a bribe of sorts but hopefully not as traceable as money. Sometimes officials were swayed by overseas jobs for their children. Maybe he just wanted recognition. Getting his signature would still be far easier than jumping through all the hoops at the UNDP.

'I can do dinner today.' Tajammul's tone was a little less inimical. He reached forward to open the door for Simon, still as eager to shoo him out. 'I love the food at La Maison.'

Tajammul Hussein wiped his forehead with a tissue, scrunched it up and threw it at the bin. It missed and fell on the floor. The cleaner could get it. He picked up the phone and dialled. 'He doesn't want to give up. He has invited me to dinner. Maybe he is going to offer me something.'

'Hey you fat cunt,' the voice on the other end of the line shouted, 'you better not be for sale. I am coming too. Where is it?'

'I am not going to give him what he wants; do not worry.'

'Where is the restaurant?'

'I will not sell you out, *yaar*, but... sure come along. It is the La Maison in F7/1.'

'I know La Maison; it serves alcohol.'

Yes, it did. He could definitely use some.

THE CALLIGRAPHY

Shakar Parian, Thursday 24 November, 10:11am

C lara ran to gather up the scrunched-up posters. She was still sobbing. She really was easily upset. Jane put a comforting arm around her.

'Thank you for cleaning them up. We can use them to start the bonfire in the evening.'

'*Mem Sahib*, no put in fire,' Clara said in a horrified voice, 'big, big, trouble.'

Clara had gone ashen. She was having an anxiety attack.

'What's wrong Clara? You don't have to worry about them. My team will be here in a few minutes, and we'll call the police.'

'It is not men; it is this.' Clara unfolded one of the posters. The glue made a part of the printed layer peel off. She held it up for Jane to see. It was the name of the Prophet Muhammad in Arabic, written large, in a circular calligraphic style. In her haste to rip the posters off her panels, she had not noticed what was on them. She had seen the image a lot throughout Pakistan and before that in Iraq. Razane even had a pendant necklace with the same motif.

'It is the name, Muhammad. You tore the name of Muhammad.'

'Yes, I can see it now,' Jane thought about it for a moment, a knot forming in her stomach. She knew people in many Muslim countries placed an enormous importance on such things. Clara was Christian, so she had not been offended. She was however beside herself with fear. Had she made a serious blunder to tear the posters? She certainly would not have torn them had she realised what they represented. Offending anyone's religion was not something she'd ever knowingly do. Her temper had gotten the better of her and had blinded her. She needed to control herself or one day she could land herself in real trouble.

'Clara, don't worry, it's going to be OK.' Jane tried to sound reassuring, but Clara did not cheer up.

As they drove back the short distance to the village, the thought gnawed in Jane's mind. The old man had recorded the whole thing. What would he do? Last time the posters were different, they were about drones and little children. They were political. This time they were religious. It was almost like a bait-and-switch, but why? Was she being set up? She walked back to her own private little outdoor bathroom to wash her hands, her mind still occupied.

Clara interrupted her thoughts. 'The food is ready, *Mem Sahib.*'

Jane ate her breakfast sitting at a small table in her hut, her laptop open in front of her, catching up on the latest news. Next to the table on the floor sat a battery pack. It had served her power needs for the last two months and was nearly empty. Just as well; it was time to go home.

As she broke off a piece of the still hot flatbread and scooped up some of the spicy and delicious omelette, she read an Australian Government travel advisory.

They were often completely misinformed. It annoyed her to think how many people were discouraged from travelling to exciting destinations because their governments were too risk-averse, and scared of being blamed for any dangerous incident, which in the scheme of things were rare.

In the two months while in Pakistan she hadn't encountered anything even remotely unpleasant. Yes, all shopkeepers tried to charge her more than they did locals. But that didn't offend her one bit. The disparity in wealth between them and her was so enormous it would be churlish of her to begrudge them a few extra rupees.

On the other hand, people were friendly and extremely hospitable. Under all the poverty they had hearts of gold. She'd never been in a place where, within five minutes, strangers could become the best of friends and divulge their deepest secrets, where they'd invite someone into their homes and offer them the last scrap of food in their cupboards.

Back home, people were far more reserved, and it took alcohol, usually lots, before they'd loosen up. Even then, they rarely connected with each other, in quite the same way.

Today's travel advisory was the same as last week's. In bold letters, it read, "Reconsider Your Need to Travel". It increased the number of zones designated as "Do Not Travel" to include the south of Punjab and the north of Sindh. This was followed by a few paragraphs that warned about terrorist attacks, sectarian violence and demonstrations targeting Western interests.

This morning's affair could be considered such an attack, even though the panels really belonged to the villagers rather than her.

It still didn't make any sense, why the men had acted the way they did.

The omelette was delicious, and it tasted even better when she ate it with her hands. She washed it down with a sip of the robustly flavoured and sweet cooked tea. This was something she'd take back with her to Melbourne. It was *chai* latte the way it was meant to be made, so much tastier than what she drank at home and was particularly well matched with spicy food. It was so simple to make, just cook milk, water, sugar, and tea leaves for about an hour on an open flame. She'd make it the first morning after she got back.

They would not rise early the first morning, not after being apart for so long. She smiled at the thought. How blessed she was? How blessed they were?

Could the poster incident delay her return? Maybe she

should send a message to Simon, her boss, and let him know what had happened.

The sound of the bus interrupted Jane's thoughts. Her team of seven engineers lived in a large company provided bungalow in nearby Mandi Bahauddin and travelled to the village every day. They'd also be happy to be going back to their homes, after tomorrow.

Mandi Bahauddin was not the most pleasant town for a lone white woman. It was small and lacked many modern facilities. It was also backward. She hadn't seen a single woman on the streets without their heads covered. Thankfully, she didn't have to live there. When the villagers had offered her accommodation in their village as their guest, she had accepted it with glee.

It had turned out to be the experience of a lifetime. Village life was extremely basic but so charming. She would never forget the neat mud huts under the tall banyan trees surrounded by the lush green fields, the calming village sounds, the smells of cooking and the earth after it rained and the feel of the cool tube well water. It would always have a special place in her heart.

Her mind was wandering, and her team were waiting for her on the bus. She got up and walked to the car park.

Before long they were all working busily. Jane decided she would not worry about the morning's events. Clara and the rest had probably overreacted. If someone had wanted to call the police, they would have done so by now. She briefly mulled over mentioning it to her team but decided against it. They were all in a good mood and looking forward to the party tomorrow. The thought of turning on the power and seeing the excited faces of the villagers energised them. Everyone in the village anticipated the event. In the last week, every few hours someone had come up to her to confirm it would all be ready on the promised day.

She was quite proud of the work her team had done. The

array of solar panels fed power through an underground cable into a bank of lithium-ion batteries, contained in a solid steel cage in the village square. They stored the charge and made electricity available all day and night. The cage had four sturdy legs to keep the batteries off the ground to protect them from flooding. Everything had been designed to be long-lasting and safe.

The battery cage was adjacent to a large gazebo Carbonon had funded as part of the development plan. It was a square eight metres on each side and made of timber and bamboo with a sloping thatched roof. During the day it would provide a gathering place, away from the hot summer sun. At night the villagers could use it to watch their communal television. The outdoor school would move into one corner of the gazebo. It would allow for evening classes for the adults.

Her team had tested the system a few times already. The panels were working, and the batteries were fully charged. A small computer monitored the installation and sent signals back to their head office if something went amiss. Today they were going to double check everything one last time, get some final readings and then tomorrow it would be ready for handover.

LA MAISON

Islamabad, Thursday 24 November, 7:15pm

S imon settled in the back seat of the Mercedes sedan. His driver closed his door and got in himself. As the car pulled away from the Marriott, he was lost in thought. He had to find a way to persuade Tajammul.

This was the most unexpected and frustrating situation he had ever encountered in his career. He was an idealist. It was a rare quality among successful entrepreneurs. He had found a niche in the market that allowed him to retain a social conscience and make money.

That afternoon he had a meeting with his staff from both their offices, in Sydney and Zurich to try to make sense of this latest development. They had decided there were only two plausible reasons for Tajammul's behaviour. He was either seeking a bribe, or someone had coerced him. Simon had asked his team to analyse both scenarios and write a report.

The first report was on Pakistan's endemic corruption. It listed examples of the types of bribes commonly asked for, the legal ramifications of bribery and the means to avoid it without giving offence. The second report was longer and made for more interesting reading.

Pakistan was an agrarian economy trying to industrialise. A small number of powerful feudal lords owned a lot of agricultural land. They controlled their workers with an iron fist. The village, Shakar Parian, was an exception. There the villagers owned the land themselves. The paper postulated that a neighbouring landowner opposed the electrification project. Any progress in one village would create a disparity that could lead to unrest and ultimately a reduction in the efficiency of their agricultural business.

He made a mental note to thank his team for the report. It gelled with something Tajammul had mentioned.

So now he had two hypotheses but no strategy on how to deal with Tajammul. He would have to play it by ear and sound him out if he wanted a bribe. If not, it would be the second reason. What if it was both? It could be. Nothing in the world was ever straightforward.

The car pulled up to La Maison. He had heard a lot about it and was keen to try it out. It also conveniently served alcohol, something very few restaurants in Pakistan did. That might prove useful. He entered the restaurant. Max, the owner, greeted him and led him to his table. As he sat, a waiter brought a breadbasket with a crock of freshly churned butter and the wine list.

Simon had just tasted his first sip of the smooth, velvety red Burgundy when Tajammul walked in with another man. The stranger was tall and broad-shouldered with a large handlebar moustache. Could this be the person pulling Tajammul's strings? Maybe this was a bit of good luck. If he could find out what the moustache man's real concerns were, he might find common ground with him.

They spotted Simon straight away and walked over to his table. He rose to greet them.

Tajammul shook his hand. 'Please meet my dear friend Jibran Ghaffar.'

Simon extended his hand. The man shook it unenthusiastically, almost as if he was doing him a favour.

'Mr Ghaffar is a member of the National Assembly and is a very big landowner,' Tajammul said in hushed tones.

'It is a pleasure to make your acquaintance, Mr Ghaffar,' Simon was at his most affable self.

Jibran Ghaffar grunted in response and looked around for

one of the waiters to help him into his chair.

The moustache man was going to be a tough customer. Somehow, he had to stay on his best behaviour and keep his temper under control. It was going to be hard because he already didn't like the fellow, and that did not bode well. He was not known as a diplomat.

The waiter came over. 'May I pour you, gentlemen, some wine?' They both nodded.

'Mr Ghaffar, where are your lands?' Simon decided to jump straight in.

'Oh, Mr Ghaffar has lands everywhere.'

'Any near Shakar Parian?' Simon tried again. They might as well get to the point. The man wasn't here because he was Tajammul's dinner date. The way he was eyeing the women in the restaurant he didn't seem to be into men.

'Mr Ghaffar is one of Punjab's big *waderas*. He has land near Shakar Parian and so many other places. He was in the Islamabad area, and I thought it would be good for you to meet him.'

Why didn't the little weasel let the man speak for himself?

The waiter brought them the menu. Simon scanned it. They would not be into snails or frog legs and he would on principle not eat foie gras because he hated animal cruelty.

'I have heard really nice things about the Beef Bourguignon. Mr Ghaffar what kind of food do you enjoy?' Simon tried to be personable. Hopefully, his mouthpiece would not order for him. The moustache man completely ignored him. How could someone be so rude? He had just asked him a direct question.

Jibran had gone into silent mode. The minister ordered for himself and his guest.

'Well Mr Ghaffar,' Simon said as the waiter finally left with their orders, 'maybe there's something my company can do for you.' He forced himself to smile.

Jibran Ghaffar smoothed the tablecloth in front of him and

brushed away some crumbs. He picked up one of the bread knives and pointed it at Simon threateningly. 'You...' he paused as a waiter walked over and refilled their water glasses.

What the fuck was the dimwit planning to do with the knife? Was it a display of extraordinarily bad manners or was he somehow threatening him? Simon was keen to find out.

'Yes, Mr Ghaffar, you were saying,' Simon said coolly when the waiter left. He was already starting to feel the anger surge through him. He had to control himself.

Jibran Ghaffar leaned forward. 'Your company...' he began again slowly.

Simon had a sudden urge to tweak his moustache. He smiled at the thought. Jibran's haughty demeanour turned to anger. His face took on a red hue.

'Your company must take your electricity and get off my land.'

Simon had not been prepared for that. 'Excuse me, what?'

'You will not switch on the power.'

'What?' Simon pretended to be incredulous.

'Are those things on the side of your head for decoration purposes only?' Jibran's voice rose in pitch and volume as he spoke.

'That's not very nice, Mr Ghaffar. Tell me the reason for yo-_'

'I can be much, much worse than not very nice. You will find out if you turn on the power.' Jibran bunched up his fists in anger. He looked ready for violence.

This was not going to end well. It was evident Jibran Ghaffar was in no mood to negotiate. At least he knew his opposition was not Tajammul. The second hypothesis had been pretty spot-on. Well, he had all the permissions in place when he began the project. It was all legal and above board, and at that time this rude cock hadn't voiced any concerns. Fuck it, he didn't need these clowns.

After his morning meeting with Tajammul, he had spoken

with his contact at the UNDP. It turned out there was a process to get the final payment without all the necessary signatures, but it was convoluted and time-consuming and meant he would have to wait at least six months to get paid. Six months would cause him a cash flow problem he would love to avoid. It was however not the end of the world.

A trio of women entered the restaurant, momentarily distracting Simon. They were all in their thirties, expensively dressed in bright, tightly fitting, local attire. They wore lots of jewellery and makeup and looked like dolls, and they smelled heavenly.

Some Pakistani women could be so achingly beautiful. For some reason, many of them thought he was good looking too. Whenever he looked in the mirror, all he saw was a pale and bony face, a slightly crooked nose, and shock of white hair. He didn't know what they saw in him, but he was not going to complain.

He needed to get out more, and, he needed a woman in his life again. That's what he should be spending the next few months on instead of chasing money. He anyway had enough to last a lifetime. Maybe he could tour the country, meet a local woman and fall in love while he still had his looks.

He was getting distracted when he needed to focus.

'Mr Ghaffar, I am afraid I really don't understand, can we talk this over and see if we can come to some common ground.' Simon kept his voice even. He knew if he lost his temper, it was a lost cause.

Jibran glowered at him. He was clearly not a man used to arguments.

'His family are traditional owners of the land,' Tajammul interjected. 'He needs to take it back. If you supply power, then the villagers will never sell and that cannot and will not happen.'

Ghaffar used his napkin to begin polishing his shiny oversized gold ring. It didn't look like any ring Simon had ever seen. It had a sharply tapered pyramid in the centre that curved as it merged to a tip. It looked like the incisor of a large cat.

Ghaffar blew on his ring, fogging it up. He polished it some more and examined it with exaggerated care. '*Yaar*, we don't owe this *farangi chootia* any explanation.'

Another woman entered the restaurant. She wore a red silk dress with subtle gold embroidery and a low-cut back that exposed her delicate shoulder blades. She moved with the effortless grace of a tigress as she headed to join the three women already seated. Simon suddenly felt suffocated. Fuck these bastards. He was not going to grovel in front of this repulsive hairy ape and his lackey. It was a lost cause anyway.

'I really don't know what to say, gentlemen. I was hoping we could have a civilised discussion. I've always believed in win-win, but I think I have just lost my appetite for food and for reasoning with you... cunts.' The blood was now rising fast in his head.

While Jibran Ghaffar glared at him, murdering him with his eyes, and with Tajammul's mouth agape in horror, Simon took out six five-thousand-rupee notes and put them on the table.

'Here you can pay the waiter, and there's a little to buy yourself some dessert.'

Simon got up, turned around and walked towards the door. He didn't look back but stole a glance at the beauties at the other table. One of the women smiled at him. He smiled back. It felt good to snub the bastards, but at the same time, he knew he had closed doors that could never be reopened.

His smug feeling didn't last long. He sighed as he sat in the back of the Mercedes. Now he'd have to spend time chasing paperwork at the UNDP. Fucking hell. The driver slowly reversed the car out of its parking spot. His phone buzzed briefly, in his pocket. Someone was trying to call him. He was about to answer, but a commotion behind the car stopped him.

'What's wrong, Raza?'

'That car block our way,' Raza said in his broken English,

as he pointed.

Simon glanced back. A black Porsche SUV blocked their path. People were shouting. What the fuck? Was it that bastard Jibran's? As Raza stepped out a man grabbed him by his shirt and began yelling in his face. A crowd gathered to watch the show.

'This is stupid,' Simon muttered as he opened the door to climb out.

He didn't see it coming. The blow struck him so hard his head reverberated like a drum. Immediately his face was on fire. He put his hand to his cheek and felt something sticky. His face had gone numb. His fingers were wet with blood. Had someone stabbed him? He slumped back into the car bleeding. Another blow knocked him out cold.

His phone beeped with a message. He did not hear it.

THE HAND OVER

Shakar Parian, Friday 25 November, 11:45am

The *dhol* player began drumming out a loud beat. He was the centre of attention. Two men stood behind him with *chimtas,* adding the high rhythm note. Men around him began swaying, engrossed in the music. He stopped and tightened the cow skin head on his drum. This was just a warm-up.

The whole village had gathered for the celebration. Everyone was bedecked in their most colourful clothes. Delicious smells of cooking wafted through the air. Sarwar the barber and Amina, his wife, were each stirring a large cauldron of *pulao* and another of sweet saffron rice. A few people around them were helping out.

Jane walked over to where the food was cooking. Amina smiled at her and scooped up some sweet rice out of the huge cooking pot. She offered the spoon to Jane, who took it gratefully. The smells were making her stomach rumble. The fragrant rice was very sweet and very yellow from the saffron. As she chewed she delighted in the distinctive aromas of cinnamon, cloves and cardamom. The juicy raisins burst in her mouth, mixing with the sweet sugary rice and the crunch of the almonds, cashews and pistachios. Yum, she had to close her eyes to fully savour the taste. Amina smiled.

'Some more please.' Jane begged.

'*Mem Sahib*, you will spoil your appetite for the *pulao*,' Sarwar said smiling.

'Then let me taste the *pulao*,' Jane said cheerfully.

It was now noon. Jane looked at her watch. Her whole team and the villagers were waiting for it to happen. Most of them were sitting cross-legged on the wooden floor of the gazebo. Simon was late. It was not like him at all to miss a celebration. Jane tried calling again. There was no answer. She had tried to call him last night. He hadn't picked up then either nor responded to the text message she had sent. He had also not updated his Facebook status nor posted on Twitter. It was all most disquieting. She decided to hold off for another fifteen minutes, but no longer. Simon wouldn't want to make the whole village wait for him. He could join the celebrations later. Hopefully, he was OK.

Fifteen minutes later Simon had still not shown. Jane walked over to Allah Boota. 'Let's begin. Simon *Sahib* can join us later.'

Allah Boota sighed with relief. He was clearly keen to begin proceedings. They both walked over to the big switch in a locked metal box behind one of the legs holding up the battery cage. Allah Boota had changed into a crisp white *shalwar kameez* and wore a bright maroon and yellow turban with a tall fan. He had to bend over so his turban would not scrape on the underside of the cage.

Jane faced the villagers. 'My dear friends my company has been paid by the United Nations and sponsored by the Government of Pakistan to provide you free electricity, powered by the sun.' She began solemnly. 'This will help you and your children live in prosperity and enjoy what people are enjoying in other parts of the world.' The whole village had gone quiet as Mahmud, her lead engineer, translated.

'I give you the key so you can start using your electricity. May God bring your village good times.' Jane waited till the translations were done and handed the key to Allah Boota. He took it and held it up for everyone to see. The villagers let out a loud cheer. They grew silent as Allah Boota put the key in the lock, opened the box, and flicked the large switch.

The lights and the four fans in the gazebo turned on. They had power. The villagers clapped and cheered. The *dhol* player started beating his drum. The loud rhythmic beat resonated through the village joined by the high pitched *chimtas*. A group of men broke into a spontaneous dance. The crowd of women and the rest of the men stood around and clapped.

Jane smiled happily. This was a huge moment for them. It was not just for their convenience or to get the Internet to do online shopping. They would no longer need to buy fuel to power their generator, nor for the diesel motors that ran their tube wells. They could use quieter and cleaner electric motors. This would save a lot of money because they needed to pump water almost continuously, in some seasons to irrigate their fields properly. They would be able to invest the savings in other things such as covers for their irrigation channels. Less water would evaporate which would save them even more. It would become a virtuous cycle to take them out of poverty.

The drumming continued. Jane had heard it before, the strong and powerful sounds were mesmerising. As the dancers moved to the beat, she felt like dancing as well, but that would have been most improper.

Eventually, the music and dancing stopped, and people began eating the delicious food. While Jane ate, people took turns to come up to her to thank her. She understood many words and all of the sentiment. It was incredible how something as simple as an electric fan and a bulb could make people so happy. What did it take to satisfy people back home? They had a far higher threshold.

The sound of several approaching vehicles interrupted her thoughts.

THE WADERA

Shisha Wal, Friday 25 November, 1:00pm

The severed head of the snake moved as it opened and closed its mouth. It was still dangerous even though it had now been dead for many minutes. Apparently, a snake's head could bite long after it was severed from the body.

Jibran paced the room keeping his distance, his mind a red cloud of fury. The villagers were bloody well not going to get away with it. Who did the worms think they were dealing with? He would crush them into the ground where they belonged. He twisted his handlebar moustache, something he always did when agitated. Majeed, the old village cobbler, had just sent him a video on WhatsApp. It was of people dancing, in Shakar Parian. They were celebrating something. Below that was a message.

'They have turned on the electricity.'

The villagers were not going to celebrate long. He was going to fix them like he had fixed Mumtaz, his wife. She was dead, the *haramzadi* bitch. The snake's head, which had finally stopped twitching, lay a short distance from her body. The axe he had used to kill the snake lay next to her on the floor.

When he was young, Jibran had read the story of Samson and Delilah. Samson was a great godlike man feared by his enemies for his strength and cruelty. His might was in his hair. Delilah, his mistress, found out and cut it while he slept causing him to lose all his power and allowing his enemies to vanquish him.

Mumtaz was his Delilah. She had started cutting little bits of his hair since the day they were married.

For a while, it even worked. Her beauty had blinded him, and he had listened to her. She tried to make him believe all humans were equal in the eyes of Allah and that he should be nice to his underlings. She told him it was the best way to buy their loyalty. She had made him soft and weak with her nonsense.

People began taking advantage of him. His servants began to brazenly look him in the eyes while addressing him, instead of at the ground. Some even made jokes in his presence. They began to presume they and he were at the same level.

Well, they presumed wrong. Everything Mumtaz had said was a lie. Allah had created lions and gazelles, the strong to rule the weak. A man in his position needed to be feared so the lower classes could be kept in their place. Nothing bought loyalty better than a whip or a stick.

If he had not listened to her, Shakar Parian would already be his. He had wanted to send a group of armed men to burn down the village, smash their tube well, beat up a few of the men and take some of the women and children hostage until they signed over their title-deeds. Five years ago, would have been perfect. Since then everyone started using social media, and suddenly nothing anymore could be kept hidden from public view. He could never afford the voting public to know how he managed his affairs.

As he realised just how much Mumtaz was holding him back, his adoration for her turned to hatred. He didn't need a useless woman who hung around his neck like a tractor tyre, questioning his every move. She was not even able to bear him a son. She was worse than useless.

There was only so far, her wiles and beauty were going to get her. The world was after all full of pussy, each one nicer, warmer, and juicier. And most didn't come with attitude.

Mumtaz was not going to hold him back any longer. He checked her pulse once more to be sure. There was nothing. Her skin had turned a light shade of blue. She was completely limp. The snake had done its job. It did not love him but had been perfectly faithful. He only needed obedience, not love. He dialled the doctor and the police then called out loudly 'Qadoos, *oey*, come here.'

Qadoos came running in. The big *Sahib* sounded angry. He let out a howl when he saw the dead body and another when he saw the snake.

'Call the cleaner and the gardener,' Jibran ordered.

'Yes, *wada Sahib*.' He was visibly shaken and ran off to call them. He guessed why they were being summoned. The cleaner was supposed to clean her mistress's room. The gardener was meant to have kept the garden free of snakes.

Jibran's mind was no longer on his dead wife but on the land, he needed to buy back. Time was running out.

It was now fifteen days since his friend Arsalan in the Mining Ministry had excitedly rung to tell him gold deposits had been found on what Arsalan had assumed to be his lands. Apparently, the government had contracted an Australian company to search for minerals in North West Punjab and a Chinese Mining Company to mine them.

An ambitious young geologist who worked for Arsalan had decided to take the initiative and survey some of the sites himself. He found sizeable gold deposits under Shakar Parian. Arsalan told him to keep it secret and went straight to Jibran.

Jibran did not tell Arsalan Shakar Parian was not his. He thanked him profusely and promised him a generous gift when gold was discovered, officially. He then sent one of his men to take care of the young geologist. He could not afford any loose ends. The geologist did not come to work the next morning. He had taken an unfortunate tumble off his roof and had broken his neck. It was kite flying season, and too many young men died falling off roofs for the overworked police to even bother to investigate. The death was treated as an accident, and the case was closed the same day.

Now he had only one month to get the villagers to sell. After that, the Australian company would begin the survey and find the same thing. They would make an official report. The government would look for the owners. It would be too late for him.

Even now the villagers would not willingly sell their lands, not when free electricity and the Internet had just been gifted to them.

He would have to destroy the solar project and the team that had installed it. But it had to be in a way that would never cast a shadow on him. As a parliamentarian in the sitting government, his public image was important. He needed to stay in the government. It would give him power and influence that would help in any negotiations with the Chinese mining company. He had to be smart, which was not at all the same as being soft.

He had come up with a cunning plan to make the villagers sell. He had celebrated with a little too much wine and in a state of complete drunkenness, had told Mumtaz.

She had gone mad with anger, threatening divorce if he harmed the villagers or the foreigners. Worse she had threatened to tell the whole world. Who the fuck did the bitch think she was? Well, she was a dead bitch now, that much was certain.

The maid and the gardener came in, their faces ashen. Qadoos had told them. The maid started bawling her eyes out and beating her chest.

Jibran slapped her hard on her face.

'Cunt, this is your fault. You cleaned *Begum Sahib*'s room!'

'But *wada Sahib*, I did not see any snake, she managed to mutter through her cut and rapidly swelling lip.'

Jibran slapped her hard on the other side of the face with the back of his hand. His large pointy ring gouged her cheek. The maid dropped to the floor in a daze.

Jibran shook the drops of blood off his ring distastefully and turned on the gardener. 'You son of a filthy whore!'

MOB RULES

Kala Shah Kaku, Friday 25 November, 4:44pm

The ride was bumpy. The hard seats did nothing to cushion the shocks from the potholes in the road. The sun was beginning to dip below the horizon, but the choking early winter smog made it darker and gloomier than it would be otherwise. Traffic on the Grand Trunk Road was hectic and quite chaotic, but the convoy of four vehicles was making good progress. Their red and blue lights and sirens doing what ordinary horns and flashing headlamps were not able to.

Jane sat in the back seat of the police Landcruiser surrounded by uniformed officers. Two Toyota pickups converted to troop carriers accompanied them, one ahead and the other behind. Each of them carried six heavily armed policemen. Mr Ali and Clara followed the three police vehicles in her Landcruiser.

They were about half an hour north of Lahore, passing through the small industrial town of Kala Shah Kaku. Their driver slowed to navigate a large, congested roundabout. Cars, rickshaws, scooters, motorcycles, bicycles, minibuses, trucks and even a tractor, pulling a trailer laden with steel for some construction site, all vied for position. Drivers were sounding their horns and flashing their high beams. Their signs of impatience were doing nothing to alter their slow, grinding, and deliberate pace.

Among all this, a traffic policeman wearing a dust mask

was making a valiant but futile attempt to guide the participants in this vehicular maelstrom, his high-pitched whistle lost in the din of the traffic. Stuck in the middle of this slow-motion cyclone Jane watched how everyone just kept on inching forward, seemingly not following any rules, yet the traffic still moved. Vehicles passed a few centimetres from each other, miraculously, without making contact. She had seen this behaviour on roundabouts in Lahore as well where the usual aggression shown by road users on a straight section of road would transmogrify into a strange harmonious accord guided seemingly by telepathy and then instantly transform back into raw aggression as vehicles catapulted out of the roundabout.

She closed her eyes. They burnt from tiredness, stress, and the effects of the pollution. The happiness of the morning seemed a distant memory. A dull throbbing ache in her temples made her feel nauseous and melancholic. The pit of her stomach was a knot. She was alone and helpless and petrified beyond anything she had ever been. Everything seemed to indicate she was in a lot of trouble.

The police officer, in-charge, had simply told her she had to accompany him to the police station in Lahore to answer questions. He refused to divulge what it was about or why they needed fifteen armed policemen and one policewoman to escort her. She was certain it was related to the men with the posters. However, she decided it would be wise not to bring it up herself. She tried remembering whether her company had ever mentioned such a situation during a training session, but her mind had gone completely blank. She could not even visualise what the trainer had looked like.

Thankfully, they had not made her wear handcuffs. Maybe they realised the presence of the stern policewoman next to her would be more than enough to make her comply, let alone that a whole army of police surrounded her. Their aloof and standoffish demeanour was in sharp contrast to the polite and friendly nature of most other locals she had met on this trip, so she had given up trying to have a conversation with them.

This was all so frustrating. She'd been hoping to spend her last day souvenir shopping in Lahore, before her flight early in the morning of the day after. Maybe, hopefully, they would only ask questions or give her a warning and let her go soon so she could get a good night's sleep.

Only two more nights alone, sleeping by herself with no cuddles and no sex. She'd not had any form of release for the last two months and was on edge. Usually, her trusty vibrator would at least dull the cravings but sleeping in the hut in the village, in the silence and without locks on the doors or windows just made it awkward. She couldn't bring herself to use it. But it was not just the sex. There was a time when she would have enjoyed being by herself, in her own space. Solitude would recharge her and renew her passions, but now, since the last two years, it was the one thing she dreaded the most about going away. She'd pine for their togetherness, the warmth, the laughter, and the conversations. Two more nights without. Then they would make up for it.

It was probably too late to go back to the village tonight so she'd have to find a hotel in Lahore for the next two nights. She would spend tomorrow shopping and sight-seeing in Lahore.

Outside the pollution was horrendous, the worst she'd seen, and it made her short of breath. The grey sky was so dense the sun was but an ineffectual orange orb. Haze even obscured the very top of the taller street lights.

It was easy to see why. The majority of vehicles around her were ancient and in poor shape, and many of them were belching smoke, tendrils of which billowed across the surface of the road enveloping everything.

People on motorcycles wore masks. Those in cars kept their windows closed. How futile.

Mr Ali had told her how the government had tried to fix pollution in the major cities, like Lahore, by banning rickshaws, horse-drawn carriages, and cars with smoky engines. It did not solve the pollution problem just moved it a little bit out of their sight into smaller towns, like the one she was stuck in at that moment.

Something bumped into their Police Landcruiser, hard. Then again. All hell broke loose. People were abandoning their vehicles and running in all different directions. Angry chanting replaced the sound of traffic. The words were unintelligible, but the raw emotion was anything but. A crazed mob formed. Men, many with beards, carrying long sticks thronged around their convoy. They surrounded the three vehicles and started banging on them. The traffic ground to a complete halt. Policemen in the troop carriers tried using batons in an attempt to keep the crowd at bay. In response the mob became vicious. Several policemen were pulled off their vehicles. One of the braver ones fired a few rounds in the air. Other policemen joined in.

The crowd appeared to be on the verge of turning and dispersing, but something made them rally and begin attacking again. The small moment of hesitation enabled a group of policemen to jump off their troop carriers. They were now using their batons to fight men with long sticks. It became a melee, a free for all.

A brick smashed into the windscreen of their Landcruiser, causing a large diagonal crack. The crowd grew even larger as it surged towards them. They were now in a frenzy, smashing and destroying anything and everything. None of the vehicles on the roundabout were spared.

The seething mob grew as more and more men joined in. The chanting grew louder. Some carried dangerous looking rifles. They were firing them in the air, the sharp report of gunshots almost painfully loud.

Jane was frozen with fear. It was all happening so fast. She was trapped. This was beyond dangerous. She couldn't help notice how some of the men had the same mad look like those she had encountered yesterday morning.

By now, the police had realised they could no longer contain the crowd by showing restraint. They started to fire short bursts straight at the protesters. Men began falling. Some tried to run, others charged forward. Complete pandemonium ensued.

A massive projectile smashed her side window, narrowly missing her. Hands reached inside and unlatched the door. She was pulled out, roughly. Her vision became strange and blurry. Her world started spinning. Her brain was working in slow motion trying to form a thought in her consciousness, but it would not come to her. Hands were grabbing at her, scratching her skin, pulling her hair, tearing at her clothes. She heard sirens and saw the smog was glowing with a pulsating red and blue light that bizarrely reminded her of a discotheque when she was a teenager. Ambush, was the word she was looking for. Something hit her hard on the side of the head. She blacked out.

IMPATIENCE

Lahore, Friday 25 November, 5:44pm

Jibran paced the room twirling his moustache. He took out his phone and checked the volume. It was on maximum. He checked his call log. There were no missed calls. It should have been done by now. But why were they not calling? He had paid enough for the job and deserved results.

The deal was she would not reach the police station alive. Three buses had been arranged to take hired men to a roundabout in Kala Shah Kaku.

Abdul Zubair had shown him the place on the map where he would ambush them. Traffic would be slow enough. It was perfect. No one would question a woman who had committed blasphemy being killed by an outraged mob. No politician or journalist would ever think of opening their mouths.

His lawyer and the *patwari* were ready with the land transfer documents. All that needed to happen now was for the woman to die. Then they could destroy the solar panels and force the villagers to sign over their land.

He took the phone out of his pocket again. It was still silent. He put it back in his pocket again. Damn it. He hated waiting.

The phone rang, startling him.

THE LOCK-UP

Lahore, Friday 25 November, 7:45pm

Jane woke with a jolt. A pounding sledgehammer was hard at work inside her head. A scratch on her shoulder and one on her arm burnt fiercely. Exhaustion made her tongue feel dry. She was sitting against a wall on a thin mat. A heavy two-metre wide steel door positioned in the centre of a thick wall made it obvious where she was. The room had an unusually high ceiling, easily the height of three men. Not that any cobwebs were visible. The harsh light from an energy saver bulb at the end of a long cord that hung halfway down from the ceiling provided barely enough illumination. The room was almost as long and wide as it was high. The wall opposite the door was even thicker and was punctuated by two small windows, with heavy steel bars, about three metres off the ground.

The heavily stained walls were coated in a glossy yellowing paint that looked like it had been repainted at least a hundred times. Thick strips were peeling along the bottom due to the rising damp. Why was she in a jail cell? Weren't they meant to just ask her questions? Her mind was too clouded to think much beyond that. What were those awful looking stains on the wall next to her head? They looked suspiciously like someone had peed there. Her nose crinkled at the sickly smell.

Through the windows, she could see the evening sky. It was not yet pitch-black, but close. She couldn't have been unconscious for long. The memory of what had just happened flooded back. Where had the mob come from? And why attack her so viciously?

She had heard and felt her clothes tear, but thankfully they were mostly intact at least enough to cover the important bits. She must have been rescued just in time. The unpleasant memory of those unfriendly hands groping, touching, and tearing at her, made her shudder.

It took her a while to notice a small form that lay below one of the windows on a mat. It was a sleeping woman.

As her awareness grew, Jane realised she could hear shouting. It sounded like the same mob. She shuddered involuntarily; fear threatened to take hold of her senses. She had to calm down. She was in a secure place.

She felt in the pocket of her jeans for her phone. Thankfully it was intact and turned on. There was data reception. With trembling hands, she wrote a WhatsApp message to Sergei, Damon, and Simon. She thought of sending it to Razane as well but decided not to. It was probably better she heard it from Sergei than reading it in a message. She then opened Google Maps and shared her location with them.

The woman on the mat began to moan. She sounded hurt. In the dim light, Jane saw her eyes were closed. What was she in here for?

'Do you speak English?' Jane said softly. '*Angrezi*?'

The woman opened her eyes as she slowly turned her head to look at Jane. She shook her head weakly 'English no no…'

Jane tried to remember her Urdu phrases, '*Aap ke sath kia hua*?' She was asking what had happened to her.

The woman looked at her perplexed. She said something in Urdu, but Jane did not understand.

'*Aram aram sey bollen*,' Jane said. She was asking her to speak slowly.

The woman opened her mouth to speak again but stopped at the sound of people running. Startled they both looked at the door. The woman sat up. The mob was still shouting angrily, somewhere outside. Another sound, of a violent scuffle, came from the hallway just outside the door. A police guard came into view followed by a huge heavily bearded man. As they watched, the huge man pushed the guard against the door and held him there. With his free hand, he hit the policeman on the jaw and watched as he crumpled to the floor. Then he took a revolver from his pocket aimed it through the bars and fired as Jane sat there, frozen.

Everything seemed to happen in slow motion. The woman's head whipped back violently as the loud crack reverberated through the cell. She fell backwards. The floor underneath her ponytail was awash in a spreading pool of dark red blood.

Jane was shocked at how fast the blood poured out of her head wound. The room was redolent with the smell of gunpowder. Her ears rang drowning out any further sounds.

In a daze, Jane looked back at the door; the revolver was now aimed at her. The policeman on the ground gained consciousness and rolled his shoulder into the shooter's legs. He staggered and would have fallen back had he not held onto a bar with his free hand.

It was her only opportunity, and she took it. With a great effort to overcome a paralysing inertia Jane got up and ran towards the pillar to the left side of the door, all the while her legs threatened to fold beneath her.

The assailant tried to aim his weapon at her, as she desperately tried to flatten herself against the wall. The bars prevented his arm from turning past a forty-five-degree angle. He swore in frustration as he pulled his hand out. At the same time the policeman, still on the ground, tried bravely to grab both his legs and topple him. The gunman almost fell but just managed to hold onto the bars and right himself. In frustration, he kicked out hard, and the policeman fell onto his back. He was now completely exposed. The brave guard was not about to give in. He sat up and made another valiant attempt at grabbing the attacker's legs.

Jane watched in horror as the big man pointed the revolver downwards and fired point blank into the top of the policeman's head. The guard's body jerked almost in sync with the way the sound reverberated, and his body slumped forward onto his killer's legs. Jane stifled a sob. The policeman had just sacrificed his life for her. The assailant braced himself against the bars and kicked the body away. He put his arm through the bars again as Jane tried as hard as possible to flatten herself against the wall.

It now seemed like a crazy place for her to stand. The pillar was barely the thickness of her body and could not shield her effectively. He would only have to twist his arm and his hand ever so slightly more. His forearm was through the bar, well past his wrist. He was straining with the effort of turning the revolver towards her. If this had been a Hollywood movie Jane would have grabbed his gun, bitten his hand, and fought back but it was real life; she was frozen with fear. The man growled in anger as his forearm got stuck again. He pulled his arm back, furiously ripped at his sleeve, hawked a big ball of phlegm, and spat on his forearm to lubricate it. Then he shoved it violently through the bars again. This time his arm was through the bars almost up to his elbow.

Slowly with great effort, he turned his weapon in her direction. Jane had another opportunity to fight back, but she couldn't take it. She should have fought back but didn't. Fear had overcome her. She closed her eyes tightly and prayed.

DAMON

Melbourne, Saturday 26 November, 2:03am

Damon tossed and turned in bed. Summer was still four days away but the night was already too warm. He had to sleep to be fresh for his interview. He needed this job, badly. Playing guitar in his heavy metal band was not enough to pay the bills, and he didn't want to ask his parents for another handout. He loved them dearly, but they annoyed him. They'd made him soft and lazy and comfort-loving by being over-indulgent. He wasn't going to let himself stay that way anymore.

No more comfort-loving, easy going, Damon. The world was going to see a new man. And he could do it. He had managed to break up with Deeba, and that had been hard. Bloody hard was a better way of putting it. He'd felt guilty and at first a little miserable. He also felt free, which was nice.

The interview was important. He had to fall asleep.

His phone, lying near him on the bedside table, rang. Shit, he hadn't switched it to silent. He turned it over. It continued to ring noiselessly. He was going to ignore it. He had to sleep. He turned over, but sleep wouldn't come. He tried thinking of warm, soft, pleasant things. He'd spend more time with Adita. There was some chemistry between them that could easily blossom into something more. Wouldn't it be funny if his next girlfriend was also from India? He smiled in the dark. Maybe he needed more variety, and even more, he needed to stop thinking and go to sleep.

Sleep of course never came when one wanted it to. The

light on his phone kept flashing. Someone had left a message. He pushed it to the far corner of his bedside table. He wasn't going to read it tonight. Nothing could be that important. The world could go on without him for a night. His smartphone addiction was another thing he had to work on. He had gotten it from his Dad, like most of his other annoying habits, and it wasted so much of his time.

Damon tried hard, but couldn't fall asleep. Knowing there was an unread message was not letting him. He wondered what the message was. He might as well check it. Maybe it was Adita. Maybe she wanted to come over or was inviting him to her place. He'd kick himself if he missed a booty call.

He turned his phone over and opened WhatsApp.

Bloody hell, it was from his Mum. Didn't she realise there was such a thing as a time difference?

'I am in jail,' the message read. He almost dropped the phone. With shaking fingers, he clicked on the message to read the whole text. Sleep was now a distant memory. His hand still shaking, he tried calling her. There was no answer.

Damon dialled his father's number. There was no answer either. He was in New Zealand on some sort of caving adventure with Razane. Even after two years, Damon still couldn't understand how his Mum tolerated his Dad's relationship with Razane. How could she let them go adventuring together, alone? His mother was not the outdoors adventure type, but this felt weird to him. His father was abandoning her, and she was letting him. In that aspect, she was the complete opposite of the clingy Deeba. Neither was healthy.

Damon tried Razane's number not expecting anything either, and he was right. In a way, it was a relief. He still found it awkward to talk to her. They were civil to each other but nothing more. To him, she was still the interloper in the family. Everything had gone wrong after she came. He dialled Ben, his younger brother. He didn't pick up. He had the sense to turn his phone off. He tried again. Nothing; Ben had switched it off.

Sleep was now out of the question. He had to do something; but what? Poor Mum. He searched for flights to Pakistan. Did he have enough credit on his card? Shit, did he need a visa for Pakistan? He checked the Pakistani Immigration website. Business visas were granted on arrival but tourists needed to apply before, and there didn't seem to be a procedure to apply for an emergency visa. He needed help. He picked up his phone and dialled Mack.

'Hey Damon, how are you son?' Mack was in a cheerful mood. Come to think of it when was he anything else? Mack was his father's closest friend and considered the two boys his nephews. He insisted they call him Uncle.

'Hi Uncle, sorry to wake you.'

'You didn't wake me. I'm in Pakistan not in Melbourne.' Mack travelled between the two countries so often it was hard to keep track.

'Uncle Mack I need to go to Pakistan today. I need help, please, if you can with the visa.'

'What's wrong? What's happened?' Mack sounded worried.

Should he tell Mack? In the end, he decided not to. His Mum might already have sorted it out. There was no use involving anyone else. At least not yet. Damon kept his voice level, 'Oh, nothing's wrong. I just want to give Mum a surprise. She'd not be expecting me at all.'

There was an uncomfortable pause 'OK. Isn't she due to return home soon?'

'Yup, but she's free from work now. I thought… maybe we could explore Pakistan a bit… before she comes back.'

There was another pause. 'You surprise me... in a pleasant way of course.'

'Well, I surprised myself. I just thought of it.'

'I can help. I will email you a letter from the Chamber of Commerce. Just show it at Immigration when you land and tell them you need a business visa.'

'A business visa?'

'Yes, just tell them you are in the rice trade and want to sample the new crop or something like that. They won't care.'

'OK thanks, that sounds easy.'

'Don't worry I have a contact in Immigration; there will be no problem.'

His father used to joke that everyone in Pakistan was Mack's contact.

'Thanks, Uncle Mack.'

'No problem, I think there is an Emirates flight leaving at 6:00 am your time.'

'You know you're a legend?'

'I know Damon, I know.' Mack was in a jovial mood. 'Just take care and if you cannot find a seat on Emirates let me know straight away. I have a good friend at the airline.'

'Yeah, of course.'

CHARGE OF BLASPHEMY

Lahore, Friday 25 November, 10:15pm

A shot rang out reverberating through the cell, then another. There was no pain or any other feeling except the need for her to pee. Somehow with great effort, Jane managed to hold it in. Her eyes were still closed, and she was still pressed hard up against the wall. The ringing in her ears muffled all sounds. It didn't feel like she'd been hit. Men were shouting. Their sounds became louder as the ringing in her ears subsided.

A violent scuffle ensued outside the door followed by another gunshot. Jane opened her eyes. The assailant's arm was pointing towards the ceiling, still wedged between the bars. His revolver limp in his hand. She forced herself to lift her head away from the wall to look. He was hanging by his arm. Blood poured out of his head and throat. He had been shot multiple times. His unseeing eyes stared at her. Two police guards pulled his body away from the door and let it drop to the floor. His facial expression did not change. He was quite dead. Jane felt both horrified and relieved. Just to be sure, one of the policemen with a revolver in his hand stomped down hard on his face. With a sickening sound, the man's nose caved in, but there was still no movement and not much blood. He was dead for sure. Jane dry retched a thin dribble of spittle onto the floor as the door opened and three policemen dashed inside.

Jane still had her phone in her hand, which was by her side. She surreptitiously slipped it into her back pocket, hoping they hadn't noticed it. Two more policemen entered. They motioned to her to accompany them.

'Why did you lock me up? Who was that man?' her voice was shaking badly and came out in high pitched warble.

'No talk,' one of them said as he grabbed her forcefully by the right arm and marched her out of the cell.

His grip hurt her, but she tried not to resist. It would only hurt more.

Jane sat in a rickety wooden chair at a steel table. The policemen had left her there, locking the door behind them. A small camera on a miniature tripod was pointing at her. A red light indicated it was recording. The room was smaller with the same solid walls and steel grate door but no windows. The same type of bulb hung from the ceiling at the end of a long electric cord.

The sounds of people shouting had diminished. It seemed she was deeper within whatever building she was being held in. Her head hurt like mad. She wanted to crawl into a corner and throw up. The ringing in her ears had become fainter. She could smell blood even though she had none on her. She tried to make sense of what had just happened, but her mind wasn't processing stimuli correctly.

Two burly grim-faced men, with the biggest moustaches, entered. From his presentation and bearing, one of them was an officer. His dark grey and khaki uniform was new and nicely pressed. He had more stripes on his upper sleeve than the inspector who had arrested her.

He sat in the chair opposite her. The other man wore an off-white *shalwar kameez* and stayed standing. From his demeanour, he seemed like a policeman as well, but junior. Maybe he was a plainclothes detective.

Their faces were grim and unsmiling. What was about to happen?

'What's going on here?' Jane tried sounding firm but also calm and reasonable. She was aware she sounded more like a whining child. 'Who was that man with the gun? Why was he shooting at me? And why are you holding me in a cell?'

'We don't know identity of man. We thinking he coming to kill dead womans.'

Jane had to concentrate because of his broken English. What he'd said was not true. The gunman had been after her. But he was dead. Her pressing concern was getting out of there.

'In Shakar Parian, they told me they only wanted to ask me questions,' she said, enunciating clearly. 'Why are you locking me up?'

The officer studied her for a moment. His companion handed him a folder. The officer opened it, picked up a paper, scanned through it and spoke in a gruff voice. 'You are arrested for violationing section 295c.'

'Excuse me what...?' her voice trailed off. The room started spinning. How could they arrest her? What was section 295c? She had to leave for home in two days.

'Section 295c, blasphemy.'

Blasphemy sounded bad. Pakistan was an Islamic country with the Shariah law. This was serious. Her throat became dry and constricted, and her breathing became ragged. The ceiling, the lights, the whole room were now spinning faster. The blood drained from her face. She was covered in sweat and shaking. Her body went weak; she was sinking into the chair. 'Sorry, there was no...' She had to compose her thoughts. 'I did not commit... blasphemy!'

The officer did not respond. He kept looking at her, unmoved. All accused people lied. The bigger the charge, the more they pleaded and tried to prove their innocence. He was yet to meet anyone who happily admitted they had done it.

'Please this is some sort of mistake,' Jane pleaded. 'I didn't commit blasphemy.' Her words came out in a whisper. She felt like peeing, but she couldn't let herself, not in front of these men. With great effort, she squeezed her bladder shut.

This wasn't happening. It couldn't be happening. The

room went dark. She slumped forward. She was so thirsty. 'Water please.'

The men looked at each other. The one standing left the room and came back with a bottle of water. He opened it and presented it to Jane who took it but her hands shook so hard she was unable to take a sip. The man helped her, careful not to touch her. Was she now dirty because she'd been accused of blasphemy? She knew Muslim men were not supposed to touch female strangers, but this was ridiculous; it almost felt insulting. She drank a few sips. The water calmed her but also made her aware of a sick empty feeling in the pit of her stomach.

'Please officer, this isn't true, it must be a mistake or a joke.' Jane tried to keep the pleading out of her voice but was unable to.

'Here is FIR, it was been signed by five peoples.' He turned the open folder towards her and pointed at a piece of paper with his finger stained brown with tobacco, motioning her to take it. 'And madam here in Pakistan nobody makes joke from blasphemy.'

Jane took the piece of paper handed to her. It was written in Urdu in some untidy scrawl.

'You must signing it,' he said after a few seconds, grabbing the paper back from her and pointing to some empty boxes, 'here and here.'

'I am not signing,' she said weakly. The room was spinning again. She had to pull herself together. 'I did nothing wrong...' she tried again to sound more forceful and assertive. She was an Australian citizen and had rights. They couldn't treat her this way.

Through the fog of panic, Jane remembered. Clara had also said it was blasphemy. She should have immediately contacted Simon or the Australian High Commission. Surely tearing posters couldn't be legally considered blasphemy. What kind of laws did this country have? She didn't even know what was on the posters when she ripped them up.

Those men had done it deliberately. Why?

'I did not commit blasphemy,' she repeated. She was going crazy. Her headache was excruciating. She remembered blasphemy mentioned in cultural training before she arrived here. It came rushing back to her. She remembered now why the consultant had placed so much emphasis on it. Blasphemy against the Prophet Muhammad attracted a mandatory death penalty. It was hard to forget anything associated with a death penalty. There was something else the instructor had mentioned about the law which she had thought was odd, but it wasn't coming to her now.

A mandatory death penalty. This couldn't be happening to her. Jane felt herself sinking again, going cold. A stronger wave of nausea washed over her. She wanted to drop to the floor on her hands and knees and throw up. She again felt like loosening her bladder but was able to keep it in, just. Not in front of these men. The nausea persisted. She couldn't help it anymore. She managed to get her head over to the side, past the chair and retched what was mainly water on the floor. That made her even dizzier. She was going to fall off the chair. Spreading her legs outwards for stability she moved her body forward and rested her head on the table. The room went dark.

The police officer looked at his junior. 'Lock her up in the small cell near the side yard by herself,' he said switching to Urdu. 'Put double the guards at her door and the main gate and notify the IG. Then clean up this mess. Tell the other woman's relatives to come and get her body. After that, I want to find out the identity of the gunman. Now move it.'

Jane heard his voice as a faraway mumble. She felt disconnected from reality and was still horribly nauseous. She had to go back to Australia in two days. Why would someone want to do this to her?

SEARCH FOR A LAWYER

Lahore, Saturday 26 November, 7:25am

It was morning. A dull pain, deep in Jane's left eye socket throbbed mercilessly, making her nausea worse. A knot cramped her stomach. She was stiff as a board; her breathing was shallow. The memory of last night rushed in and overwhelmed her. She burst into tears that pooled on the thin hard rubber mat, she lay on.

The cell, about a quarter the size of the first one, was cold and damp. The same type of bulb hung from the ceiling. It was unlit. Light streaming through two small windows illuminated the opposite wall but left the corners in shadow. A battered stainless-steel food tray, on the floor, next to her contained a flatbread, chickpeas in a sauce on a yellow enamelled plate and a cup of tea.

The noise of the angry mob had given way to normal street sounds. The police station building appeared to date back to the British era. From that and the din of the traffic, it seemed she was in an old and crowded part of Lahore.

She was still in the same clothes, but her phone was no longer with her. Someone had taken it. Ignoring the dizziness, she sat up slowly. Lack of food and the cold made her feel weak. She also badly needed to go to the toilet. A makeshift bamboo lattice screen nailed to the back of an old chair obscured a squatting type latrine.

Jane let the dizziness abate and then walked, unsteadily, over to it. She had never used one of these before, and it smelled awful. In the village, they used to dig a small pit and cover it up. Next to it in a space in the wall made by knocking out two bricks sat a roll of toilet paper. A faucet with a plastic *lotta* positioned below, provided water for washing up. To the left of the tap, another missing brick formed an alcove containing a pungent dark-pink soap.

Squatting in her jeans was uncomfortable, but she managed in the end. She flushed as best as she could and washed her hands and then her face with the pungent soap. The cold water refreshed her, and the nausea lessened a bit.

She had just finished drinking the tepid tea and eating some of the hard and cold bread when a constable opened the cell door. Two other policemen entered and beckoned her to follow.

The visiting rooms were in a row of huts in a courtyard outside the main building but within the police station compound. The huts were built up against a tall brick wall, with wicked looking hooks along the top, that separated the police station from the world outside. The heavy steel door to the courtyard was kept locked.

They led Jane to the leftmost hut. The room had nicer furnishings and cleaner walls than her cell, but it still had bars on the windows and door. Six wooden armchairs with cushions upholstered in a dark maroon vinyl were set around a large wooden conference table. A stocky, friendly looking man in a dark grey suit sat on one of the chairs facing the door. He smiled gently and rose as she entered.

'Ms Kelly, I am Sam Kitchener,' he said as he stretched out his hand, 'from the High Commission.'

Nodding dumbly, she shook his hand as she fought back the tears welling in her eyes.

He held out a business card. 'By the way, please call me Sam.'

Nodding, Jane took it and glanced at it as she sat in one of the chairs. The constables left. She waited till they were alone. 'I didn't do what I've been accused of.' Her voice was desperate, pleading.

'Ms Kelly, I am sure you're innocent, but I am not here as your legal counsel.'

'I need to get out of here. Please help me get out of here,' Jane said, aware of how frantic she sounded.

'I, I cannot do that... I'm sorry.' He had seen too many people in a similar situation, and it never got any easier. Tourists and expats often ran afoul of the law. Regardless of whether they were innocent or not he still felt sorry for them, especially when the punishment far outweighed the crime.

'Why can't you help me? What are you here for then?' Jane gripped the wooden arms of the chair hard to stop her hands from shaking.

'Our role is to offer consular assistance, but our abilities are very limited. Basically, I'm a friendly face. Here to let you know Carbonon and your family are aware of the situation and are doing everything they can to help you.'

'Yes well, I sent my eldest son and husband a message and also my boss, but they took my phone from me. I wasn't able to tell if they got my messages.' Her voice was low.

'I'm afraid, that's fairly standard. They never let people keep phones in a lock-up.'

'They charged me… with blasphemy. Do you know what that means?'

'Yes, we know. I won't lie. It's serious.' His expression was grave. 'By the way, we've spoken with your son, Damon. He had already organised to fly out.' Sam looked at his watch. 'He should have left Melbourne by now.'

'Oh!' She didn't want Damon to see her like this, in a police cell. On the other hand, if this really went pear-shaped she might not get many opportunities. She didn't want to think further along those lines. It would just lead to madness. 'What about--?'

'We got in touch with Simon Kucic. He was admitted to

hospital last night. Someone assaulted him.'

'Is, is he OK? What happened? Who did it?' Jane said in a shaking voice. What were the chances of Simon being assaulted at the same time as she was arrested and attacked? Was it a coincidence?

'The police haven't found any witnesses willing to testify. Apparently, he's mildly concussed, and needed stitches.'

'I don't understand... Why?' Jane was nonplussed.

'We don't either. I'm sorry. Also, we're trying to make contact with your husband.'

'He's in New Zealand and should be back soon. We were all supposed to return home to Melbourne on the same day.'

Sergei was caving in New Zealand with Razane. They were probably underground somewhere. Hopefully, they'd be reachable soon. She desperately needed their strength and support.

'What's gonna happen to me?' She knew she sounded scared. She was not going to fool anyone by putting on a brave face.

'Well, you are going to be presented in front of a judge where you'll be arraigned, in other words, formally charged.'

'But I'm innocent. I was set up, as in framed,' Jane said through gritted teeth. 'Can't a lawyer get the charges dropped?'

'Again, I am not your legal defence, so I can't advise you. But I must warn you such matters are treated very seriously in Pakistan. The judge will most probably not allow bail and won't listen to any arguments without a trial.'

'But... how long will that take? I can't stay here.'

'First things first; you need a lawyer. I've been informed Carbonon is working on it. It might take a few days.'

'A few days? No, don't say... I can't... there's no way...' She shook her head as tears welled in her eyes.

Sam took a travel pack of tissues from his briefcase and handed it to her. He ran his hands through his hair and rubbed his forehead. 'Ms Kelly, no lawyer in Pakistan, will risk taking this case, so we'll need someone based overseas who works in the Pakistan legal system.'

'This is crazy. Do you understand I didn't do anything?'

Sam pursed his lips sympathetically, 'Ms-- '

'Let me tell you what happened,'

'Ms Kelly-- '

'They were vandalising our panels; sticking on posters, I pulled them down--'

'Ms Kelly I'm just here to try to make them take better care of you. I've paid the superintendent a fee to make sure you get bottled water, clean food, and small amenities like toilet paper till help gets to you. I'm so sorry, I now have to leave.' He stood.

Jane let out a moan and rested her head on her upturned palms.

'I really am sorry this is happening to you. Our foreign office will be in touch with the Pakistani government to ensure you get a fair trial.'

Jane groaned. 'But... I'm trying to tell you, I shouldn't have to go to trial.' She burst into tears. 'This is such bullshit... a setup. I just ripped up the posters. They pasted them. How was I to know?' She pulled out a tissue and blew her nose.

'Ms Kelly, you must forgive me. I have to leave now, but... I'll be in touch.' Sam got up and stretched out his hand. Jane was slumped in her chair, looking down at the floor, in the depths of despair and did not look up. He turned and left with a heavy heart. He'd been in Pakistan long enough to know this wasn't going to end well.

THE LAWYER

Lahore, Sunday 27 November, 11:30am

Jane couldn't remember when she'd last felt this alone; most probably it was never. She'd certainly never been this miserable and scared. Where was everyone? Being locked up was incredibly frustrating; it made her feel so powerless. This must be how caged animals felt.

At least the food had improved. The first morning's breakfast had sickened her with diarrhoea that had lasted till the evening. This morning they had brought her a tasty Danish roll and a cup of coffee in a Styrofoam cup. Now lunch was McDonald's, a burger, French fries, and a drink. She opened the paper bag and munched on the burger. She was still unwell but had to keep her strength up. Thank goodness for the Australian High Commission.

Jane had just finished eating when the door opened again. Two constables came in and asked her to follow.

Simon and Damon were waiting for her in the visitor hut. Jane almost jumped with joy when she saw her son and gave him a big hug. Hugging him was always like hugging a bear, he was so tall and broad.

'How's my big giant teddy bear?' she said.

'I'm fine, Mum,' Damon said smiling.

Simon looked like he had stopped a truck with his face. It was all purple and yellow with a big bandage between his nose and his left cheekbone.

She hugged Simon carefully. 'How are you feeling?'

'Better now, they gave me a strong antibiotic to stave off

an infection.'

'Have they found who did it?'

'No, they haven't. I've my suspicions. I'll tell you--'

'How are you holding up, Mum?' Damon interrupted. 'You've lost weight.'

'It's the Pakistani food,' Jane said smiling, 'it's like playing Russian roulette. About one in six meals cause diarrhoea.'

Her world wasn't so bleak, now that she was in the company of people she loved and cared for. Maybe things were going to look up.

'Hopefully, you get out soon,' Damon said.

'You know, I don't think I could stand it for much longer,' Jane said. Every hour was torture.

'Well, I've sent Dad a message and have spoken with Ben.' He rubbed his eyes.

Jane looked at them both. Poor Damon looked tired from his journey. She felt guilty. He should be living his life instead of being dragged halfway around the world to rescue his mother. Simon looked unusually worried. She'd never seen him like this. Nothing ever affected him. He got angry often but never worried. What was it he wanted to tell her?

'I'm really sorry this is happening to you, Jane,' Simon said, snapping her out of her thoughts. 'We've organised a local solicitor who's--'

'Ah good so you did find a local lawyer,' Jane said.

'No,' Simon said, 'he's only willing to help with the paperwork. He won't go to court or represent and has asked for his name to be kept off the record.'

'Oh! The fellow from the High Commission said something about local lawyers not--'

'He's scared of retribution,' Damon said.

'But, why?'

'They're scared for good reason. In the last month there were three high profile murders linked to blasphemy cases,' Simon said. 'But not to worry--'

'Not to worry?' Jane said through clenched teeth.

'We've found a lawyer, a Mr Rabbani, out of Singapore and Carbonon's legal counsel is on the way as well,' Simon said. 'Mr Rabbani should be here any moment.'

Almost as if on cue, the guard opened the door. They all turned to see a smartly dressed, middle-aged, man with a slim build, and a thick beard and moustache. When he got closer, Jane noticed he had green eyes.

She stood up and offered her hand. He grabbed it in both of his and shook it warmly.

'I am Jamshed Rabbani, Ms Kelly,' he said in a clipped upper-class English accent. 'Please call me Jamshed.'

'Well call me Jane,' she said, 'it's a relief to finally have a lawyer.'

'I cannot begin to imagine how hard this would be for you,' he said in a warm voice. 'We'll try to do everything possible to help you out of this situation.' His grim look belied his encouraging words.

'You've an English accent. Are you English?' she asked.

'Well, I'm a bit of everything. I was born in England to a Pakistani father and an English mother; I live in Singapore and practice in England, Pakistan and Singapore.'

'Sorry if I… I didn't mean to be nosy or rude, I just wanted to know your background for the case. I hope you under--'

'I completely understand; it's a very unpleasant situation to be in.'

'We're really worried about what they've charged Mum with,' Damon said, 'and need to make sure you aren't affected by um, the religious emotionality.'

'I know what you mean. You don't have to worry about my legal team, and I. Most of us are Muslims. We work with the law even though we don't like how it's written. It has caused so much misery and has been used to oppress minorities. It presumes guilt and does not allow for extenuating circumstances. Its punishments are also unduly harsh.'

Every word Jamshed uttered filled Jane with ever-increasing dread. 'So, tell me please, what's really going on? What's gonna happen to me?'

'In a nutshell, the First Information Record, or FIR, has been signed by five people. They all swear they saw and heard you insult the prophet,' Jamshed said, 'You apparently tore some posters bearing his name and shouted insults while doing so. The words you allegedly used were not listed, but that is normal for here. Accusers do not want to run the risk of blaspheming themselves, so the words are never recorded. We have spoken with your maid and driver, and unfortunately, they corroborate the testimony. To make matters worse, your accusers claim they have you on video.'

Jane put her head in her hands and moaned, 'I was afraid of that, but it proves what I thought all along. This is a bloody setup; they were trying to sabotage our solar panels... and this was the second time in a week. I reacted in anger. I didn't shout insults at the Prophet. I just screamed at the men.'

'We'll look into that. This law has been used before to frame people, so we will try to use it as our defence, but for that, we must find a motive.'

'I need you to believe me. I didn't insult the Prophet. I shouted at the men.' Jane repeated, enunciating slowly, trying to keep her voice level. 'They knew what was on the posters. Why did they paste them on my panels? If anything, they've been more disrespectful.'

'Jane, we have hired a private investigator and have found out who your accusers are. The old man who led the group is a cleric. He is the self-styled leader of a religious group called the Jamaat-e-Ilahi. They are bad news. The worst. All the accusers are from the same group. Now, that Ali and Clara have put their names on the FIR they will be forced to act as witnesses. They will be driven by fear to testify what they believe the group wants them to,' Jamshed said.

'Let's then focus on proving it was a setup and have the

case thrown out,' Simon said, 'clearly the cleric fellow did it twice and he knew what was going to happen to the posters.'

'That will be my argument, but don't let's get our hopes up,' Jamshed said. 'The Sessions Court judge will take a hard-line approach and will, most likely, support an arraignment. Anything else and he would be putting his own life and that of his family in danger.'

'Who are these bastards everyone's so afraid of?' Damon asked.

'The country is full of them, Jamshed said. 'It's very hard to explain, but religion is such an emotive issue here. Pakistanis are very emotional people. On top of it, a big majority are uneducated, and reason and logic do not figure strongly in how they think. Love for the prophet is ingrained into children from a very young age. So many people would be willing to die for him.'

'But…what…?' Damon had a confused look on his face.

'They would be ready to die to prove their love for him,' Jamshed said, 'and unfortunately it means they could kill as well.'

Damon looked around for a chair. He had to sit. 'Killing for love… Sounds so bizarre,' he said. His voice sounded strange to him. What a fucking nightmare this was?

'Well, history is full of people who kill for all sorts of reasons. Love tends to be right up there along with greed and power.'

Damon shook his head in disbelief. 'Bloody hell,' he said.

'It actually gets worse. If it were just the illiterates, it wouldn't be so much of a problem. Educated fanatics have found it to be an effective rallying cry for their political ambitions. It wins them votes.'

'So, this law is used for political power?' Simon said.

'Yes sadly. The ruling party have now made it part of their platform as well, to get some of those votes back.'

'Doesn't it mean Mum won't get a fair trial?' Damon said. He felt like being sick. The way Jamshed had described it there seemed to be no way out.

'That's hard to say. The judge will go by the evidence which is all stacked against Jane,' Jamshed said, 'and no witnesses will come forward to support her. Most of these cases get bogged down for a very long time, sometimes years. Not many people have been acquitted and even if they have many are killed straight after.'

'So, you're telling me, I'm doomed?' Jamshed's words filled Jane with dark despair.

'I am saying you are in an extremely challenging situation.' Jamshed's expression was grim. 'Your life is in danger all the time, and many people in the country will be against you.'

'Jane,' Simon said taking her hand, 'we're not going to give up.' He smiled comfortingly, 'I plan to use all my contacts to make sure the Australian and American governments put maximum pressure on the Pakistani government to ensure you are safe and at least have a fair trial.'

'That kind of exposure will certainly help, and will also be her best chance of staying safe,' Jamshed said, 'Anyway let's take things a step at a time. Tomorrow is your arraignment. We will, of course, move to have the charges struck down and the case dismissed, but I don't expect a positive result tomorrow.'

Jane's mind was going numb. She was falling into an abyss of despair.

Simon sat back in his chair. He was going to have to tell Jamshed about the conversations he had with Jibran Ghaffar and the attack on him. They had to be linked. Had he precipitated this action against Jane? If so he had possibly signed her death warrant. But hadn't Jane mentioned the crazies had pasted the posters before their meeting, before he had even spoken with Tajammul? Maybe it wasn't linked. He wouldn't be able to live with himself if it was.

BEFORE THE ARRAIGNMENT

Lahore, Sunday 27 November, 12:30am

Damon stood in the police station car park. The sun pierced the haze and warmed the back of his neck. He was shaking from the effort to stay calm and collected in front of his mother. The situation was much worse than he'd imagined, but he couldn't let her see the fear he felt inside.

He watched the chaotic traffic on Charsadda Street as he waited for Simon and Jamshed to come out of the guard house. Simon's driver was busy wiping the dust off the Mercedes. It seemed like an exercise in futility.

Damon remembered he had his smartphone switched off. He turned it back on. Ben had sent a message.

'How's Mum holding up?'

'Fine considering,' Damon replied via text.

'Where's Dad and the bitch?' Ben's response was immediate. Damon had hoped he would respond fast but not like this. Ben had completely rejected Razane and had not spoken with the family for the last two years. He was angry with Damon as well, but at least he hadn't deleted him as a Facebook friend. While they had not communicated directly, they had stayed in touch liking each other's posts every now and then.

'Be nice, man. It's not the time to fight,' Damon wrote. He would call him later to explain the situation. A text message was never the best way to deliver bad news.

He could somewhat understand Ben's discomfort, but he was taking this too far. At first, he'd been extremely uncomfortable with the whole situation himself, but had eventually decided it was their life and their right to live it as they pleased. At least they all seemed happy. He still remembered the shock at his Dad's birthday celebration. They'd all gotten together to cut a cake. Ever since he could remember birthdays were only for the four of them. That time, however, a stranger joined in.

Razane was strikingly attractive, but her face had a hardness that spoke of a troubled life. During the evening, he discovered she had been a Peshmerga fighter in Kurdistan. Their mother had hired her as a translator to help with a project in Northern Iraq. During her employment, Razane had saved his Mum's life. They had been close friends, ever since.

When his Dad had cut the cake, Razane gave him a warm hug and then an equally warm lingering and very non-platonic kiss on the lips.

Ben's jaw dropped. His own expression would have been similar. They both looked at their mother, bracing themselves for an unpleasant reaction. She was scary when she lost her temper. They half expected her to punch Razane and throw something at their Dad, but the expected Armageddon did not eventuate. Instead, she gave Razane the most tender kiss on the lips he'd ever seen.

Some safety mechanism prevented his brain from going into meltdown. He remembered searching for some simple, plausible explanation. Maybe Razane was just a good friend, and that is how they greeted in Kurdistan. Ben must have processed things differently. He went silent after that.

Later that evening they all went to one of their father's favourite restaurants. It was just after the entrees their mother dropped a bombshell.

'Razane's moving in with us. All three of us are in a relationship.'

'You're letting Dad have a mistress?' Ben hissed loud enough for everyone in the restaurant to hear.

'We're both in love with her,' their mother replied.

'That's so… sick.' Ben almost pushed his chair over in his haste to get up.

'Ben it's Dad's birthday, let's talk about this like adults,' he had said, trying to calm the situation.

'They should leave me out of their sordid mid-life crisis,' Ben responded tersely.

'Ben, we all love each other very much,' his Mum's voice was calm, she obviously hoped to reason with him.

Razane had tears running down her face. 'And how exactly are we hurting anyone?' his Dad said with a steely edge to his voice. He gave Razane a tissue and pulled her close.

'It's fucking abnormal,' Ben responded. Since a young age, Ben had always behaved a bit like a priest, with a conservative outlook on life, quite different to the relaxed and easy-going nature of their parents.

'Ben, who's to say what's normal?' He tried to play the mediator even though the news had freaked him out as well. By then Ben was already halfway to the door.

'Shall I go and speak with him?' he had asked.

'No leave him, he'll be back.' His mother had replied, but she had underestimated Ben's stubbornness. He hadn't spoken to them since. Quite predictably the rest of the evening had not gone too well.

Lost in his thoughts, Damon did not notice a man on a motorcycle who had calmly taken out his phone and was taking photos of both him and Simon's driver.

SERGEI AND RAZANE

Melbourne, Sunday 27 November, 5:45pm

Sergei unlocked the front door of their penthouse apartment and held it open for Razane, 'Madame, after you.'

'Home sweet home,' she said, the wheels of her suitcase clicked over the tiled floor as she pulled it behind her. He followed letting the door close gently behind them.

'That was a lovely experience,' Sergei said as he grabbed her by the waist and pulled her close. With her high cheekbones, wavy dark hair and large brown eyes Razane was a head turner with an alluring sexiness that was hard to explain.

'What are you thinking?' Razane said in a low voice.

'You know,' he sighed. 'How I'm so lucky to have you two in my life?'

'Yes, you are. We all three are.' He was sometimes so sentimental and deep. Most men with his abilities were shallow and conceited. To her, he was the perfect combination of being grounded and confident at the same time. It was a nice bonus that he was handsome in a hard and rugged way. With his chiselled face and piercing blue eyes, he looked perpetually stern and serious, but he had the warmest smile that could light up a room. She and Jane were just as fortunate as he was.

She leaned forward and kissed him on the lips. 'Thank you for a great time, my love.'

He kissed back. 'Mmm, you're delicious...'

'You are hungry.' She smiled.

'For you, always,' he said, as he grabbed his suitcase and

walked to his study.

'Tea?' Razane called out.

'Sure, I'll come and help you as soon as I get my SIM into this new phone,' he still felt annoyed his smartphone had smashed during the climb to the surface. He was itching to log into the replacement they had picked up on the way back from the airport. Sergei never liked being offline, but today he had a strange, uneasy feeling. Something was not right. He needed to be online.

'Don't worry, my love, the world does not stop just because you are not on the Internet,' Razane guessed what he was thinking. He was the world's biggest geek. He couldn't be without his technology for a minute before he had withdrawal symptoms.

'I know, I know, I just have an unpleasant feeling something's wrong.' He heard her pottering about in the kitchen putting the kettle on.

'Serge, you worry needlessly, my love,' Razane said, raising her voice above the noise of the kettle as it was beginning to boil, 'I can't wait for Jane to get back. She makes such nice tea.' She hummed a little tune as she remembered the last few days hiking and caving in New Zealand. 'That cave is now one of my happy places.'

Sergei didn't reply.

They had spent a long time exploring a new branch of a cave on a friend's property near Hangatiki in New Zealand and were tired. After crawling through a series of tight passageways over a hundred metres below ground, they had found a large cavern that was nice and dry and decided to stop to rest. They switched off their torches to conserve power. As their eyes adjusted to the dark, they found the walls of the cavern awash with the ethereal light of hundreds of glow worms. They lay there together in each other's warm embrace, the absolute stillness only punctuated by the sounds of their hearts beating in unison and the occasional plop of a drop of water.

They were so overcome with love and wonderment they completely lost any sense of time.

Razane recited,

'When these We and Ye shall all become one Soul,
they will be lost and absorbed in the Beloved,'

Her soft voice echoed gently in the cavern. It was one of her favourite Rumi verses, and it made so much sense to her. Being lost was the only way to be truly found.

'You know you are beautiful, my darling,' Sergei had mumbled into her hair, 'more beautiful and wonderful than even this magical place.' She had smiled and turned around to kiss him tenderly, her heart full of gladness.

'That's the only reason why you can't wait for her?' Sergei walked into the kitchen.

He had taken that long to register what she had said and had missed half of it.

Razane came out of her reverie. 'So, you want a whole long list of all the things we need her back for.' She hugged him. She was too happy to let Sergei's absent-mindedness spoil her mood. He squeezed her back.

'Yes, in complete pornographic detail,' he said with a smile as he walked out of the room.

'What do you want me to… text it to you?' she said smiling. He was unusually preoccupied today.

She opened the fridge and took out the milk. It was so nice to have someone stock it for them while they were away. It was just one of the benefits of finally having some spare cash. Ever since they all had combined their incomes and assets, they were, for the first time in their lives, financially well off.

Sergei said something from the other room. His voice was different. He seemed upset. Perhaps his SIM card did not fit the phone or something else that could only be described as a First World problem. Just three years ago she was fighting the Al Nusra Front and Islamic State in Syria and her predicaments, and those of the people around her were very different and far more serious. Being too tired to clean your weapon every night, getting frostbite from the crazy winters, getting shot at and blown up. Having to huddle up in close quarters with male comrades and then having to dispel their unwelcome amorous advances.

'Jane's in trouble,' he said shuffling into the kitchen his eyes on his phone. His voice had taken on a deep dark, sombre tone.

That snapped her out of reminiscing. A knot formed in her belly. Her neck muscles tightened involuntarily.

'What happened? What kind of trouble, is she alright?' Razane's voice was like that of a frightened child. She snatched the overly large phone from his hands. It had two messages from Jane, about twenty from Damon and one from Ben. Her heart skipped a beat. It had to be serious if Ben was messaging them. She realised she had not even switched her own phone on.

'Jane's in jail in Pakistan,' Sergei said, as she began to read. His voice sounded distant like he was talking underwater. She clicked on Damon's messages.

'Oh my god!' Razane almost dropped the phone, 'blasphemy!' She had to sit down to stop herself fainting. Her world, their world, was unravelling. It had been too good to be true. Ben and so many other people had been right; they were too greedy, it was unnatural to have so much happiness and pleasure. There were so many envious people, and someone had cast an evil eye on them.

It was one of the annoying things her mother used to say. The rational side of her knew evil eyes did not exist, but panic subsumed her rational mind.

'Blasphemy?' He sat down and held her as she buried her

face in his shoulder. 'How dumb and archaic?' His voice shook. He understood the seriousness of the situation. This was no trivial matter. Far from it. In countries like Pakistan, it carried the death penalty.

'I read someplace, blasphemy carries a mandatory death penalty in Pakistan,' she said, verbalising his thoughts at the exact time as they solidified in his mind. They were often in sync like that. They sat for a few moments side by side, thinking depressing thoughts. The world suddenly a dark and morose place, their happy paradise was crashing around them.

Sergei finished looking through the rest of his phone. He had some emails and text messages from DFAT, The Department of Foreign Affairs and Trade. He dialled Damon.

'Hey Dad, finally!'

'Yes, we just got back. I'll put you on speakerphone so Razane can hear also.'

'Dad...' His tone indicated he didn't want Razane involved.

'Where are you?' Sergei's voice hardened. He knew what Damon was going to say. He was not going to let him make Razane feel excluded.

'Lahore. I just visited Mum in the police station lock-up with Simon and her lawyer Jamshed Rabbani. I have messaged you his number.' He filled them in on what had happened and told them how the lawyer was negative about her prospects.

Sergei noticed another call. Jane's boss, Simon, was trying to contact him.

'Damon, I've got a call coming in from Simon. Can you please talk to Ben? Ask him to come to our apartment.' He hung up and switched the call over to Simon.

Simon had set up a conference call with someone in DFAT. Carbonon was an Australian success story, and Jane's arrest was going to be covered extensively by the media. The government was paying attention to their case. The phone call lasted forty-five minutes. DFAT promised to do all they could to help Jane but cautioned them that they could not intervene in a domestic legal issue in a sovereign country.

'Fuckers,' Sergei said furiously as he hung up, 'our government are happy to collect taxes but won't stand up for us when we need them to.'

Still angry, he called the lawyer.

Jamshed Rabbani brought them up to speed on the case. He had been able to approach several religious leaders in the preceding few hours, one of them a former Olympic hockey player. They had promised to try and intercede on Jane's behalf and seek clemency. Sergei could sense Jamshed was trying to manage their expectations.

Razane ordered takeaway noodles. They needed their strength if they were going to get through this and she was not going to let them down by being weak.

When the intercom buzzed. It was Ben. He asked if he could come up.

Jane's arrest for blasphemy was the second story on the news. The first was a massive bomb blast in Turkey's capital Ankara.

Damon called a while later. He was using WhatsApp. 'Have you got in touch with Ben?' he asked when Razane picked up the phone.

'I'm here,' Ben said.

'Good, we need to discuss what we're gonna do, and we need to do this together, as a family,' Damon said.

MACK

Lahore, Sunday 27 November, 4:00pm

O h, fucking no, what had he done? Mack's hands shook as he disconnected the call. Feelings of guilt and remorse threatened to overwhelm him. A stream of sweat poured down his forehead. His heart began to palpitate; his blood pressure rose. His hands became clammy like they always did when he got anxious. Now he knew what Damon's strange phone call had been about. Why hadn't the boy just told him the real reason he was flying to Pakistan?

What to do first? He needed his anxiety medication and his blood pressure pills. The doctor had warned against too much stress. Apparently, he was overweight and a candidate for an early heart attack if he didn't change his habits.

This was all ultimately his fault. He had convinced Jane to take the project in Shakar Parian even though Pakistan was not yet truly safe for foreigners. The village was part of an independent farmers cooperative he was negotiating produce prices with. It helped him get a great deal, but he had unwittingly put Jane's life in danger.

He did, of course, want to help improve the quality of life in villages and to earn foreign exchange for the country but the real reason was a selfish one. Making deals was like heroin, and he was the addict. It didn't even matter if it made money or not. He had so much in so many bank accounts all over the world only his accountant was able to keep track.

In his excitement, he had not considered all the possible

dangers. While the country had grown its industrial base a lot in recent years, the main money and power was still in the rural sector. Landowners behaved like lords controlling every aspect of village life. In this case, the villagers owned their land, but there were always disputes and power plays and vendettas that went on for generations. He should have known better. In the cold light of day, it was obviously not a place for a naive foreigner. By encouraging her to do the project he had without any doubt put Jane in harm's way. It could end up costing Jane her life.

He could live an easy life in Australia, where his parents had emigrated when he was nine, but he loved Pakistan too much to stay away. He spent three months out of the year managing his rice export business from Lahore.

'You can take the Pakistani out of Pakistan, but you can never take Pakistan out of the Pakistani,' he used to tell his friends. They never understood why he kept returning even during the darkest years when bomb blasts had become a daily occurrence, and kidnappings had reached epidemic levels.

The situation in Pakistan had improved a lot since then, and a lot of credit went to the army. Over the last two years, they had managed to reduce much of the operational capacity of the terrorist cells operating in the country. People started rebuilding and expanding businesses; foreign investment began pouring back in. The economy rebounded and grew at one of the fastest rates in Asia.

He had stupidly thought Jane would be safe. He would never have knowingly placed her life in danger. It was so dumb of him and could only be characterised as gross negligence of the worst kind. His mind was wandering. He had to calm down and breathe and focus. He swallowed the pills and took a large gulp of water to wash them down. His mind was prone to wander under stress.

He remembered what he had promised Sergei. He rang his contact in the immigration department to arrange visas for him and Razane. Then he rang the Avari, one of Lahore's two five-star hotels, and booked a suite. The PR manager was a close personal friend. She always looked after him. Pakistan was all about whom one knew.

Now that he was busy he felt better. Sergei had not told him much, just that Jane had been arrested for blasphemy. She had apparently torn some posters a group of men had pasted on her solar panels.

'Jane has always had a temper,' he had remarked.

'Yes, that she has, and once she gets fired up nothing can stand in her way,' Sergei had replied with a strained laugh.

'She is a brave and courageous woman, very spunky.'

Yes, that was Jane, alright. She was slim and of average height but what she lacked in physical stature she more than made up for in boldness.

'And now she's in the deepest shit imaginable.' Sergei's voice had cracked. 'Mack, you gotta help us.'

'You don't even have to say it. You and Jane are family and Razane of course.'

Sergei took a deep breath. 'Thanks, bro.'

'How is Razane holding up?'

'She's putting on a brave face. She loves Jane like crazy.'

'And you as well my friend. I have seen how she looks at you.'

'Yes, I know. I am worried about Razane, though. She's not well. Her doctor has ordered her to avoid stress at all costs.'

Mack knew about Razane's troubled past. 'Well, she is a tough one,' he had said.

'With a soft centre…' Sergei said. 'Anyway bro, I'll owe you for the rest of my life.'

'I'm going to kick you in the head if you keep talking like this…'

'OK, see you very soon,' Sergei had said as he hung up.

Mack had read about the blasphemy case. It was front-page news for the last two days. The media had wrongly identified her as an American, so he had not connected it to Jane.

It was a massive shock to find out it was his Jane, his sweet friend, the wife of his best friend. He had a secret crush on her ever since Sergei had met her. He always told himself it was purely platonic and nothing else, but he could not help being turned on whenever she hugged him. Misgivings and guilt invariably followed these feelings. Regardless, somewhere in a small unacknowledged corner of his mind, she was his beautiful, feisty Jane.

He switched on the TV. The news was all about demonstrations organised by several Islamist groups, who always made trouble. There was a new name among them, Jamaat-e-Ilahi. He had heard of them before from an acquaintance of his, a major in the Pakistani Army Intelligence.

Jamaat-e-Ilahi was a new terrorist group, rabidly anti-western and obviously trying to rise in the ranks of Pakistani terrorist organisations. They were so new they were not yet on any global intelligence watchlist. Not many people knew about them, but he did. It felt good to be in the know; that's why it was great to have contacts everywhere.

NEED FOR PLAN B

K im's Restaurant was famous for its club sandwich. It was juicy and delicious but, at that moment, Damon did not appreciate it at all. He might as well have been eating cardboard. Unsurprisingly he wasn't in a good mood, and Jamshed Rabbani wasn't helping one bit.

Jamshed had asked for the meeting. Simon had suggested doing it over dinner. Damon had asked for it to be at the Avari, where he was staying. He didn't want to traipse over town like a tourist. He wasn't in the mood to do anything and couldn't remember ever feeling this depressed.

The route from the police station to the Avari took three times longer than it should have as traffic was diverted onto smaller roads. The police had blocked a large section of Mall Road to contain the violent demonstrations called for by several extremist groups.

His heart pounding with fear, Damon had watched from behind a police barrier. It had resembled a battle scene. Broken glass, bricks and burning tyres littered the road which was empty of traffic. Most parked cars were ablaze and many turned onto their side or their roof. Several shops were on fire, and most had their windows smashed. The crowd of angry religious fanatics were shouting and holding placards demanding the death penalty for Jane. Riot police responded by firing tear gas canisters. When that did not help they resorted to water cannon and rubber bullets.

On the way, his Dad called. They had found a flight and were headed to the airport. They'd arrive in Lahore tomorrow. That made him feel a bit better although he'd have preferred it if Razane had stayed back. They did not need a woman suffering her own trauma, complicating matters.

'Jane is standing over an abyss. Only an extraordinary effort and good luck will pull her back from it.' Jamshed's matter of fact tone snapped him back to the present.

Damon scowled. 'With all due respect I was hoping for some more positivity,' he spoke slowly and leaned forward for emphasis. Simon nodded in agreement.

'Gentlemen, I have no intention of leaving any stone unturned,' Jamshed said as he steepled his hands together, 'but you must be under no illusions and understand, exactly, what you are dealing with.' He paused to let his words sink in. 'This case will be an uphill battle. We cannot indulge in wishful thinking.'

Damon rubbed his forehead. His head was hurting. 'So, tell me, please… What do we do to maximise her chances?' He leaned back in his chair and kneaded his neck muscles. They were incredibly sore.

Jamshed's phone rang. He answered it. Damon took another bite of the sandwich and willed himself to swallow it.

'The arraignment will be tomorrow,' Jamshed said ending the call, 'at 11.15 at the Sessions Court. I have organised an interpreter. I'll pick you up on the way to court.'

'Jamshed, what should we do to get my mother out?' Damon said, repeating himself.

'I can make a list of things, but we also need to be realistic and prepare for the worst,' Jamshed replied.

Simon and Damon exchanged glances. Damon's phone beeped. He glanced at it. It was another message from Ben.

A waiter brought Jamshed's meal, a large steak with chips. Jamshed waited while he fussed with the table and refilled their glasses.

'Look, you have hired me, so that's a start. But we need something a bit more powerful to back me up. Government intervention would be helpful. If someone could get some more religious leaders to intervene it might help too.'

'We're already talking to the Australian government,' Simon interjected. 'I've spoken with our foreign office, and they assured me the minister will contact the Pakistani government directly. We're also talking to people to get a plea for clemency from other world leaders including the Pope.'

'We should also seek help from local religious leaders. Make them see these are trumped up charges,' Jamshed said. 'I have already contacted those I was able to, but we must try every possible person who can influence the outcome.'

'Is clemency possible?' Simon asked, 'what are the chances? Has it happened before?'

'Well, if we can convince the accusers it was all a misunderstanding there is always a chance,' Jamshed said, 'the case gets dropped before it goes to trial.' He paused and took a bite of his steak. 'It might seem surprising but most Pakistanis, even many religious figures are not extremists. A small number of crazies have ruined our reputation, but most of us are tolerant and peaceful,' he said wiping his mouth with his napkin.

The people he saw demonstrating today hadn't looked tolerant or peaceful, but maybe they didn't represent the majority. 'So how do we approach them?' Damon said.

'Not directly. Simon and I will work on our connections within the country and see if we can put indirect pressure on them,' Jamshed said, 'In the past, some cases have been dropped and the accused pardoned and acquitted, but the situation has gotten much worse recently.'

'In what way?'

'What do you mean?'

'How has it gone worse?' Damon asked.

'Well, the law was toughened to make the death penalty mandatory. Also, quite a few government figures and lawyers who stood up for accused people have been attacked recently. Like everywhere else in the world, extremists hijack the majority view.'

Except in other parts of the world, extremists did not kill. 'You're throwing up a lot of uncertainties,' Damon said.

'Yes, and I will add some more,' Jamshed said, 'I really want to see a good outcome here, but that will only happen if you truly understand what an uphill task this is. What I am trying to say is we don't only need a plan,' he paused as he cut into his steak, 'but also a plan B and a plan C and if possible a plan D.'

Simon ate silently, wracked by guilt. He hadn't yet found a way to tell Jamshed about Jibran Ghaffar and Tajammul, and he didn't want to do it while Damon was around. Fingers crossed the case might get dismissed tomorrow. He'd wait till after the arraignment.

JIHAD

Lahore, Sunday 27 November, 6:30pm

M aulana Abdul Zubair, the Imam of the Sabz Burj Mosque, slowly stroked his long beard as he sat, legs crossed, on a mat in the small dimly lit prayer room. The *Maghreb* prayers were over, and the congregation had all left.

Alone with his thoughts, he counted the prayer beads, one by one. Each bead a perfunctory prayer, a habit performed without conscious thought. His mind was on his mission. God's mission to wage jihad against the apostates and the infidels. It was anyway not through prayer but with his life's work that he worshipped God. His work was to build an army to force Pakistan to become a true Islamic country completely free of Western corruption.

He shifted his weight; the twinge in his left leg had flared again. Old wounds might stop bleeding and broken bones might mend but they never fully healed. It was a beautiful pain, well worth having. It reminded him of the sacrifices he had made to get to where he was now.

Many years ago he took part in a Mujahideen ambush of a small Soviet convoy in Helmand province. He had volunteered to herd goats across the road to halt the convoy. Foolishly he had also agreed to stop in the middle and open fire. His bullets did nothing but signal the rest of the ambushing party to attack. The Russians returned fire on him with a turret-mounted machine gun. He managed to dive behind a rock, escaping most of the volley of bullets except two in his lower left leg. The ambush was over in a few minutes with all the Russians dead. His leg injuries had been so bad the doctor had wanted to amputate, but he had begged him not to. He was convinced Allah would fix him and he was right. He had miraculously healed.

After that, he took part in many more battles and skirmishes. He learnt to be more cautious. His bravado, however, had earned him a reputation. Men flocked to him. He became a commander of his own group. For a few years, he aligned himself with the warlord Gulbuddin Hekmatyar, but when the Taliban swept through the country and brought in their version of Islam, he happily joined them believing he was taking part in forming a true Islamic state.

He helped in the capture of Kabul from the Northern Alliance but so did the Pakistani army and their ISI. This did not sit well with him.

It made him doubt the purpose of his fight. He realised he was merely participating in a proxy war to turn Afghanistan into a puppet state for Pakistan. Disappointed, he returned to Pakistan. He was determined to bring about an Islamic revolution. Many of his men came with him.

In Lahore, he set up Jamaat-e-Ilahi. He worked slowly and cautiously and took great care to recruit men he could trust. Pakistan was a land of opportunity with far greater potential than Afghanistan. It had a highly respected professional army and nuclear weapons. Its geographic location gave it immense strategic importance. It could live up to its promise of being the land of the pure and a fortress of Islam.

He was not alone in his thinking. The Pakistani Taliban, Al Qaeda and later Islamic State all established bases and began to compete for power, prestige and the hearts and minds of the people.

His first objective was to raise money. He soon realised jihad, and terrorism was like any business. It needed investment to ensure a return. Terrorists and jihadists needed money to finance operations to increase their media exposure. This exposure would eventually pay back in donations. The larger the exposure, the more the donations would pour in.

The larger groups received millions of dollars. The Islamic State got theirs from Saudi Arabia, and the Taliban had donors spread throughout Pakistan, India, and the Middle East. It was how they were able to fund big operations, large-scale attacks, high casualty bomb blasts and sizeable massacres.

Jamaat-e-Ilahi was always going to be small in the eyes of the big donors and potential followers until they had managed at least one noteworthy event. In terrorist circles, this meant it would need to be reported by global media outlets such as Al Jazeera, CNN, New York Times, and the BBC.

In the beginning, his income came from small donations from collection tins in mosques and small local shops and from selling protection to traders in the northern districts of Lahore. Later he began offering his services to influential people who needed someone killed or kidnapped, or protection from assassination or kidnapping. The competition was fierce, but by Allah's grace he scrimped and saved enough money to build a large truck bomb. It was nearly complete and would finally put Jamaat-e-Ilahi on the map.

Two weeks ago, he had received a gift from Allah, a rich and powerful patron. Jibran Ghaffar a member of the National Assembly and a powerful landowner had brought him ten million rupees in cash in a suitcase, ostensibly for his mosque building fund. He also offered him land in his village to build a mosque and train his men.

His *jamaat* had only one mosque. With the money, they could build more. Each mosque would include a *madrassa*, a school for young children who could be taught and trained and moulded; new followers to swell his numbers and power. Being able to train away from prying eyes was an even bigger godsend. He could now finally build a disciplined fighting force like he had in Afghanistan. With this new money, he could also start a second bomb straight away.

He knew Jibran Ghaffar would want something in return. All donors eventually did.

He didn't have to wait long to find out. A week later Jibran returned to ask for his first favour. He was worried about a foreign company that was putting electricity in one of the villages. Even worse a foreign woman, working for the company, was spreading Christianity in the village and corrupting the people. Jibran had heard she was a blasphemer who openly insulted the prophet. He had pleaded for help to get rid of the woman and destroy her work.

Jibran did not need to try and convince him. He had agreed straight away. Together they came up with a clever way to prove her crime.

It was a good plan. Abdul Zubair hated Westerners especially those spreading Christianity. When they pretended to help the poor, they were ten times worse again. They were his direct competition. He tried to pull people towards Islam, and they tried to pull them the opposite way. And when they insulted the prophet they deserved only one thing, death. For him to be able to punish her would be a real blessing from Allah. As if he needed any further incentive, Jibran Ghaffar had brought him another ten million rupees and had promised the same amount again when she was dead. Allah was smiling on him.

Praise be to Allah the plan had worked splendidly. He had made a video and given it to the police.

At the last minute, Jibran had suggested they kill her without delay to send a message about the seriousness of her crime. He had agreed wholeheartedly. The *farangi* woman should not live to see her trial.

He didn't have enough time to plan it. Both times his men failed. Two failures were surely Allah's way of testing him.

Inshallah, they would not fail a third time.

He had asked his son, Adil, to watch over the police station to keep an eye out for any visitors. He did not have to wait long. A few hours ago, Adil had sent him photos of two *farangi* men. He had immediately shared them with Jibran Ghaffar.

Jibran had been pleased and had offered an extra five million rupees for each *farangi* he killed.

The money was as good as his. He knew his men. They were tough and hard, and by Allah's grace, they would not fail. Not again.

His thoughts were interrupted by a slender young man entering the room. '*Salam a leikum*,' he said as he walked towards him.

'*Wa aleikum asalam*, Billa,' Abdul Zubair responded, 'come, come and sit.'

'It has been done,' Bilal, or Billa as he was affectionately known, said as he sat at a respectful distance, 'Saleem has volunteered.'

'You don't mean Saleem *Bhai*?'

'No no no, Saleem Bhai is too important a man to do such humble work.'

'God's work is never humble,' Abdul Zubair reminded him, 'but yes Saleem *Bhai* is a bit slow. He would most likely stab himself.'

Bilal gave a polite titter, taking care not to show teeth. Too much mirth was never a sign of piety. '*Aqa*, it is Burnt Saleem.'

'Ah, that is better. Burnt Saleem is a tiger, but I didn't know he was back from Iraq.'

'Yes, he slipped in, through Baluchistan, last night.'

Maulana Abdul Zubair loved people like Burnt Saleem. He was a true believer and straight as an arrow. If you put a naked woman and a Quran next to him his eyes and hands would only go towards the Quran. He was also an extremely useful man, lethal and deadly but still a pawn who could be sacrificed to kill the woman.

America, Britain and Australia, in fact, all enemies of Islam would think twice before sending more people to violate his villages and brainwash his people. Their soft people would be too scared once they saw what happened to this one.

By Allah's grace, he was being paid to do His work, to eradicate this filthy Christian blasphemer who was defiling his country.

Next time He would surely grant him success. Surely Allah was all wise and all seeing.

He looked upwards, 'Thank you, Allah,' he mouthed.

Bilal did the same.

'I want you to organise something else,' Abdul Zubair said.

'Just say it.'

'Find me Katha and Farooqi. I have a job for them.'

'Yes, *Aqa.*'

'I need to find out where those *farangi* are staying.'

'*Aqa*, I already know.'

'Where? How?'

'I was with Adil at the police station. I had brought him some food. Just then the two *farangi* came out, so Adil asked me to follow them.'

'Oh, and…?'

'*Aqa*, they are staying at the two big *farangi* hotels.'

'*Shabash*. I still want Katha and Farooqi here; I need them to kill those two.'

'Yes, *Aqa.*'

'Also, do we know who the judge is?'

'The judge is Nadeem Ghazali, *Aqa*,' he replied.

'He is a reasonably pious man. Yes, he will do the right thing.'

Bilal nodded in agreement.

'OK, that is all for now.'

They both got up, he, considerably more slowly than Bilal.

'Tomorrow in the court Allah's work will be done. *Inshallah.*'

'*Inshallah!*'

UNREST

Lahore, Monday 28 November, 7:05am

Recurring nightmares kept Damon awake all night. His mother was in a white robe, she wore handcuffs and was being marched to the gallows. Each time when the hangman would place a black bag over her head, he would wake in a cold sweat.

In the morning the alarm on his smartphone woke him. He had a message confirming his dad and Razane had boarded their flight to Lahore. He hated waking early, even after a good sleep, but this was torture.

He turned over to switch the alarm off and looked at Google News. An idiot in a small town outside Texas had made a video parodying the Prophet Mohammad and had placed it on YouTube. It was titled, "Free Jane Kelly".

There was also a news story about a right-wing Dutch politician demanding western countries place an embargo on Pakistan until they repealed their blasphemy laws.

Damon got out of bed seething with rage. The stupid idiotic bastards would make everything worse. It was so easy to make statements and post videos when it was not their lives in danger. Things would not turn out well today.

As if on cue he became aware of a distant roar. It sounded like a large crowd protesting angrily. He looked out of his window, but his view was blocked by tall buildings. Here and there he caught glimpses of the surrounding streets. They were empty.

He took a quick five-minute shower. While towelling himself dry, he heard many gunshots in rapid succession and the sound of explosions.

Quickly getting dressed he took the lift down to the lobby. From here he could see the front lawn of the hotel and the main boundary wall separating the hotel grounds from Mall Road. The walls were too high to see outside, so he walked briskly to the main entrance where a throng of people had gathered.

A sweeping driveway separated the hotel's front lawn from the main building. The two large wrought iron gates were closed. Several hotel guests stood at the southern gate and looked through the bars at the masses of people running and shouting on Mall Road. Like in yesterday's demonstrations they carried large banners and long sticks. On the fringes of the mob, police in full riot gear, complete with padding and plexiglass shields, ran alongside swinging their batons at any protesters moving outside the swarm. They were herding them towards Charing Cross. As Damon watched, two water cannons came into view from the left.

Several projectiles were hurled from the road towards the hotel. They landed well short of the building, but the hotel guards motioned everyone inside.

Damon looked at his phone. There was no mobile signal. 'The police have turned the mobile networks off,' a man to his right said. 'It is to stop them calling for more protesters.'

'The police are certainly efficient.' he replied politely.

Thankfully the hotel wireless network still functioned, and he was still connected to the Internet and WhatsApp.

The Nation newspaper had a live coverage of the demonstrations. Apparently, the whole Muslim world, or so it seemed, was up in arms about the YouTube video. YouTube had since taken it down, but the damage was done. People were going to be hurt, his mother one of them.

He got a WhatsApp message from Jamshed. He and Simon were staying at the Pearl Continental just down the road. 'I am trying to confirm the arraignment will still happen today,' it said.

Damon sat in Kim's restaurant and ate breakfast. He wasn't looking forward to court. He hated courts and lawyers. It reminded him of his own brush with the law. He had once lied, under oath, so a friend could get out of a fine for littering. He was caught out and had to face a magistrate. It was the most humiliating experience of his life, and he'd vowed never to set foot in a court again. He had not anticipated this.

He forced himself to eat the spicy omelette and drink the sweet tea. Outside, the noise of the shouting crowds was replaced by the rumble of heavy trucks, and the sound of running soldiers. The army had been called in. Helicopters flew overhead. Guns were fired. Eventually, the demonstrators were dispersed. Many were arrested. At 10:15 the gates were opened. Traffic started flowing on Mall Road again.

Mobile services were still down, but he got another WhatsApp message from Jamshed. 'The case is on but postponed to 2:00 pm.'

THE CLOCK STARTS NOW

Lahore, Monday 28 November, 3:50pm

Damon was tired. Even though it was late November, the weather was oppressive. Jamshed, Simon and he sat on filthy plastic chairs, in a busy open corridor outside the courtroom on the first floor of the courthouse.

Like the police station, the Sessions Court was a grand old structure built when the British ruled India. It was a square building with verandahs on all four sides on all three floors. Corridors divided each floor, equally, into an eight-by-eight grid and started and ended in a verandah. Slow moving fans hung from the tall arched ceiling along the length of each corridor. They made almost no difference to the flow of air. It still felt stifling and closed-in for the most part except for a regular burst of fresh air that wafted over them every few minutes.

Going by the state of disrepair the building hadn't been renovated since it was built. Signs of decay were everywhere. The walls were a patchwork of fresh grey cement to cover over where the original render had de-laminated. Many of the railings along the staircases had lost their wooden cappings. Naked wires poked out of holes in the walls where light fittings had fallen off.

The whole place was buzzing with activity. Clearly law, or rather the breaking of it, was big business.

People of all types, sizes and ages trudged, walked, and ran in both directions. Lawyers accompanied by peons and their clients pushed through the crowd all looking haggard and tired. A person next to him was bellowing into his phone trying to outshout the chaotic din. Every now and again a policeman would walk a prisoner along in thick arm and leg chains. Hopefully, they wouldn't make his mother wear those.

People were selling copies of the Quran and small laminated prayer cards and prayer beads. Religion seemed like the second biggest business here. A man carrying plastic bags full of what was supposed to be drinking water walked by, selling quite a few to the bedraggled people waiting for their cases to be heard.

The court was not a place of happiness. It was somewhere one hoped to be as far away from as one could possibly be. It was going to be a place of his nightmares for a long time to come.

Then it was time. The case before theirs ended and the courtroom started to empty. People outside jostled for position and began forcing their way in before all those inside had managed to leave.

Burnt Saleem looked at his watch. He was running late. Abdul Zubair would never forgive him if he failed. The police guards at the front gates were using metal detectors to check Pappu and all the stuff he carried. They found nothing and motioned them both on.

Burnt Saleem found a location just inside the main gate on the ground under a banyan tree in between a shoe polisher and an ice cream seller. It would be perfect.

'Put it down here,' he said to Pappu.

Pappu went through the motions of setting up the brazier, heating the coals and skewering the corn. A few hungry faces looked in their direction. Roasted corn was a popular snack.

Burnt Saleem looked among the skewers and found the specially sharpened one. Making sure no one was watching he carefully tucked it into his right sleeve, with the sharpened end facing down.

'*Allah hu akbar*, I am ready,' he said as he stood up, '*Allah hafiz.'*

'*Allah hafiz,*' Pappu said in reply. He would wait five minutes and then walk out of the gate.

It was time for him to do what Abdul Zubair had ordered. He went in search of the courtroom. The main notice board showed the blasphemy case was just starting. He had no time to check for any means of escape. If he did not hurry, he would have no reason to make a getaway.

He climbed the stairs and joined the crowd waiting to get into the courtroom. He needed to be at the front near the foreign woman. It would feel nice to plunge the skewer into her evil heart while he shouted *Allah hu akbar.*

With his left hand, he fingered the scars on his face, something he always did out of habit. The real pain was long gone, but the hair had never grown back, and as a result, he had a strange lopsided beard.

He had been badly burnt by the flame front from a simple diesel and fertiliser bomb he had planted at the entrance of a hotel in Islamabad. It had killed three policemen, but it had also got him. His fingers traced the outline of the burn mark. That part of his face had no feeling.

With all this crowd it would be impossible to escape. Suicide would be the only solution. He could use the skewer on himself or charge one of the armed policemen with it. Anything was better than falling into the hands of the police.

He had a high threshold of pain. He had stayed conscious while the doctor had treated his burnt face but the police throughout Pakistan had a well-deserved reputation. He did not know anyone who survived their interrogation. Even the American CIA brought them prisoners to break. He felt a strange twisted sense of nationalistic pride at the thought.

The crowd was now pushing their way into the courtroom. His path was blocked by two foreigners; one of them was the biggest man he had seen. Most likely he was a friend of the blasphemer. Burnt Saleem squeezed into a gap to the right of the giant foreigner just as he was passing the door frame.

Damon felt someone pushing aggressively from the side. It was a man with a strange looking beard. He was used to jostling in crowds since he had come here but this was downright hostile and rude, and he was already in a foul mood. He pushed back with all his might and heard a bump as the man's head struck the door frame, hard. The man let out a whooshing sound as if the wind had been knocked out of him. There was another sound like the tinkle of glass or was it metal, but that did not register with Damon. He was satisfied the man had been taught a lesson.

Burnt Saleem muttered a curse. Without rotating his head, he looked down. The knock had made him drop the skewer. It had almost gone through his foot and was now on the floor leaning against the door frame. He quickly looked around. No one else had noticed anything; everyone was hell-bent on getting inside.

He stretched his arm as far as possible and bent his knee slightly hoping to reach it without drawing attention to himself, but the crush of the crowd unbalanced him. He was pushed along with the throng into the dark courtroom.

The courtroom was huge but repressive and gloomy. Its walls were lined with a dark timber. The same wood was used for all the furniture in the room, including the bench that dominated the front. The whole courtroom had only two working lights. One was over the judge's bench. The second was a green-shaded table lamp for the court reporter who sat at a typewriter. Damon couldn't remember when and where he had last seen one of those, maybe in a museum.

People were milling about trying to find a seat. Damon, Simon and Jamshed sat in the front row. Jane waved to them.

They waved back. Damon looked haggard and sleep deprived.

She should never have listened to Mack about the project. She found it hard to say no, so people often walked all over her. But there was no point blaming herself or anyone else for that matter. The first step was to accept reality. But it was so hard. She was affecting the lives of everyone she loved. It filled her with crippling guilt. Her beautiful relationship with Sergei and Razane could end. The thought made her so unbearably sad she found it hard to breathe. She let out a sob. She had to stop her negative morose thoughts, or she'd go mad. She had to believe she would get through this. There had to be a way but as she scanned the courtroom all she saw were unfriendly faces. All were there to see the spectacle of a foreign blasphemer humiliated and put in her place. How she could use a warm hug.

Eventually, everyone found a place to sit.

The court clerk yelled out something, and the crowd fell silent. The judge dressed in a black *sherwani* and sporting a bushy beard entered from a back door and sat down. Damon's heart sank when he saw him. He did not look like a kind or merciful person. The silence in the courtroom was absolute. The crowd was obviously in awe of the judge.

The clerk announced the case. The reporter began typing furiously. An interpreter translated it for Jane's benefit into English. A few people began whispering and talking in the back. The judge banged his gavel, and silence descended again.

Damon found it hard to follow. The large room had poor acoustics, and the interpreter had a strong accent. Jamshed was arguing with the prosecutor and trying to convince the grim-faced judge about something.

Burnt Saleem was running out of time. He looked around for an opportunity. Maybe he could snatch a gun from one of the police officers and shoot the woman. He tried to calculate how he could achieve the element of surprise and from what point he would have to shoot when a policeman burst into the room carrying the skewer above his head. He shouted something unintelligible above the sudden din.

A senior police officer shouted something back and immediately the police already inside the courtroom thronged in front of Jane, shielding her. The doors were barred, and Jane was removed from the dock and taken out of the rear entrance.

This elicited a lot of muttering from the crowd.

The judge waited till Jane had left. Then he banged the gavel down hard and called out his judgement. The interpreter interpreted. 'Motion for dismissal denied. Motion for bail also denied.'

The judge leaned towards the clerk who consulted something on his desk. The clerk called out, and the interpreter translated. 'The trial is set for one month from today.'

People started heading towards the doors en masse but were ushered into a single file. The police were going to search everyone before they were allowed to leave.

THEIR ARRIVAL

Lahore, Monday 28 November, 2:30pm

Mack shifted his weight. The vinyl armchair was uncomfortable. Its cushion had sagged long ago, and he sat in it rather than on it. The cup of tea next to him sat undrunk, growing cold. It was too sweet anyway. He hated to wait at the best of times. Now it was even more frustrating.

He was in the Airport Security Chief's office. From where he sat he had a clear view to the immigration desks. Through another window, he could see one of the arrival gates. The passengers were still stuck on the plane.

He knew the chief well and regularly sent him gifts for Eid, so he was treated like a VIP. It impressed his business associates and friends no end. Impressions in Pakistan were necessary to maintain a large number of connections. Connections meant influence; influence meant power, power meant money. Besides, it was always nice to be treated special. Normally an immigration officer would meet his friends on the plane, their luggage would be taken off the carousel, and they would be driven in a buggy to their waiting car. No queues and no waiting like ordinary folk.

But not today. Today his influence was not working. Everything that could have gone wrong did. Sergei and Razane had left Melbourne at 10:30pm, Australian time. They should have reached Lahore, at quarter to eleven in the morning. A security scare in Dubai delayed the plane by two hours. When it landed in Lahore, the police did another search of the luggage and a background check on all the passengers before letting anyone deplane.

It was bloody frustrating, but he understood why they did it. The government was trying hard to eliminate the threat of terrorist attacks. Nothing sapped the confidence of the international business community more than one of them being killed or kidnapped. If it happened in the USA, it was because the person was in the wrong place at the wrong time. In Pakistan, it was because the whole country was unsafe.

Finally, at 3:15 in the afternoon, the bedraggled passengers began filing out of the aircraft. A buggy carrying an immigration official brought Sergei and Razane out first. It stopped at the baggage carousel. Mack went down to meet them, arms outstretched.

'I am so sorry this is happening to you guys,' he said as he hugged them, 'at least the case has been delayed so I think there's a slim chance we can get there on time.'

'Have you met Jane yet?' Razane asked.

'No, not yet. I know Simon and Damon have. I spoke with them, and there is now a lawyer in the picture.'

'Yes, we know that,' Sergei said. 'We spoke, and it's not looking good.'

Mack put a hand on both their shoulders. 'We are going to leave no stone unturned to get Jane out. I promise.'

'Well, we are not leaving until she is,' Razane said.

Mack was sure she meant every bit of it.

'It's very hot and humid for winter,' Razane said as she pulled a hair tie out of her jet-black hair.

'Yeah, I am sorry winter has not come yet,' Mack said. Why was he apologising? He didn't make the weather. Razane made him nervous.

Razane watched two porters argue over who was going to load their bags in the buggy as she retied her hair. She sighed. It was the most chaotic and noisy airport she had been to.

Mack's black Range Rover waited for them in the car park with its liftgate open. His chauffeur Tahir rushed forward to help them unload their bags.

'Let me *Mem Sahib*,' he insisted as he bodily blocked Razane's attempts to transfer her suitcases.

'Thank you, Tahir,' Mack said. 'After you load the bags take the rest of the day off. I feel like driving today.'

'Yes, *Sahib*.' Tahir said. He hoisted the last two cases in the boot and closed the tailgate. Razane climbed in the back as Sergei sat in the front passenger seat. She watched Tahir trudge towards the bus stop. It was outside the airport. Mack could have dropped him there. Pakistan was one of the last few countries where people treated their hired help poorly. Mack probably was not even aware of it.

'I am going to try to do everything I can to get you there,' Mack said as he slammed the driver's door shut, closing out the bedlam. 'Damon just texted me. Ours is the next case to be heard. He's still waiting outside the courtroom.'

On the way, he and Sergei made small talk. Razane sat brooding in the back staring intently out of the windows, seemingly trying to absorb every detail. Mack looked at her through his mirror, thought of saying something, but then changed his mind. She could be a little intimidating at the best of times. Right now, she looked on edge. Best to leave her be.

He remembered how shocked he had been when Sergei and Jane had first introduced her. His first thought had been how lucky Sergei was that Jane allowed him a mistress. It had taken him a while to realise Jane had an equally strong attachment to her. It was all quite bizarre and not fair. He had never found a true soul mate and Sergei had two. Being a confirmed bachelor and wealthy had its advantages. There were so many beautiful women in the world, each unique and alluring. Yet he would have given them all up for what Sergei had.

It had taken quite a while for him and Razane to form a relationship. It was awkward in the beginning. She was naturally introverted and seemed scarred by ghosts from her past, and he could not get the thought of her having sex with Jane out of his mind. It made him feel guilty, but he still could not stop.

When eventually they got a bit closer he discovered she was deep, dark, and complex, so much more than just a pretty face. But he was ever so slightly scared of her. Her past made her potentially dangerous. A killer could always kill again.

The shortest route, by distance, was through Lahore Cantonment, over the Mian Mir Bridge and onto Mall Rd but school traffic would have slowed them down. Mack took the longer but quicker route via Lahore's outer ring road. It was a newly constructed freeway, and it allowed him to push the big Range Rover to 150 km/h. He did not expect the police to challenge him and he was right.

He spotted not one, but two traffic cops on their big motorcycles with hand-held radar, by the side of the road. One noticed him, seemed to want to come after him but in the end, didn't. He could understand their reluctance. His Range Rover was easily one of the most expensive vehicles on the road, and most police knew that. Such a fancy SUV meant serious money and power and connections to high places. If they came across the wrong person, the traffic offence would not matter, but the hapless police officer could end up in a remote and undesirable part of the country. Most had learnt discretion was better than their principles. Most did the wise thing and only caught drivers of the humbler modes of transport.

Nine minutes later they were in the vicinity of Badami Bagh and a minute after they took the exit onto the N5, the main thoroughfare into Lahore from the north of the country,

The N5 was busy but reasonably free-flowing as they drove past Minar-e-Pakistan and the old walled city on their left. They hit heavy traffic as they reached the Lower Mall but by then they were only two blocks from their destination.

Finally, they reached the Sessions Court and found parking on a grassy plot outside. The parking attendant, a young boy in a light blue *shalwar kameez* and a dirty face, put a small paper slip under the windscreen wiper and gave Mack the stub. 'Fifty rupees.'

What a cheeky little bugger! Mack smiled inwardly. He was sure it was ten rupees for all other cars. He paid, and as they walked up to the security guards screening people with handheld metal detectors, they all got a WhatsApp message from Damon.

'We are now walking into the courtroom; it's room five, first floor.'

By the time they cleared the queue at the security gate, had gotten their bearings and reached the courtroom, the doors were closed. Two serious looking constables stood barring the entrance, submachine guns held across their chest, their fingers alongside the trigger-guard.

'We would like to go in,' Mack said in the most authoritative voice, 'open the door.'

'We cannot. We have orders.' The response was apologetic but firm. 'There has just been an incident inside.'

Just then their phones pinged. It was a message from Damon.

THE MAJOR

Lahore, Monday 28 November, 3:00pm

The immigration clerk finished typing out the report. A man and a woman on the watch list had slipped into the country. They were both in the E category, which meant they were to be allowed entry but an alert had to be sent out.

The report reached the inbox of an immigration analyst at the Intelligence Bureau head office in Islamabad. He had seen quite a few E category arrivals over the last few months. Many of them were high-profile businessmen who required special protection, others were people the local intelligence community needed to keep tabs on. They always let any known CIA and British intelligence personnel into the country; they were potential gold mines of information.

He compared the names with his database. One was the son of an enemy of the state, and the other a former member of a group that had alliances with a terrorist organisation. Most E category people travelled alone or with people not on any list at all. Today there were two. They appeared to be together, which was unusual. He needed to report this immediately.

He sent the report to his supervisor and added the information to a weekly immigration brief.

He also sent a separate email to Major Imran Hamdani, his contact in the Inter-Services Intelligence, also known as ISI, the feared Pakistani Army Intelligence organisation. Networks were essential for the career of any young aspiring intelligence analyst. Maybe one day he might work for them.

Major Imran Hamdani had his phone switched off. It was afternoon prayer time. He always kept his phone off while praying and found it annoying when other people didn't. Prayer time was for reflection and communicating with God.

After the mandatory prayers were over, he prayed for the souls of his departed mother and father and his wife who had been killed two years ago in a drone strike. He prayed for justice for the loss of innocent lives. He prayed for Pakistan's prosperity and for his children that they would always remain on the true path.

Feeling refreshed and cleansed and totally at peace he got up and walked outside. Most people had left. The shoe keeper greeted him and handed him his shoes. He liked the major. He was a good devout Muslim who always prayed regularly.

He went to his car and sat in the driver's seat. He was entitled to a chauffeur, but he liked driving himself.

He adjusted his rear-view mirror. He must have knocked it on exiting the car. His face reflected back at him briefly. He had not seen himself in a mirror for the last three months ever since the one in his bathroom had fallen off. He had not yet gotten around to having it replaced. As a widower, he had no use for one. But what a shock to see himself. Age was catching up fast. He looked old and pale, his hair thinner and greyer. His forehead had more wrinkles. The brown prayer mark from pressing his forehead to the ground during prayers was darker. Many devout Muslims wore it with pride. They pressed their foreheads to the ground hard to make the mark darker. He was not one of them. He did not pray to show off to others.

He switched on his phone and read the flood of emails. The one from the immigration analyst caught his eye. He had always had a knack for picking key details out of a huge pile of information.

The woman, Razane Silan, was unknown to him but he

knew the man. Sergei Markoff's father was a former KGB double agent who had caused Pakistan a lot of embarrassment. Sergei was a close associate of a Pakistani rice merchant, also in Category E. What was Sergei Markoff doing with the woman, an ex-Peshmerga fighter. He looked her up in their online database. She was an Iraqi Kurd who had spent much of her life as a soldier in the PUK Peshmerga. Later she had crossed into Syria to fight for the YPG, a Kurdish militia fighting ISIL and Jabhat Al Nusra in northern Syria. The YPG was allied with the PKK, the Turkish Kurdistan Workers Party that had been designated a terrorist organisation by some governments. It was this link that had put her on their watchlist. He was glad for it. Any person who fought in a foreign militia was of interest to him.

Why were they here? Pakistan was, unfortunately, no longer a popular tourist destination and Sergei, through his father, had a particularly unpleasant association with the country. It should be the last place he would want to visit. Everything happened for a reason, and he was going to find out what it was.

He looked for a name in his sizeable contacts list and dialled the number.

'Hello, Mack here,' the voice said. 'Oh, it's you Major *Sahib*. *Asalam aleikum*.'

'*Wa aleikum asalam*.'

'How are the children?'

'Fine, thank you, studying hard as they should be,' the major said.

'By Allah's grace they will be top achievers like their father, tell me what made you remember me?'

'Thank you for your kind words. I have a question about your friend Sergei Markoff. What is his purpose in Pakistan?'

There was silence on the other end. He was about to check whether the line had dropped.

'He is here for his wife,' Mack said finally, 'she was arrested in a fake blasphemy case.'

He had heard of the case Mack was referring to. It was splashed all over the news. Foreigners, especially Westerners did not often get arrested. Most minor crimes would get them a slap on the wrist and a one-way flight out of the country. Blasphemy, murder, and drug charges were notable exceptions. There was no way the government would brush a charge of blasphemy under the carpet.

'And who is the woman?'

'She is his wife's close friend.'

He contemplated the likelihood of a friendship developing between a Kurdish and an Australian woman. It was possible.

'Thank you for telling me.'

'No problem, anytime.'

'May God protect you.'

'May God protect you too.'

The major's office was in a large double storey house in Model Town, one of Lahore's oldest and poshest residential suburbs. The only thing that differentiated it from the others in the tree-lined street was the number of antennae and satellite dishes on the roof and security guards that looked a cut above the domestic types normally guarding the houses of the rich folk.

He called Yousaf and Fazal into his office. They were his new analysts, young, sharp and eager to please. Both were former army commandoes who had gotten mild emphysema from their posting at the Siachen Glacier. They would never take part in a military mission again, but their training and aptitude made them perfectly suitable for the ISI.

'I have a new job for you. It is completely top secret. No one even in the department is allowed to know.'

TO HELL IN A HURRY

Lahore, Monday 28 November, 3:30pm

The doors opened with a clang, and people started pushing each other to get through. Two policemen ordered the crowd to form a single line and asked them all to produce their ID cards. Sergei and Razane watched with interest as one of them began to photograph the documents.

A few men in the crowd stridently voiced their displeasure at having to go through a second check. Their protest was short lived after several policemen brandished their batons.

Eventually, Mack, Damon and Simon emerged looking glum, defeat writ large on their faces. Damon brightened as he saw them. They exchanged hugs.

'How's your Mum?' Sergei asked.

'The bail's been denied; she looked terrible, completely lost,' Damon said with a grimace.

'When can we see her?' Razane's face was a sea of pain.

'I don't know yet,' Simon said, 'all we know is the trial date's been set for one-month and--'

'Someone tried to kill Mum just now with a long sharp metal rod,' Damon interrupted.

'Fuck!' Sergei exclaimed. He realised he had shouted when people around them turned to look at him.

'Is she OK?' both he and Razane spoke in unison. Razane had gone as white as a sheet. Sergei could feel her trembling uncontrollably. He put his arm around her. She was about to fall.

'Yes, thankfully she's fine. They removed her from the

courtroom,' Simon said.

'So that's why the doors were barred!' Sergei growled, 'Tell me they caught the fucking bastard…'

'Nah, not yet,' Damon said with a scowl.

'Where did they take Jane?' Razane asked. Her voice was still trembling.

'To protective custody,' Mack said.

'Oh man, this makes me so mad,' Sergei said. He clenched and unclenched his fists. He had to calm himself down. He took a deep breath. Anger was going to get him nowhere.

'I've asked Jamshed to find out where she'll be held till the trial,' Simon said, 'then we organise to visit her.'

'Let me go and see what I can find out,' Mack said and walked off into the courtroom pushing people out of his way.

'Jamshed told me the standard policy is for prisoners to be kept in a remand centre,' Simon said, 'but he's going to try to move her to a more secure place where she's not in contact with other prisoners.'

'Hopefully, the judge sees reason.' Razane said. 'I need to sit down.' She felt weak with worry. Sergei helped her to an empty chair.

Moments later Jamshed came out of the courtroom clutching his briefcase. Mack was a few paces behind, talking on the phone.

'Nice to meet you face to face,' Jamshed said, shaking their hands., 'I do have some good news. 'In light of the attempt, someone just made on Jane's life… You did tell them I presume?' he looked at Damon who nodded. 'Anyway, the judge has agreed to move her back to the central police station she was at before. It's probably one of the best and safest locations, or so I have been assured.'

'It also means a bit of flexibility in terms of the time of the day we can meet her and for how long,' Mack interjected.

'But the other woman was shot there, right in front of Mum,' Damon protested.

'They assured me they would increase security to make it safe there,' Mack said wiping his forehead with a handkerchief. I know the top police chief, and he will make sure she is OK.'

'Don't you know a judge or some politicians who can get her out on bail?' Razane said sharply, 'I heard this country is rife with corruption. Surely a bit of money--'

'No judge or politician will risk his life,' Mack said putting his handkerchief away, 'these religious extremists are more than dangerous. Even the most corrupt know that money is no use when they are dead.'

'Dead?'

'Anyone seen to be lenient towards people accused of blasphemy becomes a target of religious nutjobs,' Mack explained. The phone rang in his pocket. He pulled it out. It was one of his business contacts. Now was not the time. He cancelled the call.

'So, do we have any news on the mediation you mentioned?' Sergei asked Jamshed.

'I was going to do that,' Simon said. 'My contact was supposed to get back to me by now. Let me call him.' He took out his phone and dialled a number.

Damon did not notice the same man with the lopsided beard standing at the end of the corridor. He had his phone pointed at them and was taking their photographs.

'Let's go somewhere we can talk,' Damon said, 'things are going to hell in a hurry.'

Razane put her arm around Damon and hugged him. 'We'll get her out,' she said, trying hard to sound certain. Comforting him made her feel better.

'Yes, or die trying,' Sergei said with a grim smile.

Damon stiffened momentarily. It was still awkward with Razane. She pulled her arm back.

'I am sorry, Damon.' Her voice was flat.

Damon felt bad. It was no time to behave like a child. 'I am sorry too Razane.' He put his arm around her and gave her a quick squeeze.

They walked back to their cars in silence.

Outside the courthouse in the carpark two men, each astride a red Honda motorcycle, felt their phones buzz. They had just received photographs of the people inside the court. They knew what had to be done.

Simon was waiting for them in the car park. 'More bad news guys,' he said with a frown, 'there will apparently not be talks.'

'Bloody hell, why?' Sergei said with a frown.

'My contact says many of the religious leaders are afraid of a backlash from their supporters if they suggest a mediation. That video posted on the Internet stuffed things up.'

'Bloody fucking hell, I knew it!' Damon said furiously. 'I got a really bad feeling as soon as I heard about the video.'

'Yes, and even without that, no legitimate religious party wants to have anything to do with Jamaat-e-Ilahi. They are considered extremists even by pretty right-wing groups.'

'Damn it, man,' Mack said. 'Doors seem to be closing everywhere. I think maybe... we break her out commando style.'

'I'll keep on trying, but like Mack said these doors have closed,' Simon said, ignoring Mack's flippant remark. It was not the time or place for levity.

Sergei tried to slow his breathing. He had to stay strong and clear headed. If he fell to pieces all would be lost. He couldn't stop a vein pulsing painfully in his temple. 'We need to take stock and understand what we can do. Can we all please meet in our hotel?'

'I will catch up with you guys later,' Jamshed said, 'maybe around dinner time. I need to organise some things.'

'OK, but can we then please go over the whole case from start to finish. What evidence was presented and who are the accusers? What do they want? Also, what are the laws and legal precedents? We need to quickly work out what our options are!'

Damon joined Mack, Sergei, and Razane in the Range Rover. Simon's Mercedes pulled out of the car park first. The Range Rover followed closely behind. They didn't see the two red motorcycles now with pillion passengers follow them.

Traffic was heavier than before. Office workers leaving for home had swelled the number of cars on the roads.

'This traffic is quite unusual for Lahore,' Mack remarked to Sergei.

'How so?'

'It's actually flowing. Most days at this time you spend more time stationary than moving.'

'If you call this flowing, Uncle Mack, then you must look at the world quite differently,' Damon said managing a feeble smile.

In the back seat Razane said to Damon, 'you know Ben gave me a hug before we left.'

'Well that's progress,' Damon said. Why did it take a family emergency for people to not behave like arseholes? 'When is he coming over?'

'Not sure. I guess it depends on what happens next,' Sergei turned around, 'we were hoping we could get the case dismissed, and go home in a few days, but that doesn't seem to be happening.'

'What are we doing to keep Mum safe?' Damon said, 'these people are truly mad. They'll try again. I can just sense it.'

'There's certainly something fucked up, going on.' Sergei pressed his palm to his temple hoping to quell the throbbing. 'Somehow having her charged is not enough. They want to kill her. Am I the only one or does it not make sense?'

'You are missing something,' Mack responded, 'it's called fanaticism.'

'Even fanatics must follow some logic!' Sergei replied.

'Well, a lot of people truly love the prophet. Many love him more than their kids or spouses. They are willing to do anything to show their love.'

'Even kill?'

'Especially kill!'

'You are not mentioning the sheer irony of it. The prophet himself was a most peace-loving and forgiving man,' Razane chimed in.

'Yeah well, fanatics getting irony is a bit of an oxymoron,' Mack said with a grim smile.

'We need to do whatever it takes so they cannot get to Jane.' Razane said.

'My friend, the Inspector General, will personally look into the security arrangements. He has assured me they were caught off guard and it would not happen again.'

'Please make sure they do everything they can,' Razane said in a pleading voice.

They had arrived outside the Avari. Mack pulled into the little slip lane to the entrance gate. Ahead of them, Simon's car had stopped behind a large black Nissan getting checked by hotel security. They all watched as the uniformed guards opened the Nissan's boot, shone torches inside and used mirrors on long stalks to check its underside.

Two Honda motorcycles pulled up alongside them. They were so intent on watching the guards they only noticed the one next to Simon's car, and it took them a few seconds to register that its pillion rider carried an assault rifle.

FIRST MAN DOWN

Lahore, Monday 28 November, 4:30pm

M ack was the first to notice the pillion rider on the motorcycle had an assault rifle. Its barrel stuck out of the black shawl draped over his shoulder.

Acting in sheer panic, Mack mashed his foot on the accelerator. The large SUV leapt forward as the pillion riders on both motorcycles opened fire.

Bullets tore into Simon's Mercedes, shattering its side windows. They missed Damon and Razane in the back of the Range Rover by millimetres, instead ripping into the rearmost pillar and smashing the back glass.

The Range Rover struck the front motorcycle and propelled it violently towards the Avari's brick boundary wall. Its riders spilt onto the SUV's bonnet. Mack, acting instinctively, braked hard, throwing them forward onto the road.

From the back seat, Razane leaned forward and flicked the Range Rover's transmission selector wheel into reverse as she grabbed the steering wheel.

'Press the accelerator, hard!' She screamed into Mack's ear. He reacted, and the SUV leapt backwards aimed at the motorcycle behind them.

The rider accelerated out of the way just as his gunman swung his rifle forward. He fired as he tried to regain balance. The bullets missed the Range Rover and took out two windows on the Avari's third floor.

The motorcycle continued accelerating, the rider

struggling to keep it in a straight line. His passenger tried to swing his gun, but he was working against inertial forces. In the end, he had to choose between aiming his weapon or staying on the motorcycle. He chose the latter. Four armed guards from the Avari came running. One of them fired towards the fleeing assailants who sped off, merging with the traffic.

Mack waved frantically at the guards to open the gate. They must have recognised him because they obeyed. Their damaged vehicle accelerated past Simon's car and the Nissan. They all felt the sickening bumps and heard the thuds as the bodies of Simon's assailants were mangled and crushed under the Range Rover's tyres. In the Mercedes, Simon and his driver were slumped forward, their heads red with congealing blood. Blood also covered a large part of the insides of their car including the windscreen.

Inside the compound, Mack pointed the Range Rover into a parking bay. His legs shook so badly he was unable to properly depress the pedal. Razane leaned forward, flicked the transmission into neutral and pressed the handbrake button, but she was too late. The SUV thumped into the back of a black BMW. The impact felt worse than it was.

Two armed guards rushed out of the hotel lobby to join their companions at the gate. Hotel staff came over to see if they needed help.

'Somebody p-p-please call the… police. The…there's been a shooting,' Mack said stammering. His voice was weak but pitched far higher than normal, his breathing coming in spurts.

'Yes, sir they have been called. Are you OK? Are you staying with us?'

'We, we, have… Just get my friends' luggage out of the back,' he said annoyed at his loss of control.

The doorman recognised Mack. 'Of course, go right in sir,' he said. If the events upset him, he didn't show it. The people of Lahore had become quite accustomed to violence.

'I have already checked in for you,' Mack said turning to

them; his breath was still ragged.

Sergei looked at him. 'I think you are in shock.'

'Nonsense, I'm not,' Mack said. He turned to a porter. 'Take the bags to the Presidential Suite please.' He handed him a five hundred rupee note, with shaking hands.

'Right away sir.'

'Fucking hell, Simon is h-h-hurt badly and his driver...' Damon said weakly, coming out of his stupor, 'will someone call a damn ambulance!' he screamed the last words. He was starting to come out of a dark fog. His vision was blurry, and he shook uncontrollably. He felt sick and weak, on the edge of insanity. This couldn't really be happening. It was a nightmare come true.

Razane leaned over; she recognised the signs of shock too well. She squeezed his shoulder. 'It's OK Damon, help is on the way,' her voice was gentle and calm.

As if on cue the sounds of sirens came closer. The gates were now closed; men were shouting orders and running outside the gate.

'Get me a blanket and some water she said to a member of the hotel staff who had come out to see what was going on.

'No. Don't worry, I am OK,' Damon said weakly.

Razane looked at the hotel boundary walls. They were solid brick, thick enough to stop bullets but no defence against a bomb. Who were the assailants? Had the threat eased? They needed to get inside where it was safer.

Sergei and Mack stepped out of the SUV. Mack looked unsteady. He held onto the door waiting for his legs to stop shaking enough for him to walk. Even her strong and tough Sergei looked pale.

'My love, we should all get inside the building,' she whispered to him.

'I want to check on Simon and his driver,' Sergei said.

'Please don't do that, I can tell you for sure, they are dead,' her voice was icy and calm. 'Please let's get inside, Damon and Mack are not looking good.'

Sergei looked at her. Razane had such remarkable control over herself. Inside she would be in turmoil, but no one would guess. No one except those she let inside. Even two and a half years after leaving the Peshmerga, the past still haunted her. She was traumatised by all the battles she had been in. Her scars would most likely never heal. She often woke in the middle of the night, screaming and drenched in sweat. He and Jane would calm her down, hold her and soothe her back to sleep.

He stroked the hair out of her face. It was always getting in the way.

'Sure, I agree,' he said sighing, 'let's get them inside.' Her strength was inspirational, and he would do everything he could to bolster hers with his own. He forced down his feelings of horror and nausea. There would be time to resolve and heal. That time was not now.

Razane reached over and patted Damon's arm. 'Let's go upstairs.'

Damon already looked a little less pale. He had a lot of mental toughness for such a young man. Mack, on the other hand, still looked quite unwell. He had to sit back in the driver's seat again.

'Are you OK?' Razane said looking into his face. He was showing the most outward signs of having been affected. That, of course, did not mean anything. Mack was a complete extrovert. He would probably bounce back the quickest as well. It was always the quiet and composed ones who took on the most damage. Like herself. But it was no time for self-pity.

A bellboy came carrying four bottles of water. Mack took one gratefully. The cool liquid instantly made him less dizzy. He had the nervous disposition of a grandmother. A sissy grandmother. Thank God, he had not seen Simon's body. He would not have been able to keep his sanity if he had. He was quite an embarrassment. Razane and Sergei looked so calm. Even Damon was now helping the porter unload the suitcases from the back. He had to pull himself together and stop being such a weakling. He took a deep breath and tried to stand again. He was going to walk. If he fell so be it. Thankfully he managed to stay upright. He was going to be OK, unlike poor Simon. Indirectly Simon's death was his fault. He had to stop thinking like that. Another wave of dizziness washed over him. He still held the bottle although the numbness in his body meant he hardly felt the pressure of his hands holding it. He took another sip. He couldn't be responsible for everything in the world. He certainly had only good intentions in doing what he had done. He needed to stop thinking. No more thinking.

While Mack and Damon sat on the soft sofas in the parlour of the suite. Razane and Sergei were in the bathroom splashing water on their tired faces. Sergei waited as Razane towelled her face dry. He held out his arms. She entered his embrace. Her cheek cool and soft against his. He stroked her hair and kneaded her neck gently. Her skin was hot and sweaty, her muscles stiff and knotted.

'Ouch, that's sore,' she said. Sergei stopped. 'Please... Don't stop,' she mumbled into his shoulder. Her breath was growing calmer as he kneaded. Her hands stroked his back and his hair. He loved his hair being stroked; it was almost an erogenous zone.

'Thank you, my love; I so needed that.' She moved her face out of his shoulder and kissed him on the lips, slowly and deeply. He cupped her face in his hands as his lips responded. Hers parted, his too. They stood there for a few seconds, eyes closed, lost in each other, and the world stood still. Finally, he pulled away and kissed her on her eyes.

'I love you so much,' he said.

'I love you more.'

'Not possible,' he smiled wanly and walked out.

She pulled her hairbrush out of her bag and began brushing her hair; her hands were shaking.

'I am glad I didn't shit myself,' Mack said touching the seat of his pants. He was feeling a bit stronger. Damon smiled.

'Please not in our suite,' Sergei said entering the room. He allowed himself to fall into the plush armchair.

'I expect the police will want to get a statement from us,' Sergei said, 'after all, we witnessed everything.' For all his composure, he was rattled to the point of feeling sick.

'Poor Simon and his driver,' Damon said. 'What's going to happen now?'

'I'll give my IG friend a call and tell him to meet us at the police station when we go and meet Jane,' Mack said. 'We'll give the statement then. By the way, Razane really kept her cool,' he said to no one in particular. 'She was like ice when we had all melted into water.'

'Razane is very human just like all of us,' Sergei said defensively, 'I imagine she's feeling just awful inside.'

'You and Jane are two lucky people,' Mack said, changing the subject, 'mainly I think you the lucky one. I would give my right nut for even one such woman.'

'Well Ben and I still think you three are weird,' Damon said not unkindly, 'but we accept you. At least I do, and Ben does too, I think...'

MOURNING

Shisha Wal, Monday 28 November, 5:00pm

The room smelled of incense. Jibran was dressed in white and sat on the floor praying with the others.

Today was the third day since Mumtaz's death. For three days hordes of people including her old parents, her sisters, and relatives and her million cousins had been coming to his *haveli*, moaning and wailing and beating their chests, offering their condolences and expressing their sorrow.

He felt free for the first time in a long time, so it had been hard to play along. But play along he did. He had gone through the motions, had cried with them, shedding fake tears. He had placed her body in the grave facing *Makkah* and put clumps of earth around her to prop her up. He had ordered a suitably grand mausoleum with a large plaque that professed his undying love for her. He had distributed food to the poor and had been at every prayer session.

All the newspapers carried the story. Wife of a member of the National Assembly found dead of snakebite. Photographs of the dead snake and the axe were in every news clip on TV. He was shown as the brave grieving widower. It was just the image he wanted. That would win him thousands of sympathy votes for sure.

He could feel the gold under the fields of Shakar Parian almost like it was a living entity calling out to him. While it was still not in his control, his plan was coming together. The gold was closer now than it had ever been.

A cunning plan executed well was one of the most satisfying experiences in life. His idea to use blasphemy to trap the foreign woman was smart. Getting Maulana Abdul Zubair to carry it out was a stroke of genius.

Now he had only a few more steps to go. He expected a phone call at any moment telling him the woman's associates were dead. The next step was to kill the woman before she went to trial. Then they would destroy the solar panels and rough up the villagers. With the woman no longer in the picture, the villagers would cave in and beg him to buy them out.

But it had to be done in the right order. The mining company was about to begin exploring. Gold would be discovered in a matter of weeks. He could not wait. But he could also not destroy the solar panels before he killed the woman. If she found out and spoke, either at the trial or before, it could raise all sorts of questions.

The woman's death was pivotal. Abdul Zubair was extremely enthusiastic about killing her, but he did not fully grasp the urgency. He would have to speak to him to make sure he understood. He had to pretend to be the man's admirer and a supporter but only till he had served his purpose. After that, he was just one of the loose ends he would need to take care of.

WHAT TO DO

Lahore, Monday 28 November, 6:30pm

A loud howling whistle and a bang made Razane jump and drop the hairbrush into the wash basin. She stood there trembling. It had sounded like a rocket but was probably fireworks. She had to pull herself together. It was no time to crack. A wave of nausea washed over her. She dry retched into the wash basin. Her head spun, her limbs grew heavy. She heaved again. There was nothing; her stomach was empty. The darkness was back and with it came the madness that brought out of control thoughts. Her face glistened with sweat. Her wavy long black hair that she had just untied covered her face.

The flashbacks came fast and violently, the killings, the explosions, images of dead people, the lives she had cut short and the friends who had died beside her. It went on through a crazy loop of fast-moving images in her mind. She had to slow it down and stop it otherwise she would go insane and never recover.

'Breathe deeply and focus on one thing,' a therapist had told her once, 'anything.'

They were on a small hilltop that was little more a tall mound of dirt. It was only slightly higher than the surrounding hills. The whole countryside around as far as she could see was undulating and covered in tall grass that had browned as spring had given way to summer.

It was near sunset, and the sun shone in her eyes. It still

burnt but a cool current of air from the north kept things from sweltering. The breeze made the tall grass sway causing the land to appear to be moving. If she squinted, it was easy to imagine they were in a dun-coloured ocean.

Razane looked through her binoculars, and all she could see was a carpet of shimmering grass seeds made golden by the sun. It dazzled her and reduced visibility. Had she been in a different situation it would have been magical but it was anything but. They were in mortal danger. She could smell her own fear. An Islamist group had just captured a nearby Christian village, had slaughtered most of the population, and were now reportedly advancing towards them.

Her unit's job was to stop them long enough for reinforcements to arrive from the north. The grass gave their group cover, but it did the same for the enemy. And because the sunlight shone towards them they were almost blind.

Kardan, the leader of their group of eight young recruits, was scanning with the second pair of binoculars. He noticed something and pointed. She looked and saw the grass move in a different direction to the wind. She thought she could see human shapes, but they were so faint it could have been her imagination. Was it the enemy? The loud crack of a gunshot made her drop her binoculars. Kardan had collapsed in a heap, his head covered in blood. His binoculars lay next to him shattered into pieces.

The world around her went mad. Her unit returned fire in the direction Kardan had been pointing, but she was transfixed on his binoculars. They had been missing the rubber hood. The sun had reflected off them and had given his position away to an enemy sniper. She could not stop thinking how such a small detail had ended the life of a human being, a good man and good looking as well. One of the few who was gentle in bed but didn't treat her like shit after.

The enemy opened fire. In the chaos, it took them a few precious moments to realise they were being shot at from a location ten degrees further south. They continued exchanging gunfire till the sun finally dipped below the horizon. The enemy lost their advantage and ceased firing.

It was after midnight and pitch-black when their first reinforcements arrived. They eventually came in sufficient numbers the next day that they were able to outflank the enemy, push them back and retake the village.

On the way, they came across a group of three women and seven small children, all girls, lying dead behind a mound. Their faces were covered in flies, their bodies already swollen and putrid. They had been shot from the front by those to whom they were running for help. Their lifeless eyes stared at them accusingly.

It was the most terrible moment in all the years she had been fighting. She had failed the people she had sworn to protect. Those eyes would forever haunt her.

It was a wrong memory to focus on. A dull ache behind her eyes replaced the nausea and dizziness. Her hands shook. She needed Sergei to hold her a bit longer, but he was now outside with Mack and Damon. She took a sip from the water bottle. It made her empty stomach rumble.

She had to find the strength herself, but she so wanted to be held and comforted by Jane and Sergei. Would it ever be possible again? She was not going to get that happiness back. She would lose both of them, here in Pakistan. Someone was going to get to them and then her new reality, this impossible happiness, would fade into a perpetual nightmare. Her breathing was becoming shallow again. The anxiety was returning. She had to stop these thoughts and pull herself together. She had to channel her despair and sorrow, into anger.

Razane unclenched her fists, her nails leaving red marks on her palms. She took a deep breath, parted her hair with her fingers and tied them loosely behind her head with a bright red scrunchie.

With a forced smile, she entered the room. There was a newfound look of respect on Damon and Mack's faces. There was something else on Mack's face. What was it? Adoration or lust. He obviously liked strong women, most men did but only for one thing. She shuddered involuntarily. It disgusted her. Men were revolting, all except Sergei. He was different.

The kettle boiled and then clicked to a stop, startling her. She needed to centre herself and breathe deeply.

'Tea anyone?' Sergei said as he got up.

'I'll have a cup please,' Damon said. 'Don't we need to talk about what we do next?'

'Make me a mint tea please,' Razane said, 'I agree with Damon. We were all almost killed. It is pure luck some of us survived, and we don't even know what, or who, we are up against.'

'I'll talk to my police friend, Mack said, 'I am sure he can help.'

'But why? What have we ever done to them?' Sergei said pouring water into the cups.

'It's what Simon said outside the courthouse,' Razane said slowly as she formed her thoughts, 'They are an ultra-extremist group, I would say easily as rabid and anti-western as anything I have ever come across. They are probably trying to send a message they will go after foreigners in any way they can.'

Sergei presented her with the handle of the mug while holding the hot surface in his hand. He was the only man who ever did so.

'Thank you,' she said, looking at him tenderly. He stroked her hair affectionately.

'I think they somehow know we are here to help Jane and are going after us because we're trying to help her,' Mack said.

'Makes sense,' Razane said.

'Surely the government will want to help us then,' Damon said.

'They might want to, but they'll not take a stand against

religious groups. Not where blasphemy is involved.' Mack said. 'No, they'll just stand on the sidelines and wait till things blow over.'

'Aren't they worried about their image overseas and getting foreign investment and all that shit?' Sergei said.

'Yes well, their overseas image is a luxury. First, they need to defeat the terrorists and improve security in the country,' Mack said. 'But you know, in an overall sense Pakistan isn't more dangerous than your average large American city but-- Hey where's my tea?'

'You never drink tea, you moron,' Sergei said.

'Yes well, maybe I've changed. Anyway, these high-profile kidnappings where people are beheaded, large-scale demonstrations that show people looting and burning, and bomb blasts, and all make it seem you have a higher chance of getting killed in Pakistan. The western media don't help either. They love to put a negative spin on things.'

Sergei got up to make Mack a cup. 'White or black?' he asked,

'I'll have mint as well, please.'

'Well to me it seems completely lawless and out of control. It is definitely not safe for us!' Razane said. Why was Mack trying to sell Pakistan to them?

'I don't blame you for thinking that.' Mack responded.

Mack was crazy if he really thought Pakistan was safe. She took a sip of the mint tea. There was nothing to be gained by arguing.

'Let's all go and see Jane and then get some dinner, then we'll work out what to do.' Sergei said.

'Yes let's,' Razane said, 'and by the way I have made my mind up. I know what our only course is.'

They all looked at her.

'We need to get Jane out of the country--'

'Well of course,' said Damon shaking his head. What was Razane? Miss Bleeding Obvious.

'By breaking her out.' Razane finished.

'Yes, and we're all James Bonds.' Damon rolled his eyes. 'Get real, please! We need a realistic plan.'

'Damon, these people will not stop until we are all dead,' Razane said in an even voice, 'so we need to find a way, and fast. By that, I mean over the next few days.'

'Razane, I understand why you are thinking along these lines,' Mack said slowly. He knew he needed to choose his words carefully. 'I know Pakistan, and I can tell you there is no way unless you came in on helicopter gunships in the middle of the night accompanied by a squad of US special forces. Even then I don't like your chances.'

'I'm with Razane,' Sergei weighed in, 'there's something scary going on. These people are not going to wait for a trial. They want Jane, and anyone who helps her, dead. I will do anything, pay any price to keep Jane and us safe.'

Razane looked lovingly at Sergei. 'Thank you, my love.' Her lips moved silently. He was her rock.

'Mack, don't you have enough connections to get her out on bail at least.' Damon said. This was getting exasperating. Razane and his Dad sounded crazy, like stupid teenagers who watched too many Hollywood movies.

'No sonny boy,' he replied, 'if I go around asking for such favours I will quickly become as popular as a leper in a fancy restaurant. Now excuse me I have to make some phone calls.'

'By the way Dad, I meant to ask how Mack makes so much money,' Damon said to Sergei in a whisper, waiting till Mack was out of earshot, 'it has to be something dodgy.'

'He's one of the biggest sellers of Indian Basmati rice in the world,' Sergei whispered with a wry smile, 'sourced cheaply from Pakistan.'

THE PROMISE

Lahore, Monday 28 November, 7:45pm

The Avari's gates were still closed to cars. Only the pedestrian gates were open. Mack had asked his driver, Tahir, to bring his second car to the Alhamra Arts Centre next door. It was where the hotel's management had asked all their guests to park, temporarily, till the police cleared the crime scene.

None of them spoke as they walked out of the Avari. Simon's bullet-ridden car was still in the same spot, but a forklift was preparing to move it. The cabin had been draped in a blue sheet of plastic. A cordon had been set up, and forensic investigators were doing their work, illuminated by temporary floodlights. Police outnumbered hotel guests and pedestrians.

Razane and Sergei both looked around nervously, scanning the crowd for anyone taking an interest in them. They saw nothing untoward.

Barriers had been placed on Mall Road to funnel all traffic into a single lane before the hotel gates, and traffic cops were using whistles and a megaphone to deter curious onlookers.

They walked the short hundred metres to where Tahir waited in the nondescript white Toyota Corolla. Sergei kept looking back expecting someone to charge at them or attack in some way. Razane scanned the pedestrians coming towards them. If they were dealing with a terrorist group, then it was entirely possible the next attack could come in the form of a suicide bomber. Those were almost impossible to guard against especially in winter when everyone was wearing a jacket or a shawl. If the enemy had returned, now was the right opportunity. But somehow, she didn't think it was likely. The gunmen who had attacked them were most certainly not working alone. They were probably part of a command structure. It would be sometime between them reporting their failure and getting new orders.

Damon glanced back one last time. A forklift had picked up the bullet-ridden Mercedes and was trundling towards a flatbed tow truck. 'I've never felt as sickened by anything in my life,' his voice shook. He'd never seen a dead person before. The image of their unseeing eyes staring at nothing would never leave him. How scarily final death was? He shuddered.

'I hope you never see anything worse.' Sergei said. It was like he could read minds.

'Razane, I seriously can't understand how you cope with all you've been through,' Damon said. He sighed as he sat in the back of the car.

'You just learn to close a part of your brain, or you go mad,' she said as she sat next to him.

Sergei climbed in after Razane, forcing Damon over to the other door. The car had dark tinted windows. It helped them feel a little more secure. Hopefully, no one would see them now. Mack climbed into the front passenger seat and gave Tahir instructions where to go.

'If no one has seen us until now, we are safe,' Sergei said. It was a bit of wishful thinking, but it made them feel better.

Mack looked back as they merged with the traffic on Mall Road. They took a left into Kashmir Road and then left again onto Edgerton Rd. The fog was starting to thicken, and visibility was dropping. Street lamps were surrounded by strange halos, and cars' headlamp beams became solid shafts of light visible as they attempted to penetrate the fog.

One by one they all turned around to look for signs someone was following them. The combination of the dark tint on the windows and the foggy conditions made it next to impossible to see. To make matters worse, most cars on the road were either white or silver late model Toyota Corollas or Honda Civics so telling one from the other was almost impossible.

So, it was not for lack of trying they didn't notice the two ISI agents in a white Toyota Corolla behind them. Yousaf, its driver, matched his speed with theirs. He was not worried though. They had managed to attach a satellite tracker to the underside of the car in front. By tomorrow all of Mack's other vehicles would have similar trackers installed. The ISI technicians were most efficient.

Traffic was reasonably light, but the fog made progress difficult. It took them half an hour to reach the police station.

Even though she had steeled herself, seeing Jane, sitting forlorn, in the visitor hut was the hardest thing Razane had faced in a long time. Jane was so good and kind and innocent at heart. It was like seeing a child being tortured. This would haunt her and if they were not successful in getting her out it would drive her insane. Their tears flowed as they rushed into each other's arms.

'My love, we are going to get you out of here,' Razane said as they embraced softly. For a moment they were one. Jane was shaking and crying, her tears warm and wet on Razane's cheek.

'I am so sorry to drag you into this, sweetheart,' Jane said as she stroked Razane's soft silky black hair. She had hoped to appear strong so as not to add to their torment, but seeing them opened a floodgate of emotions.

'Please don't say anything like that. It's not your fault,' Razane said. She turned Jane's face and kissed her closed eyes and her mouth which opened to hers, hungrily. Their lips locked and they tasted each other's salty tears.

'We'll get you out,' Sergei said, hoping he sounded as confident as he wanted to, 'I promise.' He pulled Jane gently into his embrace. Their coming together was as eager and as warm as between the two women. They had always been close, but since

Razane came into their lives, the passion between them had reignited. Razane put her arms around them both. Sergei opened his arms to let her in.

Loud coughing and the shuffling of feet announced Mack and Damon's arrival. Razane and Sergei pulled away reluctantly. The guard who had stepped back from the door resumed his post a moment later, fingering the one-thousand-rupee note Mack had slipped him. Damon saw the exchange. An uncomfortable thought entered his mind. If the police were so willing to bend the rules for Mack they would do so for anyone who paid them. Money only bought obedience, never loyalty.

They all sat. Razane took Jane's hand in hers. 'Darling, there's some bad news, we have to tell you,' she stroked her hand. Jane looked worriedly at each of them in turn.

'What could be even worse?'

'It's Simon, he… he was…' Razane felt tears well up in her eyes, 'murdered.'

'Oh no…' Jane began crying again. Razane and Sergei both put their arms around her and drew her close.

'What happened? When?' Jane sounded frantic.

'Earlier, when we were returning to the hotel,' Sergei said.

'It happened in front of us,' Damon said, 'and Razane saved us.'

Sergei looked at him coldly. He hadn't wanted to share too much information. Jane was inconsolable. She put her head on Razane's shoulder and sobbed.

'You stay with her,' Sergei whispered softly, 'we're gonna see Mack's buddy, the police chief.'

Mack's friend, the Inspector General of Punjab, sat in one of the armchairs in the superintendent's office. The superintendent sat next to him his hands folded in his lap. They both got up when the three walked in. Mack and the inspector general shook hands warmly.

'Sergei and Damon, this is Chaudhury Awan, the Inspector General of the Punjab Police,' Mack said emphasising the full title.

'Awan Bhai, please meet Sergei, he's like a brother to me. We grew up together in Australia. Damon is his son.'

The IG was a tall and dark man with a handlebar moustache, a ramrod posture, and a sombre look. His police uniform was crisply starched, and his military boots were polished to a deep shine.

'You look like a man I would rather have on my side,' Sergei said trying to lighten the mood, 'it's a pleasure to meet you.'

The IG broke into a smile. 'A friend of Mack is a friend of mine,' he said, 'please sit.'

A peon brought them cups of tea.

'Awan Bhai, you must help us,' Mack said, 'we are in so much trouble. As you know, Jane's boss and his driver were shot in front of us and someone tried to murder Jane three times already.'

'*Inshallah*, it will not happen again. I will put my best men on guard at this police station, and we will not stop till we hunt down these terrorists.'

'Sir, do you know who they are?' Sergei asked.

'The man who attacked Jane had links to Jamaat-e-Ilahi. That translates to the fellowship of Allah,' he replied. 'We know who they are and will soon discover if their leader was involved in the attacks. They are a new group. We believe they have links to the Pakistani Taliban, but it's also possible they are competing with them as well as with several other outlawed groups.'

'So why not just round them all up and arrest them?' Damon asked.

'Well son, it's not so simple. We need to collect evidence otherwise a judge will order them to be released, and then they will go into hiding. They are crafty. Their slogan is "Pure Islam without Compromise" which resonates with a lot of people.' He took a sip of his tea. 'They pretend to be law abiding and charitable and run a small religious school and collect funds to build mosques and feed the poor. We are sure they also syphon a lot of money into buying arms and planning attacks. We believe they are involved in smuggling drugs and running a protection racket.' He paused to take another sip. 'They are getting a lot of new support with this blasphemy case. Many extremist groups have expressed solidarity with them.'

'Well sir, what about today's shooting,' Sergei said.

'Had we managed to arrest the men who shot you, we could have investigated, but they were dead by the time we got there. Mack, we have reports you drove over them.'

'Awan *bhai*, Yes I did, but it was in sheer panic. I reacted to save our lives.'

'Not to worry, Mack. We are not planning any charges.'

'What about the motorcycle?' Sergei asked.

'Stolen, so useless. I will tell you honestly Sergei *Sahib* the big problem is this case is now political. Nobody in government will stand up for your wife. There have been too many assassinations of political figures who stood up for people accused of blasphemy. Everybody has a family to think of. Even I am afraid.'

'Is there any way not to lay charges or to take them back?' Sergei asked.

'I am a servant of the law. I am duty-bound to ensure it follows due process,' he said emphasising the last two words, 'but I am a husband too, and I feel your pain. So, I promise I will protect her. But I also assure you I will make sure she will stand trial.'

Just as he'd do everything possible to get Jane out of this situation. It was obvious they were not going to get anywhere with the IG. At least he seemed genuine about wanting to keep Jane safe from any further attacks.

Sergei and Razane spent another hour with Jane before the guard began to look restless and started looking at his watch.

They returned to the hotel without any further incidents. The entrance gate had reopened. The only sign of the murders was the broken glass and the sand on the road to soak up the blood. And that was it.

A great person, someone who was making the world a better place had died, and his death was marked only with broken glass and sand. By morning even this would be scattered by the traffic and the wind.

They bade each other good night with heavy hearts.

Sergei and Razane lay in bed in each other's arms.

'I've been racking my brains for a way to get Jane out.' Sergei said as he moved a strand of hair out of Razane's face. 'I can't think of anything realistic. What about you, sweetheart?' Razane was not one to indulge in facetiousness or flights of fancy.

'Just fragments of ideas, my love. I also have nothing workable yet.' She sighed. 'It's in a densely populated part of Lahore, which would be crawling with police so it will not be easy. But we also need a plan for what we do after.'

'Whatever happens, I ain't going back without her…'

'Neither am I so don't worry and just close your eyes, my love. We'll get her out,' she murmured in his ear as she gently stroked his face, 'we need you strong and refreshed.'

His breathing had become deep. He didn't reply. He was already asleep.

ICE BABY

Lahore, Monday 28 November, night

As she lay there listening to his calm breathing, she marvelled how he was able to fall asleep like a baby. For her it came harder. She had seen too many people die in their sleep. Nothing kept a person awake like the fear of never waking again. For a woman fighting among men, there were other horrors too. Horrors she did not want to dredge up, and they no longer mattered to her.

Her life had turned around. She found two beautiful companions to be with and to lie next to in a warm and safe place. Now a shadow had fallen over her again. She would have to fight like she had never fought before to save this new-found heaven. She sighed and yawned. Extreme tiredness overcame her, and she fell into a troubled sleep.

The night was moonless. They were so far from any dwellings there was no sky-glow either. That is why it was pitch black, so dark there was no difference between her closing her eyes and opening them. The grass all around moved and swayed, sounding like waves in the ocean. In the hollow between the rocks and boulders, where she lay, she felt none of the breeze. The night was warm. The sound was calming.

She was almost asleep when a grenade exploded. Her sleepy mind was jarred awake so fast it made her teeth rattle. Then the gunfire started. It sounded even more intense at night, brutal and immediate. Bullets were whizzing by, some ricochetting off rocks with a whine, others penetrating bodies, tearing through flesh and bone and sinew. Painful screams escaped the lips of those who were hit; cries choked into moans, as bodies paralysed by pain went into shock.

She lay there for the briefest of moments while her mind tried to make sense of how brutally the calm night had transcended into a frenzied nightmarish hell. Then her training kicked in. Her gun was beside her. She rolled over. Her mind automatically doing calculations to triangulate the source of the gunfire. She worked out where the enemy was and remembered she was high up and had a cover of rocks. She peered between them and saw flashes. Her mind became a sea of complete calm. She made sure her Kalashnikov was in single fire mode and aimed carefully at where the flashes had come from, now locked in her memory, and pressed the trigger again and again and again. Others in her unit began firing at the enemy as well. After what seemed like forever she heard no more returning gunfire.

She was awake again, covered in sweat. Sergei's warm body and the sound of his breathing reoriented her. He was blissfully asleep, his breathing calm and rhythmic. She had relived that night so many times it no longer caused her distress. She did, however, dream it regularly and would wake at the same part of the dream. She snuggled up to his warm form. In his sleep, he extended his arm and gently pulled her closer. It felt good and safe and secure. Nothing could hurt her.

The silence was as deafening as the gunfire. Slowly she became aware of cries and moans from the wounded. She crawled over to where she thought she had heard a bullet strike someone. It had been close to her left. The smell of blood hit her nostrils just before she touched something mushy and slippery. She tried to feel for the head and face, but there was nothing, just soft and shapeless flesh, and shards of bone and not in any shape she recognised.

Whatever had struck the person had blown their head to bits. She recoiled in horror, but she was lying on her stomach. As she tried crawling back, she realised she was covered in blood, brain and bits of flesh. She lost all touch with reality and curled herself into a ball.

Sergei held her close, stroking her hair. The bedside lamp shone in her eyes. She stopped screaming. Her neck and facial muscles were hot and tight. She was drenched in sweat. Sergei's beautiful, sensitive fingers began stroking and kneading. He knew just how and where. She relaxed against him. This was one of the memories that caused her the worst reaction. Seeing Simon's head all bloody must have triggered it.

She thought back to the following morning of that night. It had been a terrible encounter. The enemy had used soft tipped expanding hunting style bullets that had blown a huge exit hole in anyone they hit. None of the injured made it through the night. A quarter of her group was dead. If it hadn't been for her or if she hadn't been sleeping where she was there would have been many more casualties. Their commander was a no-nonsense type. He was a true believer who prayed five times a day. He had forced the women to sleep a good distance away from the men and threatened to whip any man caught in the women's sleeping area.

It was crazy how chance and carelessness had made all the difference in the outcome, but it was how life was. The enemy had been equipped with the latest American made night vision goggles, but they had forgotten muzzle-flash suppressors. It was the reason she had been able to pinpoint the location of each enemy shooter. By chance, they had approached the camp from the men's side. Only five men including the commander had survived. That gave her, the group's best shot, the time and space to retaliate.

After that attack, her unit slept in shifts which made sleep even harder because there was always someone talking or moving about. By the time she left the Peshmerga, she had become a total insomniac, and she was not alone. They had been attacked so often at night most of her unit's survivors had developed nyctophobia, a fear of the dark. Many of them became completely useless lunatics, not good for fighting or even to function in civilian life. She was hardly better herself. Her life was a wreck, and she was close to a nervous breakdown. That felt so very long ago, another universe, another life.

She felt quite a bit better. Her breathing had slowed, and the tension in her face and neck had ebbed. Sergei was, amazingly, already fast asleep again. She snuggled close to him and relaxed into sleep again.

The sun's rays shone through the tall windows and illuminated the room with a strong warm light. They all sat in a circle on a thick rug, their backs resting against pillows. It was an after-hours course in mystic poetry. They were reading love poems. Jane sat beside her reading aloud, the last poem Rumi had written for Shams of Tabriz.

'I didn't know Rumi was gay,' a woman opposite them said, in a French accent, when she finished.

'Why are you saying that?' Jane asked.

'Because of how close they were. They loved each other more deeply than most husbands and wives do.'

'I believe you can love deeply and passionately, without it being sexual. We, Westerners, have a need to put everything into boxes and label them and we have such backwards notions of sex,' Jane said.

Razane noticed how everyone was subconsciously leaning

in to listen to Jane. She was so Western, blonde, Christian, self-assured, conservatively dressed, but was speaking with such calm authority about an Eastern concept that had been lost to most people in the East.

'For us, sex is the culmination, a reward of love and loyalty,' Jane said. 'It's considered dirty and a sin unless conducted according to strict societal rules. Our views on sex haven't progressed since two thousand years.'

'Well, sex is even more taboo for Muslims,' a solemn young Iraqi man wearing thick-framed glasses joined in.

'Funny you should think that when the Quran actually encourages sex between a husband and a wife,' Jane said. 'Anyway, I believe what Rumi and Shams discovered was a love that transcended the physical limitations of the human body, of gender constructs and the rules of society... and... the constraints of historical precedence.'

'Wow,' Razane remarked, completely mesmerised by how Jane had captured her own thoughts. 'I am amazed how you put what I was thinking so perfectly into words.'

Jane turned and looked at her, 'I just feel this wondrous opening of my mind and my soul when I read Rumi's poetry. I feel reborn, like I have added another dimension to my being.'

'Yes, me too,' Razane said looking into Jane's eyes. 'I feel a peace I have not felt since I lived at home with my mother, but alive like no man has ever made me feel.'

The class tittered. She had spoken her inner thoughts, aloud. For a moment she felt a flush of embarrassment that such a private feeling had escaped her lips.

Jane gave her leg a supportive squeeze. 'Don't worry about them. I understand what you mean,' she whispered.

'But still that makes them gay, and I don't mean it in a bad way,' the French woman said.

'The way I see it,' Jane said, 'Rumi and Shams enjoyed each other's company, and they talk of kissing and physical contact. Their love had so many facets and dimensions it's possible sexual contact may have been part of it. I wouldn't say their relationship was about sex, though.'

'What it would be like to feel love like that,' Razane mumbled quietly.

Jane gazed into her eyes. 'Yes, me too.' She had sharp ears.

With their eyes still locked Jane had recited a few lines of Rumi's poetry,

'A loved one said to her lover to try him,
Early one morning, O my lover,
I wonder whether you hold me more dear,
Or yourself? tell me truly, my ardent admirer!
She answered, I am so wholly absorbed in you,
That I am filled with you from head to toe.
Of my existence, only my name remains
In my being there's only you, O Object of desire!
I am therefore completely lost in you,'

While Jane was reciting and for a brief moment after the whole world around them disappeared, the sounds and voices of the rest of the class receded into the background. It had not escaped Razane's attention that Jane had changed the gender of the lover in the poem.

Razane's eyes flickered open again. Her heart beat strongly. Her chest felt like bursting. She felt love and the fear of loss. Sergei was still breathing calmly and deeply next to her. She moved closer to him. In his sleep, he sensed her and again opened his arms. She lay her head on his chest and relaxed. Sleep was not going to come anytime soon. She thought back to that class.

Jane was the most amazing person she had met till then. That spark between them slowly developed into a flame so hot and intense it would overcome all their preconceptions and inhibitions and their respective religious upbringing. Over the days that followed their bond grew stronger and more multidimensional. They spent countless hours after work reading Rumi's poetry together and learning about him and his friend, Shams of Tabriz.

She began feeling new, reborn, transforming, growing, flowering, blooming. Jane made her want to live again. For the first time in forever, she laughed out loud. Her dark days became a distant memory. The smile never left her lips; the song never left her heart, she didn't need to sleep, couldn't sleep, her body just tingled with excitement and energy. She felt pure true love that awakened her senses and made her heart swell with happiness. Jane grew to be part of her. They became one. Later she let Sergei into her life, and their love grew even more dimensioned, beautiful, and magical. Every day was a blessing, something to give thanks for.

Now that was slipping away. Razane felt complete and total love for Sergei, but without Jane, they would both be incomplete like a beautiful song without the chorus, a strawberry tart without the strawberries. They all needed each other. How could one feel complete and yet incomplete, satisfied and yet not? How could she, they, love more than one person? Well, they did which meant it was possible. She knew if it had been the other way around; if Sergei was in a jail cell and Jane was lying there in her arms, she would have felt the same. She needed both. It was unreal but real.

It was possible to deeply love more than one person at the same time. Her mother had loved her and her three brothers equally fiercely. It proved love shared was love multiplied or something like that.

Were Jane and Sergei some sort of bizarre reverse Oedipus complex? Did they represent children she could never have? She smiled. How ridiculous. She was slightly older than Jane and slightly younger than Sergei; besides this was not the fierce love of a parent but a deep, sensuous, passionate, and yet spiritual love. Why was she analysing this? She did not have to justify it to herself, or anyone else. None of them did. It just was what it was, and sadly it was in danger of slipping away. Who was she kidding it had already slipped away. The thought was too painful; she had to sit up to be able to breathe.

Sergei stirred and muttered something in his sleep.

She had to stop these negative thoughts. She closed her eyes and took a deep breath. She would, they would find a way.

After all, she had been in worse situations. But back then she had nothing to lose except her own life. Life and death had become one and the same. She had stopped caring. There were even days when she had wished she would die, that a bullet would tear into her and release her demons.

In a way, not caring had helped her manage to always keep such a cool head. Something she had become famous and well respected, almost a legend, for. Her fellow soldiers had started calling her Ice Baby after some rap song. To tease her they would sing it while marching. It was incredibly annoying, but it also showed their respect for her. If they could see her now, they would no longer sing that song. Now that she had the whole world to lose. She was no longer an Ice Baby.

JAMSHED

Lahore, Monday 28 November, 10:10pm

'Jamshed wake up,' A hand was shaking him. He sat up startled. He must have fallen asleep. How long had he been out? He was clearly exhausted. The last few days he had hardly slept at all.

He had vigorously fought many blasphemy cases in the past. He had hated them all with a passion, but this one bothered him the most.

The law had nothing to do with Islam and everything to do with oppression and political expediency. To make matters worse, it had been written poorly, which made defending charges extremely hard. If two witnesses came forward and were able to convince the judge of their piety the case was lost. Even otherwise, most dragged on for years. On the rare occasion when his clients got acquitted, they invariably ended up murdered within a few days by some crazed lunatic incapable of comprehending the person had just been found innocent.

Yet he still did it. He had to, especially with the recent disturbing developments. Judges had been threatened. Lawyers had been shot and killed for defending their clients. Even the governor of Punjab was murdered for seeking clemency for a prisoner. No lawyer in Pakistan was prepared to take on high-profile blasphemy cases anymore, and the thought of helpless undefended people just didn't sit well with him.

Something was even more wrong with this case. He could sense it. The way Jane had described the situation pointed to a setup. The cool and calculated way the man had videotaped her was strange. These religious nuts should have been foaming at the mouth when she was allegedly insulting the prophet not calmly recording the whole event.

He had caught up with the judge when he left court earlier in the day. He had mentioned this to him, but the man had brusquely brushed him off.

'You are clutching at straws, Mr Rabbani,' he had said as he drove off.

Aneesha was smiling. 'Darling you better leave. You know my hubby is coming back in an hour, and I need to change these sheets and air the room out.'

'I love you.'

'You love my beautiful body.'

She did indeed have the most beautiful body ever. She was slender but not skinny and stood just a few inches shorter than him, which was a nice height for a Pakistani woman. Her breasts were large but firm, and her skin was soft as velvet. Her long silky black hair framed a pretty face with doe-shaped eyes and pouting sensual lips. She had impeccable taste in perfume and had the kind of beauty that made most men turn their heads for a second glance.

Jamshed leaned over and kissed both her breasts, one after the other. Then he pulled her close and nuzzled his face between them, inhaling her heady perfume. She giggled as she struggled to get away. 'Of course, I do. It is the most beautiful body in Lahore,' he mumbled into her cleavage.

'Only in Lahore?'

He straightened up and looked at her, grinning 'No in the whole of Pakistan.'

'Only in Pakistan?'

'Yes, only in Pakistan.' He ducked as she threw a pillow at him, 'then get out you miserable man, and don't come back until you appreciate my beauty properly.'

He smiled at her. 'You know Pakistani women are the most beautiful in the world.'

'OK get out now.' She tried hard to hide her smile.

He loved Aneesha. Well, he adored her body for sure and enjoyed having sex and hanging out with her. He supposed he also loved his wife but in a different way. She was too prim and proper to be any fun. She cared more about her social standing among the Pakistani expatriates in Singapore and about the parties she threw and who their daughters were going to marry. There was no fire with his wife. There never had been.

Theirs was probably a good reason why people should not have arranged marriages and why he was not going to let his daughters get married that way.

Aneesha was in the same situation. She didn't love her husband, a rich businessman who spent most of the year travelling and he did not love her either.

Arranged marriages are a real sad institution he thought as he dressed quickly. He dropped to his knees to look under the bed to make sure nothing had fallen out of his pockets.

'Such a considerate man, but I would have checked myself. I don't want to get beaten up.'

'If your husband ever beats you I'll come and kill him myself.'

'Go on; you don't have it in you to kill.'

'For you, I probably could.' He actually meant it.

That was probably the sweetest thing anyone had ever said to her. Aneesha watched him leave with sadness.

Jamshed's driver was sitting in the car, his seat reclined, reading a newspaper. The cabin dome lamp was his only source of illumination.

'Back to the hotel, *Sahib*?'

'Yes please,' he said settling into the back seat.

The night was getting foggy. Traffic was light, and everyone was driving slowly. They turned from M.M. Alam Road into the busier Gulberg Boulevard. From here it was ten minutes to the Pearl Continental, his hotel, where he could get some much-needed rest. Boy, he already missed Aneesha. He always felt withdrawal symptoms after seeing her. He resisted the urge to text her.

Tomorrow he would get his investigator to find out who owned the land in Shakar Parian and its surrounds. Most of his other blasphemy cases were actually disputes about money or property. This one might be something along those lines as well.

Up ahead the lights turned red. Their car stopped behind other traffic.

The news came on the radio. 'Two men were shot and killed in front of the Avari,' the newsreader said in a monotone.

Jamshed's blood turned to ice. The newsreader did not say who the people were. His hands shook as he picked up his phone to call Simon.

A motorcycle pulled up alongside their car. Something bothered him about this. Motorcycles always filtered to the front of traffic in Lahore. It was the last thought he ever had. The bullet shattered the glass, but he never heard the sound. The rider calmly put the pistol back in his pocket and weaved to the front of the traffic just as the lights turned green.

BEN

Melbourne, Tuesday 29 November, 4:00am

Ben closed his laptop and rubbed his sleep-deprived eyes. His head felt heavy. He had just finished reading up on what blasphemy meant in the context of Pakistani law, and it made him feel depressed. His phone notification light glowed green. It was a WhatsApp message from Damon.

Damon: We just came from Mum
Ben: How is she?
Damon: Very down
Ben: Awhhh poor mum :(]
Damon: It looks hopeless
Damon: And someone's trying to kill her, and us
Ben: Omg, wtf do you mean!?
Damon: They murdered Simon, Mum's boss!!!
Ben: Are you fucking serious, dude get the FUCK out of there!!!
Damon: Yeah man we got lucky, thank fuck for Razane
Ben: Shit... I hope you're joking
Damon: No joke man, this place is fucked
Ben: When did this happen?
Damon: 5 hrs ago...
Ben: Do they know who did it!?!?!
Damon: Not sure. I'm guessing the fuckers who accused her
Ben: Why! She's already in jail!!! Fukn hell...
Damon: Dude that's what I was thinking
Ben: What's the lawyer say?

Damon: He's not too optimistic... reckons we should figure out
    another way of getting mum out
Ben: What do you mean another way!?
Damon: No clue man... he probably thinks its bloody hopeless
Ben: This is so fucked!!!!
Damon: Razane suggested we break her out and smuggle her out
    of the country
Ben: What!?!?
Damon: She's nuts! I had a go at her and Dad
Ben: It sounds totally nuts! But ur saying there's no other way
Damon: The politics here's fucked
Damon: Everyone's backing away from helping
Damon: Even Mack's police chief friend refuses to help

There was a pause of twenty seconds.

Ben: Hate to admit it
Damon: What?
Ben: Maybe Razane's not so nuts after all
Damon: Well she is! We aren't in some fukn action movie or
    some shit
Ben: What if there's a way?
Damon: Don't u start too!
Ben: No but seriously, if there's a foolproof way?
Damon: Then yes! Anything for Mum, obviously!!!!
Ben: People do escape from places it's not unheard of
Damon: Are we criminals or CIA? How do we know what to do?
Ben: Wasn't Razane some sort of fighter?
Damon: Yeah I guess...
Ben: And Dad was in the special forces here?
Damon: Yes but 25 years ago he hasn't held a weapon since
Damon: He also wasn't too into it or he'd have gone back after
    his injury
Ben: So 2 people who can at least fire a gun or deal with pressure
Damon: And Mack's a fat businessman, me a metal guitarist

and ur an IT geek NOT confidence inspiring :)
Ben: Well, we are all Mum's got! r u not willing to even try?
Ben: U know what the death sentence means
Damon: Yes, I fucking know
*Ben: Think how fucking scared mum must be, we're the only
      people she's got*

Damon paused. He still wanted to believe all this would somehow get better and go away. He'd never get over his mother being executed for something she had not done. He would never forgive himself if he didn't at least try something. But this talk of springing her out of jail was sheer madness. He could just see the newspaper headlines. "Foreigners killed in police encounter." along with photos of them lying dead on the road covered in sheets.

Ben: Well?
*Damon: If someone could work out a plan with even a 10%
        chance I'd be in.*

Just typing that made him lightheaded. Had he meant it? Would he actually participate in something with a 90% chance of them getting killed or spending the rest of their lives in a Pakistani prison?

Ben: First, we need to stop thinking we can't do it
Ben: We are all too fukn soft

Ben was not wrong. He was outside his comfort zone. Just chatting about this made him nervous; like he was in some sort of altered reality. How come Ben acted so brave? Maybe because he was safe in Melbourne. For him, it was just an academic exercise.

Damon: So we need to toughen up!!

Ben: Yup!!!
Damon: any thoughts?
Ben: Yup a family meeting
Ben: I'll find the most secure way of talking
Damon: WhatsApp?
Ben: Probably I just need to check something
Ben: R u guys all together?
Damon: Yup, same hotel
Ben: OK call you in 30
Damon: K

Ben opened his laptop again and did a few searches on secure voice over Internet. WhatsApp was secure. That was good. Then on a whim, he typed "How to escape a country" into the Google search bar. What the fuck. He expected it to link to movies, but there were links with actual suggestions. Someone had actually thought about this. He began scanning through the search results.

FAMILY CONFERENCE

Lahore, Monday 28 November, 10:50pm

Damon's phone rang. Ben was calling him on WhatsApp. He answered, switched it to speakerphone and placed it in the middle of the coffee table. 'Hi Ben,' they all said, almost in unison.

'Is everyone there?'

'Yes Dad, Razane, Mack... me.'

'Is WhatsApp safe?' Sergei asked.

'For all intents and purposes yes, it is. The safest I know.'

'Ok, then let's keep using it for voice,' Damon said.

'Before we begin, I need to know if everyone is thinking... are we all... agreeing to try to get Jane out somehow?' Sergei said.

'I'm not because it will get us in even bigger trouble than we're in now.' Mack said.

'There is no other way!' Razane said in an exasperated tone.

'How is getting us killed or occupying the jail cell next to Jane going to help her?'

'Every country has had jailbreaks, and many were successful,' Sergei said.

'Yeah well, Pakistan is not every country. Here the police can be totally ruthless and efficient. Why do you think the CIA sends prisoners here to be tortured?'

'Of course, it's nuts, and I agree with Mack. Even thinking like this is silly but I'm not leaving here without Mum either,' Damon said. Even though he had agreed with Ben, he was not so sure anymore.

'We might just have to go ahead on our own then,' Razane

said, 'it might be better that way.'

'Razane, with all due respect this is not Iraq or Syria,' Mack said. His phone rang. 'I better get this,' he said, his brow furrowed. It was the IG.

'Ben, Mack is on a phone call, let's take a break,' Sergei said.

They watched as Mack listened to his phone. His hands shook as he put the phone down on the table. He had gone white. 'They shot Jamshed,' he said. He sat down and put his head in his hands. Silence descended on the room. 'He has been rushed to emergency and put into an induced coma.'

'Fucking hell!' Damon said. He had gone pale. 'This decides me. I'm not sitting around waiting for more of us to be killed.'

Mack's hands shook as he put the phone in his pocket. His eyes were glazed over. 'Fucking bastards.'

'When did it happen?' Razane said.

'A motorcycle ambushed him on Gulberg Boulevard.' Mack's voice was still distant.

'Poor guy, let's pray for a moment for him,' Razane said, 'he was trying to help Jane.'

They all went silent. The mood had become even more sombre. Damon got up and made everyone a cup of tea.

'Alright, I think I have changed my mind,' Mack said finally, 'they will try to pick us off one by one whether we do something or do nothing so we might as well do something.'

'That's great to hear, bro,' Sergei said, the relief in his voice evident.

'Do we all now agree? We simply have no choice.' Razane said. She looked around at them all as they muttered their assent. 'Ben?' she asked.

'Yes, yes I'm in.'

'OK then. We have next to no time so let's hear some ideas,' Sergei said, 'Razane what were you thinking of when you first mentioned it?'

'Obviously for a way to get her out of the station if possible without hurting anyone. I'm not sure of the way yet.'

'I think a lot of police have blood on their hands, they torture and are corrupt,' Mack said, 'but there are always good ones so if there is a way without creating more misery then we should try that first.'

'Look, we need to be honest here and accept there's a real possibility people will die,' Sergei said, 'it's the first thing we were taught in the army. You protect yourself and your side. Without us all understanding this we are risking ourselves, each other and Jane.'

'So, you are saying we would kill a policeman if needed?'

'I'm saying unless we are totally committed to doing so if and when needed, we might as well shoot ourselves right now,' Sergei replied.

'And don't forget we've no time to try stuff. We need a workable plan, we can use in the next two or three days.' Razane said.

'We need to treat this as war. Jane's innocent,' Sergei said. 'The police guarding her will unwittingly contribute to her death. So, it's a matter of choosing, Jane or them. And yes, Razane's right, we simply don't have time to try and find the optimal solution.'

'For a moment, let's play devil's advocate,' Damon said, 'just hear me out, 'cos I want us to be all really, really, sure about this. Aren't these policemen just doing a job, following orders? Many could be quite conflicted about this law themselves.'

'Damon, this isn't different to soldiers, in a war,' Razane said. 'Do you think all soldiers are evil just because they fight on the wrong side? You don't think they can hate their own side? They still die all the same.'

'We used to be taught rules of engagement about how and when we should use force,' Sergei said.

'So, what are you saying?' Ben said.

'We try to find a non-lethal way wherever we can. Hopefully, we don't have to kill anyone. But we do everything to keep ourselves and each other safe. Look we're not walking away from this without consequences. There'll be pain and guilt. I can deal with that, but I'd never get over leaving Jane to be killed.'

Ben was thinking how unfair this all was. He had principles. He was a good human being. He could not bear to see an animal in pain, let alone a human. But this was his mother. It was the worst kind of nightmare, one with no end.

'So, for the last time, if anyone's unsure,' Sergei said. 'Pull out. Razane and I won't ask you to do what you can't do.'

'You guys are the only family I have. You are like a brother and Jane is like a sister, so damn it I am in,' Mack said.

'Ben, we need someone to stay in Australia,' Sergei said. 'Someone who can coordinate us, do quick research, help us find solutions. You can be like our eye in the sky.' He thought he heard Ben let out a relieved sigh.

'Yeah sure.'

Ben would only trip them up. He would trip over himself sitting down. He was the perfect person to solve a technical problem, but he was clumsy and the complete opposite of Damon who was strong, physically tough and agile. Damon was also a softy. He'd been as upset as Ben, when Razane came into their lives, but had been unable to break ties with them. He would have to find a way to keep Damon out of harm's way.

'OK since I'm the brains,' Ben said, 'what's everyone think about this. We've three tasks, get Mum out of jail, get her out of the country and keep her safe in between.'

Sergei thought about it for a moment. It sounded simplistic, but there was nothing in Ben's statement he was able to dispute. Things were always easy when you broke them into chunks. Not that the chunks had solutions yet but merely stating it this way had made it suddenly seem less daunting. Sergei remembered his Dad telling him one could eat an elephant as long as one took one bite at a time. He used to giggle at this as a little boy, but it was true.

'OK I can help with keeping her safe in the interim period,'

Mack said, 'I can organise safe hiding spots within the country and transportation.'

'Sergei and I will work on how we can get Jane out of the lock-up,' Razane said.

'Damon, Mack and I can work on getting her out of the country,' Ben said.

'One more thing, I have to stress we do not have much time. Don't think a month, think days. At least to get her out and into hiding.' Razane said.

'I agree, they're probably planning an attack on the jail again,' Damon said.

'And they'll also have a go at us, so we need to think about that. We are probably safe inside this hotel but sitting ducks whenever we're outside,' Sergei said.

'We are especially vulnerable while we arrive and leave the hotel,' Razane said.

'Can I please talk?' Ben chimed in, 'First, can we all share locations on Google with one another. That way we, can all keep each other in sight. Second, what about you install some webcams near the police station? I was part of a project that installed webcams in a schoolyard to tackle bullying. We came up with some interesting places to put cameras, and they are tiny and take up hardly any space. For instance, you could rig one into a stone made of foam. I have already been looking on Google Maps at the police station, and there's what looks like a park opposite.'

Sergei loved gadgets more than most, but Ben's suggestion sounded quite inefficient. 'We'll take a look at the area and see if it makes sense to use cameras,' he said.

'Those crazy fucks will probably have people near the police station already. We need to keep an eye on them,' Ben said.

'OK we'll have a look,' Razane said. She looked at Sergei. Her eyes were saying no. Sergei nodded.

They spoke a while longer. The change in mood was palpable. Now they all had something to work on, they were a lot more positive.

PREPARATIONS

Lahore, Tuesday 29 November, 7:30am

Simon's death and the attack on Jamshed weighed heavily on their minds when they awoke the next morning. Razane looked refreshed, even though she had not slept much but Sergei appeared less so. 'I feel like I have just stepped out of a tumble dryer.'

'You were deep asleep last night,' she said hugging him, 'asleep like a baby.'

'Sweetheart, we must make sure Damon's not put in harm's way, nor Mack,' Sergei said with a serious note to his voice.

'I was thinking the same,' Razane said, 'Don't worry my love, they are also my family.'

He kissed her gently on the lips. 'I love you so much. It was the most beautiful day when you came into our lives.'

They heard a knock on the door. It was Mack. He looked like he had been up all night. 'I need a coffee,' he mumbled as he traipsed in. Sergei was about to close the door when Damon appeared in his gym clothes, looking fresh and energised.

'They have a good gym here, Mack you should try it,' he said cheerfully.

'I am too old for the gym. That is a young man's thing,' Mack replied sourly.

Damon looked at Sergei who rolled his eyes and smiled. 'We've ordered breakfast here,' he said.

'Good I'm hungry,' Damon said.

While they ate, they worked out a plan to stay safe. If they could stay out of sight, it would be hard for their enemy to launch another attack. So, they mainly focused on ways they could leave the hotel and arrive at the police station undetected.

It had become apparent their enemy were determined and organised. Jane being set up was part of a plan that included killing anyone helping her. They were not going to stop.

'What I don't get is why go to this length to frame Mum, when all they wanted was to kill her... and us?' Damon said.

'I agree. I think if we can work that out... it can help get Jane released,' Mack said as he spread some cream cheese on a toasted bagel.

'We know someone assaulted Simon before Jane's arrest so it might have something to do with Carbonon and the village...' Razane said putting her coffee mug down. Some of her hair had gotten loose. She retied it in a loose ponytail. 'So, it's probably not just about Jane.'

'Or not about her at all,' Sergei said. He stood up. 'But she's the one in danger and us getting side-tracked will not stop those fuckers trying again and again till they succeed. We should just do what we all agreed yesterday!'

'OK, but Dad don't you think Mack has a point?' Damon said, brushing some crumbs off his tracksuit pants.

'I don't think it matters,' Sergei said. 'It's not about justice or logic. We need to get your Mum and us out of harm's way. So let's focus, please!'

'I agree with Sergei,' Razane said firmly, 'and we must do it fast.'

They split up to go over the tasks they had agreed to the night before. There was a lot of thinking and researching to do. After a late lunch, they visited Jamshed in hospital. Mack's driver had found an old Honda Accord with dark tinted windows. It gave them complete privacy. Using a different car every day, they reasoned, could only make it harder for them to be spotted. Jamshed had been in surgery. He was still comatose and in intensive care. There was no point staying. They left the flowers they had bought at the hospital florist in his room and returned to the hotel.

In the evening they asked the hotel to pack them dinner for five. They ate with Jane in the visitor hut at the police station. They sat with her till they were asked to leave. It was around eleven at night. They were back in the hotel when they received the sad news; Jamshed had died of a blood clot in his brain as a complication of his surgery.

GRAND HOLLYWOOD HOTEL

Lahore, Wednesday 30 November, 10:30am

Sergei put the teacup down. He pushed the chickpeas and rice around on his plate and casually glanced at the police station. It was opposite the shabby corner restaurant they sat in. It used to be a residence. Its verandah had been converted into an alfresco dining area which was open to the street and offered an excellent view of the police station building and the parking lot next to it.

The restaurant only served one dish for which it had become famous. They had not needed to speak Urdu when ordering, which was good. Mack had done an excellent job with their disguises but someone looking like them and speaking English would definitely attract the wrong kind of attention.

Sergei's beard itched terribly and his eyes stung from the smog. He was sorely tempted to rip the thing off, but they needed their disguises. Razane in her burka was no less uncomfortable, trying to eat through the flap covering her face.

'I can't understand why so many women allow themselves to be suppressed like this,' she remarked.

'At least they don't have to worry about their appearance,' he said flippantly, 'no need for makeup, brushing your hair...'

'Yeah, or even clothes...' she said absent-mindedly.

'Now that's a way of making burkas sexy!'

She looked at him, 'well when we get out of this mess... maybe one day I'll dress up in a burka for you with nothing on underneath.'

His broad smile made his beard scrape irritatingly against his skin. 'You've got a deal,' he said looking out at the chaos. The T-intersection was abuzz with traffic. Motorcycles, cars, rickshaws, bicycles, all manner of vehicles shared the road.

Some were stationary or hardly moving; others were weaving between them at reckless speeds. Through the mayhem pedestrians diced with death, playing chicken across the road. Children of all ages walked, ran, and played among all this, some accompanied by adults and others alone. Some were begging for money, others in school uniforms were playing truant. Some, barely able to walk, were playing on the footpath, blissfully oblivious to all the dangers around them.

The air was thick with smoke and dust, and it was bedlam. The sound of engines of all types revving, horns honking, people talking, laughing, shouting, were all mixed into a strange and strident cacophony.

Among all of this, a street hawker walked by, pushing a cart laden with oranges, apples, bananas, and guavas. The sweet smell of fruit in sharp contrast to the other less pleasant odours around them.

From the little bit, Sergei had seen of Lahore, and what Mack had told him this was definitely not a better part of town.

The police station was an imposing structure that dominated the T-intersection of Sacha Saeen Street with Charsadda Street. It looked like it had been built a long time ago during the British Raj. Its architecture contrasted with the modern ten-storey office block on its left. The twelve-metre tall main building was surrounded on all four sides by a ten-metre tall brick perimeter wall topped by a row of wicked looking, inwardly curving spikes. The main building and the perimeter wall were both constructed of bricks that had at some stage been the traditional red colour. Weather and pollution had stained them a dark grey which gave the building a forbidding visage. The police station was easily the oldest building on Charsadda Street.

The structure was flanked by two tiny, neatly manicured, gardens that were part of the police station compound. Their appearance spoilt only by a thick layer of dust on all plants and trees. It hadn't rained properly for over three months, and dust covered every square inch of Lahore. Three police Landcruisers and several motorcycles and bicycles were parked in a staff parking lot between the front of the structure and the footpath.

Two four-metre-wide and three-metre tall archways in the front perimeter wall afforded the only view, at ground level, of the main building. The left archway was closed with a gate made of thick steel bars. It led to a closed door in the main building. The right archway had a similar gate that was ajar. A sign above read "Public Entry".

This was the gate they always used when visiting Jane. The other was for escorting prisoners in and out of the station. The public gate opened into a bricked off courtyard that had been made into an outdoor waiting area with a few benches around the outside walls. The door to the main building was at the end of this front courtyard. Two armed guards stood outside the main gate. A further two stood outside the door to the building. At night the guards withdrew into the main building and the front gates, and the door to the building were locked.

Behind the police station four white minarets surrounding the tall white dome of a mosque towered into the sky. The mosque fronted onto busy Sanda Road that ran parallel to Charsadda Street. To the right of the mosque and diagonally behind the police station compound was a small park, completely overgrown with ancient trees. In front of the park and to the right of the police station compound an unsurfaced plot of land was being used as a visitors parking lot. It was manned by two parking attendants. One helped people park and collected money, and the other operated a simple bamboo barrier.

A small Hindu shrine, in a tiny garden, opposite the parking lot and their restaurant seemed ridiculously out of place, seemingly unable to offer worshippers any tranquillity in the maddening rush surrounding it.

No shops on either Sacha Saeen or Charsadda Street were open when they had visited Jane, which had always been at night. Then the place had been completely deserted and quiet, the only sounds from the traffic on Sanda Road.

The night before he had counted only twelve policemen. In contrast, just then, it was teeming with them. Every now and then prisoners in handcuffs and leg shackles, each escorted by two policemen entered or exited the closed gate on the left. Three or four groups lounged outside, in the small side gardens, and others were constantly either entering or exiting the public gate. Sergei had tried counting a few times. There were at least twenty-five, all armed, some with revolvers, others with assault rifles.

Sergei cast his mind's eye into the building. The public entrance at the end of the front courtyard opened into a large administration area, a hall that included an old wooden reception desk and glass-partitioned offices and interview rooms. Two solid steel doors on the left and the back opened into the holding cells. A further door on the right led outside to the visitor huts in the side courtyard. Whenever they had visited, a guard would search them thoroughly and escort them out to the hut.

Jane would then be brought out from another steel door further along the side courtyard and almost opposite the visitor huts. Jane had told them her cell was the one closest to the side door.

Just knowing she was so close but locked in her cell and surrounded by hostile guards made him feel sick. He wanted nothing more but to see her right there and then. It was not possible in disguise. The police guards had strict orders not to allow any strangers to visit her.

He scratched his beard again; it was getting even itchier.

'Serge, stop it or it will come off!' Razane said through the mesh of her burka.

After much deliberation, they had decided they needed to study the layout of the police station and the surrounding area to work out an effective plan of escape. They could not, however, do it openly. There were too many eyes, especially on foreigners who would stand out like sore thumbs in that part of town.

Mack had suggested a disguise to blend in. He had gone shopping and had found them local clothes. With his tall build, fair complexion, grey *shalwar-kameez*, green canvas jacket, horn-rimmed glasses, wig, moustache, and beard Sergei could have passed for a Pathan from the north-west of Pakistan. For Razane it was easier. She could walk around incognito. She had always considered the burka to be a horrible garment but conceded it was useful for hiding one's identity. 'Razane the ninja,' Mack had remarked when she tried it on.

They could not very well leave the Avari dressed like that. It would have drawn too much attention there. Burkas were only worn by women in the lower economic classes, and Sergei's costume was more small shopkeeper than high-flying businessman. They had to find another place to don their disguises. So, after some searching, they found the optimistically named Grand Hollywood Hotel on Alamgir Road, not far from the police station. It was a grubby run-down motel. The two front entrances opened onto Alamgir Road, and the rear entrance opened into a small lane that ran through a busy market.

The room was small, with a double bed, and a bathroom with a washbasin, toilet and a shower. The toilet door had come off its hinges and had to be propped up in the door frame. Based on the number of shady looking men lounging around the front of the building the hotel seemed to cater mainly for short stay guests.

It was a great place to change into different clothes and to give someone the slip. It had worked like a charm. Tahir had dropped them off at the entrance to the market behind the building. They had walked into the hotel, changed their clothes and walked out into Alamgir Road where they had hailed a rickshaw.

Sergei took another sip of the tea. It tasted nice but had gone lukewarm. The food smelled good, so he took a few bites. Razane had already finished hers. Mack had warned them about only eating cooked food and drinking bottled water. They could not afford dysentery or worse.

'Stop scratching your beard, my love,' Razane said, this time more urgently. 'It will come off!'

He stopped. He hadn't even realised he was doing it. 'Sorry, it's awfully itchy.'

'Any thoughts? Other than your itchy beard.'

'First of all, I can't see anywhere to put Ben's cameras. This place is crazy. They'd get covered in dust in a day, and most likely someone would bump into them, knock them, or steal them before that happens. Also, what would they be able to pick up? This place is complete and utter chaos. Also, who has the time to analyse the feed?'

Razane sighed with relief. 'I agree. I just didn't want to challenge Ben directly,' she said.

'I understand, sweetheart. Anyway, we need to break her out at night, not during the day. We'd be completely bogged down in this traffic so we'd have to go on foot and with so many police around we'd just end up getting shot.'

Sergei had been in the Australian Special Forces in the first Iraq war. He had taken part in scores of training exercises, war games and mock raids but had never engaged in any real fighting. After the war, he had hurt his foot badly in a motorcycle accident and had left the army. Even though it was so long ago, he realised he still thought like a soldier.

He knew Razane's experience was quite different. She had seen too much combat and been in difficult and life-threatening situations countless times. What they were planning could make her post-traumatic stress disorder worse. She already couldn't sleep through the night because of bad dreams.

'What about you? Do you have any thoughts?' he asked. It was strange looking at her covered in black. 'Have you ever been in a situation like this?' He looked at her with deep concern in his eyes. He hated probing into her past and stirring up her ghosts.

'Yes, a few times.' She was annoyed. 'Will you stop looking at me like that,' she said sharply.

'Like what?' he said still gently, a note of surprise and hurt entering his voice.

'Like I'm a porcelain doll that is going to break if you ask about my past. It will not break me. What is killing me every second and every minute is one of us inside that jail. I don't care if getting Jane out makes me get flashbacks or if I cannot sleep for the rest of my life.'

He was about to say something when she continued in a gentler voice. 'You are both the sun, the moon and the stars for me. More than that. You are my oxygen. You two are my sanity. What will break me is if anything should happen to either one of you.' Her voice was breaking up towards the end.

Through her mesh, he could see her eyes were moist.

'Till then I am unbreakable. OK?' She was crying.

He knew it was not true.

'OK,' he said resisting the urge to touch her. Doing so would have made people notice. Men and women did not display affection in public, in Pakistan. He took another few mouthfuls of the rice.

'You know the Peshmerga have been fighting almost everyone at one point or another,' she said taking a deep breath, her voice now level.

He nodded.

'We had been sent over the border to Syria to help in the fight there. The Al Nusra front had captured a small town. They held the local mayor, his wife and a Dutch missionary hostage within a police station. We had to free them. I was one of a raiding party of ten who entered the police station. We were backed by a force of fifty fighters.

'While our backup force distracted, what they thought was, the main enemy position on the outskirts of town, we attacked the station. Most of us were highly trained, and the only rules we had to follow was to try and not kill the hostages.

'It turned out most of the enemy, around sixty men were in and around the police station and only around twenty of theirs faced our main force.

'The whole thing turned upside down. We ended up caught inside with them surrounding us. By the time our main force relieved us the mayor's wife and seven of our raiding party were dead.

'And that is probably the one thing the two buildings have in common. They were designed to keep people in not out.'

It was going to be the same here. Getting in was not going to be the problem, getting out was. There was one big difference. They were not going to get any help from outside.

Major Hamdani checked the weather on his phone for the tenth time. He was waiting for his boss Colonel Ali in his office. The colonel was late for their meeting. His laptop was not on his desk, so he was obviously held up somewhere, maybe in another meeting that was running over. Just then an email arrived in his inbox on his phone. It was a cancellation from the colonel.

'Sorry this meeting is running over, I wanted to talk about the person of interest who entered Pakistan, Razane Silan. She is ex Peshmerga. My sources tell me she could be acting as a gun for hire. I am concerned she may be up to no good vis-a-vis Jane Kelly. Please look into that. We cannot have a mercenary running amok in Lahore. I'll call you later.'

He accepted the meeting cancellation and replied, 'yes I am examining the possibility. She is apparently a close associate of Jane Kelly. The police guard where she's being held thought they were sisters. I will try to find out more and keep you posted.'

SACHA SAEEN STREET

Lahore, Wednesday 30 November, 11:15am

A sudden gust of cool air interrupted their thoughts. It carried lots of medium-sized dust particles but also the promise of rain. Overhead the sun had vanished behind the clouds.

'You know your beard could come off if it gets wet in the rain,' Razane said looking nervously at the sky.

Sergei had been thinking the same thing. They could not afford to make a mistake like that. People here were extremely nosy and curious, and something like that would surely attract attention. They had to get away from the environs of the police station. 'Yup, we better go.'

He pushed the plate away. The rice and chickpeas had grown cold anyway. They paid the waiter and left.

They walked up Sacha Saeen Street, away from the intersection, past various little shops selling everything from raw chicken to ladies' underwear. A small boy approached them with a goldfish in a plastic bag half full of water.

'*Bees rupiah,*' he offered as he held up the bag.

Acting on impulse Sergei gave him the twenty rupees he asked for and took the fish. It was a plain orange goldfish swimming frantically from left to right. Something about seeing creatures in captivity was affecting him more than normal.

They came to the end of Sacha Saeen Street, crossed the road to the other side, and began walking back towards the police station. Even at this distance, the building was imposing. They walked in single file because of the sheer number of pedestrians. Sergei walked ahead carrying his goldfish, Razane followed half a metre behind. It was too noisy to talk anyway, so they walked in silence.

Razane found the burka increasingly cumbersome. Everything became harder in it, eating, walking and looking around. The stupid garment made it hard for women even to talk. Maybe that was why some men forced their wives to wear it, she thought with a grimace. Whoever said it was not a tool for subjugation had never worn one.

As if the footpath was not crowded enough, hawkers had spread out their wares on canvas or bits of cardboard directly on the ground. Sellers and buyers were crouching down haggling. Sergei and Razane had to continuously shift their gaze up so as not to bump into pedestrians and down to not step on someone's livelihood, or even worse trip on a crouching shopper.

Razane was also conscious of the need to keep Sergei in her sights. From the back, he was dressed like any local and would be hard to spot in the crowd. It was so noisy he would never hear her calling out to him or even his phone ringing in case they got separated.

A fly buzzed inside her burka. She lifted her veil and shooed it out. There was something odd about Sacha Saeen Street. It was not what was there but rather what wasn't. There were no manned barriers to constrict the traffic. Every other government building, hotel and large shopping centre in Lahore had concrete or steel barriers placed on the streets leading up to them. The barriers were manned by armed police or soldiers. According to Mack, their purpose was to inhibit terrorist attacks. They had made traffic a nightmare, but apparently, they worked.

Curiously Sacha Saeen Street had no such barriers at all. The police station at the end of it would certainly be vulnerable to a bomb mounted on a moving vehicle. How odd they hadn't protected it better.

Maybe someone had come during the day, seen how busy

and congested Sacha Saeen Street was and had decided the police station did not need barriers. However, at night it was completely different. The whole place was deserted. The street, cleared of its hoardings and handcarts, was wide enough for a van or even a large truck laden with explosives. The people who had killed Simon and Jamshed might be able to rig a vehicle with a bomb.

The thought made her frantic with worry. Their enemy had so far been one step ahead of them. They might already have something in the offing. She hoped not, but they had to assume the worst.

What about other security? She looked around for cameras and saw none. She looked again, carefully, at all the poles and the sides of buildings for any sign of a camera installation. There were none she could see.

They came to the small Hindu shrine that took up the corner at the end of the street. It was essentially a three-metre square garden with a few plants in pots and a small water fountain in the middle. A tiny trickle flowed from the fountain's spout. Sergei dropped the goldfish into the water with a sigh of relief. He had been wondering what he would do with it.

'Hopefully, the people looking after this place will take care of it,' he murmured.

They looked both ways before turning right onto Charsadda Street. The shops here were bigger, and the footpath was clear of hawkers. Perhaps the proximity to the police station presence kept them at bay. They walked past three chemists in a row followed by a doctor's clinic, then a tailor and a printing shop. Similar buildings continued one after the other all the way to where the street ended in a T-intersection.

'You know, this street can be boxed off easily,' Razane remarked.

'You mean by the police?' Sergei mulled it over. Thank goodness for Razane. 'Yeah, I see,' he said.

'If we get held up or get unlucky we would be in deep trouble,' Razane said. 'We cannot have the getaway car on this street.'

They had to find another way, a foolproof way to escape. They crossed Charsadda Street carefully, looking left and right to avoid being run over. On the other side, they turned left and walked slowly back towards the police station. As they reached the visitors parking lot, they looked at the overgrown park behind it.

'I wonder if there's access through to Sanda Road through that park there,' Sergei said. 'If there is we could be on the main road within half a minute, jump into a waiting car and not be boxed in.'

'Well spotted,' Razane said.

Walking through the parking lot to explore the small park would have drawn attention from the attendants, so they decided to walk along Charsadda Street in the direction of the police station, hoping to find a shortcut to take them to Sanda Road. Thankfully, five shops after the police station, they found a narrow alleyway only suitable for pedestrians and cyclists.

The little park abutted the large mosque. It was completely overgrown with mostly tall fig trees with thick buttressed trunks and dark leathery-leaved canopies. They looked like they had been planted in another era. The ground was bare except for dead leaves, and litter that must have blown off the street. The park was separated from the footpath by a small steel fence. It could easily be stepped over, but at night it would be a trip hazard, with disastrous consequences.

'We don't wanna be tripping over this,' Sergei said grimly, pointing at it.

They stepped over the fence and entered the park. The trees completely blotted out the sky and made the park dark and gloomy. They walked up to what seemed like the middle. From here they could see the back of the public parking lot and the side of the police station building.

'I believe we have our escape route,' Razane said softly. We ask Damon to wait in the getaway car outside this park on Sanda Road. If we run, it should take us twenty seconds to get from the police station entrance to this park and another fifteen to pile into the car.'

'The only thing that needs to be worked out is how exactly we bring Jane out,' Sergei muttered as they walked out of the park back onto the footpath.

Sanda Road was a busy and fast flowing three-lane road with a low central divider that could easily be driven over. Hopefully, it would help them get away fast.

Sergei spotted a rickshaw and hailed it. He gave the driver the address of the Grand Hollywood Hotel. On the way, he called Mack's driver.

'*Salam aleikum* Tahir, we are ready.'

'OK sir, I'll be right there.'

At the hotel, they changed out of their disguises and walked out of the rear entrance through the marketplace to the waiting car.

Fazal put away his binoculars. 'I don't think they are coming back.'

'Yes, I think you are right, they have left,' Yousaf said.

They were standing at a window on the fourth floor of a building at the end of Sacha Saeen Street. The police station loomed large in the distance. The major had asked them to watch and record all suspicious comings and goings. A little while after they had begun their shift the major sent them an image of Sergei Markoff and Razane Silan in disguise.

'They could be headed your way,' the accompanying note read.

Apparently, a fellow ISI agent had followed them from the Avari to the Grand Hollywood hotel. He had observed them go up to their room and had been quite taken aback when they emerged dressed differently. Fortunately, he had the presence of mind to take a photo and send it to the major, who had forwarded it to them.

The major had predicted correctly. Fazal spotted the pair entering the little restaurant, not long after. Later they watched them as they walked around before they disappeared left along Charsadda Street.

'Why do you think they are in disguise and watching the police station?' Fazal asked.

'I am not sure, but they are strange people, and complete amateurs,' Yousaf said as he yawned and stretched his arms over his head to ease his weary muscles.

'Yes, they are not very professional.' Fazal smiled.

Yousaf dialled the major. 'Sir, we think they have left.'

'OK, good. We have just heard their driver is on the move. I think they are heading back to the Grand Hollywood.'

'They are strange people, sir. They were watching the police station like we are.'

'Hmmm... Yes... Good work. Now keep watching. I want to know if anyone else shows a similar interest.'

'Yes, sir. No problem, sir.'

THE FINAL SOLUTION

Lahore, Wednesday 30 November, 12:30pm

The sound of prayer beads clicking was the only thing that disturbed the tranquillity of the prayer room. It was just him in communion with Allah, the most magnanimous and magnificent, the most forgiving and awe-inspiring. Zuhr prayers had ended, but he always liked to sit another half an hour in contemplation. It was when he was at his most serene and he could think most clearly.

He stood up feeling a little dizzy, both his knees clicking painfully. His left foot hurt badly today. He straightened his back with some difficulty. It hurt as well. Maybe there was rain on the way, but most likely it was just old age. He did not complain. The pain was only a test and temporary like everything in this world. It was Allah's way of reminding humans the body was on loan. Only eternal life was real. One day he would die and make his way to *Jannat-al-Firdous*. However, it was not going to be today. He and his group still had a lot of work to do. Important work that would soon send non-believers to hell, in small pieces.

He walked out of the room into the large yard. Small drops of rain were beginning to fall. It smelled fresh. He looked up at the sky. Allah be praised.

A large tent stood in the middle of the courtyard supported by tall bamboo poles. Excitement building, he made his way inside. The Bedford truck stood in the middle looking purposeful. It had seen better days and was bruised and battered with a few rust holes in the front mudguards. Apart from that, it appeared straight. He had asked Bilal to buy a good truck, and he was sure he had done just that. Bilal was his most trustworthy man, even more so than his son, Adil. The raindrops were now large enough to make pattering sounds on the canvas. The wind had picked up speed causing the tent to flap noisily.

Babur emerged from under the front of the truck, his hands completely covered in grease. He had been servicing the engine to make sure it would not break down. He moved the hair out of his eyes with the back of his hand. A bit of grease transferred to his cheek.

'It is ready, *Aqa*.'

Abdul Zubair had waited almost three months to hear those words. He patted Babur affectionately on the head. '*Shabash*, well done! Show it to me then.'

This truck bomb had cost him almost five-years of savings. But money would not have been enough had it not been for the sheer good fortune Allah had bestowed upon him in the form of Babur.

Babur was known as one of the top five makers of bombs and improvised explosive devices among jihadi groups in the world. If they gave prizes to bomb makers, Babur would have received one. He was well-read with a double-degree from a top university in America in mechanical and chemical engineering. Instead of finding a well-paying job he had returned from the land of the *Shaitan* with the fire of Allah in his heart.

His speciality was converting cheap and commonly available items into dangerous weapons. One of his biggest achievements for which he became famous was modifying easily accessible drones into remotely guided aerial bombs that caused havoc among the Syrian and Iraqi government troops.

When the Islamic State executed his wife for using a mobile phone, he left Syria in disgust. ISIL's loss was a boon for all the jihadi groups in Pakistan and Afghanistan. His improvised explosive devices helped the Taliban take back many small towns in Afghanistan.

When Abdul Zubair heard of Babur, he made a special trip to Nauzad, northwest of Kandahar. He managed to convince Babur with the help of his old Taliban contacts to return to Lahore to build a bomb for him.

Over the three months, Babur worked tirelessly, sometimes not sleeping for days. Fatigue and working with explosives were never a good combination, but Babur was so imbued with the fire of Allah he didn't seem to need sleep like ordinary men.

Abdul Zubair had seen the plans for the truck bomb and then bits and pieces of it as it came together. Today was his first chance to see it complete. He was excited. He felt power coursing through his veins. His dizziness was all gone now. This was indeed an auspicious occasion. Allah's presence was much in evidence today.

He placed his right foot carefully on the steel step and using the handle pulled himself up into the front passenger seat. The austere cabin lacked the ornate decoration found in most Bedford trucks.

He fingered the large pipe made of one-inch thick steel that sat above the transmission tunnel. It started from the load area in the back of the truck, poked through the rear cabin bulkhead and abutted the dashboard.

The gear lever had been moved to the steering column to make way for it. He knew the pipe was a shaped charge designed to explode forward into a building, opening up a huge hole and killing everyone inside.

He looked back at the bulkhead separating the cabin from the rear load area. In place of steel was plywood painted in the same grey colour as the rest of the cabin. He tapped on it carefully. It sounded hollow. From outside it was indistinguishable from the real thing.

He climbed out and looked underneath. The chassis was reinforced with plate steel that had closed most of it off making it incredibly strong and at least twice the weight of a standard

Bedford.

He walked to the back of the truck. Here he saw the rest of the pipe containing the shaped charge. Behind it was a simple propane bomb designed to incinerate any survivors from the first explosion. A cage held eighteen gas cylinders containing the extremely flammable gas. The cylinders were individually encased in many layers of hessian containing thousands of ball bearings. More ball bearings were packed in the spaces between the cylinders. Behind the gas cylinders at the back of the load area was a solid parabolic dish made of eighteen-millimetre-thick steel plate. He knew because he had paid for the steel himself.

It all looked impressive and deadly.

Babur stood beside him watching his face, waiting for him to ask something.

'Show me what you have done since last time.'

'Well *Aqa*,' he pointed at the large parabola at the back of the truck. 'I have built this reaction plate to shape the propane explosion and the ball bearings forward into the police station.

'How did you make the dish?' He had done some welding work as a younger man, and that looked impressive indeed.

'*Aqa*, I did not have a roller, so I made it by cutting the plate into small shapes, grinding an angle onto their edges and welding them into a parabola. It was a lot of work.'

'*Shabash*,' Abdul Zubair said. Babur's dedication was inspirational. 'Tell me again how this is all going to work. From the beginning.'

'Well *Aqa*, as I promised this truck is a new kind of a bomb. It will burst through any defence. When the truck hits the target the trigger at the front of the pipe will make that bomb explode. It contains UNX in a shaped charge and will be most powerful. It will open up a big hole inside the building, kill everyone inside and most likely make it collapse.

The pipe bomb will be the trigger to make the propane tanks blow up. They will send flames and ball bearings into the inside of the building. Every person in the building not already killed by the pipe bomb will be roasted alive and shredded to pieces. The explosive force of the propane will cause any part of the building still standing to collapse. It will all be reduced to a pile of rubble with no survivors. It will take rescuers days to sift through what's left. There will be nothing left to be buried.'

'And we will have men in a van just outside who will arrive with machine guns and a video camera. If there are any survivors, they will take care of them.'

'*Aqa,* your men will not need guns but rather spades.'

'You are marvellous Babur, the best engineer in the world.' He smiled and patted Babur on the shoulder. 'And don't worry about what I need. Those men are only to make absolutely sure...but... I trust you are correct.'

Babur knew he was right but did not argue. There was no point. The Maulana would find out himself.

Abdul Zubair had selected Ishaq to be the driver. He had joked with Bilal about asking Burnt Saleem to do it just to see his reaction. But he knew Burnt Saleem was not suitable. Allah had chosen him for other things. He would learn from the mistake he made in the courtroom. Allah would forgive him for his past errors and failings as he forgave all true believers.

Ishaq, on the other hand, was most suitable. He was a believer, but dim-witted. Where Burnt Saleem was Allah's tiger, Ishaq was Allah's sheep. He spoke slowly and was a slow learner, but what he lacked in brains he made up with dependability. He had learnt to be a good driver after many years and did not get easily flustered. He would not be nervous if the police stopped him. His brain just did not work fast enough for him to process panic.

He had the fire of Allah inside of him. It was all that mattered. The burning desire for martyrdom made up for all other shortcomings.

He almost envied him his quick ascension to heaven with

all its pleasures. But Allah chose his generals, who shaped the destiny of the world, just as he chose his foot soldiers.

He was sure the truck would demolish the police station. Babur had designed it to destroy a much larger cinema complex before Jibran had insisted they use it on the police station. He had been delighted to discover Abdul Zubair had a bomb ready to go and had promised to pay him enough money for two more of the same.

Jibran had insisted on the second part of the plan. He wanted to be sure this time.

Jibran was right. They could not allow another failure. The woman and all her friends should already be dead by now.

Jibran had warned him of dire consequences if he did not succeed with the bomb. The man had no manners. One moment he would cajole and beg, and the other moment he would threaten.

Right now, he needed all the money he could get from Jibran so he would continue to stay quiet and let Jibran throw a tantrum like a badly-behaved child. But one day when the time was right he would send Jibran to hell where he belonged.

In a way, Jibran was even worse than the non-believers. He pretended to be a true Muslim but was not. He wore the right clothes and prayed and said all the right things but he was known to drink alcohol, gamble and commit adultery. He lusted after power not to serve Allah but for his own glory. He was the worst kind.

They had decided to attack at night because the truck needed to build up speed. It could only happen when Sacha Saeen Street was empty. If they timed it right, they would get all the woman's companions when they visited her.

The only regrettable thing about an attack at night was the reduced casualty rate. He needed a lot of dead bodies to make the right headlines around the world. Fewer than a hundred dead people in a poor country like Pakistan rarely made it into the big newspapers in America and Europe.

He knew most of the people who would die with this bomb would be innocent, but he did not worry about them. Life in this world was temporary and never to be cherished or treasured. If they were true believers, they would go to heaven. If they were sinners, they would go to hell where they belonged. In any event, they would reach their final destination a little earlier. What was wrong with that?

He just had to pray to Allah the newspapers would pick up the story.

JIBRAN

Lahore, Wednesday 30 November, 2:00pm

Jibran had almost sent his apologies for not attending the Intelligence Sub-Committee Briefing. At the last moment, he changed his mind. He would be glad he did. This whole situation was getting beyond frustrating. He was used to getting his way, and fast. Now everything had bogged down. Abdul Zubair's men were a constant disappointment, and the foreigners had turned out to be more resourceful and resilient than expected.

They were taking precautions and outsmarting them. Abdul Zubair's men had been unable to properly follow them since Monday night.

The foreigners had started using different cars each day, making them harder to spot when they left their hotel. In traffic, they would zigzag all over the place and run red lights making them almost impossible to follow. They had worked out a way to switch their mode of transport and dress before arriving at the police station so yesterday they were not spotted until they left. Abdul Zubair's men might be good at demonstrating in the street and using brute force to kill, but they could not do so on command, and now they had also lost the element of surprise.

God only knew if they would be able to blow up the police station. He had seen the bomb yesterday, and it looked promising enough, but he was just not sure about them anymore. So, he needed a backup plan. He now had his own men doing what he was paying Abdul Zubair to do, and they had not failed so far. The lawyer was dead, and they would get the others as well.

But he could not kill the woman himself. For that, he needed Abdul Zubair. Her death had to be tied to religious extremism and the blasphemy case.

He had tried to find out who the other foreigners were and how they were connected to Jane Kelly but had been unsuccessful.

The fat Pakistani was a rich businessman, a rice trader. Why was he helping them? Did he have a business stake in Carbonon?

In any event, they all had to be eliminated. He could not afford any loose ends.

He had joined the Intelligence Sub-Committee partly because his uncle, also a career politician, had advised him to and because of the connections he made within the intelligence community. It meant access to privileged information before anyone in the general public knew. It also came with a certain prestige. It made him a part of the establishment.

It was through one of these briefings he found Abdul Zubair and his group. They had been characterised as a low-level terrorist network with an unknown risk profile. They were perfect for what he needed. The only problem was they had not yet lived up to their intelligence rating. Any number of firebrand *mullahs* in most local mosques could have done something similar. Except, of course, they did not usually have access to powerful bombs.

The weekly intelligence briefings were for the most part tedious, four hours of endless talking about mostly useless stuff.

At each meeting they would go through lists of people under surveillance, people of interest, who had entered or had left the country and people who had been added to the various lists the government kept. Only slightly more interesting was information on Indian and Afghan troop movements and assessments of their state of combat readiness.

It was all dull but apparently necessary. Pakistan's intelligence agencies had become a law unto themselves. This hurt Pakistan's image which the present government was working on to improve. This committee was meant to make them accountable to the government and to provide some semblance of political oversight.

The ISI was Pakistan's largest and most powerful intelligence agency. They had been directly responsible for setting up the Taliban in Afghanistan and the various extremist groups in Kashmir to harry Indian troops. Extremists were by nature, not a species particularly renowned for their reasonableness or loyalty. Anyone not following their narrow worldview invariably became an enemy. So over time, those groups became a headache for Pakistan. In hindsight, the ISI chiefs should have known better. Maybe they had never read the story of Frankenstein, how the monster had killed its maker.

He had to be careful Abdul Zubair did not get out of hand and turn on him. The safest option was to string him along till the land was transferred to him, and the foreigners were dead. Then he would arrange an accident for the bearded fool. He would be the last loose end.

Bored, he thumbed through the pages, scanning ahead. Many of the people of interest had photographs attached. He reached the middle when he saw it, his body stiffening involuntarily. It was a photo of the older foreign man and the Arab woman in a one-page report. He was so keen to read it he almost knocked over a bottle of water.

"Persons of interest Sergei Markoff and Razane Silan who entered the country through Lahore Airport are now established as associates of Jane Kelly who is charged with blasphemy. They have been observed visiting the Charsadda Street Police Station. They are under surveillance and have been seen engaging in behaviour of dubious and unexpected nature. On several occasions, they have acted to evade surveillance. Consider raising risk level".

He had read such reports in these meetings before. It meant a caseworker would be assigned to track them 24/7. Their hotel rooms would be bugged and their telecommunications hacked.

He scanned the pages ahead. Only these two were mentioned. There was nothing about the younger man nor the Pakistani. Were they not on the ISI's radar?

What was the unexpected behaviour referred to in the report? What were they up to? Why were they on the watchlist in the first place? Were they CIA or Mossad or something else? The foreigners were obviously not ordinary people but professionals. It explained why they had been so successful at evading Abdul Zubair's men.

He had a disturbing thought. If the ISI were watching them, then any attempt to kill the foreigners would be observed too. Thank God, he had found out.

He had to use men who were not his direct employees and could not be traced back to him. He knew just the man.

And he had to make Abdul Zubair move the day of the bombing forward.

OPTIONS

Melbourne, Wednesday 30 November

Some people are decisive, others are not. Ben was somewhere in-between. He had found five possible routes out of Pakistan. They all had advantages and disadvantages.

None of the options was perfect. He forced himself to rank them from one to five. Was his mother even aware her son, Ben, who'd forsaken her for the last two years was making these life and death decisions?

Children often complain about being constrained by parents. But children constrain parents just as much, with expectations of how they should behave. In this case, he was the guilty one.

To a great extent, he'd reacted out of shock when they'd introduced Razane as their partner. Till then they'd always been the perfect family. The thought of the three of them together sickened him for reasons he could not explain, even to himself. Maybe it was a part of being an awkward teenager that he couldn't countenance anything unconventional.

But two years in a young man's life was like a lifetime. His mother's arrest had made him take a different perspective.

There was a high chance she could be executed. He could lose her. He felt a pang of remorse. He was desperately sorry, and unable to tell her. Hopefully, it wasn't too late to let her know he supported her right to live the way she wanted. Who was he to decide what was normal anyway? Fuck normal!

He took a deep breath and created a WhatsApp group. He

called it "Family". The escape route would be a family decision.

> *Ben: The 5 choices in order of best to worst are:*
> 1. *Escape by sea. It's the second furthest away but has advantages too. It's patrolled by the Pakistani navy and coast guard. Pakistan's maritime boundary extends 350 nautical miles (630km) into the Arabian Sea and abuts those of Iran, Oman and India and International waters. The bulk of Pakistan's navy patrols the maritime boundary with India, its key military threat. The rest of the zone is patrolled by modern cutters and fast missile boats. The proposal is for a luxury yacht to visit Karachi. On the way out it will meet a fishing vessel with Mum onboard. I've already researched a few vessels we could hire in Dubai. One issue is cost. The voyage to Australia is around $600,000. Risks include needing to travel 1250km to get there. Getting stopped by the coast guard during an inspection. Usually, the coast guard leaves people alone once they've been inspected. So, if the boat picks Mum up after their inspection, we should be fine.*
> 2. *India is the closest escape route. The nearest border is an hour away. It's heavily protected with fencing, and due to its length, not all is patrolled. Whatever is not patrolled is monitored electronically. Where fencing isn't possible, e.g. in ravines and cliffs they use laser walls with alarms. The problem here's finding the optimal place to cross. The risks with this option includes dealing with people who know smuggling routes and being betrayed by them. Being shot by armed forces on both sides, being killed on Indian side by a fanatic Muslim soldier or civilian. Mum's face has been in the news all over the world.*
> 3. *Afghanistan's border is far more porous but is fraught with danger. The only safe places to cross are at the immigration checkpoints. Any other crossings require*

local knowledge. Same risk of betrayal as India. The terrain is difficult. There will be a need to pass through no man's land. Finding a guide to trust is tricky. The risk of betrayal and of being caught in an armed conflict is high. If caught by Afghan authorities their response is unpredictable.

4. China. The only way to go into China and not get arrested is to go through a proper border checkpoint. These are manned by Pakistani immigration who will arrest her. Her name and face will be on an exit control list if she escapes. Entry into China is no issue as long as done properly. Since this is not being done legally, it's virtually impossible. We could apply for a visa. However, China has an extradition treaty with Pakistan and could hand her back.

5. Iran comments are similar to China. Higher chance of extradition. Also, the risk of fanatics as per India and Afghanistan. It's also the furthest option from Lahore.

Within two hours everyone replied. They were unanimous.

JANE

Lahore, Wednesday 30 November

A gentle breeze blew. It was just cool enough to keep the perspiration from building on her skin and just warm enough to carry the heady scent of eucalyptus. She reclined, legs crossed under her, on a large burgundy divan on their timber deck under the massive seven-hundred-year-old river red gum tree. Condensation had formed on the outside of the tall glass of iced tea she held in her hands. Every minute or so another water drop would roll down the side of the glass and pool on the deck below. Her eyes took in the scenery of what had become their happy place.

Their land was mostly a small wooded hill in the beautiful Yarra valley on the outskirts of Melbourne. The area around their log cabin had been cleared and landscaped with European trees that contrasted beautifully with native species growing further up the slope. From where they sat they could see horses grazing in a paddock on their neighbour's farm. Someone far away operated a ride-on mower. Crickets chirped as a cicada droned a rhythmic mating call. She was in a state of deep relaxation.

Razane was reciting their favourite Rumi poem about love, in her quiet, solemn voice. The setting sun, shed of all its heat and glare reflected on her face and formed glowing orange pinpricks in her lovely dark brown eyes. She was leaning against Sergei, and her legs were in Jane's lap.

It was the same poem she had read out to Razane and the rest of the poetry class at Zakho University.

The poem ended. They were now talking about what Rumi had meant and how his concept of love could be interpreted as love for a person or for the divine and how both were the same in a way. If you loved a person, you loved the divine whether the divine was, in fact, a singular entity like God or a pluralistic concept like the universe. It was a beautiful discussion and argument because there was no right or wrong way to look at it.

They all approached it from a slightly different angle. Razane was Muslim, Sergei was an atheist, and she was Christian. All three were profoundly spiritual; it was how they connected so strongly. Their love ran so deep they desired nothing else but to spend time in each other's company. Their discussions did not need a beginning nor an end and this place, their favourite spot to relax on a warm summer evening, was the perfect place to do it.

A metallic clanging sound startled Jane. She looked around. It did not fit in with the surroundings. There it was again. Her happy place faded away. The hills and Sergei and Razane were gone and in its stead, the dirty yellow ceiling, and the naked light bulb at the end of the long cord. She had a knot in her stomach and felt like throwing up. Her breathing became ragged, and she felt short of breath. She fought hard to quell the panic, to get a grip. Today was the sixth day of her nightmare. One she no longer believed she'd wake up from.

Jane tried slowing her breathing, forcing her mind to go back to the divan on their deck but it eluded her. The clanging sounded again. A guard was banging on the bars looking at her.

'Yes, what?' she said, gesturing with her hands.

'OK?' he said pointing at her, 'you OK?' He looked concerned.

It must be late. She had overslept. Her watch showed it was eleven in the morning. The breakfast tray lay on the floor next to the door, untouched.

'Yes, thank you,' she said giving him a weak smile.

He was one of the friendlier guards and acted more like a concerned uncle than a policeman. He was in his mid-fifties, tall and straight with a wrinkly face and ink black hair and moustache, that were a bit too dark to be his natural colour. He always smiled and spoke respectfully to her in his broken English.

He was just doing his job. She didn't blame him. 'Thank you,' she said forcing a smile. He smiled and sauntered off.

Jane sat up slowly, feeling dizzy. Mornings were always the hardest. Waking up and realising she was still in the police lock-up was almost as bad as when they had first read out the blasphemy charge.

The lumps in her bedding had formed painful knots in her back. She tried moving her neck and her arms. They felt leaden, her energy levels almost depleted.

She had to keep her spirits up and keep fighting, but it seemed quite hopeless. The spark she had always been able to summon appeared to have been extinguished. What made it worse was the hurt she was putting her loved ones through. The haunted look in Razane's eyes and the worry on Sergei's face had been almost too hard to bear. They needed her as much as she needed them. Their amazing companionship seemed doomed.

With some effort, she splashed some water on her face and wondered what her family were up to. Every day they said the same thing. They were looking for ways to get her released. They sounded confident and hopeful, but it was most likely an act for her benefit. If they had a plan, they would have told her.

Was the Australian Government doing anything? Could they? On their traveller website, they warned about the need to follow local laws, and that they couldn't intervene in criminal cases. Would it apply to her? She hadn't done anything illegal, at least not knowingly. Would they treat her differently if they knew she'd been set up?

Jane ate a few bites of the burger. It was cold and tasteless.

She washed it down with the tepid coffee. After a while, she couldn't manage any more. Her mouth was dry even while she was drinking, and she had no appetite at all.

She got up and did a few painful stretches followed by a few forced push-ups, trying to get her heart pumping. Workouts had always made her feel better but not this time. Her joints ached, her muscles felt sluggish like she was moving in a vat of molasses. Maybe she was coming down with something. She touched herself on the forehead. There was no fever, and her skin felt cold and clammy.

What was Jamshed doing and why hadn't he visited since the day before? He was supposed to be working on her case and keeping her abreast of progress. It was strange Sergei, and Razane hadn't mentioned him last night.

Jamshed had never been positive about the outcome, which was worrying. The two occasions they'd met he'd assured her he would leave no stone unturned. Only people who had no clue what they were doing turned over every stone.

She had to stop this. Thinking and waiting was driving her crazy, making her doubt the very people helping her. What anguish poor Razane and Sergei must be going through? A wave of nausea washed over her. She didn't have the strength to even walk over to the toilet bowl to throw up. When was this misery going to end?

But she couldn't stop thinking. To top it off a tension headache started and grew worse till it felt like her skull was going to explode.

Jane wasn't able to manage lunch either. The guard took it away after it got cold. By five she was bent over double, dry retching into the corner as the blinding headache caused stronger and stronger waves of nausea to engulf her whole being.

It was seven o'clock when the guard came again. He beckoned to Jane as he unlocked the door. 'Visitors,' he said.

Jane took a quick sip of water, rinsed out her mouth and washed her face. Sergei and Razane were early today. Thank goodness. She stood with difficulty as her trembling legs threatened to give way. The guard waited with a sympathetic look on his face.

He escorted Jane outside to the visitor hut. Razane and Sergei rushed forward. Jane collapsed into their arms, crying. Razane kissed her all over the face. She too had tears streaming down her face.

Jane noticed the look of puzzlement on the guard's face. There were questions in his eyes. He didn't quite understand who was related to whom and how. She didn't care.

Razane stroked her hair and kissed the furrows on her forehead as Sergei held them both close. After a while, Jane stopped trembling. The tension left her, and she felt lightheaded. If Sergei had not been holding her, she would have fallen. He guided her gently onto the middle of three chairs Razane had pushed together. Then they sat either side of Jane, holding her close. She closed her eyes and drifted into a short sleep, relaxed.

After a while, Jane opened her eyes and smiled weakly at them, 'you're my angels.' They responded with more gentle kisses.

'Where are Mack and Damon, are they OK?' she asked after a while.

'They're fine. Both are busy working on ways to get us out of this situation,' Sergei said.

'So, you are working on something? What? Please tell me.' Jane sounded desperate.

'We are looking at many options--' Razane said forming her words slowly. How much should they tell Jane?

'And where in the world is Jamshed?' Jane interrupted.

Sergei and Razane exchanged glances.

'What aren't you telling me?' Jane said, apprehensively.

'You aren't supposed to hide anything from me?'

'We didn't know how to tell you,' Razane said placing her hand on Jane's arm to comfort her. 'Jamshed... he was attacked... shot. He's... dead!'

Panic gripped Jane. She felt weightless again and would have fallen had she not been between Razane and Sergei.

'They're going after everyone trying to help me,' Jane said in a weak voice. 'You guys need to leave Pakistan at once,' she said, the pitch in her voice was rising. 'Please, please, please tell me you'll go.' Tears were streaming down her face.

Razane and Sergei held her tightly between them. Each took one of her hands in theirs. Razane kissed her on the forehead and then on each eye. She continued gently kissing Jane all over her face till she calmed down.

'Do not say that. You know we cannot leave,' Razane said. 'Our lives are here where you are as long as you're stuck here.'

'And we're taking serious precautions whenever we leave the hotel so don't worry,' Sergei said.

Jane started sobbing softly as they both held her in a close embrace. She knew Razane was right. She'd never be able to leave any of them behind anywhere either. No matter what the personal cost to her. She'd die for them and they for her.

'I love you both so much,' Jane said, 'and I'm so, so sorry to put you through this...'

'I love you too,' they both replied in unison.

'You know I was dreaming of our log cabin,' Jane said when she'd calmed down again.

'You'll be there sooner than you know,' Sergei said into her hair.

'If I get out, I want us all to never leave Australia again.'

'When you get out.' Sergei corrected her. 'And yes, we'll stay put.'

'But you are more the wanderer then Serge or me,' Razane said smiling gently. They both knew what Jane had said was never going to happen. She had a heightened sense of responsibility for all the problems in the world. She loved people, and her heart bled whenever she saw human suffering. She was not the type to hide in a safe place. At least not for long.

'Nah, no more,' Jane said forcing a smile. 'With Simon...gone I... I just can't work there anymore.' Her mood darkened again. 'I can't believe he's dead,' she sobbed.

Sergei and Razane sat with Jane till after ten. They had brought dinner which they ate together. They talked about everything and nothing, and for a short while, Jane was in her happy place.

The guard had given up looking at them. Maybe they were just desperate people behaving desperately. He felt sad for them.

Eventually, the superintendent came out and politely but firmly asked them to leave.

Jane returned to her cell much happier. She was the most loved person in the world, and Sergei and Razane had seemed a bit more positive. Maybe there was hope. She had to believe there was. If there were a way, they'd find it. She knew if one of them were in her place she wouldn't rest until she'd gotten them out either.

But this was Pakistan, and here people got murdered for even proposing clemency for a person accused of blasphemy. Her lawyer had told her not to expect leniency and to prepare for the worst. And he was now dead. What could Sergei and Razane do to get her out?

The assassin watched as Sergei and Razane climbed into a waiting taxi. According to Jibran, they always travelled together. Even though they varied their times, they had never failed to visit Jane, every day. Most likely, they would visit tomorrow as well. He would do the job then.

STAIRWAY TO HEAVEN

Lahore, Thursday 1 December, 9:00am

Allah was never closer. He could feel His presence, His radiance filling every part of him.

'Almighty thank you for blessing me with this gift of martyrdom. Your love is in my heart and in my soul,' he whispered. He sat there for the next two hours in deep contemplation, praying.

Soon he would meet his maker, the all-seeing, all benevolent, giver and taker of life, creator of the universe and of heaven and hell. He would be rewarded even more in the afterlife than he had been in this life. Infinitely more.

Would he enjoy the seventy-two virgins? What would he say? The *Aqa* had told him he would not need to say anything. He would be their king, and they would exist only to serve and please him. It would be quite a change from his wife who refused to let him touch her and beat him up on the few occasions he tried. Not that he blamed her. He was a nobody in this world, worthless and undesirable.

But he was not a nobody. Allah loved him. Why else would he have chosen a lowly worm, such as him, for martyrdom? He was going to be a hero of the jihad the Maulana had promised was coming. A jihad against bad people who blasphemed the beloved prophet, bombed little Muslim children, and fornicated with animals.

He fingered the envelope in his pocket. In it was a letter to his wife. Bilal had written it for him because he did not know how to read or write. He had dipped his finger in ink and had made a thumb impression to prove it was him, even though his thumb impression looked like everyone else's. Bilal promised to post it after he had departed this temporary world.

Along with the letter was a cheque for three *lakh* rupees.

He thought of all the stories Bilal had told him of the great martyrs of Islamic history, *Hazrat* Umar, *Hazrat* Ali, Saladin and many who were nameless. He was going to join their exalted ranks.

He thought about what he needed to do. Gullu had spent a lot of time teaching him to drive the grey truck. It now felt quite easy. He was not always able to drive in tight spaces and reversing into them was almost impossible, but he was good enough to drive on open roads with little traffic. All he had to do was to get in the truck and start it and drive to where Bilal had shown him and not stop.

He was not afraid in the least. There would be no pain. The *Aqa* and Bilal had told him, Allah would immediately take him in His cool embrace straight through the doors of heaven because for martyrs there was no waiting. His hands trembled in anticipation. He could not wait.

WHATSAPP MESSAGES

Lahore and Melbourne, Thursday 1 December

Ben: *I need some serious cash. $728K. It's a bit more than I thought. What to do?*

Sergei: *Is that for the yacht?*

Ben: *Yup, for option 1*

Damon: *Wow crazy amount of money!*

Mack: *Send through payee details. I will transfer straight away. @Damon it's actually quite reasonable. You know superyachts are around a hundred mil to buy*

Sergei: *Thanks, I'll pay you back. I'm good for it*

Mack: *So am I and I don't want it back*

Sergei: *Yeah we'll see about that but thanks. I owe you*

Mack: *Fuck off idiot*

Ben: *The bank details are 5634-9873 9871604 for bank transfer. Add comment "Shalayla for Ben" or attached is a credit card invoice whatever you choose*

Mack: *No problem. Check in two hours to confirm they received it*

Ben: *Thanks, Uncle Mack!!!*

Mack: *That's more like it! We're all family*

Damon: *Thumbs up*

Razane: *Hugs*

Mack: *BTW, if anything should ever go wrong. I've got two safe houses with cars. They are both properties owned by a subsidiary of my company. Both in Lahore. Each has a late model Corolla and a small stash of weapons and the fridge and pantries are full of food. My weapons cache is now empty :)*

Mack: *Google position of house 1*

Mack: *Google position of house 2*

Damon: *Ur a legend!!!*

Sergei: *Those houses might help us on the way to Karachi. But your plan to Karachi needs a bit more detail. We still owe you our plan. How to spring her out.*

Ben: *Dude. Stating the obvious*

Sergei: *We've got a plan. Meet tonight at the hotel!!!*

THE PLAN

Lahore, Thursday 1 December, 4:00pm

B en was on speakerphone. 'The boat's booked and fully paid for. They're waiting for final dates, but they need to leave Dubai no later than the seventh of December,' he said.

'It gives us a drop-dead date,' Sergei said.

'OK, but let's not use the words drop dead, please,' Razane said shivering. Sergei gave her leg a gentle squeeze.

'Anyway, the boat is the Shalayla. It's a forty-two-metre luxury superyacht. The cruising speed is twenty-five knots with a top speed of thirty knots.'

'What are knots compared to kilometres?' Damon asked.

'One knot's around 1.8 km/h,' Ben responded, 'anyway from Karachi it's around fifteen hours to reach international waters. Then it's around twelve days to Darwin, give or take. I've told the yacht company we plan to visit a few Asian ports before we reach Australia. Once out of Pakistani waters we can always change our mind and take a more direct route.' He paused to take a breath. No one spoke. 'So, here's what I'm thinking. I fly to Dubai as soon as you get Mum out. I'll book flights every day to make sure I can leave as soon as I need to. Meanwhile, you head to Karachi.

'From Dubai, I'll set sail for Pakistan as soon as possible. It'll take me thirty hours to get to Karachi so bear it in mind. I'm right now organising the visit with the Pakistani High Commission in Canberra. I've told 'em we're doing a documentary series on the great deep-sea ports of the world.

Apparently, a visa won't be a problem.

'We'll dock somewhere in a marina and clear customs and immigration. On our way-out, you guys all get on a boat and head out to sea. We'll pick you up a suitable distance offshore. Because immigration will already have checked us, they'll have no reason to do so again. That's basically it.'

Razane was the first to speak. 'Wow, Ben that is a really clever and well-thought-out plan,' she said.

Ben smiled. That was a nice compliment. Maybe Razane was not so bad after all. 'Thanks.'

'Bloody spectacular,' Damon said.

'I think it's brilliant, Ben,' Mack said.

'My thoughts too,' Sergei said. 'That's a great plan. Now if we can solve the other two major problems as well we stand a really good chance.'

They, of course, knew what problems he was talking about, but Sergei verbalised them anyway. 'We need to get your Mum out of the police station and then…' he paused and sighed deeply, 'and then get her to the boat while the biggest manhunt, probably in the history of the Pakistan, gets underway…'

'Jane's escape will make religious nuts foam at the mouth,' Mack said.

'That will make it twice as dangerous,' Razane said. 'Many people will happily kill us or hand us over to the police; we have to be super careful.'

'Here's an idea. You leave maps and all sorts of info in the hotel room. It'll seem you're crossing into Afghanistan. So they look the wrong way, and you can slip out of Lahore,' Ben said.

'Ben, I think you are secretly a spy,' Mack said smiling, 'I just know it.'

'Nah, just a steady diet of spy movies.'

'Let's then be clever in how we leave clues,' Damon said, 'if you make it obvious they'll not fall for it.'

'That's good, Ben,' Razane said diplomatically. She didn't want to say it, but unlike his first plan, it was downright silly.

Even the most amateur investigator would spot such a ruse. Sergei raised his eyebrows and smiled at her. He felt the same. Thank goodness.

'Given we have two safe houses in Lahore let's lie low for one or two days till things die down,' Sergei said.

'I disagree, Serge,' Razane said. 'We should head straight towards Sindh and not stop in Lahore. The sooner we're near the ocean, the better.'

'Razane is right,' Mack said. 'One of the first things the authorities will do is put up road-blocks, everywhere. They could last for weeks. They can also order a shut-down of all telecommunications and then we are fucked big time.'

'OK, we leave straightaway,' Sergei said. 'Ben, you should leave for Dubai as soon as possible. Don't wait for us.'

'The problem is Dubai's banned the use of voice calling on WhatsApp. I don't trust the old-fashioned phone call. That's why I was thinking of staying in Melbourne at least till Mum's out.'

'OK, then leave immediately after,' Mack said. Everyone nodded their assent.

There was a pause of a few minutes while they all sat, lost in thought, contemplating the momentous events that were going to unfold. Regardless of how it ended none of them would ever be the same again.

'Well, the running plan sounds great,' Damon said breaking the silence, 'as long as we give ourselves four or five hours head start we can maybe steal a march on the police, but... the big question... how do we get Mum out?'

'And that's our department,' Razane said. 'Thanks to Mack, Jane is always brought to the same visitor hut in the courtyard. That will help us a lot. It means we are only one locked door away from freedom.' She paused to take a breath. Everyone was looking at her. 'One guard brings Jane into the visitor room. Then he always stands outside chatting to the duty guard in the courtyard. If Mack can keep the police in the administration area busy, Sergei and I will overpower the two guards in the courtyard.'

'We take their weapons and incapacitate them,' Sergei said, 'We use their keys to unlock the door to the admin area. Then we disarm and force the policemen at gunpoint through the courtyard and into Jane's cell. We cut the phone lines and leave straight away. The next shift changes over at nine next morning. If we can get outta there by eleven, we'll have a maximum ten-hour head start. That'll get us only halfway to Karachi. Then all shit will hit the fan.'

'What do you mean maximum ten hours?' Damon said furrowing his brow.

'Things could go wrong,' Sergei said. 'Someone could check on them. If there's an emergency and someone calls the police station and finds they cannot get through, we'll have less time.'

'And that is a chance we will have to take,' Razane said as Sergei nodded.

'The good thing,' Mack said, 'here it's very common for phone lines to be down. So, I think there's a high chance no one will bother. Pakistan is not like Australia.'

'So, what about any emergency calls. Surely in a big city like Lahore--' Ben said.

'That would be handled centrally and by mobile units. If they can't get through they'll call another station,' Mack said. 'The IG told me the police station is going into lock-down at night. No new suspects will be allowed in.'

'That is a bit of good luck,' Razane said, 'it also makes getting to Karachi easier.'

'Yes, it makes up for there not being a proper plan to get to Karachi,' Sergei said.

'Mack, do you know anyone who has a plane? Maybe a friend in a flying club?' Ben said.

'Oh, yes, as a matter of fact, I do,' Mack said grinning as they all smiled and rolled their eyes, 'I have a friend with a Cessna. He's always complaining how expensive his hobby is. Let me call him; maybe I can contribute to his running expenses.' He dialled a number as he walked out of the room.

They all went silent. 'You two, your plan is good,' Damon said, 'scary but it could work.'

'It has to work,' Sergei said gravely. He was not happy with it. It wasn't the best plan. It wasn't even a good plan. There were too many uncontrolled variables. So many things could go wrong. They always did in real life.

'Hey, what am I doing?' Damon said.

'Ah, we didn't forget you,' Razane said, 'you're the getaway driver. You'll be on Sanda Road outside the overgrown park. We walk out of the police station through the park and get in your car, and you drive us off.'

'It almost sounds too easy,' Damon replied under his breath.

It was a big elephant in the room. They all thought the plans were overly simplistic, but none of them could come up with a way to improve them.

Just then Mack returned, 'my friend will fly us till Multan.'

'Ah, that's great,' said Damon.

'What did you tell him?' Razane asked.

'Just that I have overseas visitors with very little time, who want to visit Multan before they leave.'

'Hmmm, it's kinda true,' Sergei said with a smile. 'Is he OK to fly at night?'

'Yes. He just wants twelve hours notice.'

'So, Dad, This means we have a plan to get to Karachi,' Damon said.

'Yes, I agree. We have the three plans we need. One's a great plan, and the others need a bit of luck and us staying focused, but it's better than nothing.'

'This deserves champagne, Damon said. He walked over to the fridge. 'Here's some Coke instead,' he threw them each a can.

Razane was quiet and lost in thought. She caught the can

and put it on the table unopened. It did all seem too simple, and that made her uneasy. Things were never straightforward and no matter how clever, plans never worked out exactly as intended. Except for Ben's idea of meeting the yacht, the rest were quite amateurish. But she could think of no way to improve on them and time was running out. At least Damon would not be in any danger.

'So last question. When do we do it?' Ben asked.

'There's no benefit in waiting,' Sergei said.

'Yes, and there's everything to lose, so let's plan for tomorrow.' Damon said.

That did seem soon. 'It almost seems rash,' Mack said, 'but I am trying to think what we could do if we had more days.'

'We'd just worry and get careless, and our enemy will get lucky and kill us,' Razane said, 'but I would prefer we give it at least one more day. Tonight, and tomorrow when we visit Jane, let's keep an eye out for anything we haven't thought of. We need to look for flaws in each part of the plan.'

'OK, then our visits tonight and tomorrow are like dress rehearsals,' Mack said.

And that was it. The plans their futures hinged on, were set.

THE GENTLEMAN

Lahore, Thursday 1 December, 8:00pm

A brar, slid back the mirrored door. Lights flickered on to reveal a row of dark suits. He caught his reflection in the mirror. He loved how he looked. Just muscled enough in all the right places, a flat stomach, and decent sized shoulders. A physique that looked nice in top quality clothes. A physique designers designed for.

So, what should he wear? He liked to match clothes to his choice of transportation, the job, and his mood.

He would be in the rougher part of town, and he needed some space to crouch in the back. He would take his Black Overfinch Land Rover Defender. That would require an English suit. He selected a midnight grey double-breasted Saville Row, a black Henry Herbert shirt, a pair of black double buckle Cheaney shoes and last of all an Omega Seamaster with a black leather strap. He left the tie. He would go open collar.

He finished dressing and looked at himself again in the mirror. He was quite the dapper English gentleman like his late mother used to say. She used to consider herself the quintessential English lady even though the only English blood in the family was his grandfather's. His late father, a rich Punjabi landowner, used to not mind it for the most part. Upper class is upper class like land is land, he used to say in his thick Punjabi accent that had often made his mother cringe.

Abrar was never sure what his father had meant, but he didn't care. He had left more than enough wealth for him to live out his life in luxury. How could he begrudge him a few cringe-worthy memories?

He was an only son. His line of the family would stop with him. He was sure of it, mainly because he was not going to dip his wick in any pussy.

His mother had made sure his father had never found out he was gay. He would have gone off the deep end and would have blamed her. He was always critical of him being a little too refined. 'Why you encourage him be soft? Why he spend so much his time on clothes?' he used to growl at his wife in his bad English.

For all their faults he missed them. They had died in a car accident five years ago. With that, his anger for his father had died as well.

At least he no longer needed to pretend anymore. The social circles he moved in celebrated his gayness. It was seen as cool. Even heterosexual men clamoured for invitations to his lavish parties. In a country as homophobic as Pakistan that was quite amazing, but then high society in every country functioned with a different set of rules and standards.

He walked over to his gun cupboard. He would have loved to have used an English rifle to match his clothes and his vehicle. His Accuracy International L115A3 was also his favourite. Sadly, it was bolt action, and he would need at least a semi-automatic for today's job. He chose the Swiss SIG SG550 Sniper. It was his second favourite.

The job was for a former Aitchison college classmate. Jibran was one of the few people who knew he was the feared assassin known throughout Pakistan as The Gentleman. Jibran had called yesterday asking for a favour. He had dressed in local clothes and had taken his small black Suzuki Swift to survey the location and sight his targets. He could have finished the job yesterday, but haste made waste. It was another thing his father always used to say. That he believed in.

He normally charged twenty thousand dollars per hit and

required payment upfront in a Swiss bank account. For Pakistan where one could get a person killed for a lakh rupees or less, he was expensive. But as in everything else in life, one got what one paid for.

Apart from the cachet that came with his reputation, he offered a no kill, no pay, money back guarantee. He had never had to return a payment yet.

Today's job for Jibran was for free. It was not right to charge one's former classmates. Of course, he didn't do any of the jobs for the money. After all, he had all the money in the world. But life in Pakistan could get boring. There were only so many parties he could throw, so many late-night drag races he could organise and so many men he could fuck.

The killing was what got him up in the morning. He had started out hunting deer in Swat. It was the one activity he and his father would enjoy together. It was how he discovered his natural talent. He was a top-notch marksman. Killing animals was fun, but it did not compare to the pure joy of killing a human. Nothing quite felt like lining up a man or a woman in his scope, the target completely unaware he had them in his crosshairs, their life, their future in the palm of his hands. Only God would truly understand what it felt like, not that he believed in God.

The exultation from pulling the trigger and watching them fall was visceral, primitive, almost erotic. He would pay to do it but getting paid was better. It showed his art and skill were appreciated.

It was a cool moonless night. The day had grown steadily colder. A few drops of rain had fallen and were dotting his windscreen. The weather was finally changing, winter was on the way. He was glad it wasn't quite here yet. In Lahore, winter nights were generally, extremely foggy to the point of it becoming opaque. Fog had a way of interfering with a sniper's vision for everything but small distances unless he used an infrared spotlight to go with his night vision scope. He didn't have one of those.

Abrar estimated Sacha Saeen Street was around six hundred metres long. This part of town was old, and all cables for electricity, telephone, TV, and the different Internet providers had created a mad jumble that made every electricity and telephone pole look like a person with a bad hair day. To make matters worse every square inch of space on every pole was covered in advertising billboards, some of which stuck out half a metre. It made getting a clear line of sight to the police station next to impossible unless he parked in the middle of the street.

It was more by luck than anything else that he had found the perfect spot the night before. It was next to a particularly ugly looking transformer stuck halfway up an electricity pole. It would give him the line of sight he needed while still allowing him to park on the footpath.

He drove slowly up Sacha Saeen street till he finally found it again. Satisfied, he parked the Defender on the footpath, facing away from the police station.

Along its entire length, Sacha Saeen Street had a total of three working street lights. He was almost halfway between two of them and in deep shadow.

He draped his jacket over the passenger seat and climbed into the back. Here the dark tinted glass helped ensure he was completely invisible from the outside.

He took out his rangefinder which showed he was 293 metres from the police station. That worked out well. It was close to the maximum range of the SIG. He relished the challenge. He looked at the brightly glowing hands on his Seamaster. The time was 8:47.

He opened a small hatch in the back-glass window by sliding it sideways and rested the silencer on the rubber-lined edge. He used a clamp rest to hold the barrel in place and adjusted it upwards ever so slightly till the silencer was no longer in contact with the glass. This was important so the rifle would not kick when he fired. He looked through the Schmidt and Bender optical scope and zoomed in till the closed gate of the police station came into focus. He could read the words Public Entry even though no light was reflecting on it. He was all set. He arranged some memory-foam blocks to sit on and waited.

Fazal and Yousaf watched and waited as well. This was getting boring. How many more days would the major make them continue their surveillance? About the only thing that had moved or changed all evening was the black Land Rover. They had not observed it on previous nights. It was probably someone visiting his mistress. It was most likely a strange coincidence another black car, a small hatchback, had parked in the exact same spot the night before. In the interest of being thorough, Yousaf noted down its license plate number.

AN HONEST POLICEMAN

Lahore, Thursday 1 December 2016, 9:30pm

According to his wife, God bless her departed soul, he, Qaiser Majeed, was either a simple or a stupid man. Whether he was stupid or simple on any given day had depended entirely on her mood and how kindly she felt towards him.

He knew he was not stupid. He had taught himself to read a newspaper even though he did struggle with some tricky words now and then. He had learnt to use his new phone with the big screen and no buttons. He had also caught many criminals, by being smarter than them. Stupid people could not do that. But he agreed he was simple, and there was nothing wrong with that.

Everything considered, he would still rather be simple and honest than crafty and dishonest. Dishonest and crafty people had destroyed his beautiful country. They had made it the laughing stock of the world. The worst were the politicians who lined their pockets instead of spending on schools, hospitals, and roads. Thanks to them Pakistan was now the top country in the world for corruption.

Qaiser Majeed had never been to school, so he hadn't encountered the word "irony", but he had an innate understanding of the concept. He had never risen higher than constable because he was honest. From his rank, he could never catch the real criminals, the people who lived in palaces with big flashy cars, gold watches, and bodyguards. The only criminals he had ever arrested were people who stole and cheated because they were dirt poor and desperate. People he felt sorry for. He had resigned himself to the reality he would never catch the big crooks. The only policemen who could rise high enough to do that were crooked themselves.

He would continue to do his job and would continue to be the best person he could be. He would try to be a candle in the darkness. Hopefully, the country would one day improve, *Inshallah.*

There were more people like him, and there was hope. When he had seen the flyer from a new government department, the Police Anti-Corruption Office, he had almost cried with gladness. Here was hope. There was now a way for the common simple man like him to report corruption. The flyer promised action would be taken the same day. The person who made the report could stay nameless.

He wished he had been able to show the flyer to his wife. His eyes welled up a bit as he thought of her. She had been a good woman, a good mother, and a hard worker.

She had been a cleaner in a big factory and had worked ten hours a day for six days a week and then she would come home and look after the house. With both their wages they had been able to send their two sons to college. His eldest had just started working in a bank in a well-paying job.

He hoped she was watching him now. He would contact the Anti-Corruption Office and report all the goings-on at this police station.

Last year the IG and the governor along with many journalists had visited the police station. The IG had given a speech and had called it a model of honesty and efficiency. The next day the newspapers had run articles with photographs that told how they caught the most criminals in Punjab and that the poor people of the neighbourhood felt safe. He knew it was not true. Here they still treated poor people like dirt and rich people like kings.

The foreign woman got special treatment because she was rich. Food was brought for her from a good restaurant. She had a cell to herself, she got visitors every day, and they were able to stay for many hours and even eat with her. Normally in a police station, visitors were not allowed at night and the maximum time was only ten minutes unless they were lawyers.

He liked the woman. She had a nice and honest face, and she smiled at him sometimes. He was sad she would be hung for blasphemy. It was quite possible she had been blamed wrongly. It happened a lot. She certainly did not look like a blasphemer. She had not raised her voice once or complained or done anything unpleasant. Being a foreigner meant she was most likely Christian. He had nothing against them. Christians and Muslims both believed in the same Allah.

Even though she was nice and maybe innocent, no one should get special treatment. The Pakistani who came with her visitors each time handed out thousand rupees to each policeman like it was tissue paper. He had refused to accept it. Of course, he still carried out his order to escort her to the visitor room after hours. He always obeyed a superior officer.

But he was not going to sit quietly and do nothing. Wrong was wrong. He was going to go home after his shift and ask his son to help him with the computer so he could send the report to the Anti-Corruption Office. Then Allah would do the rest.

He looked up. The sky was black. Just then a single raindrop fell and landed in his left eye. He blinked, and a tear dropped down his cheek. It felt nice. He smiled. Was it a sign Allah was on his side? The yard was gloomy and dark with just a single spotlight shining on the solid steel door that led inside to the cells. A roll of thunder that sounded like someone was moving heavy furniture around, reverberated in the narrow space between the outer perimeter wall and the main building.

Maybe Allah was not happy after all. He shivered; it was getting cold. The visitor huts were dark and unlit. The foreign woman's visitors had not come today, which was strange because the way they embraced showed they loved her. He looked at his watch. He was doing a double shift today. He needed to go back to his post, but Afzal, the constable on yard duty, had still not come back from the toilet.

His radio crackled, 'Qaiser Majeed bring the foreign woman to the visitor room.'

THE DRESS REHEARSAL

Lahore, Thursday 1 December, 9:45pm

The low rolling rumble of thunder sounded ominous, like a big angry growling dog in the sky. The taxi cab turned into Charsadda Street. Razane and Sergei sat in the back seat looking out. It was much later than usual. Jane must be wondering where they were.

They had timed their arrival to after the start of the new shift at 9:00pm. Escape at this time would give them longest head start.

Today they had to focus on every detail even more than they had in the past, looking for anyone or anything that could get in the way of a clean escape. Murphy's law was a bitch. If something could go wrong, it would and at the worst possible time.

Whenever they had visited at night, the whole street appeared empty. Lahore was one of the most densely packed cities in the world. It had a lot of homeless. If people were asleep in doorways or in the park, they would be tough to spot. Someone could come home late, or return to check on their shop or even take a detour.

As the taxi pulled up to the front of the police station, Razane slipped off the burka, scrunched it up and stuffed it in her bag. Sergei took off his wig and beard and handed them to her. 'I'm glad I have a big bag,' she said smiling.

The taxi driver turned around for the fare and gave a start. Two completely different people looked at him. 'You rich people do strange and wonderful things,' he muttered to them in Urdu, the smile returning to his face. Sergei dropped an additional thousand rupees in his hand, and he beamed even more brightly. '*Salam Sahib*,' he said.

'*Salam, bhai*,' Sergei said. He was starting to use local phrases he had learnt, with more confidence.

They stepped out of the cab. The wind had picked up. The taxi's headlights illuminated bits of flying paper. A white plastic bag was caught in an updraft and did a funny dance near the clinic building before getting stuck on an electricity pole, its dance coming to an end.

Razane shivered. 'It's freezing.'

It was indeed suddenly wintry. Yesterday it had been decidedly warm and closed in. Today the air was fresh and cold like it had been washed in icy water.

Sergei gave her a quick hug as the taxi pulled away. Apart from a lone cyclist slowly making his way towards them on Sacha Saeen Street the whole area was deserted. The two intersecting streets were poorly lit. The electricity company had obviously given up trying to maintain the street lighting. Much of both streets were in shadow as the young moon passed behind a cloud. Everything was dark and gloomy. The shadows made him nervous. So much could be hidden in them. Their escape route, the park leading to Sanda Road, was in almost complete darkness as well. Hopefully, those shadows would help them during their escape.

He checked Google Maps. The red dot showed Damon on Sanda Road near the park. He was waiting to pick them up.

'Damon is in place. Let's not forget to time how long it takes to walk through the park when we leave,' Sergei said.

'Yes, my love.' Razane nodded.

They walked quickly into the police station.

The guard at the door greeted them sullenly. He hated foreigners. At least these paid generously. Considering the blonde woman's crime, they should pay more. He would be happy to see her hung. How dare she come to Pakistan and insult the Holy Prophet.

Mack had arrived earlier and sat in a circle around a brazier with several policemen and the station superintendent. They were all drinking tea and laughing at a joke. The brazier did not seem to have much effect on the temperature in the cavernous room. If anything, it was even colder than outdoors.

Mack saw them and waved. He placed his cup on the floor and got up. He was shivering. Razane was glad she had brought a light but warm pashmina shawl for Jane. Their poor darling would be cold.

The superintendent stood up, greeted them, and shook Sergei's hand. He motioned to one of his men to search them; then he spoke something into his radio.

'They are fetching Jane,' Mack translated for them in a low voice.

The constable unfolded and inspected the shawl Razane had brought and had a cursory look inside her handbag. It was clear they would not be able to bring handguns into the station. He asked Sergei to empty his pockets and proceeded to pat him down. Satisfied, he unlocked the side door to the courtyard. Sergei put his things back in his pockets and followed Razane through the open door. A light misting drizzle began to fall as Razane silently counted the steps to the visitor hut.

Outside the hut, they waited as their escort unlocked the door and turned on the light. They entered and sat at the table. The constable left, no doubt keen to get back to his warm cup of tea and the brazier. They heard the sounds of his footsteps recede down the courtyard, then the door opened, closed and was locked. Razane looked at her watch. 'That was eighteen seconds.'

'Let's not forget their radios,' he whispered. Razane nodded. They would have to overpower the guard and take the radio off him before he had a chance to use it.

'Jane is taking her time,' Sergei said.

'She looks so pale and sad,' Razane said, 'It makes me cry

whenever I see her.'

'It won't be for much longer, hopefully,' he whispered.

Outside on Sacha Saeen Street, Abrar shifted his body. He was starting to get a little stiff from crouching in the same cramped position. He had turned the Land Rover's engine off to prevent any vibrations from the engine affecting his shot. A tiny 12V electric heater kept him warm. It wouldn't do to let his fingers go numb at the last moment.

Earlier he had first observed the portly Pakistani man arrive. He was dropped off outside the police station in a white Toyota Corolla. The car drove off. He was target number one. Where were the others? He hadn't been there the night before. Only Sergei and Razane had visited. The Pakistani walked into the police station, and the door closed behind him.

Another five minutes passed before a taxi pulled up. At the same time, a whirring sound next to him made him jump. Abrar looked left. A lone cyclist rode past him. What the fuck was this idiot doing out at this time? Back at the police station Sergei and Razane climbed out of the back seat of the taxi. Thank goodness, they were here. The cyclist was weaving a little; the drunk bastard was going to obstruct his line of sight. Could he shoot all three? He would have to do the cyclist first, which could alert the other two. Jibran had told him they might be CIA. If he shot and missed them now, he would not get another chance from this position. It was better to wait till they came out of the police station hopefully along with the Pakistani. Even better, the young man might show up by then.

From the photos, Jibran had sent him the young man was handsome and well built. He would have loved to have gotten his hands on him in another way. The young gay men around here were mostly skinny runts. Lahore had only slim pickings for those into men.

His younger cousin Ayesha and him often played a game

they both enjoyed. His chauffeur would drive, with her in the back seat of his old black Mercedes, around the streets near his home, where young people hung out. She was strikingly beautiful and could easily entice a young fellow into the car. They would make out for the time it would take for the car to reach his house. When the young man, by then, convinced he had entered heaven, was all steamed up, and near bursting at the seams, Ayesha would surreptitiously pull a hanky, soaked in chloroform, out of a ziplock bag. The young man would wake up naked in bed with him at his side instead of the lovely Ayesha. He would have photos of the young man on his phone to threaten him with, just in case. Invariably, confusion would turn to outrage, fear and finally acquiescence. Sometimes the more exuberant ones were so horny they didn't care who they fucked or who fucked them.

His dick was now uncomfortably hard from reminiscing, forcing him to shift and adjust himself. Stay sharp idiot! He looked outside. The taxi was turning around. The cyclist was nowhere to be seen, and the gate to the police station was closed. He eased his finger off the trigger and cursed himself. Bloody unprofessional of him to daydream on a job.

Abrar fished for a chewing gum in his pocket. Fuck there was nothing. Outside it started to drizzle, a fine misting kind that was bad for visibility. Even though his scope was fully inside the car, the wind still picked up a few fine water droplets and deposited them on the lens. The glass had a special coating. It was supposed to make water bead off, but it was ineffective against the tiny drops. He took out a lens cleaner and polished the glass clean. It wasn't necessary, but being obsessive was a common characteristic of a sniper.

He took a deep breath. He had to be patient. Patience was the most important quality of an assassin. All the talent and marksmanship were of no use without it. He adjusted the foam blocks he was sitting on and waited.

A low subsonic rumble made his hair stand on end. It rose

in frequency till it became audible. It wasn't thunder; it sounded mechanical. A shadow flitted past as he heard a grinding sound and a pop and tinkle. The Defender shook. For the briefest moment he was disoriented, then he saw the rear brake lights of the massive truck that had just destroyed his passenger side mirror. Its headlights were turned off. No wonder he hadn't seen it. The dickhead must be on *charas*. He had an almost overwhelming urge to shoot out his rear tyres. It would teach the bastard. But that would not do. The truck would end up stuck on the road, blocking his view. Dropping his guard once a night was more than enough. For the second time that evening he relaxed his grip on the finger trigger. He needed to breathe, deeply.

How odd the truck driver had still not turned on his lights. It was almost completely dark. Was he that stoned? He heard the truck shift gear and accelerate. It dawned on him. The truck wouldn't be able to turn at the intersection. The driver didn't want to. He was going to ram the police station. The meant it must be carrying a…

He didn't have time to duck.

In the police station courtyard, Razane and Sergei waited for Jane. They heard the metal door being unlocked. Razane glanced outside. It was Jane waiting just inside the courtyard as the constable slammed the door shut and locked it. Their footsteps grew louder as they approached. Hers light and unsteady, his heavy and deliberate. Sergei and Razane stood waiting expectantly. Jane was just outside the hut. The policeman said something to his colleague who sat in a chair near the end of the courtyard. He was on guard duty. He got up and sauntered over. Jane entered the hut and rushed towards them. Razane met her halfway, they embraced, and the world exploded.

Damon was parked illegally on the side of Sanda Road next to the little park. The Australian in him was on edge for doing that. The floodlit mosque ahead of him had a car park, but a steel gate barred entry. Thankfully, traffic was light, and other drivers were driving around him.

He was in a WhatsApp call with Ben who'd put him on hold to make himself a cup of coffee. A fine drizzle fell, creating a light mist in the air. Traffic had picked up a bit. A few people were now tooting their horns at him as they drove around. Sooner or later someone would come by and yell at him to move the car. He'd have to do this again tomorrow. It'd be the biggest disaster if he weren't there to meet his parents.

Maybe he should find a spot further back where he could park legally but still see them emerging from the park?

He tried remembering the road's features. There was a bus stop further back. He could stop there. It was not ideal, but at least he would not block traffic.

Google Maps showed his Dad, Mack and Razane represented by three red dots. They were in the police station. A blue pulsating flash lit up the road, reflecting off buildings. A siren blared. It was a police car somewhere in the traffic behind him. It approached at high speed and drove past.

He needed to relax, this wasn't Australia. He took a deep breath and the world went crazy. A loud mechanical crash was immediately followed by an earth-shattering explosion, louder than the loudest thunderclap he'd ever felt and heard. The car shook violently and moved sideways. The trees in the park leaned over as their branches shook with violent convulsions. The floodlights on the mosque went out. Its dome seemed to shift.

Objects of all sizes flew all around him; many struck his car with terrifying force. One by one the four minarets tumbled down, almost in slow motion. The two front ones crashed onto Sanda Road. One fell on top of a taxi, crushing its cabin flat.

Cars swerved and fishtailed before coming to a shuddering stop, the screech of their tyres drowned out in the bedlam. A big concrete block from one of the minarets broke off, careened across the road, and smashed into the side of a bus waiting at a bus stop. Passengers were flung out of the other side like limp dolls.

His car still shook as debris began raining down. Rubble was strewn across the road. Fear gripped him. He was in a daze. His vision blurred. The fate of the crushed taxi filled him with crippling dread. The tall glass office towers on the other side of Sanda Road were bereft of windows, their insides exposed. His windscreen was covered with a thick layer of dust and stones. Something hit his windscreen. A star-shaped crack appeared just below the mirror. He turned on his wipers. A dense cloud of dust and smoke was rolling onto Sanda Road, enveloping the whole area. Then all of a sudden it went quiet. What was going on? His brain had switched off. He tried starting the car and remembered it was already running. He couldn't hear. A ringing in his ears blocked out most other sounds.

Damon fought through the fog of shock and despair. What the fuck had happened? A thought nagged him from the corner of his mind. It was a thought that involved Mum, Dad, Razane and Mack and was too scary to bring to the fore. The explosion had destroyed half the mosque. The police station must have fared worse. He sat there paralysed. Outside, a few people were starting to move and pick themselves up. Others lay on the road motionless. From somewhere someone let out a loud pained scream. His phone, where was it? It had fallen on the floor. The screen was still on. Google Locations showed only one red dot.

In a panicked state, he got out of the car. The world was still strangely quiet. His ears were still ringing. He started towards the park then changed his mind, came back, picked up his phone and ran back towards and through the park. As he did so, he almost tripped over the low railing that separated it from the footpath on Sanda Road.

The explosion had destroyed all light bulbs in the vicinity. It was almost completely dark. The moon struggled to break through from behind the clouds. Dust and smoke billowed in the air making visibility even worse. The small manicured garden and the outer side wall were the only parts of the police station not damaged.

Feeling sick and dizzy with fear and panic he ran to the footpath on Charsadda Street. The wind picked up a bit. The loud revving of an engine alerted him to a van approaching fast, down Sacha Saeen Street. Its headlights on high beam, illuminated the ruins shrouded in a cloud of swirling dust. The damage to the police station was even worse than he had feared. Most of the front perimeter wall and the front wall of the main building had collapsed. A huge crater had formed in place of the parking space at the front. Around the crater were bits of twisted metal, pieces of which were also strewn over the width of Charsadda Street, along with chunks of masonry and bricks.

The cloud of dust and smoke swirled around but stayed put. Small objects contained within the rubble of the building smouldered. A terrible, strong burning smell, chemicals mixed with the stench of burning hair and flesh, hit his nostrils. It made him want to gag. He felt even sicker.

With a squealing of tyres, the van skidded to a halt. Men, carrying assault rifles, piled out. The van's headlights projected their moving shapes in the smoke and dust cloud making them appear twenty feet tall. They were shouting as they ran towards the building. They stopped at the crumbled perimeter wall and opened fire into the inky chasm, moving their weapons in a slow sweeping motion.

Damon had till then been rooted to the spot, but this shook him into action. Still not thinking clearly, his head pounding, the sound of blood pumping in his ears, he ran back towards the park, his footsteps masked by the gunfire. He half expected one of them to look in his direction and shoot him dead, but that did not happen.

Damon took one last look back. Four more men got out of the van. They carried strong flashlights. Then all together they clambered over the smoking heap of rubble into the blackened interior of the building.

Further up Sacha Saeen Street, Abrar viewed the scene through his night scope. He noticed a shadowy figure emerge from the park on Sanda Road, but he was more interested in the van load of gunmen. When they began strafing the inside of the police station building, the figure ran back towards the park. He seemed unusually tall and broad. Oh, shit, was it one of his targets? Abrar aimed his scope and tried focusing on his new quarry. When Damon turned back, Abrar was just able to make out his face. It was the big young, well-built hunk of a man he'd been looking for. Shit, double shit! What was he doing on Sanda Road? He had to get over there and fast.

In one fluid motion, he pulled his rifle back, closed the hatch and clambered into the driver's seat. He started the engine put the car into gear and took off, tyres chirping.

Damon was now back on Sanda Road. People were standing outside their cars, dazed. Sounds of gunfire still came from the police station building. Where were the fucking police? Where was his family? A wave of nausea rushed over him. He knelt on the ground and vomited.

It was completely pitch black. Razane opened her eyes, her brain desperately trying to kick into gear. She was on the floor. Jane was on top of her, their faces touching. Jane was limp.

Jane's hair was covering her face. She tasted blood. Her mouth hurt like hell. God, don't let it be Jane's blood.

Dreading what she would find, she tenderly felt Jane's body with her hands. There was nothing untoward. She felt Jane's head and gently moved her hair out of her face. Jane groaned and stirred. Razane's heart started beating again as relief rushed through her. The love of her life was alive. Holding Jane's head she gently rolled her off herself, making sure her head did not strike the ground. Jane groaned again and feebly lifted her head.

Beside her, Sergei stirred. He sounded in pain, worse than Jane. Razane felt for her phone in her pocket and turned the screen on. Its faint light illuminated the swirls of smoke and dust that covered everything in the room. She coughed, and so did Sergei.

Razane reached out to touch him. He was clawing at his eyes which were covered with a fine layer of dust and tiny stones. She needed water. There was a bottle in her bag which was still on her shoulder. It took a lot of effort to move, her body was sluggish and wracked with pain.

'Keep your eyes closed my love, let me wash them!' Razane carefully blew the dust off his face, paying close attention to his eyes. Poor Sergei, he was in a lot of pain, his eyelids flickering madly.

'Is Jane OK?' He moaned.

'She's fine. Now keep still,' Razane said as she carefully poured some water over his closed eyelids. His eyes flickered open and closed again. She had managed to get some water inside. He groaned and opened them again. She kept pouring. 'Turn your head sideways my love.'

After a few more drops he was able to keep his eyes open. 'Thanks!' There was relief in his voice.

'Don't rub them. And try not to blink too much.'

Sergei sat up. A layer of dust sloughed off him. His eyes still burned, but at least he was able to keep them open. There was something more. His left arm hurt when he moved it. He felt under his armpit. Something hard was sticking out the side of his chest. Panic gripped him. Was it a rib? He touched it again. It shifted slightly. Wincing, he pulled at it, and it came out. It was a thick pointed splinter of wood. He moved his arm. It still hurt but the sharp pain had diminished.

He moved over to Jane who still lay limp on the ground.

She had a purple bruise on her forehead. Razane poured a bit of water over her face. Her eyes stirred. She looked dazed and disoriented but seemed uninjured. He looked at Razane. She had a cut on her lip. Her hair was grey with dust, but otherwise, she looked unhurt.

'I'm OK,' Razane said sensing his concern, 'Jane seems concussed.'

'Can you move darling?' Sergei said to Jane, 'does it hurt anywhere?'

'No... I'm...I'm fine,' Jane said trying to sit up but unable to lift her head more than a few centimetres off the ground.

Sergei stroked her hair and gently helped her sit. With his free hand, he felt for his phone. It was dead. Damn! He grunted as he picked Jane up, cradling her in his arms. The effort made his head spin.

A dreadful realisation dawned on Razane. The blast completely changed everything. Their plan to break Jane out would no longer work. She would be moved to another, possibly more secure facility.

Razane stood, unsteadily, and walked outside to survey the scene. Only the light of a new moon, filtered through the fog, shone into the courtyard. She turned on the LED light on her phone. The courtyard was littered with bits of masonry in all sizes. The two policemen lay on the ground just outside the hut. Their bodies, unnaturally twisted, their clothes were blackened, and their hair still smouldered. A horrible smell of burning flesh emanated from them. There was no use even checking; they were dead beyond any shadow of a doubt.

A flame front had blown through the courtyard with the shockwave. The steel door to the main building from where Jane and the constable had emerged was badly buckled and twisted. The ground around them and the wall of the visitor huts were charred black.

Only a few seconds earlier and Jane would have been lying there too. The hut had saved them from an almost certain death.

The thought made her mind reel. The courtyard was otherwise largely intact and seemingly still closed off from the outside. The main perimeter wall around the police station also stood apparently unscathed.

The main building had fared worse. The roof and the top third of its walls had been blown off, but the lower portion still stood. The small grille in the buckled door revealed a yawning blackness inside.

A little nugget of hope formed in Razane's mind. Maybe the outer walls had been breached. If so they could escape today.

Smoke and dust hung in the air and blocked the view of the front end of the courtyard and the door to the administration area. A man-sized chunk of masonry lay at the rear of the courtyard partially blocking it. From where she stood the rear perimeter wall looked intact as well. It was not a good sign. It meant they were still stuck inside the outer perimeter wall.

Sergei slowly emerged from the hut carrying Jane. He saw the scene. 'Oh shit,' he wheezed, coughing. 'Call Mack, please,' he said in a panicked voice.

Razane's phone buzzed. It was Ben.

'Dad and Mack's signals dropped. What's wrong? I can't see them anymore.'

'Sergei's here with me,' Razane said, so is your Mum. 'Call Damon and see if he's OK, there's been a bomb attack on the police station.'

'Oh, fuck!' Ben said.

They looked towards the front of the courtyard again. The dust was slowly settling. The forward part had collapsed into a tall pile of rubble that blocked any passage. The door to the admin area, if it still stood, was on the other side.

The bomb had hit the front of the building. That's where Mack was. Sergei felt sick at the thought. His legs weak, he staggered. Had he not been holding Jane, he would have fallen. Tears welled in his eyes.

'Oh, fuck, Mack's out there...' All the strength drained out of him as the awful realisation sunk in. His friend was probably badly hurt, or dead.

Razane turned to him. She touched his face, damp with tears, and looked into his eyes. My love, there is nothing we can do from here to help Mack.' Tears were flowing down his face.

Mack was most likely dead. This was many times worse. If Jane was moved and Mack was not there to help, then all was lost. Razane had an almost overwhelming urge to curl into a ball and cry, but she fought back. They could not give up, not while there was a glimmer of hope.

Razane had never seen Sergei so lost, and her heart sank at his pain. She wanted to cry as well. She wanted desperately to hold him, but he was carrying Jane. Both the loves of her life were hurt. She had to be the strong one and fight through her own fog of pain and confusion.

The deafening sound of gunfire reverberated through the remaining shell of the building and shook them out of their torpor. Razane almost dropped her phone. With trembling hands, she switched off the light. They had to get out of there, or they would die tonight.

The rear of the courtyard offered the only hope of escape, however slim. At least it didn't look blocked. The gunfire stopped. Men were now running and shouting inside the building. They were there to finish whatever the bomb hadn't. Strong shafts of torchlight shone from inside the main building into the sky.

Razane put her finger to her lips and motioned for Sergei and Jane to be quiet.

Still carrying Jane, Sergei followed Razane as she walked towards the back wall. The men inside approached the buckled metal door leading to the courtyard.

There was more firing and the sound of bullets hitting metal. They were trying to get into the courtyard. Sergei and Razane squeezed past the fallen chunk of masonry and were now at the back wall. Here the courtyard turned left as it ran behind the main building. Their eyes slowly adjusted to the near darkness. A large section of the main building had collapsed towards the outer perimeter wall. A large gap had opened up into the police station building. If they had wanted to, they could have entered it, but it was full of hostile armed men. Soon it would be teeming with police.

Thankfully, the gunmen inside had not yet realised the wall had been breached. They were still trying to get through the side door, but it wouldn't be long before they gave up and looked elsewhere.

They had to escape before that happened. Razane slowly walked forward hoping against hope to find a hole in the outer perimeter wall. Carrying Jane, Sergei followed carefully. He could not afford to trip over any unseen debris.

Damon stood and wiped his mouth. The gunfire had stopped. Now the predominant sound was of people moaning, punctuated by screams and wails. Still feeling nauseous he walked towards the mosque hoping to find a way in.

He felt the rush of wind and the sound of an engine and a powerful impact with something massive and hard. He went flying onto the footpath. His head hit the pavement, and everything went black.

Abrar jumped out of his Defender and rushed over to where Damon had fallen. He took out his Beretta and aimed it at Damon's head. He could kill at least one of them tonight. Sirens blared in the distance. The gunfire had stopped. The gunmen in the van must have retreated. He had to leave himself.

What about his other targets? Were they still alive? It was unlikely, but he couldn't be sure. For the third time that day he willed his finger off the trigger. He had no time to look for them and until he knew, either way, the young man would have to stay alive.

He opened the Defender's tailgate. A bystander looked at

him in a daze.

'Help me with my friend. I need to get him to a hospital.' Together they loaded Damon into the Land Rover. 'Thank you, my good man,' he said to the helper and shook his hand.

Damon was still out cold. Ideally, he should have tied him up, but there were too many people milling about. He would have to keep his wits about him and listen for him waking. Somewhat reluctantly he closed the tailgate and ran to the driver's seat, put the Land Rover into gear and drove off, threading his way through the debris and stranded vehicles on the road. The police sirens were getting nearer.

'Oh my God,' Razane whispered and pointed at a huge breach in the perimeter wall. It lined up with a corresponding breach in the rear wall of the main building. It was the main path of the blast. Through it, they could see all the way into the mosque and beyond it Sanda Road and freedom.

Sergei whistled under his breath. 'Wow, it took out the mosque as well.' He followed Razane as she carefully stepped over the rubble.

Jane could sense he was struggling. 'Let me walk,' she whispered.

Sergei had no choice; he had finally run out of strength. He put Jane down, carefully. Men were still shouting inside the building, but there was another sound, sirens. Following Razane's lead, they clambered over the piles of rubble barely managing to keep their footing.

They were in the mosque compound now. All the glass in the building had been blown out. They ran through the main prayer hall. At the front, the boundary wall of the mosque had collapsed onto the footpath on Sanda Road. They walked over the fallen boundary wall to freedom.

A scene of utter devastation met them. Broken cars and bits of the mosque's minarets were strewn everywhere. People covered in dust, many bleeding, lay, sat, and stood on the road and walked around in a general state of confusion. To the right, a long line of cars were banked up. Several policemen were directing traffic into a side street.

Their Corolla stood on the side of the road next to the park. It was completely covered in dust and small stones. They ran to it. The keys were still in the ignition. Jane and Razane got in the back seat. Razane gave Jane the burka, from her bag, and wrapped herself in a shawl, leaving only her face exposed.

Ben rang. 'Where are you guys? You look like you're outside the police station. Are you out?'

'Jane, Sergei and I are in the car on Sanda Road. I don't think Mack made it. And we can't see where Damon is,' Razane's voice was hurried. She turned on the speaker so they could all hear.

'I tried calling Mack. There was no answer,' Ben said. 'Oh shit! I can see Damon. He's about a kilometre away and moving... further away. Holy shit, he just turned onto the N5. Let me call him.'

'Wait, don't!' Razane shouted.

'Why?' Ben sounded alarmed.

'Damon is obviously in a vehicle... We just saw a black SUV speed away,' Razane said, trying to work it out as she spoke. 'Maybe he was in that vehicle.'

'Why?' Ben said.

'I have no idea,' Razane said.

'After the bomb, men with automatic rifles entered the building,' Sergei said. 'They were trying to make sure everyone was dead.'

'So you think they...?' Ben's voice trailed off.

'How else do you explain where Damon is?' Razane said. 'Maybe they were watching us all along... Someone took him captive. We don't know.'

'What the fuck!' Ben said.

'Yes, Ben that sort of makes sense,' Sergei said, 'I just can't think of a reason Damon would be driving away from us on his own accord?'

'There is really no other explanation. Even if there is let's just follow,' Razane said in an urgent voice.

'OK, you guys get out of there. Follow Damon. I'll help you track him.'

MASHA'ALLAH

The subsonic rumble shook his mosque ever so slightly. Moments later the sound of the explosion reached him. Then the mosque shook again as the blast wave hit.

'*Masha'Allah*, God has willed it.' Abdul Zubair smiled and looked up raising his hands in prayer. '*Inna Lillahi wa inna ilaihi raji'un*, we surely belong to Allah and to Him we shall return.'

Bilal ran into the prayer room. '*Masha'Allah*, it is done. *Inna Lillahi wa inna ilaihi raji'un*. It is done! Ishaq is *shaheed*!'

'Yes, Ishaq has become a martyr.'

'Gather everyone, we need to be ready to leave for the village when Adil and the rest return. We have work to do.'

As Bilal left he pulled out his phone and called Jibran.

'*Mubarak ho*, it has happened.'

There was silence on the other end of the line. 'You have outdone yourself. You are a true servant of Allah.'

'Allah has graced me with this opportunity.'

'Have your men reached the village?'

'We are leaving now,' Abdul Zubair replied. There was more silence.

Jibran replied, speaking slowly, with a great deal of control. '*Maulana Sahib*, you agreed to have your men waiting near the village!'

Abdul Zubair tried to mask his annoyance. 'Are we celebrating a victory or a defeat? Why are you addressing me with discourtesy?'

'Forgive me *Maulana Sahib*--'

'We have only one van. You asked me to send my men to make sure no one was left alive after the blast. Maybe if esteemed people like yourself would be more generous, then we would have more means. But Allah will always provide in his wisdom.' It was now his turn to be irate.

'I apologise profoundly,' Jibran replied taken aback, 'but the woman did not only blaspheme the Prophet, peace be upon him, but also gave the villagers the tools of the *Shaitan*, the Internet. They already switched it on!'

Abdul Zubair hated the Internet. It was the devil's work and spread pornography and other cancers of Western countries. The Internet was not even good for teaching the word of Allah because Indian and Israeli agents had spread wrong teachings to confuse people. When the revolution came, it was the first thing he would shut down.

'Jibran, son, you did not mention the Internet before,' his tone softened. 'You told me to punish the villagers for not discouraging the woman from sinning.'

'Yes, I asked you to destroy the work she did.'

'We will do that, *Inshallah*. I can hear the van outside. We will leave now. I will come to your *haveli* as soon as it is done.'

'Very well, I will give you some more donation for the mosque then.'

'*Allah hafiz.*'

'May Allah protect you.'

Jibran slammed the phone down. Fucking son of a filthy whore. He had expected the work to be done, all of it, and it still was not.

They all piled into the van as soon as it returned. Abdul Zubair sat in the front while his son drove.

'So Adil, tell me everything.'

'*Masha'Allah*, it was successful.' Adil handed his father his phone with the photographs he took.

Abdul Zubair smiled as he flicked through the images. He noted with satisfaction the Hindu shrine on the opposite corner was no longer there. *Masha'Allah*!

'*Masha'Allah,*' came the echoing cheer from the back.

ABRAR

A brar drove carefully, but fast. He was now on the N5 heading out of Lahore. Flood-lights illuminated the grand Badshahi Mosque to his right like a diamond in the dirt. This was the older and poorer but also the historic part of Lahore. It was low-lying and prone to flooding, whenever the Ravi burst its banks, which was every rainy season.

It hadn't always been like this. Five hundred years ago this was the centre of Lahore. It was a walled city right next to where the Mughal emperors built their palaces in the magnificent Fort of Lahore. But then the river had changed course, and Lahore had grown away from it till what was once the centre became its northern entrance.

Abrar loved Lahore, but he hated this about it. All other great cities built themselves around their historical monuments. Lahore had egested its grandest and most historic part to the outer rim. Now poor people lived there. Poor people who didn't mind getting their houses inundated every monsoon. And why would they? They hardly had anything that could get wet.

He changed lanes and accelerated to get around a smoky bus. It was empty of passengers, probably on its way back to the depot.

The streets were now quite deserted for Lahore, and the breeze was losing its battle to keep the fog at bay.

As he crossed the river, the fog became pea-soup thick, and he was forced to slow to a crawl. The taillights of the car ahead of him were barely visible until he was within a few feet of it. The queue of cars inched forward, slowed by poor visibility and the toll booth ahead.

He now had time to think things over. What the fuck had just happened? One thing was obvious, he was just the backup plan to the bomb. But then who were the gunmen? Was he the backup to the backup plan. Now that was truly insulting. He had a good mind to put a bullet into Jibran's forehead, right smack in the middle of it. He was a fine surgeon, a master of his craft. What he had witnessed were butchers. The two did not mix.

He did not approve of butchers. Despite having eighty-two kills he hated violence, and he certainly did not approve of bombs. They were so messy. They were also the tool of people he hated, radical Islamic fundamentalist bastards.

He handed the toll booth operator the money and drove on. The traffic began to pick up speed.

Assassins, like him, were at the top of the food chain, like lions, an essential part of the natural human ecosystem. They had a proud and long history. They killed the weak, the slow and the stupid; the greedy and overreaching who had forgotten their place. His victims were never good people. Ordinary innocent people going about their ordinary lives did not make enemies who paid big money to have them killed.

Terrorists, on the other hand, killed indiscriminately, like virus or bacteria. Was Jibran mixed with extremists? He had never expressed any such views; he drank and smoked and fucked like the rest of them. Of course, he was a politician, and he pretended a lot. He made speeches about the need to impose Shariah Law more completely and for the country to be more Islamic. That of course was fake like most things politicians said and did, the opportunistic bastards.

Grabbing the young man had been a spur of the moment thing. He needed to stay in the game a little longer and see it play out a bit but he had to work out a plan super fast. He could put a bullet in the back of the young man's head and dump him in a ditch by the side of a road if nothing came to him soon.

Shit, he swung his wheel hard to dodge a bicycle that was trying to get around a pothole in the road.

'Almost got you, fucker,' Abrar shouted at the cyclist. They were outside the city limits now and into open countryside; it was no place for a bicycle.

Abrar was about to call Jibran when the young man groaned. Bugger, he was coming to. The kid was much bigger than him. He had to stop him waking.

Abrar pulled to the side of the road where the verge was a bit wider. A drainage channel, dry and chock full of weeds, ran alongside it. In his haste to get off the road and stop he had almost run into it.

He opened the glove box and took out a bottle of chloroform, daubed some into a wad of tissues and folded them over to stop the highly volatile liquid evaporating. He walked to the back of the Defender and opened the door. The young man was sitting up, looking dazed. Abrar unfolded the tissue in his hand, leapt inside and pressed the opened wad over his face. Acting instinctively, the young man pushed back hard. Abrar had managed to lock his free hand around the back of his neck, but his fingers were not able to hold on, and he felt himself fly out the back of the Land Rover.

He landed in the dirt with a thump and had to stop himself rolling into the ditch. A bit too strong, motherfucker! Thankfully the chloroform had worked. The huge man was on his back, out like a light. The effect would only last a minute at the most.

Abrar fished in a side pocket for some cable ties. He used two thick ones to tie the young man's wrists together behind his back and two for his ankles. Then he got a length of rope and passed them between the two loops, effectively hog-tying him.

A huge truck drove past shaking his four-wheel-drive, its horn blaring. The Land Rover's side opening door prevented passers-by from seeing what he was doing but the road conditions were poor and sooner or later someone would ram up the back of him. Not in a welcome way.

His prisoner was a good-looking fellow, eminently fuckable. He might just have some fun before he killed him. His eyes strayed to his crotch. How would his cock taste? Shut up monkey brain. This was not the time. Next to it, he saw another bulge, rectangular in shape, his smartphone.

'Oops, what have we here.' Abrar fished it out and tried to turn it on, but the screen was locked. He was about to fling it into the fields but stopped himself.

A plan was beginning to form, a cunning plan. Abrar got back in the driver's seat and drove off. As soon as his vehicle made a Bluetooth connection with his phone, he dialled Jibran.

FOLLOW

Lahore, Thursday 1 December, 11:07pm

Jane sat in the back seat, Razane's arms wrapped protectively around her. She was breathing in Razane's warmth and the familiar perfume she always wore. Razane's smell always turned her on.

She became aware of other things. Their car was moving slowly and turning. People outside were shouting at each other and honking their horns. It felt strange to be outside the lock-up, free. It seemed unreal, almost too good to be true, like a dream.

Dreams rarely felt this good. Could it be a dream inside a dream or rather inside a nightmare? For the last six days, she had been in a nightmare she had wanted to wake from. If this was a dream, she did not want to wake from it. A dream she did not want to wake from inside a nightmare she had been desperate to wake from. That was crazy. She reached out and touched Razane on the face. Razane kissed her hand. That felt real. Dreams did not include tactile senses. That meant it was real. She squeezed Razane tightly, a smile on her face.

The police were frantically trying to clear cars away from the bomb affected part of Sanda Road. More police cars and ambulances were on the way, and they needed to get through. Other police had blocked traffic five-hundred metres up the road and were diverting cars into Ittehad Street. Those already ahead of the diversion were being made to reverse. It was taking far too long. They were still right next door to the police station, or what was left of it. The tension in the car was building up.

Ben was on the phone. He was speaking, but Jane could not hear clearly.

'What's Ben saying?' Jane asked. Her voice sounded strange to her, disjointed like she was outside her own body.

'He's tracking Damon's phone and telling us where to go,' Razane answered softly.

'Don't worry, sweetheart, we'll get Damon back,' Sergei said.

Razane was in a turmoil of emotions. She was elated Jane was no longer a prisoner. It was nothing short of a miracle they had escaped from a highly secure building that had, for the most part, been destroyed by a powerful bomb.

They had not escaped unscathed. Mack was dead. She was processing it a bit too clinically. His death did not grieve her directly. Instead, she felt the pain Sergei was going through. Had death ceased to have any meaning for her? Maybe she was permanently damaged inside. Come to think of it Simon's death had also not upset her. Her only sorrow was for Jane's loss.

Mack's death troubled her for more pragmatic reasons. He had been the only one with local knowledge. He would have known how to get past all the police checkpoints, that would surely spring up on the way to Karachi. They also had no means of getting in touch with the Cessna pilot.

To make matters worse, Damon had been taken, prisoner. Now, they were driving in the opposite direction to Karachi. It seemed like they had taken one step forward and two steps back.

Theirs was the last car to be guided out of the traffic jam. From her repose, Jane saw traffic lights and the tops of some of the taller buildings and trees. She also saw whenever anyone came close to the car. There was a lot of shouting. It put her on tenterhooks. She half expected someone to stop and challenge them. But the police were not interested in them. They were trying to clear a bomb site and make way for the influx of emergency services. In her confused state, she couldn't comprehend she had no reason to worry. At least not yet. No one was looking for three people in a Toyota Corolla.

Her body felt so weak she was dizzy even lying down. Lifting her head felt as tiring as running a marathon. Something was wrong with her. Had she been hurt in the bomb blast? Her ears were still ringing, and she could not hear Razane or Sergei clearly. The only thing stopping her panic was Razane's comforting touch.

Her eyelids were heavy and sleep beckoned, yet she resisted. Did she have a brain injury? She vaguely remembered something about keeping people with head trauma awake and not letting them sleep. She had to fight the lethargy, the clouds in her mind. Damon, her baby, had been kidnapped presumably by the same people who'd killed Simon and Jamshed and maybe Mack. If so, he was in grave danger.

It still did not make sense. Why target her with such viciousness? What had she ever done to them? Why attack her family, like mad dogs?

Warm tears welled in her eyes. Nothing seemed to quite make sense. What was going on? Why was their car there and where was Damon when he was kidnapped? Was it all part of her being disoriented? She couldn't think clearly. She was exhausted. Maybe a small nap wouldn't hurt after all.

'Poor Jane is in shock,' Razane said in a worried tone.

'Keep her warm and calm,' Sergei said looking back. 'I'll turn the heater up.

Razane squeezed Jane tight. She kissed her face tenderly and stroked her hair. 'I love you, my sweet darling!'

'I love you so, so much, too,' Jane muttered. 'I need to just close my eyes and sleep for half an hour. Wake me then please.'

'Sure, my love, have a rest.'

She watched Jane's breathing get shallow and felt her body relax.

'What do you think's wrong?' Sergei said in a worried tone.

'She got hit by the blast, the shock wave. It can injure a person quite badly.' Razane had seen people with no visible wounds die a few days after being in a blast zone. They had acted like Jane did now, and from there they just got worse and worse and then died. But she could not say that to Sergei. She could not let herself think it. Hopefully, Jane had not experienced the full severity of it.

Sergei turned his head around to look at Jane. He was pale. He was in shock too. Razane reached forward and touched his face. His skin was clammy.

'Look forward please, my love,' she said gently as she stroked his cheek. He had not yet processed Mack's death. When he finally did, it would hit him hard.

Still holding on to Jane she pivoted the left side of her body forward and wrapped her arm around Sergei from behind. He was shivering.

She alternated between squeezing his left arm and stroking it. Some of the stiffness left his body, he seemed to calm down, but then he started to shake again. Warm tears dropped on her arm. He was sobbing. She took her arm away and fished in her bag for a tissue.

'He was like my brother,' Sergei choked back a sob. His driving was becoming erratic.

'Would you like me to drive, my love?' she asked.

'No, I'll be fine.'

He calmed a bit. At the next set of lights, she could feel and hear him break down again. Deep sobs wracked his body. The shock and the grief were both manifesting themselves at the same time.

She stroked his hair, 'I'm so sorry, Serge!' She leaned forward and kissed him on his neck.

'OK, I got the signal again.' Ben's voice startled them. The signal from Damon's phone had been dropping out every so often. 'I hope his battery doesn't go flat.'

'Where's he now?' Sergei said.

'Still on the N5. He's just crossed a bridge over the River Ravi. You guys are some way behind him. There's a bit of congestion at the toll booth, but then it clears. I'll keep taking screenshots in case I lose him.'

'Good work Ben,' Sergei said, 'I'm glad you're still in Melbourne.'

They drove in silence. The bridge came, and they joined the queue of cars waiting for what seemed like an eternity to pay at the toll booth.

Razane watched for signs the booth operators were taking any special interest in them. Nothing. It seemed no one was looking for escapees. It was a suicide bombing after all, and the perpetrator of the crime was spread over Charsadda and Sacha Saeen Streets.

The traffic began flowing again.

Jane opened her eyes. The dizziness and ringing in her ears seemed to have subsided a little. Her head rested on Razane's chest. Razane had an incredible way of remaining calm in the most stressful situation. Her gentle breathing and the sound of her heart gently beating reminded Jane of the first time she had heard Razane's heartbeat.

ZAKHO

Zakho, North Iraq, 2 years 2 months earlier

Slowly, Jane opened her eyes and tried to orient herself. They had spent the previous week touring the region, enjoying the beautiful but rugged mountains, their snow-covered peaks contrasting with lush green valleys. They'd slept in so many different hotels and inns it was easy to get disoriented in the mornings.

Jane's mind cleared, gradually. They were in the charming little town of Zakho with its beautiful ancient bridge over the River Khabur. It had gotten late on the way back from Turkey to Sharanish. An unexpected cold weather front had moved in from the mountains, and a light dusting of snow had made the roads too treacherous to continue.

Razane's soft breast cushioned her head, the side of her face ever so slightly damp where their skin touched. Razane's slow rhythmic heartbeat echoed in her ear.

She was naked. They both were.

Last night it had finally happened. Jane blushed at the memory. It was the deepest most sensuous experience she'd ever had with anyone. She'd been like a wild animal on fire; they'd both been. Something inside of her had awakened. Something she had, till then, never even been aware of.

The details flooded back, how they'd kissed and nibbled and tasted one another, their emotions overwhelming them. They had devoured each other to the point of orgasms that rolled on and on and on till they fell totally exhausted in a heap. And then again and again till finally, sleep came.

Just the memory aroused her. She was wet again, in fact, she was drenched. Razane would be able to feel it too, where her leg rested between hers.

She reached down and felt Razane. Yes, wet, soaking wet even more than she, if that was possible. Razane stirred. Jane licked her moist fingers. The smell was heady, the taste divine.

'I need more. I want to go again, please,' Jane murmured breathlessly.

'Oh yes, yesss!' Razane whispered. They were moving together, but it was slower and less frenzied but still as intense as the night before, and when they'd finished they lay holding each other, their hearts beating as one.

Outside the sun rose in the sky. Jane looked at the clock on the bedside table. It was eight in the morning. It was still a bit early.

Razane's breathing slowed. She had dropped off to sleep again. Jane lay there deep in thought, thinking about Sergei and the strange way her life was unfolding. Hopefully, it wasn't unravelling. Amazingly there was no feeling of guilt or remorse or shame, no dread of what was going to happen. There was only an easy feeling, of happiness and pure optimism. Everything was going to be OK!

She gazed at Razane. Here was the love of her life. The person she was meant to be with. She knew it with utmost certainty. In fact, she'd never been surer of anything in her life. It was strange because Sergei was also the love of her life and she did not love him any less. Even as she lay there spent and satisfied she missed him and longed for him. He completed her in the same way Razane now did. That, of course, didn't make any sense. How could something or someone be completed twice? She almost laughed out loud at the craziness of it.

But life had stopped making sense ever since she'd met Razane.

Jane had always been a straight-laced person, neat,

predictable, dependable, boring. Her life, a rigid box, with everything clearly labelled and defined. Order and predictability represented happiness and comfort. That had all changed, totally! Her box was gone, smashed to smithereens but she wasn't uneasy or unhappy, rather the complete opposite, her spirit soared on a current of air, higher and higher, her soul, light as a feather!

There was so much more that didn't make sense. She'd never had sexual feelings for a woman. Yet the first time she set eyes on Razane a frisson of excitement had run through her. One kindred soul had reacted to another, unencumbered by rules and inhibitions. And what they had last night, and just then, was even more impossible, unthinkable! She'd never been able to stand her own wetness. After Sergei would go down on her, she'd not be able to kiss him until he rinsed his mouth. Yet last night she couldn't get enough of Razane, drinking her in as if she was imbibing the nectar of the gods.

Jane smiled as she remembered. She would return a different woman.

For some strange reason, she wasn't worried how she'd break the news to Sergei. Things would work out. She was totally at peace, in complete submission to the universe. Her relationship with Sergei was special. Sergei was her rock and her soul mate. He was loyal to a fault. He would never leave her. It might get a bit tense and complicated, but she'd work it out, somehow. They would make the impossible happen.

It was getting close to check-out time. They both took lukewarm showers to wash away the smell of sex before they went downstairs for breakfast. Then they drove the scenic route to Sharanish, an hour away. On the way, they sang songs and talked and smiled, carefree and happy, like children. The happiness of new love, in one of the most dangerous places on Earth.

Their relationship had blossomed over the last months in the most incredible way. Jane had hired Razane as a guide and translator, while she worked on a project to bring solar power and the Internet to the remote but picturesque Sharanish, a village nestled in the mountains of northern Iraq. People here were dirt poor with no heating, light bulbs or running water. They were completely cut off from the rest of the world with not even a regular postal service. This project would change their lives.

Over a month Jane and Razane had become close friends. They travelled all over the region and spent hours in conversation, enjoying what they had in common and delighting in what they could learn from each other.

Like herself, Razane was deeply spiritual. She had been a fighter in the Kurdish Peshmerga but left after a tragic incident in which a group of innocent people were caught in a crossfire between her unit and a jihadist outfit. Many died. She had blamed herself, and the guilt and shame made her an emotional wreck.

Razane introduced her to Rumi, the great 13th-century Sufi poet. Jane was fascinated with his poetry and philosophy and his controversial relationship with Shams of Tabriz, a mystic dervish. The two men had become soul mates. It was rumoured Shams was murdered because of their relationship and after his death, Rumi went on to write the most beautiful heart-rending poetry in memory of his lost friend.

Jane and Razane spent long hours in the evenings, listening to music, drinking Turkish coffee, talking, and reading poetry. On many occasions, the conversation would swing to the love between Rumi and Shams and how it transcended the narrow human constructs of gender and family and possessions and even life itself.

Razane was a non-practising Muslim, Jane a non-church going Christian. The spirituality of Rumi brought them to a new place that allowed them to bond. With every passing day, they grew closer and more intimate. Unbeknownst to both, they were falling in love.

One day Razane saved their lives. They had gone to Mosul,

140km south of Sharanish, to interview final year university students for the job of maintaining all the equipment she was installing.

All day long they had heard gunfire in the distance. This sound had become so commonplace in Iraq, since the American invasion, people just accepted it as normal. But that day it was different, more intense. All around them people were on edge. Something was amiss.

Sensing danger they decided to leave as soon as the interviews were over.

On their way home, they reached the outskirts of Mosul without seeing a single car on the road. The whole northern part of the city looked abandoned. Something was badly wrong.

As they approached the interchange to Highway 80 to head north back to Sharanish, Jane noticed four pickup trucks behind them carrying the black Islamic State flag. Each carried four men in the tray, all armed with machine guns.

The pickups surrounded their Landcruiser in a V-formation with two either side and two hemming them in from behind. The men in the nearest pickup on the left fired in the air and shouted at them to stop. Both women had a pretty good idea what fate would befall them if they were captured.

Screaming at Jane to hold on, Razane slammed her foot on the brake. The two front pickups, their drivers unable to react in time, overshot them. Before their drivers began braking, they were many car lengths ahead of their Landcruiser.

The pickups behind them had to swerve hard to avoid a collision. As they also passed forward of them, they began fishtailing badly, their drivers failing to regain control.

By the time the Landcruiser had pulled to a stop all the ISIL thugs were about a hundred metres ahead of them. The gunmen, in their efforts to stay in the trucks, had forgotten about the women. Three of the men were unable to hold on and were ejected violently onto the road.

Razane saw a side street on the right, turned the

Landcruiser and raced into it. Fortunately, they ran into a group of Iraqi soldiers on a tank who stopped them and directed them to a safer route out of Mosul. They never saw the ISIL men again. They also never returned to Mosul. Within days it was overrun by the Islamic State.

When they were safely out in the countryside, Razane pulled over, staggered out of her car and threw up violently. Jane got out and held her hair and give her a tissue.

'That was the bravest thing I have ever seen anyone do', she had said resisting the urge to throw up as well.

On the side of the road with the hot sun blazing overhead, they had embraced each other, both of them were still shaking. They smelled of fear and sweat, and Razane smelled of puke. But they held each other for a long moment, and it felt good and blissful. Even though Razane had just saved her, she had a distinct feeling Razane needed saving just as much as she did. It was the first time Jane knew she was in love with Razane.

THE CHASE

GT Road, Friday 2 December, 12:01am

The headlights pierced the night. Sergei drove as fast as he dared. They had just passed through the small town of Kamoke. It was a messy sprawl of buildings typical of most small towns in Punjab. Kamoke was famous for its rice market. Sergei only knew about it because Mack had an office there.

He felt short of breath at the thought of Mack. The fact that his friend had just died had not yet fully sunken in. He was still in shock. The immense feeling of sadness and loss would come later. There would be time to mourn. Now he had to focus, or more of his family would die.

They were out in the countryside again, among the fields. The N5 Motorway used to be the Grand Trunk Road. Sergei remembered reading about it in a Rudyard Kipling book, Kim. His mother had given it to him when he was a kid, in bed with the chicken pox so many years ago. He had looked the road up and had been surprised to find it was real. It was one of Asia's longest and oldest and ran from Chittagong in Bangladesh, through India, Pakistan all the way to Kabul in Afghanistan. As a child, it had seemed so exotic and far away.

Now he was driving on it; though, not by choice. He desperately hoped Damon's phone didn't run out of battery and stayed on the network so they could keep following his signal. The connection had already dropped a few times, but on each occasion, it came back within a few minutes.

He was increasingly certain Damon had been taken

captive. Either that or someone had robbed him of his phone, and he was lying in a ditch somewhere, perhaps on Sanda Road, maybe in the park. He couldn't let himself think that. It also didn't make sense. Damon was huge and unusually strong, not a good target for a mugging. Besides Damon's phone had started moving north after the bomb had gone off. It was implausible someone would steal a phone after something like a bomb blast and then travel out of Lahore. The only sensible explanation was his captors were connected to the deadly attack on the police station.

If so why take Damon? Why not just kill him like the fuckers had been trying to ever since they had got here? That's where the logic in his thought process broke down. Maybe, and this was a horrific thought, they were going to but just hadn't had the time.

The road was a dual carriageway with two lanes in each direction with a concrete barrier in the middle. It was poorly lit, with no street lights except at intersections.

It had started raining again, this time more heavily. The wipers were smudging the windscreen more than clearing it. To make matters worse, it seemed trucks in Pakistan all had their headlights stuck on high beam. They appeared to all be playing an arms race with other trucks using spotlights powerful enough to illuminate low flying aeroplanes. Each approaching truck temporarily blinded him.

Sergei tried flashing his headlights to get them to dip but gave up in the end. He remembered Mack telling him most truck drivers in Pakistan smoked hashish to keep awake. Drugs and sleep-deprivation were a deadly combination.

Their car was taking a battering as well. The road surface had not been well maintained and every so often their car banged hard into a pothole. Hopefully, their suspension and tyres would hold out.

Thankfully, there were no pedestrians about, at least, none he could see. He was sure not going to be able to spot them if there were any.

'OK, his signal's back again,' Ben's voice startled him. 'Damon's in Gujranwala on the outer ring road. Wait, he's turning onto Alipur Chatha Road. He looks to be heading in a westerly-ish direction.'

'Gujranwala,' Jane piped up. She had just woken, 'we used to turn west on the Gujranwala Ring Road to go to Shakar Parian.'

'Oh shit, I wonder if that's where they are going?' Sergei said, sounding puzzled. 'But--'

'Ben, can you find Shakar Parian on the map?' Jane cut in.

'Yup, wait a sec, umm... I can see it here. It's a tiny little village on the map. Oh, I see photos Mum has uploaded--'

'Why would they be taking Damon there?' Razane said.

'Hey, aren't we jumping ahead of ourselves?' Ben chimed in. 'Shakar Parian is a tiny dot of a village and the whole of western Punjab is accessible by turning west from Gujranwala. They could be going almost anywhere.'

'My gut's telling me there's a connection...' Jane's voice trailed off. Speaking made her feel weak. A wave of nausea swept over her. She gripped Razane tightly.

Razane looked down. Jane had turned pale. She was shivering. Razane touched her forehead. She was warm.

'Please be OK, my love,' Razane murmured under breath as she took her own shawl off, wrapped it around Jane and pulled her close.

'Guys, the bomb blast is in the news already,' Ben said anxiously, 'I just saw a headline pop up.'

'What's it say?' Sergei asked.

'Wait it was here. Fuck, let me look for it.'

Sergei turned on the radio. The inspector general was at a press conference. He spoke in English.

'A bomb has destroyed Lahore's top police station on Charsadda Street. There are no survivors. All on-duty police and prisoners in the cells were killed as well as many passers-by.' He paused and took a deep breath. 'Eighty-three people have died, and over one hundred and seventy have been injured, many severely. The police are contacting family members for DNA samples to identify the victims.' He paused again. 'Are there any questions before we wrap-up?'

A reporter spoke up. 'Sir, has anyone claimed responsibility?'

'No. No group has come forward yet.'

'Is Jane Kelly among the victims?' Another reporter asked.

'Jane Kelly was held at that police station. Due to the state of the bodies, we are unable to identify anyone. That is why we are seeking DNA samples.'

'Sir, can you comment on reports of firing after the blast?'

'At this point, we cannot comment until further investigations have been made,' The IG said. His comment was met with a tumult of voices.

'That is all the time I have for questions,' he said loudly. 'Let me assure all members of the public. We will leave no stone unturned to bring the perpetrators of this heinous crime to justice.'

Sergei turned off the radio.

The silence in the car was palpable as they all struggled to comprehend what they had just heard.

Ben had heard it too, 'they think you're dead, Mum.' No one spoke.

'Why do you say that?' Jane said, weakly.

'They said there were no survivors,' Sergei said.

'Oh.' Jane said.

'Do you know what it means?' Ben said. 'The police won't look for you.'

There was silence while the implication sank in. The emotions that flowed too complex for them to verbalise. A sense of relief washed over Jane. A pang of guilt almost immediately replaced it. Mack had just died, Simon too, and Jamshed and all the police at the station.

Sergei's feelings were in turmoil as well. His closest friend had lost his life for the woman who was the love of his life, one of the loves of his life. He hadn't chosen for it to happen of course but the thought reverberated in his mind like a billiard ball gone crazy. How could one compare the worth of two humans? It wasn't possible. Yet one life was gone, expunged from this world, and one was saved, redeemed. What if he had to make that choice?

He was unable to suppress the answer. He'd have chosen Jane, of course. The certainty made him feel even more guilty. Why was he thinking these dark thoughts? He had to firmly close that door in his mind and focus.

'Is there any way they can find your DNA?' Razane asked.

'Huh?' Jane came out of her thought bubble.

'Your DNA, the man on the radio...'

'Oh, there'd be DNA on my things in my hut back in the village. My clothes, toothbrush, hairbrush...' Jane said, trying to sit up.

'We'll have to go to the village after we get Damon,' Razane said, 'before the police realise this as well.'

'If the police get Jane's DNA we're back to being fucked.' Sergei said, 'we don't have Mack to help us get to Karachi!'

'Anyone know how long a DNA test takes?' Razane asked.

'I saw a show on TV. Apparently, it depends on the state of the bodies.' Ben chimed in.

'They'd have been pretty badly burnt, but we can't be sure,' Sergei said, 'so we must go to the village and fast, right after we rescue Damon!'

'Oh, yes. We must,' Razane said.

'Is it OK if I keep resting my head on you?' Jane said in a low voice, 'I'm still dizzy.'

Sergei heard and looked back, his expression worried.

'Every fibre of my being is yours,' Razane said gently, 'do you really need to ask?' she pulled her close. Jane rested her head on Razane's chest and fell asleep again while Razane softly stroked her face.

Sergei winced as he straightened up. Every movement

hurt. The whole side of his chest below his armpit burned furiously. The splinter must have penetrated deep, or maybe the wound was infected. He'd read someplace cuts got infected quickly in tropical countries. He touched around it gingerly. He would need to have it looked at. At least it wasn't bleeding.

They drove on into the night following a GPS signal relayed to them by Ben over another Internet signal. Hopefully, the gods of technology would shine on them tonight.

THE THROUPLE

Melbourne, 2 years earlier

Sergei wondered whether Jane would be annoyed with him. He'd acted a bit silly around Razane all evening, like he was infatuated with her. He normally never flirted. Maybe he was just mirroring how Jane was behaving. His beautiful strait-laced Jane, usually shy and reserved was acting like a giggling teenager with a bit too much to drink. Not that he minded in the least. He'd always hoped she'd loosen up and enjoy life a bit more. Tonight, she'd been flirting with the guests and most of all with Razane.

They'd invited a few friends over to celebrate Jane's homecoming after three months in Northern Iraq. However, Razane ended up being the centre of attention, especially of the men.

Razane and Jane had worked together in Iraq and had become close friends. She'd returned with Jane and was staying at a nearby hotel.

Razane was stunning. Her wavy black hair framed a striking if not a classically pretty face, with high cheekbones, dark eyes, and a flawless olive complexion. She wore bright crimson lipstick that accentuated her full sensuous lips. Her dark almond-shaped eyes were deeply expressive and looked like she'd experienced the depths of sadness and the heights of joy.

She wore a strapless crimson chiffon dress complemented by a slender silver bangle, a thin silver necklace and flimsy silver high heeled shoes. She looked so elegant and poised it was hard to visualise her in the drab military uniform of the Peshmerga.

Not that Razane didn't look like she could fight. She was lithe and muscular. In some ways, she reminded him of a leopard. Maybe it was the way she moved in a fluid and deliberate way.

Her manner made her even more alluring. She was quiet and intense and a bit aloof with everyone except Jane and him. She looked like she got what she wanted when she wanted it and in the meantime, didn't indulge in frivolity. Whenever she spoke, it was with calm authority and in a lovely Middle Eastern accent. By the end of the evening, he was totally turned on by her. Most likely the other men were too.

She and Jane had obviously developed an intimate relationship. He noticed them touching often as they exchanged banter and giggled together like schoolgirls.

That was, of course, natural, what they'd gone through would bring anyone together. Jane had told everyone about Iraq and how Razane had saved her life in Mosul. That had elicited oohs and aahs from around the dinner table.

After an evening spent laughing, drinking wine, telling jokes, and dancing, their friends, except Razane, finally left at around midnight. A post-party high made the three of them restless, so Jane suggested they go for a walk.

It was a lovely spring evening. A pleasantly warm breeze blew gently through the neighbourhood. It wafted through leaves and swayed tall grasses, creating a calm, soothing whisper that harmonised with the chirping of the crickets. The soft blanket of sound was so peaceful it could have lulled even the most chronic insomniac into a blissful sleep.

Jane walked between them, their arms interlocked. Sergei was aware of how good she felt. He'd missed her. He could smell her and Razane's distinct perfumes, Jane's was sweet fruit and bubble-gum, Razane's sandalwood and musk. He heard the rustle of their dresses, and their breathing becoming laboured as they climbed to a park at the top of a small hill.

'Razane I haven't told you... I can't tell you how grateful I am... what you did in Mosul,' he reached over with his free hand.

Razane took it in hers and squeezed it softly. They all slowed to a halt.

'I just reacted… mostly out of fear,' she said softly in her lovely accent. She still held his hand. Her grip firm but her skin soft. It was hard to imagine her holding a gun.

'Still--'

'Those ISIL thugs have a most terrible reputation, how they treat women and Westerners, and I...' Her voice trailed off.

'It doesn't matter... most people would have frozen; it's the bravest thing anyone I know has done and... you two survived.'

They were both looking at him. Jane put an arm around his waist. Her other arm was around Razane's. She gently pulled them in a tighter circle till they stood so close their breaths mingled.

'I'll be indebted to you for the rest of my life,' he said, swallowing hard, their proximity made him giddy. The world around them, the breeze, the crickets, the odd car in the distance, had suddenly gone silent as if someone had thrown a woollen blanket over the world.

'If something had happened to Jane I'd have died inside,' he said, his voice thick with emotion, 'she's the most special person in the world.'

Razane smiled, 'I know, I feel the same way...' Her voice was low, almost breathless. He heard it catching in her throat. It was obviously emotional for her too.

'I feel a connection, a bond, a feeling of love and warmth towards you,' he said trying to choose his words carefully. He didn't want to offend her or sound like he was coming on to her.

He didn't resist the gentle pressure as Jane gently squeezed them closer. They came together in a warm embrace, 'And… I'll always be there for you, always…' his mind was now decidedly foggy. He'd better stop talking.

He expected Razane, and even Jane, to push them apart after a few moments but neither of them did. Their embrace lasted a few more moments and then a few more. Surprisingly it didn't feel awkward in the slightest. He had a fleeting feeling Razane and Jane had melded together, and he was becoming part of their singularity. It was an odd thought to have, but he'd never felt more at one with the universe.

This wasn't a casual contact, it wasn't sexual either, just simple love that felt natural and good. Before moving apart, Razane brought her face closer to his. He saw the reflection of a faraway street light in her eyes as she looked up at him. Her breath was warm and sweet. She kissed him on the cheek and whispered, 'You are welcome, I too am grateful I was able to do what I did.'

He nearly burst with elation. The brush of her smooth cheek, the dampness of her lips left a memory on his skin. He resisted an almost overwhelming desire to kiss her passionately on the lips, but he'd been turned on for quite a while and couldn't let his erection think for him.

They finally separated and walked on. The brush of her cheek, the feel of her breath, the smell of her perfume and the sound of her throaty voice continued to linger in his memory. He guiltily realised he wanted her badly and not only sexually. He would have been content to hold her gently and close for a long, long time. He'd never felt that way about any woman apart from Jane.

They sat on a park bench and talked a bit more. Then they strolled home, laughing, and chatting all the way. A casual observer might have mistaken them for teenagers from their buoyant effervescence.

The thought of how unexpectedly Jane had behaved kept playing on his mind. She'd never been jealous or possessive, but she had pushed them together, encouraged their closeness. She'd have felt his arousal, heard it in the way his voice became hoarse. Yet she had continued to hold them in the embrace, and there was no hesitation or discomfort, rather quite the opposite; Jane had glowed with happiness.

It was two in the morning when they returned.

Later in bed, Jane had one arm around his neck and was stroking him with her free hand. He was running his hands all over her. They were both naked.

'You were turned on by Razane, I could feel it,' Jane said out of the blue.

She'd always been direct with him. It was something he loved about her but the question still startled him.

He was super horny, and Jane was obviously aroused too. Was she talking dirty or was this a serious question?

Well, of course, he had been, hugely, and Jane was helping him take care of the enormous sexual build up, but it was more. He was not just sexually turned on but emotionally as well and that, of course, was harder to own up to.

He might as well be truthful, well at least partly. Dirty talk during sex was like a confessional in a church. One should be able to say anything. Besides if she ever expressed hurt later, he could always downplay it.

'Yes, I was turned on, a bit. Razane is very sexy,' he said trying to play it by ear. 'All the guys were turned on by her.'

'I noticed it too,' Jane said as she sat up and straddled his chest, one arm behind her; her hand still gripped his erection. He sensed she was smiling.

She thrust her hips close to his face. 'Come on do what you're so good at,' she ordered, 'It's been a long three months.'

Slowly he rotated and moved her onto her back. Now he was on top, her legs entwined around his torso. He began kissing her, first slowly then hungrily, like an animal. His tongue moved over her body. Her skin smelled heavenly and tasted divine. She stiffened as he made his way lower. She was now writhing, delirious. 'Hey I should be the one complaining, you had Razane,' he mumbled mischievously, 'I was the one alone.' He put two fingers inside her and felt for her G-spot.

'You have your uses, and she has hers.' Jane moaned ecstatically. She wasn't backing down.

Wow, she was getting good at this. Jane was becoming

naughty. About time!

'Does she have a nice tongue?' he said smiling and then pushing it a bit further, 'does she taste good?' He knew he'd taken it just a bit far as soon as the words came out. He expected Jane to sit up and say something like 'yuck,' and then the dirty talk would stop for the night.

But she didn't. After a pause long enough for him to think she hadn't heard, she mumbled deliriously and ever so softly said, 'yes...'

She'd spoken so quietly he wasn't sure he'd heard her reply. Was it his imagination? No, she'd said yes.

He lifted himself off her, reached over, flicked on the bedside lamp, and looked at her.

'What?' His tone was incredulous, his mind spinning. The strange slightly awkward half smile on her face told him she was serious. She sat up too. The smile was gone from her face. His mind raced trying to comprehend what this profound revelation implied.

'Did you say... yes?' he was aware of the expression of incredulity on his face. Her silence was enough of a reply.

'But I thought you could never have sex with a woman? You can't even stand--'

'I thought so too...' Jane's voice was quiet, almost childlike, she was now looking distressed, vulnerable, and scared.

His heart immediately went out to her. 'Then how? When? Why?' he softened his tone, not wanting to sound like an interrogator. Even in a daze, his overwhelming emotion was of love and tenderness towards her. It always would be. He was justifying her actions to himself. She'd been alone, and scared. She was a softy who loved everyone, but he felt adrift, at a loss for words and meaning.

Jane reached out and touched his arm. He remained motionless. She sidled up and put her arms around him. He didn't move but also didn't push her away. He wanted her to make him understand.

'Serge, I need you to know... I love you so... so very much. I have never loved you more, and you'll always be the centre of my universe.'

He looked at her, confused, the image of Jane naked with Razane all he could think about. He was unable to decide if it aroused him or made him feel betrayed.

'And you of mine...but... What are you saying?'

'I am,' she paused to take a deep breath, 'also in love with Razane!'

He stayed silent. Contextually this was where the conversation was heading, but it still did not resolve his bewilderment. His mind was just not catching up.

'So, what do you wanna do?' he said after a long pause.

'Nothing,' Jane said, 'I want you to make love to me so we can go to sleep. We can talk more in the morning. Just know this doesn't change anything between us. It doesn't need to. Like I said I love you and want you in my life forever. Now shush. Shut the light and perform your husbandly duties.'

He had not lost his erection. Their lovemaking was hotter than usual, almost animalistic. This was a completely different Jane.

They eventually fell asleep, naked, in each other's arms.

When he awoke Jane and Razane were busy laying the table for breakfast. It had been too late for Razane to return to her hotel so she'd slept on the couch but seemed none the worse for it.

'So, she told you?' Razane said coming up to him and taking his hands in hers.

'Yes, she did,' he said, a bit awkwardly.

'I'm so sorry you got a shock, I asked her to wait to tell you, but she is so... impulsive.'

'Yes, she cannot keep a secret,' he looked over at Jane. She was frying an egg and looked like she wasn't ready to be part of the conversation.

'It was not meant to be a secret,' Razane said gently, almost inaudibly. 'We just grew together, and it just happened.' She was watching him as if trying to gauge his thoughts.

He realised he didn't feel anything but warmth and empathy towards Razane. It was strange because she'd just upended all the paradigms in their lives. 'Well, it's a bit of a strange situation.' He didn't really know what to say. What did one say when one met one's wife's female lover for the first time. He wasn't sure there was a protocol.

'I am so sorry you were hurt. Jane told me so much about you. You seem like the nicest man.'

'I am not hurt, just a bit, umm, taken aback, I suppose, I don't own Jane. I just love her and don't want to lose her. That's all…' he said.

Jane came over and took his hand in one hand Razane's hand in the other. 'This doesn't need to change anything, Serge. You'll never lose me.'

'I also don't want us to grow apart.'

'That's never going to happen,' Jane said, kindly but firmly.

They were having this intimate, heartfelt conversation in front of Razane but somehow it seemed OK. He'd only just met her twenty-four hours ago, but she didn't feel like a stranger at all. There was something warm, magnetic and enchanting about her in the way she made him feel serene and aroused at the same time. It was something he'd only ever experienced with Jane.

He could feel the warmth of her hand and felt a connection that was more than just physical. He knew so little about her, yet she felt closer than a close friend, almost like a kindred spirit. It was all so confusing!

Of course, it was easy to rationalise. Razane was an amazing woman. He could understand how someone could fall in love with her. The same went for his beautiful lovely innocent warm-hearted and kind Jane. She was and always had been about love and warmth and giving. Falling in love with her was so natural. In fact, it was hard to know Jane and not fall in love with her. However, understanding it at the intellectual level did not help with or explain the emotional turmoil he felt.

'So, what do you want?' he asked Jane finally.

'Both of you in my life forever!' Jane had been ready with the answer.

They talked more over breakfast. It was the weekend, so they didn't need to go anywhere. They just lazed about and talked and got to know one another. Jane told Sergei about her new passion, Rumi's poetry.

Later that night when they were alone, Jane said, 'so what do you really think of Razane?'

'I like her a lot. She's warm and funny and so interesting. I feel relaxed with her and enjoy her company.'

Jane smiled and didn't say more. In her mind, she must have done a little victory dance. The first day was over, and they were all still friends.

He subsequently discovered that Jane had asked Razane the same thing the following morning while they were out for a walk.

'Sergei is adorable. You have got a great man,' Razane had said.

'Thank you,' Jane had said squeezing her arm.

'He seems open and honest and decent, so unlike any man I've ever met. I feel at ease, and like I can be myself around him. Like I can say anything, and he won't judge me.' She had put an arm around Jane. 'And he is so secure and confident.'

'That's Sergei. He's very comfortable with himself.'

'So many men are not.'

'Well, he's very talented and has always been with everything, including what's most important.' Jane had said with a twinkle in her eyes.

'I never knew I'd ever say this about a man, but I could so easily have sex with him,' Razane said, 'he just seems clean and pure and... uncomplicated.'

'I've never been bored with him. Actually, I've... never not come.'

'You know you would make a great saleswoman.' Razane had smiled, 'I would most likely buy anything from you.' They stopped in the middle of the street and hugged.

Over the next weeks, he and Razane grew close. Jane's intentions were obvious. She did everything she could to encourage it along. In any other situation such intervention would have backfired but somehow there was magic in the air, and it didn't. Razane was great fun to be around, deep and insightful and super sexy. Knowing her was like entering a whole new world he knew nothing about. It didn't hurt that she was a lovely person, decent, caring and non-judgemental.

Then like it had happened between Jane and Razane it also happened between Razane and him. He never did remember when he actually became aware of it, but it didn't matter. He fell in love with her and she with him. They became what Jane called a throuple. It was a strange word but far better than when she'd later jokingly called them his harem. He hated that word.

PRINCE CHARLES

Alipur Chatha, Friday 2 December, 1:30am

The back of the Land Rover was cramped and uncomfortable. The second-row seats were stowed up against the sides of the cabin. Damon lay diagonally in the awkwardly shaped space between the back of the front passenger seat and the tailgate.

The floor was not flat. A hard lump stuck in his back, every bump in the road sending a jolt of pain into his ribcage. His legs were elevated by a block of foam which put even more weight on his back. His knees and palms burnt savagely where they had scraped on the road. His wrists were on fire from the cable ties that bound them.

He tried moving his hands and wiggling his fingers to relieve the numbness. It didn't help. The cable ties were too tight.

He turned his head to look at the driver. He only saw his silhouette. He didn't look like what he had expected. The man was clean shaven, slim, and seemed in his late thirties. He wore a dark, open-collar shirt and expensive cologne. From his appearance, Damon would have judged him to be a doctor or a dentist rather than a kidnapper.

Damon was unable to see past the passenger seat backrest but by the way it was shaking over every bump it didn't seem occupied. It was only the driver and him in the vehicle.

If he could somehow get out of these restraints he could easily overpower the man, but how? He tested the ties but didn't have the leverage to do anything more than to make his wrists burn even more fiercely.

The sickly-sweet stuff the fucker had shoved in his face earlier had left an unpleasant metallic taste in his mouth. Whatever it was had knocked him out cold. He was still groggy and aware of a dull headache. He tried guessing how long he'd been out for but gave up. It probably wasn't for long, but he couldn't be sure. He had no idea of the time, where he was nor where he was going.

As his grogginess subsided, it was replaced with a sick feeling of worry for his parents, Razane and Mack. Out of the three, only Razane's phone had still been on the network. Hopefully, it was because his Dad and Mack had dropped theirs and not something far more awful. And where was his phone? Did he have it in his hands when he fell or was it in his pocket? He vaguely remembered putting it in his pocket just before he was struck by something. He must have been hit by this man in his vehicle. The bastard had sideswiped him. Why?

He tried moving his leg to feel for the phone. It was massive and bulky, and it would have made its presence felt by the way it tightened his pocket. It wasn't there. The fabric felt quite loose. Either he'd dropped it, or the man had taken it.

Fuck! Fury overtook him, momentarily but he managed to fight it. He had to stay calm and not antagonise the fellow.

'Hey man, where are you taking me?' Damon waited for an answer. There was no reply. Had the man heard him? The interior of the vehicle was boomy.

'Hey, mister, who are you and where are you taking me?' Damon said louder this time.

'Oh, hello there.' The man had a clipped and cultured British accent and sounded more like Prince Charles than an arsehole Pakistani kidnapper. 'I'm terribly sorry I had to restrain you. You kick like a mule.'

'Well alright, I won't kick. Can you please untie me? We can work this out...'

'Yes, well I'd love to but... I'm afraid, I cannot do that.'

'Can you at least loosen my hands?'

'Sorry, there old chap. But don't worry we're nearly there.'

'Nearly where? Who are you? And why are you... Why the fuck are you doing this?'

'It's what I do! I take care of problems for clients.'

'Mate, I've not done anything to you... What clients?' Damon knew the answer already.

'Of course, you haven't, dear. It's never personal.'

'Then tell me who your client is.'

'Sorry. Client confidentiality, old boy... It's something I take great pride in.'

'OK, what are you planning to do to me...?' Damon tried to keep his voice even. The man didn't reply. He tried to think of a way to gain the upper hand. Nothing came to him. It was always so easy in the movies. Sadly, this was real life. He was sure Ben would have thought of something.

'Let's not worry about that, my young fellow. My employer will probably just ask you a few questions, and then he might send you on your way.'

The man had heard after all. Could he believe him? He badly wanted to. Maybe it wasn't so bad after all. This guy didn't seem like the other people trying to kill them. Still who the fuck was he?

'Does he work for the government?'

'Who, my employer?'

'Yeah,'

'You can say that,' he said with a chuckle.

Just then the car went up a slight rise. What seemed like expansion strips in the road, reverberated through the cabin. Thrumming sounds indicated they were driving alongside a fence or a wall with gaps. Damon lifted himself and stole a glance out. The headlights of a truck passing in the opposite direction illuminated the bridge they were on. In the distance, through the fencing, he saw a lone boat on the water, fishing by floodlight or maybe dumping a body.

'That is the River Chenab, in case you're interested.'

Oh, the prick was a tour guide too, and he worked for the government. They were only going to ask him questions. That, at least, was a bit of good news, or was it? Didn't the CIA send terrorist suspects to Pakistan for questioning? What did they call it now? Advanced interrogation methods? No, the term was extraordinary rendition. It sounded terrible. Shit, he was fucked. He had a low tolerance for pain. Was Ben able to see his phone on the network? Even if he did what difference would it make? Maybe he could call the police. What if his parents followed? That's if they were alive. This could all turn messy. If only he could work out how to escape. He tried straining at the ties on his wrist. The burning in his wrist became unbearable, and he gave up.

After what seemed like an hour, the vehicle slowed and turned off the smooth bitumen onto a bumpy road. The pain in his rib cage became excruciating as the bumps became bigger and more frequent. After a while, the man dialled a number and said something in the local language.

The bumpy road ended in a rise, a dip then a slow climb. As soon as the vehicle stopped, the man jumped out. Damon heard voices and saw he was in the driveway of a large double storey house with huge glass windows.

The tailgate opened, and a light blinded him.

Jibran scowled at Abrar. 'Why bring him to me? I paid you to kill him.'

Abrar stiffened then realised Jibran had spoken in Punjabi. The young man wouldn't have understood. There was nothing to be gained by making him panic.

'You didn't exactly pay me, my friend,' Abrar said patiently as he showed Jibran the smartphone.

Jibran's brow furrowed. He didn't want to admit he didn't understand. 'Why you show me the phone?'

'Because you dum-dum. We can use it to see who else this

man is working with. We then call them and ask them to come and pick him up. Then we take care of them once and for all.'

Jibran brightened considerably. 'You are very clever, *yaar*,' he said, clapping Abrar on the back enthusiastically.

'*Oey*,' he shouted to his guards, 'Take him to the basement and lock him in the cage.'

'Come inside and let's look at the phone,' he said to Abrar and walked back into the house.

THE PASSWORD

Shisha Wal, Friday 2 December, 2:30am

'You dumb cunt motherfucker, sisterfucker, give me the password, or else I'll get my biggest man here to fuck you in the asshole till you bleed to death.' Jibran said as he hit Damon, again and again, his face livid with anger and frustration. His moustache twitched as he shouted.

Damon's face began to swell up. His left eye had closed, his lip was cut, yet he stayed silent. There was no way he could let them have the password. He wasn't sure who these people were and whether they were connected to the fuckers trying to kill them. His life was already in danger. He couldn't risk the others too.

'Ouufff,' Damon doubled up in pain, unable to breathe as the man punched him in the stomach.

He wasn't sure how long he could hold out in this cage, his hands tied to rings above his head. They'd removed his jumper and shirt and his shoes, and it was freezing cold.

Abrar wasn't enjoying the vulgar display of violence one bit. It was quite uncivilised, and Jibran seemed to be enjoying himself a bit too much. It was the first time he had visited Jibran in his village. In his house in the city, he was quite different, a bit crude and ostentatious but still reasonably civilised.

He'd been shocked when he saw the cage. It looked like it was built for a gorilla in the zoo except it had all manners of hooks and rings welded to it.

'Whatever do you need a cage for, *yaar*? I didn't know you were into S&M.'

'*Oey*, you city people, do not know the trouble we have with our workers,' Jibran had replied earnestly.

'You lock farm workers in there?' he'd asked, shaking his head in disbelief, 'whatever happened to just firing them?' He'd seriously considered walking out of there, but Jibran was not the type who forgot or forgave, ever. He decided to grit his teeth and bear it.

On one level Abrar felt sorry for the young man. He seemed like a kid from a good family, well-spoken and everything. But business was business, and a cup of tea was a cup of tea, like his grandmother used to say.

Jibran's tender mercies weren't working. The young man was resisting valiantly.

Was there another way to get the password? Abrar was not going to try and guess himself. Too many incorrect attempts would lock the phone and render it useless. He'd had that bad experience just recently himself.

Sometimes people wrote their password, or a hint of it, on their phone. This man didn't seem that stupid. Still, he turned the device over and tried looking for any writing. The lighting in the basement was dim, and a flickering tube light annoyed him, so he climbed the stairs. He was now in Jibran's private weapons room.

It was a huge space roughly six metres in length and four metres wide and laid out like a mini-museum. Rifles, pistols, and machine guns sat in racks along the far wall, grouped by era. The opposite wall held swords, knives, spears, maces, and pieces of armour. A glass case in the middle contained a dizzying array of torture implements. Jibran loved his weapons even more than he did. His gaze fell on the wall opposite the huge window and his collection of sniper rifles, the precision instrument of war. Jibran loved to show them off and lord his collection of rare sniper rifles over Abrar. Crowing that he had better and rarer guns than he did. He wasn't concerned he could not shoot straight. He did not have the temperament for it. The only weapon suitable for Jibran was a grenade, but ironically, he did not have any.

Here the lighting was better, and Abrar was able to examine the phone carefully. He took off the rubber cover but there was nothing apart from some scuff marks, and what looked like an ink blotch.

Then he noticed the screen. It had a plastic screen protector. He noticed the outline of a pattern on the surface, an area where the shine had dulled from wear.

It was a faint but nevertheless distinct M. He turned the phone on and entered the pattern on the screen. The phone unlocked.

Damn, he was clever. He looked through the phone. The young man's name was Damon. He went into the settings and turned the phone lock off then he noticed the Google Locations app. It showed a map of Jibran's village. The phone he was holding showed up as a blue dot blinking over Jibran's mansion. He checked for red dots to see who else was sharing their locations. One was in Australia. When he saw the other, he nearly dropped the phone.

'Shit,' he exclaimed as he ran back down the stairs. Jibran was out of the cage. He held an electric cable in his hand. One end went into a wall plug. The other end had been stripped down to the bare copper wire. He was going to electrocute him.

'Hey wait! I have managed to unlock it.' He was breathing heavily.

Jibran turned. A smile crept across his face. 'Wonderful! yaar.'

'Don't celebrate just yet. This young man, Damon has two people tracking him; Ben in Australia and Razane very near here.

'Wah yaar! that is amazing technology,' Jibran said enthusiastically. 'Very near here? Where?'

'On Phalia-Mandi Bahauddin Road. Maybe half an hour away.'

'That is fantastic technology.' He was like a broken record.

'Razane is the woman you wanted me to kill,' Abrar said.

'Yes, and Sergei, Mack and this man.' Jibran pointed at Damon.

'Well, I was waiting for them to leave the police station but you had to blow it up.'

'That was to kill Jane, the blonde woman,' Jibran said. 'But, *yaar*, let us talk after. First, we must welcome our visitors.' He ran upstairs. Abrar followed.

THE TRAP

Shisha Wal, Friday 2 December, 3:05am

'Move your fucking backsides, you sisterfuckers,' Jibran thundered at the men as they hurriedly clambered into the back of the pickup truck.

Abrar looked at him, disapprovingly. 'Do you have to be so crude? The upper classes need to be benevolent to those who serve them.'

'Fuck you too, *yaar*! You don't know these imbeciles. If you give them even an inch, they will take your whole arm... They are lazy and useless.'

'Well if you lock them in cages and torture them, they'll hardly be your willing subjects,' he said under his breath.

'How far away are they still?' Jibran asked, looking at the phone in Abrar's hand.

Abrar looked at the map. The red dot was still in the same place, on the main road to Mandi Bahauddin. It hadn't moved. It meant one of two things. Either Razane and Sergei had stopped for whatever reason, or more likely it was the last place they had a good signal. Abrar was willing to put money on the second. This part of Punjab had patchy mobile Internet coverage.

'They were on the Phalia-Mandi Bahauddin Road twelve minutes ago, but if they keep going at a hundred, they--'

'Stop talking your techie nonsense,' Jibran interrupted, 'what does it mean?'

Abrar had to restrain himself from slapping the man, 'did you go to school only to look at your teacher's tits?' he hissed. 'It means the closest they could be is about here.' He pointed to the map.

Jibran looked at it. It took a while, but finally, it clicked. 'Oh, now I understand,' he said.

'You want your men in place there… so they can block off their escape and… I would say… they need to hurry like mad.'

The road from the highway to their village had no name. It was a narrow track, part bitumen and part compressed dirt, and barely wide enough for a small car. Trucks had to drive slowly and navigate potholes and ruts on the side of the road. Only a capable off-road vehicle could confidently drive on it at anything close to speed.

Around four and a half kilometres off the highway the road branched into three at an intersection the locals called Panjo Katla Chowk. It translated to five murder intersection. Abrar was sure the five murders had something to do with Jibran's family. The *chowk* was around a kilometre from Jibran's village and mansion.

The middle road from Panjo Katla Chowk led to their village. The northern branch ran towards Shakar Parian and on to Sargodha Road. The southern was a dead end and led to more of Jibran's fields.

They planned for Jibran's men to wait on the southern road till their quarry had passed Panjo Katla Chowk then seal off their escape. A second group of armed men would wait for them in the village.

He and Jibran would be on the rooftop of his mansion, a massive double storey house built on a butte that gave it a commanding view of most of the surrounding countryside.

The road approaching the village from Panjo Katla Chowk ran through a divide in a small tree-covered hill, around two hundred and fifty metres from Jibran's mansion. It was slightly taller than the hill the mansion was built on. To see the road beyond the hill they had to climb to the mansion's rooftop. In the daytime, Panjo Katla Chowk was easily visible from that elevated position. At night, because there was no street lighting, it needed specialist equipment.

He was glad Jibran had night vision binoculars that used the latest technology with a range of twelve hundred metres. Jibran had boasted they were the only one of their kind in Pakistan. It made sense. They were banned from being exported out of the US.

Abrar lay on a blanket on the rooftop looking through the night scope of Jibran's Barrett MRAD. It was an awesome 50 calibre sniper rifle with a far greater range than his SIG. This gun made him want to cream his pants. It was another one of Jibran's rare weapons and had apparently been smuggled from Iraq, where it had been captured from the US military. It was also fitted with the latest night scope that enabled the rifle to have an effective range of over nine-hundred-metres in near darkness.

Unlike Jibran, he could put it to good use. He'd asked him a few times to sell it, but he had a better chance getting Jibran to suck his dick. What a terrible waste that this bumbling amateur had such great weaponry and didn't even know how to use it.

'Hey Jibran, I need you to get me one of these Barretts with the same scope.'

'Sure *yaar*, no problem. You just can't have mine,' Jibran replied.

'So, when's that going to happen, before or after the cows come home? You dimwitted fuckface,' Abrar muttered to himself.

They waited on the rooftop and watched the lights of the pickup truck as it slowly made its way past the row of huts that marked the end of the village proper. As it crested a rise between the two sides of the small hill, it began picking up speed.

Jibran looked through his binoculars and Abrar used the scope to focus on Panjo Katla Chowk. 'We're lucky there's no fog between the *chowk* and here. It was becoming thick in Lahore on my way here,' Abrar muttered.

'Well, it shows Allah is with me,' Jibran replied, brightly.

'If Allah were with you, he'd have given you more brains,'

Abrar muttered under his breath. Come to think of it if Allah were real he wouldn't have made Jibran in the first place.

The pickup was now approaching Panjo Katla Chowk. Their quarry was nowhere to be seen. In the distance, a faint row of car and truck lights marked out Phalia-Mandi Bahauddin Road.

Abrar stiffened. He thought he'd seen something. He took a deep breath to steady his scope. It was incredibly hard to do because more than ninety-nine percent of his field of vision was complete blackness. Finding a car's lights without at least getting a reference from the surrounds was like finding a needle in a haystack.

Then he saw it again. It was a car, its lights on, just visible through the trees. It was halfway between Panjo Katla Chowk and the highway. The undulating countryside had hidden it till then.

'I think I see something, can I have the binoculars please?' Abrar said.

He looked through them. The vehicle was still too far outside the range of the binoculars to be seen clearly, but he could make out the headlights and around it an indistinct white shape.

They would be at Panjo Katla Chowk in about two minutes. He checked the map. The red dot was still on the highway where it was before. He'd been right.

He handed the binoculars back to Jibran and lay down on the rooftop. He looked through the Barrett's scope, aimed it at Panjo Katla Chowk and waited.

'Sergei we've lost Ben's voice call and GPS signal,' Razane said.

'Damn.' That was a bit of bad luck. The map had shown a right turn off the highway. Now they'd have to find it without the help of GPS.

Sergei strained to look for it. Visibility was poor. There was no overhead lighting and, no painted lines or cat's-eyes to delineate the lanes or even the edge of the road. To make matters worse, it had rained some time ago. Every car that passed sprayed a fine mist of muddy water on their windscreen. They were out of washer fluid, and the wipers were smearing a fine brown slurry across the glass.

Sergei almost overshot the turn. He'd been keeping track of the odometer from the last intersection and was expecting the road. Even then, at first, he didn't see it. It wasn't signposted nor marked in any way and just looked like a big ditch on the side of the highway. If he'd been driving any faster, he'd have missed it for sure.

'Hold on,' he shouted as he braked hard. He stepped off the brakes and as the car levelled out he swung the wheel sharply right. The front tyres squealed in protest as the car squirmed and threatened to understeer into the fields.

The road turned out to be hardly better than a mud track with patches of bitumen at irregular distances. Had he taken the right path?

'What do you think sweetheart?' he asked Razane who was now sitting back calmly pretending not to have noticed the dangerous turn.

'I say, let's keep going,' she said. 'If it's the right road we'll come to an intersection in around five kilometres. If we don't, we turn back.' She tried dialling Ben again. There was no response.

Jane moaned in her sleep. Razane placed a hand on her forehead. She had a slight temperature.

Ben was beside himself. He'd lost them. Their signal had been stuck since the last ten minutes. Goodness knew where they were. He could still see Damon's position. It had stopped in what looked like a small village with a large building at the end of a narrow road among the fields. Did they even have a plan to rescue him? He was about to ask when their voice signal dropped.

Like Sergei and Razane, he was quite certain his brother had been taken captive. Damon had described the men who'd attacked the police station after the bomb. They'd fired indiscriminately into the destroyed shell, determined to kill any survivors. It made little sense the same men would take Damon captive unless they'd realised his Mom had survived and Damon was an insurance policy. Or his kidnapper was someone new.

Nothing made sense anyway. It hadn't from the beginning. Why would someone go to such lengths to try and kill his family in the first place? Was his mother hiding something? She'd done other strange things like be a lesbian with Razane.

What if Damon's captors had been able to access his phone? They'd be able to see Razane's position on Google Maps and prepare an ambush.

Never underestimate your enemy. Wasn't that the first rule of war? Or the third, or whatever. It didn't bloody matter. The more he thought about it, the more plausible it seemed. Suddenly he was certain. What a bunch of fucking amateurs they all were, not to have thought of it before.

Ben tried dialling again and pressed the refresh button on the map location app again and again. There was nothing. No reply. His fingers moved feverishly as he typed out a message.

'STOP! DANGER! GO BACK IMMEDIATELY!'

He copied the message onto every messaging app he had. He sent the messages a second time and a third. He redialled again and again. His breath was coming in fits. He was shaking. Why the fuck hadn't he thought of it before?

THE REALISATION

Shisha Wal, Friday 2 December, 3:15am

M ajor Imran Hamdani drove as fast as visibility through the fog allowed. They needed to hurry. It was early morning, and thankfully, traffic was light. Only shift workers and night owls would be out at this time. Fazal and Yousaf were in the car with him.

In better circumstances, he would have enjoyed the early morning drive. It reminded him of happier times when Lahore was cleaner, less hectic, and people smiled more often.

He loved his city. He had travelled to Washington, New York and London for work, so he knew what a developed city in a rich country looked and felt like. Lahore was dirty and disorganised, overcrowded, and polluted but it had a special feel few other cities had. It had a deep connection with its past, beautiful food and lovely people; well, at least some of them were. It was not just his blind patriotism. Most of the overseas intelligence agents he had hosted over the years had been uncomfortable at first when they arrived. After they left they almost always missed it. A CIA contact had compared Lahore to an old but graceful woman sleeping under a dirty blanket.

Sadly, her blanket was getting putrid, and she was close to suffocating.

Lahore was growing uncontrollably. A sizeable number of young people were unemployed or wrongfully employed. Worryingly it had become a base for several new terrorist groups, and the government was not doing enough to root them out. Too many were too busy stuffing their faces and lining their pockets to care.

He looked over at Fazal. 'Where are they?'

'I'm checking... This phone is stuck. I am going to restart it.'

They had just left Mayo Hospital. A bandage covered Yousaf's right eye. The doctor had removed a thin shard of glass from his eyeball. The rest of his face was peppered with cuts and nicks.

Fazal had been luckier. He was in the toilet when the bomb exploded. Its window had no glass in it, so there had been nothing to shatter. He had nearly jumped out of his skin and had peed on himself in the process. The major had not let him go home and change, and he felt unclean and was sure he stank. He could still feel wet patches in his trousers and almost wished he could have traded places with Yousaf.

'OK, one more moment. I have started it,' Fazal said. 'One... second sir. Yes... the foreigners are on... Phalia-Mandi Bahauddin Road.'

The app was the ISI's internal software that had recently been adapted to a smartphone. It used the country's military satellites rather than the commercial ones the public depended on for their navigation. It was far more accurate and covered the whole country.

'Good, keep an eye on it,' the major said as they turned into Charsadda Street, 'and let me know if they change route.' With any luck, they would catch up with the car and its occupants in the morning. He would then discover why they had driven to the middle of Punjab just after the bomb had gone off. It didn't make sense, not unless they had a hand in it.

His thoughts were interrupted by a police constable gesticulating furiously for them to turn around. He ignored him and stopped, a few metres away, at the temporary barrier. The constable ran up to him shouting angrily but immediately quieted down when he saw his badge.

'Sorry, sir!'

The major ignored him. 'You two come with me,' he said to his underlings.

The building had been cordoned off with police tape. A noisy generator was providing electricity to four powerful floodlights. The whole scene was a hive of activity. Forensic teams were sifting through the debris, taking photographs and marking things. He had to flash his badge several times to be allowed through.

What he saw left him reeling. The police station was utterly destroyed. The front of the building had a gaping hole about twenty metres at its widest. The inside was all blackened. A strong and unpleasant odour, a mix of chemicals and burnt human flesh and hair dominated the senses. The back wall of the building had an even larger hole. About half the roof had completely collapsed and lay on the floor. Through the hole in the rear, he saw another larger pile of rubble. It used to be a mosque. He had prayed there several times. It had collapsed as well.

The major carefully stepped inside what remained of the building. About two-thirds of the left wall, a third of the rear wall, the whole of the right wall and about half the front wall still stood. Inside the smell of burnt flesh and hair became overpowering. He had smelled it before, but it always turned his stomach. Yousaf and Fazal both looked queasy.

'If you want to be sick, do it outside,' the major said a bit more firmly than he had intended.

He took a small torch out of his pocket and shone it around. No internal walls were left standing. The fallen portion of the roof had crushed half the cells as well as the administration area. Dust covered bodies, including some in police uniform, lay among the rubble. In the remaining cells bodies were shrouded in white cloth stained red and black. The rest of the roof looked precarious. It would not take much to bring it all down.

The major walked over and lifted a sheet. The body was badly charred and not recognisable as a human.

'Are they all like this?' he asked a technician with a camera.

'Yes, sir. I have never seen a blast this bad. It was a multi-stage device. They even used ball-bearings.' The man looked positively unhappy to be there.

The major didn't blame him. He wondered which cell Jane Kelly had been held in. There was no way to tell. The records would have been kept in the administration area which had been obliterated. It would take days to remove all the bodies and get their DNA samples analysed. There wasn't going to be another way of identification. The bodies were mangled and burnt beyond recognition.

Further in, the steel door to the courtyard had buckled and distorted and was peppered with bullet holes. It was ajar. The major walked out into the courtyard. This was the only part of the police station that had not suffered structural damage. The visitor huts still stood. Two bodies, police guards, lay under sheets in the courtyard near the door. He uncovered them. Their necks were twisted, and their hair and uniforms had been singed.

'The flame front must have come through this door,' he said to Fazal and Yousaf who looked like they were going to be sick again. 'You can see how it has burnt this big patch on the side of this hut.'

'Was this side door open when you got here?' the major asked a second man taking photographs.

'No sir, we had to break through. We were hoping to find survivors.'

The huts in the courtyard were undamaged. The door to the rearmost hut was open. It was empty, and apart from a layer of dust, there was no sign of damage inside. Anyone in there could have survived.

Yousaf had told him the bomb had gone off while Jane's visitors were in the police station. It meant they were probably either in the administration area or in her cell or even, quite possibly, out here in the courtyard. It could explain why one of the huts was unlocked. What arrangement had they made with the superintendent to visit out of hours? There was no respect for the rule of law.

The major walked to the back of the courtyard and through the hole into the mosque compound. The mosque would have to be pulled down and rebuilt.

'Be careful sir, the dome collapsed just after we got here,' a duty officer said, 'by how it looks it could collapse further.'

He could see no reason for it not to. Nothing substantial was holding the large dome up any longer. 'Thank you,' he said as he picked his way around the outside of the destroyed building. Fazal and Yousaf followed him like shadows.

They were now on Sanda Road, which resembled a war zone. Work crews were using shovels, bare hands, and a bulldozer to clear the debris from the road.

'Sir, they have just turned west off Phalia-Mandi Bahauddin Road and are heading down a small track.'

'I, I can see the intersection,' Sergei said.

There was no reply from the back seat. Razane was staring intently at her phone. Their GPS location was still stuck, and there was barely any phone signal. A new message appeared on her screen.

'Oh my God! Stop!' Razane screamed. Jane opened her eyes in surprise. 'Stop, stop, please!' Razane repeated.

Sergei applied the brakes hard. Their bodies strained against the seatbelts as the Corolla ground to a halt.

'Why, what happ--'

'A message just came through,' she said speaking rapidly, 'it's from Ben. All he said is stop immediately You are in Danger!!!.'

What did that mean?

'Serge, I am scared. We should get out of here.'

In the village, on the mansion's rooftop Abrar watched as the Toyota approached and stopped just short of the intersection. A large bush obscured most of the car except for the bonnet. He made a final adjustment to the scope. He had done all his trajectory calculations using the ballistics calculator app on his phone. Even then this was going to be a real challenge, for him and the Barrett.

'Now move forward a bit more so I can see you,' he muttered. They had stopped, for some unknown reason. Had they somehow realised? He had to take the shot now. He aimed at where the driver's seat would be and fired. The bolt-action was deliciously smooth, he fired twice more in rapid succession.

Sergei put the car in reverse and floored the pedal. The tyres chirped as the Corolla lurched rearwards. Something struck the front with a loud metallic clang just as three shots rang out. He swung the wheel around; the car pivoted sharply. It now faced the direction they'd come from. He put it into first and accelerated hard.

South of Panjo Katla Chowk, Guddu, the pickup driver, answered the phone with trembling hands. It was the *wadera*.

'Catch the car you son of a bitch. Do what I sent you for!' Jibran shouted.

Shaking, even more, Guddu put the phone down. He had been waiting for the car to pass the intersection just like the *wadera* had ordered but he had not seen it. He was sure he had not fallen asleep.

'Did you see it, Ali?' He asked the man beside him.

'No, I did not see any car,' Ali said. Of course, that was not going to matter to the *wadera*. They would all be in big trouble when they got back if they did not catch them. Guddu started the engine and drove to the intersection. The tail lights of a car were heading towards the highway, opposite to what he was expecting. Guddu turned the wheel and accelerated as hard as he could, after them. The pickup lurched awkwardly. He could not let them get away.

UNDERSTEER

Shisha Wal, Friday 2 December, 4:10am

The night was still pitch black. Their headlights illuminated the bumpy road, the heavily rutted verge, and the green grasses on the edge of the fields on either side. A huge cloud of dust billowed behind them, lit red by their tail lights. Through the dust, a pair of headlights, a car or truck, was following them.

Sergei drove as fast as he felt safe, but their pursuers were managing to keep up, neither gaining nor falling back. The Corolla's suspension was getting a real workout as it struggled to cope with all the undulations in the road.

Did the bullet hit something vital? There were no unexpected sounds from the front of the car, just the hum of the engine and the staccato of gravel hitting the car's underside. Touch wood, it hadn't damaged the car in any critical way.

'To me, that sounded like a large calibre round,' Razane said shifting so she could better cushion Jane's head against the bumps.

She had an uncanny way of picking up on what he was thinking.

'I wonder where they were firing from,' Sergei said.

'I distinctly heard the shot after the bullet hit the car. So, it must have been from quite a distance away...'

'In this pitch-black darkness?'

'Yes, that was very scary,' Razane said. She hated snipers. It was the stuff of her nightmares. They were the silent, grim reapers who could snatch anyone's life in the blink of an eye. For most victims, there was no awareness of death. One minute they were the next minute they weren't. Maybe that was why she became one herself. The best to fight fear was head-on.

'What in the world are we up against?' Sergei muttered quietly.

'A highly skilled sniper, for sure,' she said.

'Army?'

'Out here it could be anyone. Maybe… it is a militia group.'

'They obviously were expecting us,' Sergei said.

'Oh, yes. You are right. But--'

'The only way they'd have known is if they were able to get into Damon's phone. They would then have seen us approaching.'

'We were very lucky back there,' Razane said.

Fuck, she was right. But luck sooner or later ran out. They had to act smarter from now on. He had to shake off whoever was following them. From the lights, it obviously wasn't a modern car. Lights on newer cars were all funny irregular shapes and almost white. These were circular and yellow. They were also quite a bit higher than on a car. It must be a pickup truck, an old one. Shame on him if he couldn't lose them in a modern car.

'Hold on, it's gonna get bumpy,' Sergei said as he pressed his foot on the accelerator.

The potholes were coming frighteningly fast. He had to focus hard to avoid some of the deep ones, but slowly their lead increased.

Sergei was concentrating so hard on getting away from their pursuers he forgot about the highway. There were also no road signs or signals to warn him. They were at the intersection and going too fast to stop. He managed to do a quick head check, saw a gap in traffic and aimed for it, hoping the car would handle the change of direction as well as the change of road surface.

The little Toyota shook and became airborne for the briefest moment as it left the dirt road and came crashing down on the bitumen. He had the presence of mind to wait till the wheels loaded up before he steered to follow the highway. The tyres squealed as they scrabbled for grip, the car understeering like mad, threatening to spear into oncoming traffic.

Thankfully, a gap in the cars coming from the opposite direction allowed Sergei the space to let the Toyota drift into the opposite lane just enough to take the pressure off the tortured tyres. As soon as he regained control, he straightened back into their lane.

Fuck, that was close. He took a deep breath and gunned the engine. The car surged forward. Razane looked back. The pickup had not yet reached the intersection.

'I have a feeling we're OK,' she said, 'our white Toyota looks like the ones in front and behind us.'

Sergei looked back and smiled. They were in a group of four other light-coloured Toyota Corollas.

'I never thought I would find a use for a white Corolla,' Sergei said.

'Or a black burka for that matter,' Razane said. She was breathing hard from the excitement of the chase. 'That was good driving, but I almost fainted back there.'

'One does one's best...'

The phone rang, startling them. It was Ben. They had mobile phone coverage again. 'Are you guys OK?' He was almost screaming.

'Yes, yes, calm down. We are,' Sergei said.

'We were almost ambushed,' Razane said, 'someone shot at the car.'

'What happened? Are you OK?'

'Yes, thank goodness. We were lucky,' Sergei said.

'So, you drove down the small road to where Damon--?'

'Yup,'

'Did you get my messages?'

'Yes, just where we stopped. It's why we stopped,' Razane said shuddering at what had almost happened.

'You know how stupid we all are?' Ben said. 'You could

have been killed.'

Sergei wasn't sure how to respond. It did seem like the dumbest thing he had ever done. He wasn't even sure what he had been expecting would happen if they had made it to Damon's location.

'Yeah, I am not sure I was even thinking,' he said in a monotone. He felt deeply embarrassed.

Razane sensed his thoughts, leaned forward, and squeezed his shoulder, 'don't be too hard on yourself, my love, I stopped thinking too.'

'I have been Googling a few things,' Ben said. 'Firstly, it seems Mum has a concussion. She needs to rest. Also, I looked at the map and thought of something we could do. But it depends on whether you can buy some smartphones. If you can? Buy two with two external--'

'What are you thinking... External what?'

There was no reply. Razane fished the phone out of her pocket. It was dead. The battery had run out, and they had no means to charge it. They were flying blind, again.

'We have to buy a charger, and we might as well get ourselves some new smartphones from the nearest town.' Sergei said.

'Yes,' Razane said, 'then let's find a place to sit down, gather our thoughts and come up with a plan.'

A plan sounded like a good idea. The nearest town was Mandi Bahauddin. Fifteen minutes later they entered its outskirts. They drove through the narrow streets while the small town was still fast asleep, following signs to the city centre.

At that time of the morning, it was nothing much to look at, just a collection of mainly drab rendered brick houses and shops built around a walled city, dating back to the Mughal era, and a magnificent mosque. The roads in the centre of town were laid out in a gridiron pattern with a notable absence of any street lights or traffic signals.

A few stores advertised the latest Samsung and Apple

phones, but they were closed.

The only shops open were a bakery and a tea stall. Sergei bought some sweet buns and cups of milky *chai*. They ate in the car. The *chai* was robust and sweet and woke them up. Jane felt a bit better. Her fever and headache had subsided a bit, but she still felt dizzy and drained.

'My darling, finish your tea and put your head back in my lap,' Razane said, 'You have a mild concussion from the blast.' Jane obediently complied.

Sergei tried to think of what to do next, but his mind drew a blank. He could not remember the last time he'd felt this powerless. Who were they dealing with? What did they want?

Even if they knew, they had no way of contacting them to negotiate and no means to fight either. It was like a game of chess, and they had run out of moves.

When the shops opened, they could get back online. What to do till then?

'We should not just sit around feeling bad,' Razane said interrupting his thoughts, 'Shakar Parian is close. Can we go and get Jane's things?'

'Huh, yes, good idea,' he responded.

'By the time we get back, the phone shops will be open.'

'You know you're amazing,' he said looking back, 'how you can sense what I'm thinking.'

She reached over and stroked his face 'It's called love,' she said softly. 'I'm inside of you, and you're inside of me.'

'Rumi?'

'No Razane,' she said smiling.

THE VILLAGE

Shakar Parian, Friday 2 December, 4:30am

E ven though dawn was over two hours away, the sky had just started to lighten slightly, but the low cloud cover meant it was still almost completely dark at ground level. The van pulled into the Shakar Parian car park. As was common with many villages in this part of Punjab the residential zone of the village was for pedestrians and cycles only. A low mud wall kept cars out.

The men piled out, closed the doors quietly, and walked quickly and silently through the gap in the wall towards the collection of huts. No one heard them. They were all fast asleep.

Eight men took up positions around the village square while two doused the large wooden gazebo with petrol from the jerry cans they carried.

The flammable liquid sloshed onto the wooden structure and soaked into the dry timber. A strong smell carried by the volatile fumes spread through the village.

A few sleeping people stirred. The men stepped back. Abdul Zubair gave the signal, and Adil flicked a match onto the soaked timber structure.

The flames caught with a huge 'whoosh' that resonated through the sleeping settlement like a thunderclap. Within seconds tongues of fire were licking the rafters. Ten seconds later the whole gazebo was alight. The wood around the batteries burned furiously.

The villagers were among them; their sleep filled faces

showing bewilderment and shock as they stood transfixed by the blaze.

Abdul Zubair lifted his AK74 rifle above his head, pointed it skyward and fired a short burst. The gunfire would have sounded like the skies were falling to those still asleep. More startled people appeared in the square.

'Death to the blasphemers, death to Americans,' he shouted and fired in the air again.

Two villagers brought buckets of water in a feeble attempt to put out the fire, which by then was licking the canopy of the tall banyan tree.

Burnt Saleem stepped forward and smashed the nearest man in the head with the butt of his rifle. He collapsed. The other immediately put his bucket down. A few rushed to help the fallen man, but no one made any further moves to extinguish the flames. They just stood and watched, horrified, as their great pride and joy, went up in flames.

'Who is the headman of the village?' Abdul Zubair called out loudly.

Allah Boota stepped forward, the expression on his face a mix of fear and hate.

Abdul Zubair went up to him. 'You have one day to leave this village,' he said imperiously. 'If there is even one man still here tomorrow morning we will return and kill you all.'

Allah Boota was momentarily speechless at the sheer brazenness of his demands. '*Maulana Sahib*, these are our homes, our fields,' he implored, 'why are you chasing us away? Where will we go?'

'You can go to hell,' Abdul Zubair was getting furious at this villager, 'You cooperated with a blasphemer. We could file charges against you all.'

'*Sahib* we did not know what the woman was going to do. We did not help her.'

'You kept her amongst you. You are all guilty,' he snapped.

'*Sahib*, please have mercy on us. We have small children;

they have not done anything to you.'

'One day! Or we return and kill your small children. Tell me you understand.'

Allah Boota stood there, nonplussed, saying nothing.

'Tell me you understand.' Abdul Zubair walked over to where a young girl stood holding on to her mother's legs and aimed the rifle at her.

'Yes *Sahib*, yes. We will do as you ask,' he said hurriedly but in a resigned voice.

'To make sure you obey, I will leave two of my men here. Adil and Osama you watch them. The rest of you... we leave!'

He pulled the two to one side. 'If they give any trouble start shooting them one by one,' he said loudly, making sure the villagers could hear. He was looking at Allah Boota as he spoke.

Dawn was now an hour away, and the sky was starting to lighten. Dense clouds still veiled the ground in darkness. The glow of the fire became visible as soon as they turned off Sargodha Road. It was magnified by the light wispy fog that blanketed the countryside.

'Oh my God!' Jane put her hand to her mouth, 'that's the village.' She was looking a bit better and was sitting up.

'Something's on fire there!' Sergei said, 'what could it be?'

'All the huts have straw roofs, and there's the timber gazebo we built.'

As they approached, a beaten up old Suzuki drove out of the village car park and headed in the opposite direction. 'That's Allah Boota's car. He's the village chief,' Jane said sounding concerned. 'Something's wrong.'

'He seemed in a hurry,' Sergei said.

'Maybe going to get help or taking someone to hospital,' Razane said.

'I wonder how the fire started,' Sergei muttered. 'I guess we're gonna find out soon enough.'

They turned into the car park. It was empty except for an old flatbed Daihatsu truck and a small white Suzuki Alto.

'Do these belong to the villagers?' Sergei asked.

'Yup.'

'My darling, you should stay in the car and out of sight,' Razane said as she felt Jane's forehead again. 'Thank God, your fever has gone down a bit.'

'I feel a lot better,' Jane replied. 'I'll stay, but please be careful.'

'Yes, of course, sweetheart,' Sergei said. 'By the way, how do we find your hut?'

'Hmmm,' Jane thought for a moment, 'if you follow the path through that gap in the wall you come to the centre of the village. It's a largish space where everyone gathers to socialise. The gazebo's in the middle of it, and all the huts are in a kind of a rough circle around it. My hut was a bit more towards the centre of the circle. There's a tree behind they didn't wanna cut, so they moved the hut forward. You'll notice it straight away.'

'What should we tell them if they ask who we are?' Sergei said.

'Just say you're a grieving relative collecting my things. You look white, they'll believe you.'

It sounded simple but so many things could go wrong. They usually did. Something strange was going on here. For one, fires didn't just start on their own.

'We should stay out of sight until we can be sure it's safe,' Razane said. She was thinking about the fire too.

Jane lay on the back seat and covered herself with the burka. Razane checked from outside. She was invisible. Sergei locked the car with the key. The remote would have made the car beep and given them away. He was glad he thought of it. Then he and Razane walked towards the village centre along the narrow path.

They heard the hubbub of a village already awake and soon saw the flames through the trees. A large structure had collapsed into a black burning pile of wood and ash like a large scattered bonfire. They could just make out the shape of the roof which was the last thing still burning. 'That was Jane's gazebo,' Razane said in a hushed voice. 'I saw photographs she posted on Facebook. This will crush her!'

Trying to keep out of sight they turned off the track and made their way through the undergrowth behind a cluster of huts. From here they had a direct line of sight between two huts into the village square. The villagers were talking animatedly to two armed men, holding what appeared to be assault rifles.

'That's trouble right there,' Sergei said quietly, 'I don't like the look of those men one bit.'

'Nor I,' Razane replied, 'they don't look like from this village.'

The two men looked most unpopular just then. The villagers had made a semi-circle around them and were starting to speak louder and more aggressively. The men had backed up against the front wall of one of the huts.

'The only thing stopping a lynching are their guns,' Sergei remarked.

'I believe we have no choice but to disarm them.' Razane whispered, 'otherwise we are not leaving with Jane's things. That or someone gets hurt.'

'Got a plan?' he said.

'Follow me, my love.'

'To the ends of the fucking earth and beyond, my darling,'

'What, only the earth?'

'The Solar System,'

'Only?'

'The galaxy,' he whispered

'Is that the extent of your love?'

'The universe, the multiverse, beyond infinity, to the end of time...'

Razane did not reply. She saw a log pile. Next to it was an axe with a long handle. She selected a sturdy stick thicker than her forearm.

'This will suit you,' she said. Sergei swung it in an arc to test its weight and balance.

'Careful!' she picked up the axe and felt its blade. It was razor sharp.

His reply was drowned by a loud succession of gunshots. The men had fired in the air. The sudden silence was broken by falling leaves and branches.

There was never a time like the present. Razane sprinted forward.

'Oh shit,' Sergei muttered, quite unprepared, and followed on her heels, trying to be as quiet as possible.

The two men now aimed their guns at the villagers, who had moved back a few steps, as one. Their assailants advanced, menacingly, weapons still pointing at the crowd, shouting something. The villagers backed away a few steps more.

Razane was almost level with the front of the hut. Sergei was right on her heels. The men fired at the ground in front of the villagers. The crowd broke and ran. Several stumbled and fell. Women screamed.

Razane and Sergei burst through the gap between the huts. They were now three metres behind the men. Some in the crowd noticed them and turned. With a fierce cry, Razane leapt towards the man further from her, swinging the axe viciously. Sergei charged his partner. They both half turned, eyes wide in shock. Razane's axe cleaved into his forehead before he managed to turn his gun around. He dropped like a stone. Blood began gushing out as she tried unsuccessfully to rip the axe back out, but it was stuck solid. She had to let go of the handle, Sergei needed her help.

Sergei meanwhile hadn't been close enough. The second man had almost completed turning, and Sergei was still half a metre short. Razane kicked the man from behind just below his knee then threw her weight against his back. He stumbled and fell to his knees, the barrel of his gun digging into the ground. The impact left Razane badly winded.

The man tried straightening and lifting his gun. Sergei was now in position but was unable to swing his stick for fear of hitting Razane. Instead, he leapt up and kicked the man in the head with all the force he could muster. The man's head snapped back. Sergei managed to check his forward momentum and in the same motion stamped down hard on the stock of the rifle causing him to drop it.

Razane fell against Sergei, but he caught her and helped her straighten up. The first man with the axe still embedded in his skull was still twitching on the ground. Before any of the villagers could move Razane scooped up both rifles and handed one to Sergei.

'I knew our Taekwondo would come in handy,' Sergei muttered.

The first man was now still. Razane placed her boot on his head and wrenched the axe from his skull. The gushing blood became a brief torrent that spread across the dusty ground. Then his heart stopped pumping, and the blood stopped.

The other man lay on his back, his legs folded beneath him, groaning.

'This is one of the men who attacked us in front of the hotel,' Razane said in a flat icy voice, as she looked at the bloody corpse.

Sergei was stunned how, in the blink of an eye, Razane had changed from a soft and loving woman into a cold-blooded killer. She appeared calm and in control, and he was shaking like a leaf.

'Tie him up,' she said to no one in particular. 'Do you have rope?'

Someone came running with a few coils of blue and yellow nylon cord. Sergei turned the injured man onto his stomach as Razane tied his arms and then his hands firmly behind his back.

'Wow, you can try that on me one day, my queen,' Sergei whispered to her. He always used humour when he was stressed.

Razane acknowledged him with a grimace. She'd gone

completely pale and looked positively ill. As soon as she had tied the last knot, she ran behind the hut and vomited. Sergei went with her and held her hair back gently. Someone came running with a bottle of water. Razane accepted it gratefully and took a few sips. She still looked a bit woozy, but the colour returned to her face.

Her control had been a facade. He should have known. 'Are you OK?' He murmured. His hand lay comfortingly on her shoulder.

'I, I just killed another man...' there was a pained look on her face.

He knew what she meant. Razane had told them how she'd had to leave the Peshmerga. Years of trauma had led to violent nightmares and depression. She had frozen during combat, and her comrades had died as a result. It was only after meeting Jane and then him that she'd started feeling human again. But she was not completely cured. In spite of weekly treatments for her post-traumatic stress disorder the nightmares still tormented her. She often woke in the middle of the night screaming and gasping for air. He and Jane, would hold and comfort her and soothe her back to sleep.

He remembered a conversation around a campfire on their weekend property. They were telling each other ghost stories. Jane had just finished hers. Razane then said something that sent shivers up his spine. 'Every life I have ever taken stays with me. It is like their spirits hang around, angry with me for ending their lives.'

Jane had reached over, 'it's because you are such a warm kind soul,' she had said gently stroking her back. 'You were not meant to be a fighter.'

'Not many people choose to fight, sometimes fights choose people,' Razane had replied.

That's what had happened to them now. They hadn't asked for any of this.

It was awful to see Razane in pain. In a way, she was far

more delicate and fragile than Jane. Jane got hurt easily but also bounced back fast. Razane was deeper; she bottled everything up.

He had to be the strong one and not put Razane in such a situation again. Bloody hell, he should have taken the lead just then. But how would he have handled it? He would probably have gotten both of them killed in the process. Being a third Dan in Taekwondo didn't prepare a person for a real fight; only combat experience did. He also didn't have her killer instincts. She had moved like a leopard and killed like one. But he couldn't let his beautiful, lovely Razane, the love of his life, one of the two loves of his life, continue to be what she no longer wanted or was able to be. He had to step up.

The villagers were debating amongst themselves what to do when Sergei and Razane joined them.

'I am Sergei, Jane's husband. This is Razane, her sister.'

'I am teacher of children in here village,' a small skinny man dressed in a singlet, and a loincloth said. 'We are thanking you for help with bad men.' If he looked relieved, he wasn't showing it. None of them were. Maybe they were worried about repercussions

'What happened?' Sergei asked.

In a few words, the teacher told them what had happened in the early morning and how their chief had gone for help. The rest of the crowd nodded along. In the meanwhile, three men placed the body on a *charpoy* and covered it with a sheet.

'We are very very sad… for Jane. She was big sister for whole village. May Allah grant her *Jannat ul Firdous*,' the teacher said.

'Yes, may Allah grant her *Jannat*,' Razane agreed as Sergei nodded too.

Jane's hut was small and neat. The red suitcase, she had been living out of, sat on an empty metal trunk. It was closed but unzipped. Razane switched on a battery-powered camping lantern as they examined her room. A half-read book lay on a mat on the floor beside the bed. Next to it was a compact charger pack for her phone, a charging cable, and a battery-powered reading lamp. On a small chair in the corner, two water bottles and a toiletry bag lay on a neatly folded pile of towels and pressed clothes.

The suitcase was already partly packed. Jane's wallet and passport were in a side pocket. Razane packed the rest of her things. 'Check the pillowcase and the bedding,' she said, handing Sergei the lantern.

Sergei looked carefully over the bed sheets; they seemed freshly laid. He found nothing that could be used to test for DNA. Not wanting to take chances, he removed the pillowcase and gave it to Razane to pack.

After another glance around the hut, they said goodbye to the villagers and walked back to the car. Razane had a sudden thought and stopped. 'Keep going; I will only be a moment,' she said and ran back.

Jane stood outside the car waiting for them, beside herself with worry. She ran over and hugged him. 'I heard shots. Are you OK? Where's Razane?'

'She's just coming.' He told her what had happened. 'We got these guns from the men who killed Simon,' he said loading the suitcase and the rifles in the boot.

Jane looked worried. 'Where are they?'

Razane joined them, breathing heavily. 'They will not need these.' She held out two mobile phones. 'It will save us buying SIM cards.'

'Oh, great.' Sergei smiled.

'Where are the men?' Jane asked again.

'One of them is tied up, and the other is, um... dead,' Sergei looked at Jane, knowingly.

Jane caught his glance. 'You poor darling,' she pulled Razane into an embrace, 'this is so wrong. I am so sorry.'

'I am OK, my love,' Razane said into her ear, 'don't you dare apologise.'

Jane kissed her tenderly on the forehead and lips. 'You

know I can't bear to see you in pain.'

It was time to go. They piled into the car. Sergei started the engine, and they drove off.

'Who were those men?' Jane said after a period of silence. 'What did they want with the villagers? Seems it's not just me they're after,'

'Maybe it's something to do with the village,' Razane said, 'most violence happens because of money or land.'

There was more silence as they contemplated this.

'At least we now have weapons,' Sergei said after a while.

'Yup. They're Kalashnikov AK74s. We used to use them. I know them like I know you guys. I used to sleep with mine,' Razane said with a wry smile.

As they neared Sargodha Road, Razane remembered Jane's battery pack and plugged in her dead phone. It took a few minutes before they were able to call Ben.

'Did you run out of battery?' Ben said when they finally made the connection again.

'Yes, the battery died. We just found a power pack,' Sergei replied.

'Great. I was worried.'

'You were saying something about a plan with phones... just before...' Sergei said.

Ben told them.

THE BENEVOLENT LORD

Jibran placed the glass on the table. His servant refilled it. Another walked into the dining room, '*Wada Sahib*, men from Shakar Parian are here. They have been waiting since before six in the morning outside the gate to see you.'

'Good.' He had ordered his guards not to allow any villagers to even ask for permission to see him before nine.

'They beg to speak with you. They say big emergency,' the servant was looking anxious. This was clearly against the big *Sahib*'s orders.

He smiled inwardly. He was expecting the villagers. 'OK, go tell them I will come and see them when I am ready.'

The servant rushed out.

He would let them sweat a bit longer then he would make them an offer, they couldn't refuse, as their benevolent and rightful liege lord. Abdul Zubair, the bearded goat, was finally showing his usefulness. Maybe he needed to continue the alliance a little longer.

MANDI BAHAUDDIN

T he shop was tiny. The walls were lined with floor to ceiling glass cases filled with mobile phones and accessories of all brands and price points. A lone salesman sat behind a glass counter reading a newspaper. He had a cup of tea in front of him.

'*Asalam Aleikum*,' Sergei said.

'*Wa aleikum asalam*,' the man was understandably delighted with such an early customer, he switched to English, 'come in, sir. Please, sit down.'

'Thank you.'

'Are you American?'

Sergei was a bit taken aback at such directness; he smiled, 'No Russian and Australian.'

'Oh Australia, I have a son he lives in Australia. Very nice country. Can I get you a cup of tea?'

Sergei was impatient to get on with it, but he didn't want to be impolite either. 'That is kind of you sir, but I am sorry I am getting extremely late. Could I please buy some phones and some external power packs?'

'Of course, of course, my whole store is in front of you. We have the best and latest, all guaranteed new and fresh stock, sealed and unopened.' He rattled off his sales pitch without taking a breath.

'Give me four latest and best Android phones, four external battery packs and four cables, four headsets and one SIM card.'

'Sorry sir, I cannot sell a SIM card to a foreign national.' The shopkeeper replied. 'Please bring a friend with a Pakistani ID card. I have everything else.' He picked up the calculator and tapped in some amounts.

'OK, I understand.'

'Here is the price,' the shopkeeper said turning the calculator towards him.

Sergei walked out of the store with his package.

He logged into his new phone using a new email address. He established contact with Ben and made sure Ben could see him on the map. Then he logged out of Razane's old phone. He took one of the new phones, logged into it using Razane's old email address and again made sure Ben could see it on his map.

Razane's identity and location were now linked to the new phone. He could see it on his map and Ben could see it too.

They looked for the local courier service and found it just a few shops away.

'How long to deliver to Lahore?' he asked the lady behind the counter.

'We have Normal, Express and Super Express,' she replied.

'I'll take whatever is same day delivery.'

'Sir, that is Super Express.'

'OK super express it, please.'

He connected the phone Razane was logged into to an external battery pack and used tape to secure them together. Then he placed it into the sturdy padded bag the woman had given him. He sealed it, addressed it to Mack Hameed, Hotel Avari, Mall Road, Lahore, and handed it to the woman.

Back in the car, he was able to see the phone's location in its Super Express bag inside the courier store. Hopefully, Damon's captors were watching as well.

VICTORY

Shisha Wal, Friday 2 December, 9:15am

Jibran took a deep breath. How good it felt to win. He watched from his gun room as Allah Boota drove off in his old car. He felt like jumping up and down with joy, but that would not do, not in front of the servants.

Allah Boota had finally agreed to sell. As head of the village, he had the power to act on behalf of all the villagers. In return, he had magnanimously offered to let the villagers live in their huts rent free and keep half the profits from the crop they sowed. He had of course also agreed to protect them from Abdul Zubair and his thugs.

His was an extremely generous offer. Allah Boota had almost wept with joy as he signed the piece of paper Jibran had placed in front of him. He never shared profits with other villages, but there would not be a crop in Shakar Parian for much longer. Soon it would be a gold mine.

He typed a text message to his lawyer instructing him to complete all the paperwork by the end of the day.

'Hey *yaar*, the signal just came on again,' Abrar said, walking into the room. He held Damon's phone in his hand. 'They are in Mandi Bahauddin.'

'OK go there then, bloody find them and finish the job,' Jibran said, 'I will get one of the men to put a bullet in the kid… Maybe I will do it myself. My pit bulls will eat well tonight.'

Sergei looked at his watch as he and Razane got out of the car. It was half past nine. A fresh wind was blowing, picking up dust. The sun shone feebly through an overcast sky. They were back at Panjo Katla Chowk. The memory of the bullet hitting the front of their car was still fresh.

He had inspected the car. The bullet had pierced the driver's side front guard and had been stopped by the door hinge. Thank goodness it hadn't hit anything important, but it had been too close for comfort.

Sergei took the phone and battery pack out of his pocket and turned on the screen. The signal showed three bars.

'Hey Ben, can you hear me?' He said.

'Yup, I can see you're at the intersection. You must have a signal because I can see all three phones.'

'Great!'

'Just turn the surveillance app on like I told you. And point it in the direction you want to keep an eye on.'

Sergei found a small, sturdy shrub and taped the phone to the stem just above ground level. Then he broke off some twigs and covered it making sure the camera was unobstructed.

'How's the view?' he asked Ben.

'Looking good.'

Razane was looking westwards. 'I can see a satellite dish and the top of a house. It looks like the one visible on Google maps.'

She took the phone from Sergei, put her finger to her lips and pressed the mute button.

'I have a bad feeling about this, Damon may be in serious danger,' she said as they started walking back to the car.

'Yes, and we need--'

'We do not know what they are planning, she said interrupting him, 'or what they have already done. I did not want to say it in front of Ben, but he is too much of an IT geek, a bit like you.'

'I'm worried about Damon as well,' Sergei said as he

opened the driver's door, 'what are you suggesting?'

'Well… I do not like Ben's idea to just wait until the people in the mansion leave to follow the parcel.'

Sergei frowned. He'd thought the idea was good, but he trusted Razane's instincts over his own. 'OK sweetheart, I am listening.'

'Sergei my love, so many things can go wrong,' Razane said, her voice softening. 'They could send only a few people or ask someone in Mandi Bahauddin to follow the parcel. What if they are happy to see us leave and not care to follow?' Sergei had no ego when it came to her and Jane. She loved that about him. It was one of the things that helped make their little triangle work so well.

'Or the parcel is put in a container from which it can't send out a signal,' Sergei said. He could see where Razane was going with this. No plan was ever foolproof.

'I just don't think we should sit and wait hoping to see them go past this intersection in hot pursuit,' Razane said.

'Razane is right, Serge,' Jane said, 'I didn't want to say anything, but I am really scared about Damon. Every second we waste--'

'What do you suggest? We just attack the mansion without knowing who we're dealing with?' Sergei said scratching the stubble on his chin.

'I believe, we don't have a choice,' Razane said, 'not if we want Damon back alive.'

'So, what should we do, sweetheart?' Jane asked.

Razane explained her plan to them.

DNA

Shakar Parian, Friday 2 December, 9:30am

M ajor Hamdani pulled into the car park and eased the Corolla into a space next to two police pickups. 'Trouble precedes us,' he muttered.

'I want you both to take lots of photos. Interview as many people as you can. Remember what I taught you. Record everything.'

He flashed his badge at a sub-inspector about to challenge them. Four paramedics walked past, carrying two stretchers. The first carried a man groaning in pain, on the edge of unconsciousness, his face bruised and swollen; his features were unrecognisable.

The major pulled back the sheet covering the body on the second stretcher and froze. He recognised the face even with the gash on the forehead. 'One of you take a--' He was interrupted by a flash from Yousaf's camera.

'Did they have IDs?' he asked one of the policemen.

'Ask the duty officer sir; we are just constables,'

The village square was a mess. A police inspector with a large stomach and a cropped white beard was barking orders at some of his men. The smouldering ruins of what was once a large wooden structure dominated the square. Three constables were taking statements from the villagers who had been herded into three queues.

'I am Major Hamdani,' he showed the inspector his badge.

'*Salam* sir, I'm Akhtar, this is a police investigation. What has this to do with ISI?'

'The dead man is a known terrorist.' The inspector gave a start. 'Give me the story. What happened here?'

'This is the village where the American woman was arrested for blasphemy. The villagers told us a religious group came with guns and burned down their new village hall and ordered them to leave.'

'To leave?'

'Yes sir, within twenty-four hours.'

It sounded bizarre. 'That was a large... structure,' the major motioned at the smoking pile of ash. 'I wonder where these poor villagers got the money to build it,' he said.

'They say it was the American woman. Seems very strange, sir. Must be black money,' the inspector said.

Everything that could not be explained easily was always black money to some people. Black money or black magic. 'OK thank you. By the way who is the village chief?'

'Allah Boota, sir. He is over there.'

'OK, and what happened to the armed men? Why is one dead and one almost dead? These villagers don't look dangerous.'

'Apparently, a man and a woman, sir, came just when these men were about to shoot at the villagers. They attacked them, and during the fight, this one died.'

'Oh, really? What weapons did they have?'

'I was told, they were unarmed, sir, just a stick and an axe.'

'Very brave of them but I meant what weapons did these men have?'

'We only know they were rifles, sir. We do not know what type.'

'Did you get descriptions of the foreigners?'

'Yes, sir. They were foreigners. One was the blaspheming woman's husband and the other her sister. They came by to collect her things. They also took the guns.'

It was not something he had wanted to hear. He did not need armed vigilante foreigners, obviously capable of killing, running amok. 'OK thank you for your help. Tell me, what are you going to do about them?'

'About who? One is going to the morgue and the other the hospital.'

'No, the foreigners.' How had this man made it to the rank of inspector?

'Nothing sir. The villagers insist they were defending them. I would put it down as justifiable homicide in defence of others.'

'That is good. I was going to suggest the same.'

He had no doubt the foreigners were Sergei and Razane. For them to get out of the police station alive meant they were resourceful if not also incredibly fortunate. If Sergei was indeed Jane's husband and she was dead, he would be in mourning. Why would he come all the way to get her things? Unless he had heard the police were looking for DNA to identify her. Whoever had written that police press release needed their head examined. That pointed to only one thing. Jane was alive. No one did anything for no reason.

That also applied to the people who had tried to kill Jane. Something bigger was going on. There had to be. The terrorist group was small fry. Why pick on a foreign woman building a solar panel installation in a remote village and then bomb the police station to kill her when she was most likely going to be sentenced to death anyway?

And that also with such a powerful bomb. It was almost a waste on the police station. The effect on something like a hotel or a large government building would have caused fifty to a hundred times more casualties. Yes, there was something else going on and until he understood what, he did not want the foreigners arrested.

The village chief Allah Boota was nervous. He was grey-haired, short and of slight build. '*Salam Sahib*,' he said, offering his hand.

'Allah Boota what an unusual name you have. Are you

Christian or Muslim?' the major asked shaking his hand firmly. Asking direct questions was a tactic he used often. It helped to unsettle people. It made them forget any story they had fabricated. He wasn't expecting Allah Boota to have any reason for lying, but aggressively interrogating everyone had become a bad habit. His wife used to castigate him for it when he used it on her or their children. Now with her gone, there was no one to moderate his behaviour.

'I am Christian *Sahib*. Why?'

'That is OK,' he said in a friendlier tone, 'I am just wondering if that is why they attacked your village.'

'Most of the villagers here are Muslim, only my family and one more family are Christians. We also have one Hindu family, sir.'

'Right,'

'But those people were not from here. I have never seen them before.'

'Do you have any disputes with anyone?'

'No sir. We live peacefully. We work hard and raise our children, and do not trouble anyone.'

He thought for a moment. 'Tell me, who is the landowner here?'

'The landowner, sir?'

'Yes, who owns the land?'

'We do, sir. We are a village cooperative, but we may sell it soon.'

'OK, well apart from your village who owns most of the land around here?'

'Oh, Choudhury Jibran Ghaffar does,'

'The member of the National Assembly?'

'Yes sir, he is the MNA from this area.'

It was a sad irony that the feudal classes, who exploited the farmers, were their representatives in government. No wonder things never got better.

'Where are his lands?' he asked.

Allah Boota pointed all around, 'he owns most of the land between here and Mandi Bahauddin. All except our village, sir.'

He had meant to ask him something else, but it had slipped his mind. It was something Allah Boota had said.

'May I ask who you are, sir?' Allah Boota said.

'I am from the ISI.'

'The police?'

'Yes the police,' he lied. It was easier than explaining.

'OK, one more thing. Where did the woman live?'

Allah Boota showed him.

Jane's hut was tiny and dark inside. He took out his torch and shone it inside.

The room was empty save for a chair, a steel trunk, a *charpoy* with a thin cotton mattress. The pillow was missing the cover. A light blanket was folded at the foot of the bed. She was quite a spunky woman for sleeping on a *charpoy*. Even he would not do it. They were uncomfortable and creaked too much.

It was funny how foreigners loved things Pakistanis turned their noses up at.

He shone the torch on the bed. It was freshly made. He got on his hands and knees and looked on the floor. Something bright caught his eye in the corner, near the head of the *charpoy*, a filament of blonde hair.

'Hah!' he pointed it out to Fazal, who came closer. 'Carefully bag this.'

'Well done sir. Your eyes are very sharp.'

THE MANSION

Shisha Wal, Friday 2 December, 10:15am

The smell of petrol in the confines of the little Corolla, even with all the windows open, was almost unbearable. With such a concentration of fumes their car was a mobile bomb. Any spark could blow them sky high. The tension was palpable.

They were on Phalia-Mandi Bahauddin Road five minutes from the turnoff to Shisha Wal village.

Razane held an empty glass coke bottle in one hand, and a funnel in the other. Jane carefully poured it half full of thick tractor oil. Then she filled the other half with petrol, leaving a small gap at the top. Razane screwed the cap shut and carefully pierced it with the blade of a scissor rotating it to make the hole round. Jane fed a length of cotton rope into the bottle. Razane sealed the hole with a blob of five-minute epoxy smeared around the rope and carefully placed the Molotov cocktail into a plastic shopping bag that sat in the crate on the floor. Five more to go. The smell of epoxy added another layer of stink and made the back of Jane's throat burn.

If the clerk at the service station was surprised at what the two foreigners and the woman in the black burka were buying he hadn't shown it. Hopefully, he wouldn't report them to anyone.

'You have to time these precisely,' Razane said, 'the rope will burn super-fast. Just throw it as soon as the rope catches fire.'

'Don't worry, sweetheart. I'll be careful,' Jane said. She coughed and put her head out of the window to take a breath of fresh air.

'Also, I don't trust this epoxy to seal,' Razane replied, 'so hold the bottle upright.'

'Sweetie, I grew up on a farm,' Jane said, 'I used to make pipe bombs and other crazy things, and I'm still in one piece.'

Razane went quiet. Jane leaned over and kissed her tenderly on the forehead. 'I'll be careful, I promise,' she said.

'Thanks,' Razane brightened up. The strain was starting to show. She had never been in a battle with people she loved. It was obvious Jane and Sergei had never seen action. Otherwise, they would not be as cool as they were now.

Sergei turned onto the little road. Here it was bumpier. Razane had to hold on to the funnel more carefully as every large bump knocked it out of the neck of the bottle. The floor of the car was already wet with motor oil and petrol.

Sergei slowed right down. He didn't want to make it any harder for them to fill the bottles. There was also no point arriving before the Molotov cocktails were finished.

Outside, in the distance, a few people were working in the fields. A tractor was tilling the soil. Overhead, birds of prey were circling something to their left, maybe a dead animal.

Thankfully so far, there was no other traffic on the little road. Compared to the masses of people everywhere else in Punjab, it all seemed strangely unpopulated.

They approached Panjo Katla Chowk and pulled over to the side. Sergei killed the engine.

Till now, they could have been visiting Shakar Parian. However, beyond this point, they were in enemy territory and much more likely to arouse suspicion.

'OK, ze last Molotovs ist almost Komplet, mein darling Kommandant.' Razane said. 'Fraulein, ze kotton rope pleez.' Jane smiled and fed the last piece of rope into the hole in the cap. Razane sealed it and placed it in the second plastic bag. They had used nearly two litres each of tractor oil and petrol.

'We'll do a lot of damage with these,' Jane said. She had a knot in her stomach and was trying not to think of what was going to happen.

Sergei got out of the car and walked over to the phone they had left behind, taped to the shrub, and retrieved it. So much for that plan. Thank goodness Razane had come up with a better idea.

He walked back to the car. 'Jane honey, you need a phone too,' he said handing it to her along with a spare earpiece, he took out of his pocket.

Sergei dialled Ben. 'Ok, we are ready to go in.'

'You guys are... crazy,' Ben protested in a worried tone, 'I've only seen two men leave on bicycles since you placed the phone there. The house and village could be full of terrorists.'

'Yup, I understand, but we don't know what to wait for,' Sergei said. 'For all we know, they've already left to follow Razane's signal back to Lahore, or not. And Damon could be badly hurt or worse.'

'Ben these people are ruthless,' Jane said. 'I'm really scared, but... just can't see another way.'

'Let's not debate this any further,' Sergei said. 'We don't have a choice. We've gotta get Damon out. Now let's focus on what we have to do.'

They discussed the plan again.

From the aerial view on Google maps, the road they were on bisected a hill on the edge of the village. The hill was visible from where they stood. Trees ran along the ridge of the hill blocking most of the view to the mansion. Only the roof was visible. It meant unless their enemy had posted someone on the hill or the roof, their approach would not be observed.

'The sniper last night was probably on that roof,' Razane said pointing at the satellite image on the phone.

'He'd be shooting at us now if he was still there,' Sergei said.

'Yes, that makes... sense,' Razane said. 'I can't see anyone on the roof at the moment.'

'Thank goodness,' Jane said, shivering at the thought.

The map showed the village had thirty-one huts in two rows. Twenty-two were to the north of the road and the rest to the south.

The mansion was on a second hill at the end of the road they were on. From where they stood it appeared higher than the rest of the village.

'Well, I am OK with the plan,' Razane said, 'but Sergei I really, really don't want you to go inside the mansion.' They had argued about it, and Sergei was adamant.

'I know you don't, sweetheart, but I'm not going to let you go. I know you can handle yourself... far better than I can, but I'm not putting you through the trauma. I'm just not. Besides I have a feeling you are a better sharpshooter than me.'

'But you do not have any combat experience. It can make all the difference in a fight,' Razane continued, 'if anything would happen to you, I would die.'

Sergei muted the call to Ben. He didn't need his disapproving son hearing this part of the conversation. He could just visualise him pretending to gag. 'I can't let you go either,' he said, 'I can see how badly this affects you. Not physically, but mentally and emotionally. It would kill me if anything... happened to you.' His voice caught in his throat.

'Razane there's risk for you, for all of us,' Jane said. Let's go with the plan where Sergei goes in the mansion, and you cover him from the hill.'

Razane knew it was futile to argue more. She shrugged her shoulders and sat back in the seat. She had a few minutes to get into the zone. Feeling frustrated and angry and anxious was not going to help any of them.

Sergei put the car into gear, and they drove on again. No one spoke. The enormity of what they were about to do was weighing on their minds. They reached the foot of the small hill just east of the village. Sergei pulled over and stopped. He put the car into neutral and pulled on the handbrake. The road ahead rose sharply to a crest a third of the way up the hill. From where they now stood the mansion and the village were completely hidden.

He turned around to face Jane and Razane. 'You know, all of us have the world to lose today,' he said. His voice was thick with emotion. 'I intend for us to continue to be together for a very, very long time.'

'Yes we can't let Sergei lose his harem,' Jane said smiling. Now that they were doing it, her fear was receding. Razane smiled too.

'Go on get out of the car,' Sergei said with a chuckle. 'You are impossible.' Inside though he was in turmoil. This could be their last time together. He had to push such stupid fucking thoughts out of his head.

'Let's stick to the plan, and we'll pull through,' he said, 'please check your headsets work. Keep your phones on and let's stay connected... and... Remember unmute Ben.' He said as they opened the doors to leave the car.

'Yes captain, sir,' Jane said.

Sergei unmuted his phone. 'Ben we're going in.'

'OK, I can see you all. Good luck and guys, thanks for sparing me all the yucky conversation.'

Jane picked up the two plastic bags with the ten Molotov cocktails and a lighter before she stepped out. She had not put on the burka this time. It would be a trip and a fire hazard. Razane grabbed her Kalashnikov and joined her.

Keeping out of view of the village and the mansion, Jane started up the hill. After only a few metres she began to feel dizzy and was soon out of breath. She still had a bit of a fever, and her head hurt from the after-effects of the bomb and the fumes in the car.

The hill was only fifteen or so metres high but quite steep, and she had to use protruding tree roots to pull herself up in a few places. By the time she was halfway up, she saw double. As she got near the top, Sergei put the car into gear and slowly drove forward up the slope. Razane took a position beside the road just below the crest. She lay flat on her stomach and inched forward till she was able to see the rear of the huts, as well as the mansion gates.

Her first task was to cover Sergei and make sure no one attacked him. Then she would head to the mansion even though it was not part of the plan. There was no way she was going to leave him to deal with whatever was inside, by himself.

The Corolla crested the rise. Sergei's eyes were peeled, focusing, taking in every detail possible. He was going to prove he could take the lead in situations like this. He had after all trained in the Australian special forces, even if it was over twenty years ago. He was sharp and fit, and he was fighting for everything precious to him.

He was now past the cutting in the hill. The road levelled off as he passed the first row of huts. Shisha Wal was different to Jane's village. Shakar Parian looked inviting and homely. This looked more like a prisoner-of-war camp. The huts all faced the mansion, which dominated the village with its position and size. The whole layout seemed to have been designed so the village chief could look down and keep an eye on everyone.

The ground stayed level for around a hundred metres, between the huts and the climb to the mansion. It was grassless and covered in sparse shrubs and a few stunted trees. Four charpoys were arrayed in a square in the centre of the ground. An old man lay on one of them. A few naked children played around the charpoys. Three elderly women sat outside one of the huts preparing a meal.

'Most of the adults must be working in the fields,' Sergei spoke into the earpiece. The village is almost completely empty.'

'Jane, hold off on the bombs until we've started shooting and people return to the village.' Razane said.

'Understood! I can see lots of people in the fields from here,' Jane replied.

To his left, beyond the last hut, a tube well pumped water into an open channel that ran parallel to the huts and flowed towards the fields on both sides. A large steel grate bridged the water channel. Sergei's teeth rattled as the car bounced over it. A branch of the same watercourse ran parallel to the road, curved away behind a clump of trees and shrubs and drained into a small lake. A few women were washing their clothes on its banks. To his right on the edge of the fields, a large open shed housed two tractors, a pickup truck and some motorcycles. Could that have been what their pursuers had followed them in last night?

The road started climbing the short distance to the mansion gates. This part was nicely metalled and in top condition. Tall and slender yellow-golden conifers grew on both sides. Ahead of him at the top of the hill was a two-metre tall brick boundary wall topped with a row of metal spikes. An imposing steel gate stood open. Two guards, with rifles, watched him. Their plan had only included one man. It was the first hitch. This was going to be harder to get right. Sergei's hands shook, he badly needed to pee.

'Razane can you see both guards?' He tried hard to keep the tremor from his voice.

'Yes, my love. Just don't block my view.' her voice calmed him a bit. Oh, how he loved her!

Easier said than done. Sergei looked in the mirror at the cutting. Razane was not visible. As the car began climbing, the guards gesticulated angrily, waving him back. He braked lightly and slowed to a crawl, his left foot unsteady, shaking. He stuck his arm out of the window and waved to them, smiling. The men, unsure how to respond, stopped and waited. As the car reached the gate, the road became almost level. Sergei put the car in neutral and put the handbrake on. Beaming brightly, he stepped out of the car, 'Asalam Aleikum, I am here to see your master,' his voice was loud, overly so.

The first guard, initially taken aback, collected himself. He tried to find the words in English to respond.

'Big Sahib not say you come,' he managed after a moment, 'you go!' He pointed his rifle at him, almost poking him in the chest.

Sergei had to maintain an assertive stance and look like he was in control otherwise it was all lost.

The second guard stared at the hill. What the fuck was he looking at? He said something to the first guard and pointed. Sergei turned to look. The first guard looked as well. Shit, had they spotted Jane? The second guard lifted his rifle.

'Razane he's seen--' A bullet whistled, a loud crack rang out, and the second guard fell, his rifle clanging against the Toyota's front guard.

It had started, Sergei's vision narrowed. Everything to either side of him darkened. What was happening? Shit, he had to do something. The surviving guard now in two minds, whether to stay or flee, chose the latter and turned on his heels to run inside. Sergei remembered what Razane had said and ducked. Another shot rang out, and the first guard fell as well. Blood gushing out of his massive head wound began slowly trickling downhill.

'Great shot,' Sergei said breathlessly into his mouthpiece as he grabbed his AK74 from the front passenger footwell. He still had a strange kind of tunnel vision as he ran past the open gate.

He had to think differently, much, much faster or get killed. First order of business, look for any threats and not charge in like a crazed loon. Observe, identify threats, act, his special forces training came to him. The driveway opened into a large brick paved courtyard that spanned the width of the house. The house had two large open garages on either side. One contained a black Mercedes from the nineties, the other a black Porsche SUV and a small red Nissan 370Z sports car.

Sergei looked up, it was a bad habit to only look ahead. Enemy fire could come from anywhere. Each floor of the mansion had four very large windows. They reflected light. He couldn't see inside. That was dangerous. Razane was obviously thinking the same. Two shots rang out and then two more. All the four large windows on the top floor shattered and fell to the ground in a shower of glass. Amazing how she was in sync with him at this distance. Or maybe she thought like a fighter and anticipated and recognised threats in real time, unlike him. Maybe both. No wonder she was almost a legend among the Peshmerga. He could now see inside. There was no one there.

Time to swing into action. He ran across the courtyard towards the front door and tried the handle. It was locked. The sound of barking from around the side of the house grew louder. Dogs, big angry ones, getting closer. This was also not in the plan.

The gunfire had alerted the villagers. Shouting could be heard from the fields. 'Sergei, lots of people are coming this way. They must have heard the shots. Some of them have guns,' Jane said. 'Wish me luck.'

The first subsonic whoosh echoed through the village as a Molotov cocktail burst into flames. The sound was almost masked by the barking of the dogs getting nearer. Thankfully he remembered them. They were the largest most vicious pit bull terriers he had ever seen, and they were running fast, straight at him. He aimed and fired. He got three and missed one. The fourth was now only three metres away when it leapt at him. He pressed the trigger and fired a burst of three rounds point-blank into its chest. The momentum of the bullets swung the dog's body away from him. It dropped to the ground and was silent.

People began to scream. Sergei looked through the gates. Some of the villagers were running towards the huts, several of which were on fire. Jane had a strong arm. That part of the plan was working.

Shots rang out peppering the walls around him. Someone was firing in his direction. Must be from the village.

His adrenaline kicked in. He ran towards the double front door. He was about to aim the rifle at the lock when he remembered how dangerous a ricochet could be.

More shots rang out.

'I've got them,' Razane whispered.

He gave the heavy door a mighty kick. It flew inwards

violently. The shock jarred his leg, but thankfully there was no damage. He was in a large hall. Inside, two men and a woman, servants, shock writ large on their faces, cowered next to an open double glass-door against the back wall. Their arms were over their heads, palms towards him. No threat there.

He took in the rest of the layout, trying to stay calm. His mind raced crazily. He was going to die and get Razane and Jane killed. He fought his runaway thoughts. No time for thinking nonsense. Focus! A stairwell on his left ran up to the second floor. It was empty. Beside the staircase, two closed doors led to goodness knew what. To his right, an open set of French doors led to a spacious drawing room. That was it. There was no one else.

Keeping his rifle trained on the servants, he sprinted to the French doors and looked inside. The drawing room was empty. Back in the hall, the front courtyard and the gate were visible through the large windows. There was no one outside. More shots rang out in the village, and more petrol bombs went off. So far no one from the village had reached the mansion. Razane was doing a great job keeping them at bay.

Sergei crossed the hall to the other side looking up the stairwell as he went. He opened both closed doors and looked inside. One was a study and the other a smelly toilet someone had just used. Both were empty.

Jane's voice crackled in his ear. 'I am out of bombs. People are running to put the fire out. There are lots more men in the fields on their way back. I think we might have achieved the opposite effect.'

'Jane, go back to the top of the hill and hide among the trees there. I am just entering through the gates, Razane said, 'Sergei tell me you hear me.'

'Yes, yes, I do,' he said, breathing heavily. She shouldn't be here. She must have run all the way through a village of angry crazed people. That was reckless and also not part of the plan. He ran towards the glass double-door. The servants hadn't moved.

The doors opened into a large space, part lounge and part hallway that led to other rooms. The lounge was sunken and full of leather sofas arrayed around a large TV.

This must be the proper home part of the mansion. The front part was probably for receiving visitors. He had heard in some traditional Pakistani homes, women observed purdah and kept themselves separate from men who were not family.

Four wooden doors opened into the lounge. All were closed. To his right, a passage ran to an outside mesh door. To his left, another staircase led to the first floor, and a passage next to it led to a closed door. How many staircases did these buggers have?

'I am in the front hall,' Razane said, breathing hard. 'I can see you in the back part of the house... this place is a maze. Have you checked the front rooms?'

'Yes, I have. Careful of the stairway.' He was starting to feel a bit more normal. His vision returned. Having her in the house was reassuring.

'Where is Sahib?' he could now hear her without the earpiece. She had moved to the glass doorway 'Sergei she's pointing upstairs.' 'Where is the boy?' she asked the servants again. 'She's not answering.'

'Maybe she doesn't understand.'

'Check the back of the house. I will cover you,' Razane said as she stood astride the glass door. From there she was able to see the front door and both staircases. Sergei ran and checked the four doors. Three led into empty bedrooms. One was locked. He kicked it open. It was a kitchen. A young servant girl, cowering behind a fridge, let out a scream when he entered. He signalled to her to stay quiet. He tried the external security-mesh door at the back of the kitchen. It was locked.

'Ben, what is a tall young man in Urdu?' Razane asked.

'Lamba jawan admi,' the reply came back almost immediately, and the word where is kahan.' Ben was focused.

'Lamba jawan admi kahan?' Razane said.

Despite the gravity of the situation, the servants smiled at her accent. Their expressions of fear and bewilderment were softening. Razane smiled too, unable to help herself. The woman pointed through the glass door towards the left passageway.

'Sergei, check the left passage. Damon should be there. A shot rang out, deafening them. A spray of plaster hit Razane in the face and neck. Ouch, it stung, but thankfully it had missed her eyes. Someone was shooting at them from the top of the inside stairwell. From where she stood, Razane could just see a bit of the landing on the top floor. She aimed and fired a burst of three rounds.

'Are you OK?' Sergei shouted.

'Yes! Get Damon. I'll cover this,' she said, in a much calmer voice than his.

Sergei ran down the left passageway. The door was locked. He kicked it. It swung inwards; his momentum caused him to topple forwards. At the last minute, he grabbed the door frame to steady himself. A set of stairs led downwards. Thank goodness, he hadn't fallen down them. He flicked the light switch on the wall to his right.

It was an enormous basement. He descended the stairs. Tube lights along the unpainted grey concrete walls cast an uneven light. Some of the tubes buzzed loudly, and one flickered creating a macabre feel. His hair stood on end. The purpose of the basement was not to store wine or keep food fresh. It was a dungeon, a place of torture. A large cage stood in one corner. It took him a second to register that Damon was in the cage, his hands tied over his head. He was shirtless, and his face and torso were covered in bruises and cuts. Damon stood silently as his eyes adjusted to the light. When he saw Sergei, his expression of fear turned to amazement and then relief.

'Dad,' he said in a hoarse voice.

'Damon, are you all right? Wait, I'll get you out.'

Sergei's relief was short-lived. The cage door was locked. The key was missing.

He was tempted to shoot at the lock but again thought the better of it. The risk of a ricochet was even higher.

'Who has the key?' he asked in a voice laced with frustration.

'A big bastard with a huge moustache.'

'How many others are there?'

'A few… One, this fellow with a moustache, some men with guns, and this bloke with an English accent. He's the one who brought me here in a black Land Rover. There are also--'

'There's no Land Rover outside. Are you sure? I only saw a black Porsche, a Mercedes and a red sports car.'

'Dad I know the difference. It was a Land Rover, a Defender. I'm sure,' he said, exasperation in his voice.

More shots rang out.

'I'll be back with the key.' Sergei rushed up the stairs.

'I might have hit him. I heard a man scream after I fired.' Razane whispered into his earpiece. Sergei ran to the bottom of the stairwell that led to the second floor and cautiously looked up. He heard groaning. Crouching low, he crawled up the stairs, rifle at the ready. A large heavy-set man dressed in white, with the biggest moustache he had seen, sat on the floor holding his leg. He was groaning in pain, his leg covered in blood. When he saw Sergei emerge up the stairs, he picked up a revolver lying on the floor next to him. Sergei aimed at the wall next to his head and fired. The man dropped his weapon. Sergei ran up the rest of the way, looking around cautiously. There was no one else. He picked up the fallen revolver and put it in his pocket.

'OK, I have him.'

'Guys, I need help here,' Jane said in a worried voice. I've been spotted. Some men are coming up the hill.'

'Sergei, can you manage?' Razane said.

'Yes, you go, I have it under control.'

'Jane, I am on the way, hold on. Razane ran out of the house and to the gate. Three men carrying large sticks were halfway up the hill.'

'Jane, how many can you see?'

'Three men with pitchforks, and there's a crowd at the base.'

Razane aimed and fired. The first man fell. She fired again. The second man fell. Then she fired a last time. The third man fell. 'Jane get back out of sight. You are easily visible.'

More men were heading towards the cutting. They were going to try and climb the hill from the other side. She was running out of ammunition. Working rapidly, she fired single rounds at each of the two men in the lead. They both dropped like stones. The rest ran back towards the huts. She had to get to Jane. She climbed in the Toyota; thankfully Sergei had left the keys in the ignition. She reversed down the driveway as fast as she dared. The car's exhaust scraped on the ground throwing up sparks before it levelled off.

'Jane, I'll meet you on the other side of the hill,' Razane said as she executed a sharp 180-degree handbrake turn. The villagers were busy getting buckets to put out the fires. Jane had amazingly hit seven huts. Razane raced past them. A few men, sticks in hand, stood between the back of the huts and the hill looking up. The Corolla launched up the slope to the cutting. A shot rang out and hit the back of the car. It crested the rise and was airborne for a brief moment before slamming down the other side.

Jane came running towards her, amid a mini avalanche of rocks and stones. Razane braked hard. The car stopped on the downward slope, the camber of the road pushing it onto the grassy verge. It was now no longer visible from the village. Another shot rang out.

'Jane stop where you are and take cover behind that rock.' Razane screamed. She had to reorient herself and work out where the shots were coming from. She got out of the car keeping low. Another shot. Someone was shooting through the cutting and hitting the cliff face on the opposite side of the road. It must have come from the northern part of the village. This village chief used armed men to keep his people working in the fields. What a bastard.

Keeping low she crawled to the crest and peered over. Three men armed with assault rifles were running towards the south end of the village. They were heading towards the pickup truck. As they ran, they fired in her direction. Several bullets whizzed over her head. These men were different. They aimed well, which was hard to do while running. They were no ordinary village folk.

She peeked again. Two armed men were heading up the slope towards the mansion. Things were rapidly getting out of control. There were just too many of them. She ducked as one of the running men pointed his rifle in her direction.

THE BONUS OFFER

Shakar Parian, Friday 2 December, 10:40am

Major Hamdani felt like smashing the phone, but instead, with a great deal of restraint, he hung up. He needed to breathe deeply. It was all part of God's plan.

'Fazal, Yousaf, we are leaving,' he called out.

'But boss, we have not yet interviewed everyone,' Fazal said.

'We have to return to Lahore at once. Lieutenant General Akram's orders,' he explained. 'All down to major rank must be present. It is about the bomb blast.'

'OK, Sir.' They looked dejected. He didn't blame them. It was their first field work since they had started with him.

He handed the inspector a card, 'please send me a copy of the transcript of all the interviews.'

'I will do sir,'

'Yousaf you are the expert in directions. What is the quickest way to go back to Lahore?'

'Sir, two choices. One is a shortcut through farmland to Phalia-Mandi Bahauddin road. Or return via Sargodha Road.'

'What does your Google say?'

'Sir it says the second way. Sargodha Road to Phularwan saves an hour in traffic.'

'Then why are you giving me...? Oh, never mind' Yousaf was a frustrating contradiction. He wasn't stupid, but he sure acted that way sometimes.

Yousaf shrugged, unsure how to respond.

'Fazal you drive,' the major said, 'I will take a rest. We go to Lahore then come straight back to visit the wadera.'

Both Yousaf and Fazal looked at him. He ignored their alarmed expressions and thumbed through the newspaper. Yousaf began to read through the interview notes as Fazal drove in silence. Traffic on Sargodha Road was light. It was a little warmer than yesterday but felt fresher. Winter would come earlier this year.

They made it to Phularwan in forty minutes. From there they turned south onto a feeder road. Eight minutes later they were on the M2 Motorway to Lahore.

'Sir, when are you going to arrest the foreigners?' Fazal said.

'When it is time.'

Sergei looked at the man on the floor. 'If you lie to me and someone comes through one of those doors,' he said in a steely voice, 'I'll execute you before anything else. So, you better be damned sure you're alone.'

'I only have my domestic servants in the house.' He was breathing heavily, clearly in a lot of pain.

'Where's the key to the cage?' Sergei asked.

'You do not know who you are dealing with,' the man growled, ignoring him. He grimaced as he shifted his leg carefully. 'You dumb sisterfucker! Whatever happens, you are dead. You can kill me and still, you will end up dead.'

'Well we'll see about that,' Sergei kept his voice level. He wasn't going to let this fucker get to him. But what the heck did he mean, even if he killed him? 'I'm only going to ask once more. Where's the key to the cage?'

'Huh?' The man looked at him, his face expressionless.

'Alright don't tell me I didn't warn you. Where's the fucking key?' Sergei said slowly, placing the barrel of the rifle close to the man's leg.'

He could see the conflict in the man. There was vanity behind the moustache. He wanted to express more anger and defiance, but fear held him back. Maybe he had never been at the wrong end of a gun before. It was easy to be brave when you were holding a gun, but not the other way around.

'This injury will heal,' Sergei said, 'but if you delay another second, I will shoot your knee off. That, I promise, will never heal.' He placed the tip of the barrel on the man's knee and pressed down hard.

Jibran sighed in frustration as he slowly reached into the pocket of his kameez and pulled out a key.

'If it's the wrong one, I'll come back and blow off both your kneecaps and your ankles. I promise,' Sergei said with menace.

'I know who you are. My men do too. You are Sergei Markoff. When I catch you, and I will. I am going to do much worse. I will rape your butthole myself. I will have Razane stripped naked and raped by every man in my village, and then I will feed you two to my dogs.'

Sergei stamped down hard on his injured leg. As Jibran convulsed with pain, Sergei smashed him in the head with the butt of his rifle. He went limp.

Hoping the man hadn't tricked him with the key he ran down the stairs through the passage and down into the basement. How the hell did the fucker know their names?

He put the key in the lock. It fit. He turned it; the tumblers clicked. The door unlocked.

Someone was behind him; he could sense their presence. He spun around. It was one of the servants, holding a knife. Sergei was about to sidestep and raise his rifle when he realised the man was offering it to him.

Shit, he was panicking, calm down. The knife was for Damon's rope. He took it gratefully. 'Shukria.'

The lighting was poor, and the rope was tight. He worked slowly and carefully so as not to cut Damon. The wound in his side throbbed like crazy.

Outside more gunfire raised his anxiety levels. He needed to hurry.

'I'm cutting Damon free as we speak,' he said into the earpiece.

'Is my baby OK?' Jane said.

'Yes, your baby... is OK,' Sergei said with a smile as Damon rolled his eyes.

Sergei grunted with the strain as the last strand of rope gave way. Damon was free.

'Are you able to walk?'

'Yes, I think so,' Damon said as he rubbed his wrists. 'Thanks.'

The servant came down the stairs again. They hadn't noticed him leaving. He handed them each a bottle of water.

'Thank you. Shukria.' Damon said.

Sergei picked up Damon's clothes and shoes from the floor. The pain in his side was flaring up making him dizzy. 'You better put these on.'

Damon shivered as he dressed. He winced as he did up the shirt.

'Those look like nasty bruises.'

'That man was a total animal. I hope you shot him!'

'Razane did, and I roughed him up a bit, but he's still alive.'

'I hate to say it, but we should kill him. He's a complete psycho,' Damon said.

More shots rang out.

'Serg, we have five armed men outside,' Razane said. 'Two are running towards you. Another three are going towards the shed with the pickup. They have pinned me down. Please help.'

'OK sweetheart, I'm on my way.'

'Follow me but stay well behind,' he said to Damon as he ran upstairs, across the lounge, and through the glass doors.

The front door was still open. Sergei could see the dead dogs on the grass where they had fallen. There was no sign of any men yet.

He ran towards the door. Still no sign of anyone but there was more gunfire from below in the village.

'Razane, are you OK, what is happening now?'

'I am still pinned down and low on ammo. These men know what they are doing. They are not farmers. I need some fire from your direction, but please be careful. Two men are halfway up the driveway. They will be through the gate in seconds.'

'Thanks.' Sergei sprinted fast towards the gate, keeping in line with one of the pillars for cover, his rifle at the ready, finger on the trigger.

The men came into view. He fired a short burst. They had no time to react. Both fell on the spot.

'I got them, what amazing teamwork?' He said breathlessly. A rush of adrenaline prevented him from reacting to the horror of killing two men.

More gunfire. This time from the southern part of the village. The three men were taking turns firing at Razane's position in the cutting, giving her no time to respond. They had almost reached the shed with the pickup.

'I'm in position and am engaging them now,' Sergei said as he took careful aim and fired. One, two, three, all three shots missed. The men turned towards him. He took cover behind the pillar as they raised their weapons in his direction. 'Razane now,' he said flinching as shots punched into the brickwork, spraying him with debris. Two more shots rang out from a slightly different direction.

'I got two.' Her voice, a whisper. He laughed with relief. She was an unbelievable shot. He glanced up. Two men had fallen and were not moving. The last man had dropped to one knee and had turned his weapon towards the cutting.

Sergei steadied his rifle, took aim through the sights, and fired. The man jerked violently, crumbling in a heap, one knee under him. But he was not dead. He still held his rifle and lifted his head again. Slowly, he aimed it at the cutting. Sergei fired. The man's head twisted, the gun dropped from his hand. He fell sideways and was still.

'I got the last one.' His pride was mixed with relief. He wasn't that bad a shot.

He heard a car's engine and saw the black Porsche backing out of the garage.

'There is someone in the first window on the left,' Razane shouted a warning. Sergei turned around, looked up and noticed a flash of white in the window opening, the barrel of a rifle pointed at him. The bullet ripped into the side of his head just as he heard the loud bang. He heard it slice into him and went numb. The ringing in his ears drowned out Razane's shot. It took less than a second for the searing pain in the side of his face to floor him. His stomach felt weightless, everything went dark, and he stumbled and fell. His earpiece fell out.

'Sergei my love,' Razane cried out in an anguished voice, 'no, no, no please...'

There was no reply. This couldn't be happening. Not to her Sergei. Did she hit the target? There was no one in the window. She kept her rifle trained there just to be sure.

'Sergei please, please, please talk to me, my love.' She was sobbing. Sergei was still lying on the driveway. For a second she lost her mind. Her eyes were not seeing. She felt like dying. Jane came running down the slope towards her.

'Sergei,' Jane was crying too as she looked towards the mansion. Razane turned towards Jane. Her madness vanished. Jane was exposed. There could be more gunmen.

'Stay down, Jane!' she screamed.

Jane dropped down next to her. They both looked back at the mansion. The black Porsche stopped in front of Sergei's prone form. Damon got out and ran towards him. He picked him up and put him in the back seat of the SUV. Razane's brain kicked into full gear again. She had to cover them. There was no one in the window. Damon closed the door and jumped in the driver's seat.

Now a scan of the village. The villagers were all taking

cover behind whatever made them feel safe. The fires were forgotten. There were no more men with guns. The Porsche's engine roared as it raced down the driveway.

She had to move the Toyota, or the Porsche would ram straight into it leaving the road blocked and them without a means to escape.

'Stay off the road,' she yelled at Jane and climbed into the front seat. The engine was still running. The Porsche was only metres away. There was not enough time. She floored the throttle and dumped the clutch. The Toyota's front tyres scrabbled for traction as it darted forward just as the Porsche came over the crest.

Damon saw the Toyota at the last moment and managed to slam his foot on the brake. They were going to hit.

The bump as the Porsche hit the left rear corner of the Toyota was softer than Razane had expected. The force propelled the car into a ditch by the side of the road. It came to rest at a precarious forty-five-degree angle.

Holding her rifle, Razane clambered out of the driver's window and ran up to the Porsche. 'Sergei.'

Jane was right behind her.

'He's alive,' Damon said smiling with relief. 'A bullet scraped the side of his head, but nothing went in. Thank goodness for Dad's hard head.'

Razane opened the rear door. Sergei was sitting up looking dazed holding the side of his head. His hand glistened with blood. Jane opened the other door and climbed in beside him. She was about to take his hand away to check his wound when a gunshot rang out. It whistled over their heads.

'Hurry,' Razane said, 'let's get out of here.' She hopped in the front next to Damon. They took off fast.

Jibran put down the Barrett. They had escaped. Fuck the motherfuckers, sisterfuckers. He sat back down. His leg was on fire. His right shoulder was throbbing. His head felt like it was going to explode. He could feel himself go faint. He had to lie down. The room spun. They had made the biggest mistake of their lives. No one dared cross Jibran Ghaffar. A servant came running with a bottle of water. He took a few sips and the world spun less.

The sisterfuckers. The world was now spinning the other way. He had to lie down. 'Bring a pillow and go and fetch some men. I need to go to hospital.'

He dialled Abrar.

'Hey cunt,' he groaned into the phone. 'You wanted the Barrett?'

'Hey. Oh good, you finally truly value my friendship,' Abrar said. There was silence on the other end of the line. What was Jibran up to? Hopefully, he wasn't expecting him to return to his village?

'Where are you now?' Jibran grunted after a moment.

'On the M2 motorway, following the signal.'

'I don't know who you are following.'

'What do you mean?' Abrar was puzzled now.

'They were here in the village.' He sounded in pain.

'Who?'

'Sergei and Razane and a blonde woman. It must be Jane,' Jibran said in a weak voice.

So, they had all made it out of the police station alive. He almost felt like laughing. It served Jibran right, using something as crude as a bomb. But how the hell did they escape that devastation?

'You don't sound too good. Are you OK?' Abrar asked more out of curiosity than concern.

'No, I am not fucking OK. They shot up my village and killed my dogs.'

What the fuck? His mind flooded with questions. How was that possible? Jibran had at least ten armed men in the village. Who was he following to Lahore? Was it the fat Pakistani?

Did he have Razane's phone? Was he a decoy?

'Also, they have my Porsche.' Jibran spat the words out.

'Wow.' Abrar suppressed the laughter till he had pressed the mute button, but then he couldn't stop. It couldn't have happened to a more deserving person. Tears started running down his face. He had to stop. Jibran wouldn't take kindly to him making light of his predicament.

'Hey, are you there?'

'Yes, I am,' he unmuted the call. His cheeks hurt. He coughed to stop himself laughing again.

'Kill them all, and you can have the Barrett. It is my bonus offer.'

'Consider it done today, brother,' Abrar said, 'The stupid fucks. They must not know who you are,' he continued in a flat voice, 'consider them dead.'

'Why are you waiting? Finish them now.'

'I can't pinpoint their location. The mobile coverage is not good out here; I need to wait till Lahore. By the way, you don't sound good. Are you OK?'

'No. I am on the way to the hospital. They shot me.'

These people were doomed. There was a good lesson in there for him. Never shoot Jibran without making sure he was dead.

'Sir, their behaviour is strange. After Shakar Parian, they went to Mandi Bahauddin and then near the village of Shisha Wal. Then they drove back to the main Phalia-Mandi Bahauddin Road, and back to Shisha Wal. I wonder what they are up to?' Yousaf said.

'They were so near us we could have arrested them,' Fazal said.

'All in good time,' the major said. 'I want to know who they associate with and why someone is trying to kill them.' Too many things just did not add up. Why blow up a police station to kill the woman? Why were all her associates in the police station at the exact time of the explosion? How come they were still alive? Was it possible the bomb was meant to help Jane escape? If so it would have to be the foolhardiest prison break in history. Yet somehow it had worked.

'Sir, do you think they were responsible for the bomb?' Yousaf asked.

The question came out of the blue. He tried to remember. He was sure he had not spoken his thoughts aloud. It was a rare example of Yousaf demonstrating he could be sharp and insightful.

'But how does that make sense?' Fazal said, 'it was such a powerful bomb, it was a miracle anyone survived and--'

'You are right. It is most mysterious,' the major said.

'I wonder if the bombing was the work of the mullahs who witnessed the blasphemy,' Fazal offered.

'If they wanted them dead why get them arrested in the first place?' Yousaf responded.

'Good points. Also, what is the connection to the village? And why are the foreigners in Shisha Wal? Who are they visiting?' He hoped this was all sinking in. 'See boys, if we arrest them now we will never know the answers.'

'Allah,' Abdul Zubair wailed, 'why such a cruel test of your humble and always faithful servant?'

Bilal sat next to him. His head bowed. He had brought him news of Adil's death. The man's face had fallen. He suddenly looked sick. Abdul Zubair was one of the hardest men he had ever known. In Afghanistan, he had forged a reputation for being a cold-hearted and ruthless commander who won his battles and skirmishes at any cost. Bilal had never seen any weakness in him.

'May Allah, bring him into heaven straight away,' Bilal said hoping his words would give some comfort.

'What happened? How did he die?'

Bilal told him. He knew he was talking about dead people. They were dead, but they just did not yet know it yet.

'Is Dad OK?' Ben's voice startled them. They had forgotten he was listening all along.

'He's hurt, but he's going to be OK,' Jane said.

'I could almost not bear listening to you guys,' Ben said, 'I nearly shat my pants a few times.'

Jane smiled. 'It's time for you to head to Dubai.'

'OK guys, I am going to hang up now. Talk to you in a little while.'

There was silence in the car. Razane was leaning forward, her head in her hands. Her shoulders were shaking.

'Damon, stop, please, I want Razane to come and sit in the back.'

'I am OK. Please keep driving. It's too dangerous to stop.' Razane's voice sounded strained and hollow.

Jane leaned forward and tried to put her arm around her as best as she could. Razane was shaking almost uncontrollably. 'Damon do as you are told now.'

Damon knew when his mother was serious. He checked the rear-view mirror. No one was following them. He pulled over to the side of the road. Jane jumped out and opened the front passenger door.

'Sweetie, the sooner you come to the back, the sooner we can be off,' she said with a determined set to her jaw.

PIGEONS

Lahore, Friday 2 December, 12:45pm

He had never been in such a situation before. Usually, his targets lived and worked in Pakistan. They had fixed home and work addresses, most often an address for a mistress, and they would regularly visit the same mosque or club. He would use his network to find everything about them he needed to know. Then he would plan and prepare. Meticulous planning and preparation was the secret to his perfect success rate.

Now the situation was different. These targets knew someone was after them. They knew how to fight. They had given Jibran a bloody nose, which was no mean feat. They would try and leave the country fast. But how? The airport was too risky. Jane's face had been in every newspaper in the country. Sergei and Razane were on an immigration control list.

He knew next to nothing about these people, their habits, their weaknesses. They couldn't have escaped before the bomb went off. He'd been watching the only entrance the whole time.

Unless they were long lost relatives of Houdini, they must have been in the police station when the truck hit. It beggared belief his targets had simply walked out of there.

The blast had been unbelievable. His ears were still ringing, even now. Time had slowed as he watched the truck smash into the police station, mesmerised, he had forgotten to duck. Thankfully his Land Rover's glass stayed intact, even though the blast wave shattered windows in the buildings around him. His poor Defender's lovely black paint job was quite a bit less lovely now from the broken glass that had rained down on it.

The strangeness of this whole situation didn't start or stop there. Even more peculiar were the lengths Jibran was willing to go to kill them. He didn't often ask his clients what their motives were so he hadn't this time either. Maybe he needed to. There were too many unknowns and loose ends. He was in way over his head, and it was almost as dangerous to proceed as it was to pull out.

Jibran was dangerous, a narcissistic maniac with a serious god complex. The type who lusted after power. The seriously rich and seriously powerful in the country were all bred this way. To some extent, he was as well. When the British left India in 1947, the waderas and the big moneyed families just took their place. They saw themselves as the new masters. They aped British customs and manners and pretended to be civilised and benevolent.

Jibran was different, an outlier. He could be most convivial with his friends and equals, but his sadistic and cruel streak was never far from the surface. For those who crossed him, all hell would break loose. One could not reason with him, let alone argue or disagree. Every slight progressed to a grievous insult all in his head. Before long, one of his gunmen brought the argument to an abrupt end.

Jibran was responsible for killing many more people than he had. Most for reasons even he could not remember. Many were innocent, in the wrong place at the wrong time. Some were servants or villagers who disobeyed him. Others were opponents. None of his victims ever got justice. Jibran had the money, power, and influence to stop any of it ever washing back on him.

Maybe he ought to assassinate Jibran. It would make the world a better place. But he didn't think he ever would. If something were to go wrong, nowhere would be safe. The thought alone made him queasy. He lowered the side window and took a deep breath to calm himself.

The air rushing in was mixed with rain droplets and tasted and smelled fresh. The wind had shifted again, and with it, the temperature had dropped. The seasons had definitely changed. Winter had well and truly set in.

By the time he entered Lahore, the fat Pakistani was already at the Avari. If he felt safe enough to return to the hotel, then they all would. In that case, he might just have a plan to get them this time.

Given they had raided Jibran's village a short while ago, they wouldn't arrive at the hotel for at least another couple of hours. Enough time for him to dash home to freshen up a bit. It was important he was comfortable while he worked, and he was dirty and tired.

Traffic was light for Lahore. It took him ten minutes to travel the three kilometres to his comfortable home in leafy Scotch Corner. He had a quick shower. He made himself a coffee and spread orange marmalade on thick warm buttered toast, his mind on the plan. His phone rang.

'I have a new plan,' Jibran said. Abrar listened with growing unease.

They entered Lahore from the east and stopped at the first chemist. Razane bought some supplies to tend to Sergei's wound. It was still bleeding so they decided to stitch him up in the chemist's parking lot. Besides, a hotel guest dripping blood on the marble floors would attract the wrong kind of attention.

Razane stitched the gash in the side of his head while Jane held him in her arms and stroked his hair. Even with a double dose of the strongest painkillers Sergei almost fainted with the pain.

It was obvious Razane had plenty of practice. She was quick and efficient but gentle. Working on Sergei helped her steady her nerves and regain her composure. It was no time to be weak. Sergei and Jane depended on her. She would deal with the pain later.

'We're really lucky this only grazed you,' she said as she cut the suture, 'a tiny bit closer and you wouldn't be sitting here.'

'C'mon, we all know I'm the luckiest man alive,' he said through gritted teeth.

'And you better not forget it,' Jane smiled.

'I don't think we'll let him,' Razane said as she applied an antiseptic cream and a dressing.

He felt whole again but dizzy from the pain and loss of blood and from the realisation how close they had come to being killed. What they had attempted would have been sheer madness had it not been borne out of desperation. It was probably best to not dwell on what could have happened. Nevertheless, they were incredibly lucky to have gotten away alive.

'You can come back inside,' Jane said to Damon with a smile. He had been pacing outside, unable to watch.

They debated what to do next. Razane wanted to bypass Lahore and head straight to Karachi. Jane and Sergei wanted to go back to the hotel for their passports. Razane reluctantly agreed. Not having passports would make leaving the country next to impossible.

Lahore was reeling from the shock of the enormous bomb blast. According to the news on the car radio, the official death toll had climbed to ninety-eight. Over a hundred people were still in various hospitals. Many were still critical. It was expected the death-toll would rise further. The army was putting Lahore into lock-down to prevent any follow-up attacks. A public day of mourning had been declared for the day after, and people were asked to stay away from the city centre.

They drove along the nearly empty roads unhindered and reached the Avari fifteen minutes later. Army units were busy setting up checkpoints in many streets and installing barriers in front of buildings.

'Phew! That was close,' Damon said as he handed the Porsche's keys to the valet. 'I got the impression… had we been five minutes later we'd have been stopped at every intersection.'

'Yeah, and us without passports, we'd all be in lock-up,' Sergei said.

Abrar looked up at the unfinished eight-storey tower. He was OK with heights, but he hated this building. He had climbed it a few times before. The concrete had weathered badly and had started crumbling. Every grip and foothold was precarious, not made any easier by pigeon excrement that seemed to cover every square inch.

Construction had started over twenty-five years ago to build the glamorous headquarters of the now infamous Bank of Credit and Commerce International. When they were found out to be the world's largest money laundering operation, work had stopped. It stayed that way for many years.

A rich Arab bought it and restarted construction, hoping to turn it into residential apartments. Not long after it was discovered the original work was as shoddy as the bank's practices, construction stopped for good. The new owner abandoned his plans, and the building sat under the weather slowly crumbling and decaying.

Creepers now covered the lower five storeys. A few trees had put down roots inside its grounds and had broken through the temporary fencing.

After a family of homeless people were found with their heads bashed in, the city forced the owner to erect a permanent brick wall around it. However, the trees were left unchecked and soon undermined it. Large fissures opened up in the brick-work. Abrar entered through one of the gaps and found himself in a small jungle.

The trees had blocked out the sky. A rustling nearby made Abrar's skin crawl. It was probably a feral cat; the place was most likely crawling with all sorts of creatures. Many people believed it was haunted by spirits of the murdered family.

He shivered involuntarily as he walked up the crumbling concrete staircase built around a central tube, the spine of the building. Almost every tread had some part missing, leaving rusty steel bars sticking out at all angles.

Staying as close as possible to the inside of the steps, he made his way carefully upwards. He carried his SIG in a light shoulder bag, making sure it did not snag on any wayward piece of the building.

He was fit, but by the time he reached the top, he was breathing heavily from the exertion. At least heights did not bother him. He checked the roof carefully for any new cracks and found a spot to set up. The last time he was here was to assassinate a member of the provincial parliament. He had been a particularly noxious fellow who'd made a few too many enemies among the rich and powerful. He'd been fortunate to get a good view of the parliament steps which had allowed for the perfect shot. New foliage now blocked that view.

The hotel was not far from the parliament building. The only part of the Avari visible was the part he needed to be, the exit gate. Beyond the gate, in the valet parking area, he could just make out Jibran's Porsche. Its distinctive front bumper and headlights made identification easy.

A contingent of the elite police Eagle squad stood at the gate watching traffic. He counted them twice. There were eight. Eight men who could shoot in his direction and raise the alarm, sending people to block his escape.

The silencer on his rifle would only muffle the muzzle-blast of the gunpowder. It would not stop the sonic-crack of the bullet breaking the sound barrier. The policemen would be fooled into thinking the shots were coming from the opposite direction

At first, they'd run towards him. He would pick them off one by one. After a few were killed, the rest would realise their mistake and run back towards the hotel gate. It would give him enough time to finish them all.

But his first kill had to be the Porsche's driver. The rest

would then be sitting ducks in the disabled vehicle allowing Abdul Zubair and his men to grab them.

He rang Jibran, 'OK I can make it work.'

'Wonderful, yaar.'

'Just tell your bearded friends to be in place. There's no room for mistakes.'

He hung up and looked for other breaks in the tree cover. There were a few. Police and army units were all over Mall Road. The authorities were clearly nervous. He would have a minute, no more, to take all his shots. Then he would have to leave. Abdul Zubair's men had better manage their end of the bargain.

It was a shit plan, borne out of Jibran's massive ego, and completely driven by anger. Why could the fucker not just let him kill the foreigners as they left the hotel? Why get Abdul Zubair to kidnap them to satisfy his sadistic tendencies?

The Porsche was still at the Avari, carelessly parked in plain view. These people were unbelievable, part brilliant, part dumb. Did they really think the matter had ended? With Jibran, it would never end.

He found a good spot for his SIG, not too near the roof's edge. He screwed on its silencer, balanced it on the bipod and zoomed in on his target. He was ready. He moved his neck to relieve his stiff muscles and grabbed his binoculars. A pigeon flew overhead, a few metres away. 'Don't you drop a shit on me!'

Abdul Zubair was lost in contemplation. His son had been martyred too soon. Even worse he had been killed by a woman. 'Oh, Allah give me the strength to avenge your faithful soldier,' he prayed silently.

His phone vibrated in his pocket shaking him out of his thoughts. He was sitting in the front passenger seat of the van. Bilal was in the driver's seat. His men were in the back. They were ready to leave, waiting for the signal. The phone vibrated again. He took it out of his pocket. It was Jibran.

Jane stepped out of the shower carefully so as not to slip on the wet floor. She was still dizzy. She put on the bathrobe and wrapped a towel around her hair. After eight days, it had felt so good. Now she was hungry. Razane had ordered room service. She sat next to Sergei and grabbed a sandwich and a Coke. Boy, was she hungry?

Sergei kissed her on the side of the neck. 'Mmm, you smell nice,' he whispered as Jane crunched into a cucumber. She heard Razane start the shower and smiled at the sounds of domestic bliss. She closed her eyes and imagined they were back in Melbourne. She opened them again. There was still a country and an ocean to cross, literally, but she felt more confident than she had been since her arrest.

Hopefully, they would not become careless now.

A disturbing thought occurred to her. 'Darling, what if the villagers who saw me report me to the police?'

'Yeah, I didn't think of that,' he frowned, 'but I hope not... We better keep an eye on news feeds.' He thought awhile. 'You know the man with the moustache was likely involved in the bombing and... don't forget he kidnapped Damon... maybe he will not want to call the police.'

'I'm just scared. I can't go back to the lock-up.'

'I won't let it happen.'

'Oh, Serge, I just don't get what's going on... The blasphemy charge, the killings, the bomb, burning the village, all the madness... there has to be some reason for it, something we just don't understand.'

'Yeah, of course, nothing happens for no reason, but I'd rather live a long life wondering than risk finding out... I do though wish I'd done what Damon suggested... and killed the moustache man in the mansion.'

'Seeing what he did to Damon, he deserved it… But I don't see you able to just kill, in cold blood.'

'Well, we'll probably never know. Anyway, all I care is getting outta here, fast.'

'He's undone everything we worked so hard for in the village...' Jane sighed.

Sergei put his arm around her and gave her a comforting squeeze. A bolt of pain shot through his side. He saw black in front of his eyes. If he hadn't been sitting, he would have fallen.

He focused on breathing to regain some control. Razane came out dressed in a towel as well and sat down on the other side of him. The colour had returned to her cheeks, but the strain was showing in her eyes. 'Your turn to shower, my love. Just be careful of your stitches. You don't want to get them wet.'

Sergei got up slowly and walked to the bathroom. Thankfully Razane and Jane were absorbed in each other and didn't notice him moving awkwardly. He closed the door and leaned against it. He felt like collapsing. The whole side of his body was on fire. Lifting his arm to remove his sweater and shirt caused white hot pain to lance through his torso. Everything went dark. He sat on the edge of the tub till his dizzy spell abated. He went closer to the mirror and looked at the source of the pain. Like he suspected, he had a gash under his arm. It was covered in pus. The skin all around was intensely inflamed.

He should have asked Razane to look at it when she stitched the side of his head, but he had been so dizzy then. He couldn't ask her now; it would delay them. He tried washing it under the shower. The pain was so bad he had to sit on the floor so he wouldn't fall. It burnt like hell but eventually, a lot of the pus washed out. The skin all around the cut was as red as a tomato. It needed stitches, but he'd have to wait. He wouldn't endanger his family by being a baby. Gritting his teeth, he finished the shower, shaved, and put on a loose long-sleeved t-shirt, a clean sweater and pants. By the time he was dressed his forehead was wet again from perspiration.

Jane and Razane had dressed and were sitting on the couch packing a rucksack with some essentials.

'I've decided,' Jane said while Sergei put on his shoes, 'Damon is flying out from Lahore.'

'I was thinking the same thing myself,' Sergei said making an effort to keep his voice normal despite feeling light-headed. The shower had not refreshed him. He felt drained and shiverish, 'with his size, he stands out.'

'He is not cut out for this.' Razane said.

'You're right, he isn't,' Sergei said.

'Actually,' Razane continued, 'before seeing how you handled yourself in the village, I would have said the same thing about you.'

Sergei stopped and looked at her. 'And now?'

'You surprised me, how you kept your head. I was scared but most proud of you.'

'Thanks, sweetheart.' He beamed. It meant a lot coming from her.

'Me too. You were our strong, tough hero,' Jane said.

He didn't feel like a tough hero. The room spun in two directions. He was going to throw up. He sat down and took a deep breath, trying to quell the nausea.

'I'm still not a shadow on Razane, her marksmanship is out of this world and… you were also amazing. For such a softie, what you did took real spunk.'

'OK agreed, we're all amazing.' Jane smiled.

By the time Damon arrived, all showered and clean, they were ready to go. Jane had used her phone to buy him a ticket to Dubai.

As Damon ate hungrily, Sergei told him of the new plan.

Damon thought about it. 'Are you sure? You might still be in danger?'

'I believe the danger has passed,' Jane said sounding more confident than she felt, 'we probably put the main man in hospital.'

'And the bomb guy will not do it again,' Sergei observed.

'What do you mean?' Razane asked. She never understood

humour. Jane hadn't gotten it either.

'I meant that specific guy who drove the truck...oh, you people are hopeless.'

'Trust Dad to tell a Dad joke.' Damon observed dryly.

'We are hopelessly in love with you but not your silly jokes,' Jane said bending down and kissing him on the top of his head.

'Anyway, Ben might need some help, negotiating with Pakistani border people,' Razane said, 'and you never know what will happen at sea. Two will be safer than one.'

Damon didn't put up much resistance. He was pleased to be leaving.

Bilal was sweating. There was no parking anywhere near the front of the hotel. The police had cordoned off everything. A policeman watched them closely as they passed. The way he looked at them made Bilal uncomfortable. Now Abdul Zubair wanted him to go around again. The same policeman would remember a van full of bearded men circling the hotel. He would stop them for sure.

Was Abdul Zubair thinking clearly? He had never seen his leader so on edge. He was always so sanguine and calm. Now, even his face had darkened along with his mood, and he was speaking in a higher pitch. He seemed close to breaking down.

He did understand Abdul Zubair's distress to some extent. His son had become a martyr.

But he always told other people to celebrate if their relatives died for the cause. Maybe it was easier said than done. Perhaps it was never the same for one's own family.

He hoped Abdul Zubair would not make them do something stupid and get them all killed, with no benefit. He did not mind dying for Allah and his prophet. Embracing death in a glorious struggle with a high purpose would be sweet. He just did not fancy being cut down in a hail of police bullets without achieving anything. That would be wasteful and foolish.

Traffic on Mall Road was bumper to bumper but only in the lanes heading out of the city. The others were empty. The shutdown had come into effect in the middle of the day, and all businesses had been given two hours to close. People were leaving their workplaces for home.

Army checkpoints on many streets and police cordons around all the big buildings meant the traffic was constantly starting and stopping and shuffling between lanes.

Driving past the American hotel had so far yielded no result. What would, going around a second time, achieve?

'Aqa, that policeman was watching our van very closely,' he said.

Abdul Zubair looked at him with bloodshot eyes, 'I will take care of the policeman, go around again,' he growled.

THE OUTRAGE

Wah Hospital, Friday 2 December, 2:41pm

Painkillers made him relaxed and sleepy, so he had refused any. He wanted to feel every cut of the surgeon's knife, the intense burning as he debrided the wound on his leg and his shoulder, the astringent agony of the disinfectant and the searing pain of the needle as it stitched his inflamed flesh together. He wanted to feel it because it was nothing in comparison to the outrage that had been inflicted on him. It was also going to be nothing compared to what he would inflict on the foreigners when he caught them. He had almost bitten through the rubber block the doctor had given him to bite down on. He had sweated and had nearly fainted, but finally, it was done.

The bullet was out of his leg. The good news was, there would be no permanent damage. It had only nicked his shoulder, but had destroyed a large patch of skin and tissue. The doctor had to remove more so it would heal. He would still be able to use his arm, but he would be in pain for some time.

The sour-faced nurse was fussing with the bandages on his leg. He felt tempted to send her flying with his other foot, but somehow, he did not think the doctor would approve. So, he gritted his teeth some more and waited. Then he waited some more while she cleaned and dressed his shoulder. Finally, she finished and walked off.

The insult was simply too much to absorb. He still could not believe what had happened. They had dared to set foot in his village without his permission. The rest was blocked off in his mind. It was incomprehensible.

People trembled when they heard his name. They averted their eyes when they saw him. He had made people disappear just for bumping into him in a crowd and not immediately apologising. If anyone found out someone had walked into his house and killed his men, he would be finished. The shame would be unbearable, his family honour, mud.

He would think about all their brazen trespasses when they were dead. Abrar would kill one. Abdul Zubair would bring the rest to him. When he had them in his basement, he would think about the outrages they had committed while he showed them real pain. Then he would heal and be complete again.

He dialled Abrar. 'Are they still in the hotel?'

'Yes.'

'Call me as soon as they make a move.'

'Sure, I will.'

'Not after you have tried to kill them but before. I want to hear you firing the bullet.'

'OK, I'll put you on speaker.'

'Remember, kill only the driver so the rest cannot get away. My men will do the rest. If you are a good enough shot, by all means, shoot the others but only to injure. I need them alive.'

'You have already told me that before,' Abrar said sounding frustrated.

He called Abdul Zubair. 'Are you ready with your men?'

'Yes, but we have no place to stop and park.'

'My man is watching the hotel. I will call you to let you know when they are about to leave. He will shoot the driver and all the police. Then you grab the rest of them. It is important you do not kill them. I need to show them what pain means.'

'Do you think I do not know how to do that?' Abdul Zubair said.

'I do, but for me it is personal.'

'What is more personal than my son being killed?'

'Your son?'

'Yes attacked in Shakar Parian and killed. My other man was badly hurt.'

There was a long silence as Jibran digested this. It was the first time he had heard about it. When were the foreigners in Shakar Parian? He did have Allah Boota's signature, so the villagers could not back away now. 'Inna lillahi wa inna ilaihi raji'un, you have my deepest condolences,' he said, finally remembering his manners. He needed this man's cooperation.

'Do you understand why it is personal for me?' Abdul Zubair said his voice rising in pitch.

'Yes, yes I do. Of course, I do. Bring them to me, and you can join me in killing them slowly. We will both make them suffer so much they will pray for death.'

'OK.'

'Now listen very carefully again to how you are going to do it.'

Abdul Zubair listened even though he had heard it just an hour ago. It was a good plan. 'Inshallah we will do it and bring them to you.'

Jibran put the phone down. He had to restore control in his village fast. For that, he needed armed men.

Eight out of his twelve bodyguards were dead. The rest were not there at the time of the attack.

The truth was he had underestimated his enemy and had paid the price. He should have taken the intelligence briefing more seriously. They were dangerous. They had to be, to kill all eight guards including three of the most experienced fighters he had ever employed. If he had been better prepared, the outcome would have been different. He could not change the past, but he could repair the future, and he could have his revenge.

He also had to organise a backup plan in case Abdul Zubair or Abrar failed. He knew just the man who could help him.

He dialled a number.

'Asalam Aleikum, Saeen,' the gruff voice said.

'Wa aleikum,' he made his voice sound as deep and authoritative as possible.

'How may this servant be of assistance?'

'I need a problem taken care of,' Jibran said. The man on the other end listened without interrupting.

'OK. It will not be a problem. Send me photographs and the payment. I will put the word out.' The man was a broker. He controlled an Internet site where members put in quotes for the jobs he posted. All members were anonymous, but they numbered in the thousands. Pakistan had no shortage of cutthroats and murderers looking to make money. Within an hour Sergei, Razane and Jane's photographs would be on the site.

'No problem.' He would get Jane's photo from a newspaper article. Sergei and Razane's photos were on his phone.

'One more thing. I need eight guards for Shisha Wal,' Jibran said.

'I shall send some men this afternoon.'

THE BUS

Lahore, Friday 2 December, 3:00pm

Razane loved trees and Lahore had so many, especially in this part of town. She hadn't noticed when they had first arrived, but then she had been in a depressed frame of mind. Most battles she had fought were either in urban areas or in open terrain such as grasslands or desert. Both were dangerous in their own way, but they had one thing in common, snipers. A well hidden long-range sniper could end everything without warning. One moment a soldier could be alive looking at the sky and the clouds feeling the earth beneath tired legs, shoes hurting from all the walking, laughing or cracking a joke with a comrade, or pondering an argument or the last fuck. The next moment a bullet could explode through their skull mushing the brain, extinguishing life. Trees and forests were safer. There were so many more places to hide and fewer lines of sight.

She took a deep breath. Her runaway thoughts were going to drive her mad. She had to force them out of her mind. She was no longer a Peshmerga. Her life was not a continuous battle, day in day out. She had put that life behind her.

The trees here were indeed beautiful, but on second thought it was dangerous to consider anything safe. So many battles had been fought in jungles. Trees could hide an enemy just as easily as a grassy plain. She scanned them again. On closer observation, the tree cover was not complete. Here and there buildings were visible through the foliage. Any of those windows could hide an assassin.

That was not a pleasant thought, but she was glad for it. Pleasant thoughts were a luxury she could not afford at the moment. She was at war with an unknown enemy. She had to keep treating this as war until they were out of Pakistan even if she lost her mind doing it. Better crazy than dead.

The bullet that had hit their car last night had come out of nowhere and had been fired by an expert sniper. The moustache man wasn't a good shot, thank God. It was most likely the man who had kidnapped Damon in the Land Rover. What if he was in one of those buildings?

The constable had his rifle pointed straight at them. Another was waving them over.

'Aqa did I not say this would happen,' Bilal said through gritted teeth.

'Tell them I have had a heart attack and you are looking for Mayo Hospital,' Abdul Zubair said.

Bilal pulled over. 'Help us,' he said in an anxious voice as the policeman opened the driver's door, 'I am so confused. My uncle is having a heart attack.' Abdul Zubair groaned loudly, his hand on his chest. 'And I can't find the way to Mayo hospital.'

The constable looked at the six men in the back of the van. 'Who are these men?'

'We are a missionary group on our way to our mosque.'

His senior officer wandered over. Abdul Zubair groaned again and faked shortness of breath.

'Let him go and tell him the way,' the officer said.

'He needs to go straight past Edgerton Road and turn right on Montgomery.'

Bilal had his head out of the window listening intently, 'Thank you, sir, thank you.'

'Now go fast and do not let me see you again,' the constable said sternly.

Razane turned around to see Sergei, Jane and Damon step out of the lift. They all looked exhausted, but Sergei looked positively ill. Hopefully, his head wound was not infected. Did she look as bad as him? She certainly felt it. It had been the most harrowing eighteen hours in a long time. She walked over and pulled Sergei to one side.

'You need to let me drive.'

'Why sweetheart?'

'I am worried about the sniper; he could be out there.'

Sergei thought it over. Extreme paranoia was the best survival mechanism. 'Look, I agree. It's very possible, but tell me how can I let you be the target.'

'But we'll all be in the car.'

'Yes, but any half-intelligent shooter will target the driver first to stop the vehicle.'

'You know my love, you have a sharp mind.' She was impressed. He was learning quick.

'Well, thanks but you know buttering me up won't make me change my mind,' he said gently, 'I can't put you in harm's way.'

'Sergei please, I've had a look at all the possible buildings someone could be in... I have an idea of the angles a shot could come from. Remember, I've been a sniper. I think like one. I have a plan that... I, I just need you to trust me.'

'Tell me what it is and let me do it,' he said as he gently grabbed her by the shoulders and looked gravely into her eyes, 'please.'

His face was wet, he looked feverish. His head wound couldn't have become infected so soon. She had cleaned it well. She would need to look at it again as soon as they were out of the hotel.

'Sergei, my love, please don't make a scene.' She reached out and touched his forehead. It was burning. 'You have to trust me.' God, please don't let there be anything wrong with him.

Jane came over. 'What's it, guys?'

Sergei told her. Jane looked at them both. 'I don't know what to say. Do you think I want to lose either of you? But Sergei, seeing how you look you shouldn't be doing anything let alone drive us.'

He had lost the argument. 'OK but I'm sitting in the front with you,' he said firmly.

'Just trust me, OK.' Tears welled in Razane's eyes. She blinked them back furiously.

Sergei put his arm around her. He felt dizzier and wondered how he would have driven if he had managed to convince Razane. 'Of course, I do... with my life. I just… couldn't bear it if something would happen to you, that's all.'

'I believe we're all in the same boat,' Jane said, 'Razane is the most skilled and experienced. If we were in the army, she'd outrank you, so please stop being so bossy.'

Sergei knew she was right.

The parking attendant offered to bring them the car, but Sergei handed him a thousand rupee note and told him not to. They would get it themselves.

Abrar stiffened. The Porsche was reversing slowly. He dialled Jibran. 'It's time.'

'OK, hold on.'

Abrar put the phone on loudspeaker. On the other end of the line, Jibran made a phone call, 'they are emerging from the hotel,' he heard him say to Abdul Zubair.

A shiver of excitement ran through him. In twenty seconds they would be at the gate. Eight policemen were still guarding it. He flicked the safety switch on and off. If was definitely off. He always went through this ritual, just to be sure. He put his eye to the scope. The exit gate pillars loomed into view. The Porsche was now obscured behind the left one. Only its roof was visible. They were waiting for something.

'Turn around and go back down Nisbat Road and drive fast,' Abdul Zubair said to Bilal in an urgent voice. Bilal braked hard, found a gap in the central divider, and swung the wheel hard to the right. The van tilted alarmingly as it turned, threatening to roll over. The men in the back grumbled loudly. Thank Allah, their vehicle righted itself. He completed the U-turn and accelerated hard. They were now approaching the intersection with Edgerton road. The lights were red. He thought about running them, but at the last moment realised a police motorcycle was riding alongside and the sergeant was looking at them. Reluctantly, he braked to a stop.

'Don't look,' Abdul Zubair said quietly. Nothing must stop them now. After the lights turned green, they were at the most fifteen seconds from Mall Road and the hotel. They would get to the foreigners easily.

'Now, you all listen carefully,' he said without turning around. 'We have a man in the trees opposite the big hotel. He will kill the driver and start shooting the policemen at the gates. We will drive to the hotel going up the footpath. You, four men, shoot any remaining police and the rest of us will pull the dead driver out of the foreigners' car. Bilal, you get in their driver's seat. I will get in the back and keep my gun on them. Once we drive off, you all get back in the van and follow us. Do you understand?'

'Yes, Aqa.' Their replies were loud and enthusiastic.

'You are good men, real soldiers of Allah.'

They sat in the Porsche, their thoughts on the sniper, as their black SUV inched slowly forward. Near the gate, Razane braked gently and put the transmission into neutral. From where they sat most of the road was obscured. The convex mirror high on the right-hand pillar showed a steady stream of distorted cars making their way along Mall Road. Razane waited, concentrating, deep in her zone. Sergei watched her intently but said nothing.

A large tall Daewoo tourist bus came into view. It was travelling slowly in the middle lane. The lane closest to the hotel was empty. The police had put up traffic cones just after the entrance gate so cars could leave the hotel without being snagged by traffic. Razane put the Porsche into drive. The bus inched forward a bit more till it was directly in front of the gate. Razane released the handbrake and drove forward.

Sergei smiled. She was smart. The bus blocked any view a potential sharpshooter would have.

On the roof, Abrar saw the bus. 'Please no.' He groaned. But he was sure. The bastards would do it again.

'What is it?' Jibran had heard him.

'They are getting away. A large bus is covering my field of view.'

'Fuck, motherfuckers, sisterfuckers...' Jibran screamed. He made a call on his other phone.

The bus passed. The Porsche was gone.

Abdul Zubair heard the phone ring. It was Jibran. He was about to answer when another police motorcycle, sirens blazing, pulled up next to him. The traffic lights turned green. A police car overtook traffic on the wrong side of the road and screeched to a halt in front of them. They were wedged in. Four constables jumped out, guns drawn. The two sergeants on the motorcycles on each side had their revolvers pointed at them. Cars behind them started honking. Traffic began banking up.

Abdul Zubair answered the phone. 'Wadera Sahib help us.' He explained what was happening.

'Hand the phone to the policeman,' Jibran said.

Abdul Zubair started winding the window down, but the sergeant opened his door. Behind him, another slid the rear door open. Bilal's door was opened as well. A policeman reached in, turned the ignition off, and removed the key.

'We told you how to get to the hospital,' the sergeant who had opened his door said gruffly.

Abdul Zubair said nothing but handed his phone to the man.

TAKING STOCK

Lahore, Friday 2 December, 6:30pm

42 Zaitoon Street was nondescript and similar in size and design to most other houses in the street. It was double storey, made of solid brick and covered in a smooth light green render. The front had a verandah on each floor that extended the width of the house and was supported by four green marble pillars that stretched from the ground to the flat roof. The roof and the verandahs were enclosed with steel railing. The house was surrounded by a two-metre-tall light green boundary wall and a dark green gate that spanned the double width driveway. A massive mango tree stood outside the boundary wall, its canopy stretching from the road to the house.

Razane beeped the horn. They waited. She pressed the horn again. The lights atop the gate pillars came on. Someone came running. A large bolt was slid sideways, and an old man looked out. He was dressed in a shalwar kameez. Sergei got out of the car, a little too quickly. He could almost not feel his legs. He waited for the world to stop spinning before he addressed the man.

'I am Mack Sahib's friend, his dost.'

'Ah OK,' the man replied in broken English, 'come, come.' He went back inside and pulled the large gates inwards.

Razane drove down the long driveway along the side of the house and stopped behind a white Toyota Corolla.

'How many people are in the house?' Sergei asked him.

'Two. Me. I cook. My wife clean.'

Sergei took out ten thousand rupees. 'You and your wife, go home. Come back five days,' he said showing him five fingers to help him understand.

The servant beamed happily as he pocketed the money.

'Go now, fast, fatafat,' Sergei said waving to him, remembering another Urdu word he had heard Mack use. The man ran inside calling out to his wife. She came to the door to look at them and then went back inside.

After a few minutes, they both emerged in heavy jackets, carrying a small suitcase, and left on an old Vespa, his wife sitting side-saddle behind him. Sergei shook his head as he closed the heavy gate behind them, struggling with the weight. Razane came to help.

'Damon's flight just took off,' Jane said as she emerged from the car.

'Good. It's a relief he's left.' Sergei said weakly. He was finding it hard to stay upright. He needed to lie down, or he was going to fall.

'We should dump the Porsche,' Razane said, 'before we make ourselves comfortable.'

Jane sighed. 'Sweetheart, Sergei doesn't look too good.'

She was not wrong. He felt like shit.

'It could have a tracking device,' Razane said. 'Jane you remember in Iraq, all our vehicles had them.'

'Yes,' Jane said, 'the engine could be disabled and the doors locked remotely.'

'None of that's happened...' Sergei said feebly. He swooned and steadied himself, 'so far.'

'Maybe they are waiting for us to stop in one place so they can come calling,' Razane replied.

Knowing their enemy, it was a scarily realistic possibility. She tried listening for any untoward sounds coming from the street. There was nothing. 'I'll come with you in the Toyota,' Jane said, 'but let's help Sergei inside first.'

Sergei wanted to protest but couldn't find the energy.

They helped him inside and lay him on the couch. 'You're burning up, darling,' Jane said in a worried voice. 'You rest. We'll be back in five minutes.'

He lay on the couch in the front living room and dozed off. When he woke, they were back.

'Where did you leave the Porsche?'

'In the car park of a McDonald's around five minutes away,' Razane said, 'now let's check what's wrong with you.' She felt his forehead again. If anything, he was even hotter. Worried, she peeled away the bandage on the side of his head. 'This is clean.'

'I hurt myself in the explosion,' Sergei said, 'it was a large splinter of wood. It didn't feel so bad then, but it's bad now.'

'Why didn't you tell us before?' Jane said, shaking her head.

He was too weak to answer. Razane and Jane helped him out of the sweater and his shirt. The wound was covered in pus and all around was bright red.

Jane went looking for a first aid kit and returned with cotton swabs and a bottle of disinfectant. Razane bathed the wound liberally till the pus and blood encrusted scab softened. Underneath was more pus. Sergei winced as she continued cleaning it.

'This needs an antibiotic and painkillers,' Razane said, 'I saw a chemist nearby. I'll be right back,' she said and rushed out. Jane busied herself in the kitchen. The fridge was well stocked with eggs, milk and fresh fruit, and she found fresh bread in the pantry. By the time Razane returned she had cooked up an omelette and brewed a large pot of tea.

'You are not going to stick that in me,' Sergei said eyeing the needle.

'It's amoxicillin,' Razane said,' it should help clear the infection faster than tablets.'

'You got it without a prescription?' Jane was looking at the packaging,' did you have to bribe them?'

'No. No bribes. I even got morphine. It's a very free country in some things it seems,' Razane said with a wry smile.

After Razane injected the antibiotic and the morphine, she stitched his wound, covered it in antiseptic ointment and placed a dressing on it. Then she gave him paracetamol for his fever.

By the time they finished dinner, Sergei was feeling a little better.

They all sat on the couch together and watched a re-run of a British sitcom on Netflix.

It was nine-thirty when they decided to go to bed.

The master bedroom was on the top floor. It contained a large bed neatly made with fresh linen.

'I dreamed of us sleeping together again,' Jane said excitedly, 'it kept me sane.'

'We were never going to leave without you,' Sergei said as he stroked her hair. Razane joined in.

'I'm in the middle,' Jane said.

'Of course,' Razane said as she led her to the bed.

It was a normal queen-sized bed and felt tiny compared to what they slept in back home.

'How's the pain now?' Jane said, as Sergei got in beside her.

'Yeah, it's more comfortable. I feel human again.'

'We are all walking wounded,' Jane remarked as Sergei tried to find a comfortable position next to her.

'Well, it's better than the walking dead,' Sergei grunted with a smile.

They were cramped, but no one complained. It was the first time they lay together after two and a half months. Jane had given up hoping she would ever be able to snuggle with the two people she loved the most in the world. For all their bravado Sergei and Razane had their moments of doubt as well.

Jane took deep breaths as her body relaxed and tension ebbed out of her muscles. She giggled as Razane slid her hand under her shirt and brushed her fingertips lightly across her erect nipples. Sergei lay on his good side facing them both. He kissed

Jane and nibbled on her ear. Razane did the same. Sergei looked into Razane's eyes and reached across and kissed her warmly on the lips. Then they went back to running their tongues in Jane's ears until she begged them to stop. Sergei and Razane had brought her close to orgasm that way before. Today her ears were toe-curlingly ticklish.

They stroked one another, enjoying the closeness and the touch they had been craving. Even after two years, they were still giddy with love, and sex was as exciting as the first time.

Tonight, however, they would go no further than foreplay. They were just too tired.

One by one they fell into a peaceful sleep dreaming sweet dreams. Their whole world, the galaxy, the universe, time itself had shrunk into the small space on that bed in that nondescript house in Lahore. Three interconnected souls at the centre of creation, joined by friendship and love, as simple and pure as it was deep and spiritual.

BACK ON THE TRAIL

Shisha Wal, Friday 2 December, 6:30pm

Major Imran Hamdani frowned. What was the Toyota doing in the ditch? They had almost missed it in the deepening dusk. 'Stop the car,' he said.

Fazal pulled to a halt just before the road started sloping upwards through a cutting in the little hill. According to GPS, they were just outside Shisha Wal village.

'Well, that is their car,' the major said, 'but, where are they?'

'Maybe still in the village,' Fazal said.

'No, I don't think so,' Yousaf said. 'This car was leaving when something made it end up in the ditch.'

The major climbed out of the passenger seat. 'Fazal, you stay here. Be prepared to move our car in case someone comes along. I want to check it out. Yousaf, you come with me.'

The Corolla was perched at a precarious angle. A strong man could easily have pushed it over onto its roof. The interior stank of petrol. The keys were still in the ignition. He turned them. The engine fired up. He switched it off. Yousaf fished out a roll of cotton rope, a fuel, and an oil container from the rear passenger footwell. 'Look at this sir. There is also a tube of epoxy.'

'Molotov cocktails. They were making them. This gets more interesting every minute.'

'Should I take it with us?'

'No point, it will just make our car dirty… and dangerous. Put it all back,' the major said. 'I think we have seen enough,' he added as he got back in their car.

The village of Shisha Wal came into view as they crested the rise. A noisy generator powered a bank of lights that illuminated a hive of activity. People on ladders worked on the roofs of several huts removing blackened straw. A burnt smell filled the air. There had been a fire, several of them. The mansion on the hill was also being worked on. Two men were atop a scaffold doing something to the windows on its front facade.

'What happened here, sir?' Fazal said.

Major Hamdani curled his lip and looked at him. 'Why don't you Google it like you Google everything.'

Yousaf shook his head, 'that's what we are here to find out, idiot.'

'I meant, I wonder what happened,' Fazal said with a sour face.

'It is connected to our foreigners,' Yousaf said, 'I am sure of it.'

'You boys love to talk and state the obvious... but when your mouths talk your eyes stop looking, your ears stop listening and your minds stop thinking,' he said, tapping his forehead to reinforce the point.

'That will not bother Yousaf; he doesn't have a mind.'

Yousaf did not respond. Fazal's bickering was getting out of hand. He was going to show them both, who was more mature. 'May I step out of the car and talk to the villagers?'

'Good idea, Yousaf, just watch these people,' he pointed at four bearded men armed with Kalashnikovs and dressed in white shalwar kameez and skull caps who came running up to them. They reminded him of the two in Shakar Parian. What had they stumbled upon? The foreigners, this bunch and the wadera, what was going on?

Fazal brought the car to a stop as the major rolled down his window. Yousaf got out. The men slowed to a walking pace when they saw their government license plate. The major stuck his badge out of his window, and their demeanour changed.

'This is private property,' the man in the lead said with

exaggerated politeness, huffing slightly.

'Hey, we are on government business. I am with the police.' These people did not need to know they were ISI. 'Now get out of our way.'

He put up his window as Fazal drove up the slope to the mansion. 'Look, there are bullet holes in the plaster and on the pillars. There was a gunfight here,' Fazal said.

A Toyota Hiace van and a black Land Rover Defender stood in the driveway just inside the gate. In front of them was a truck carrying window panes. Six workers were manipulating a large pane of glass up two ladders and onto the scaffolding.

Fazal stopped the car on the level part of the driveway just outside the gate.

'Let's stay clear of the glass,' the major said to him as they both made their way between the parked vehicles.

Two armed guards came running out to meet them.

'This way, the wada Sahib is expecting you.'

'That is nice of him.'

They were ushered, through French doors, to a luxuriously appointed drawing room.

'Please have a seat here Sahib. Wada Sahib will be out shortly.'

A servant came in carrying a round silver tray. He offered them each a bottle of Pepsi with a straw in it.

Major Hamdani looked around the room as he sipped his drink. It was large, its walls lined with carved walnut panelling. Sumptuous leather settees, ornate decorations and thick Persian rugs gave it an air of opulence.

Fazal poked at the cushions. 'These are comfortable,' he said feeling the soft leather, 'it smells like an expensive shoe shop in here.'

'You can live like a prince when other people do the work for you,' the major said just loud enough for Fazal to hear.

They did not have to wait long before Jibran hobbled into the room with the aid of a walking stick. He was dressed in a starched white shalwar kurta adorned with elaborate silver embroidery.

Major Hamdani and Fazal rose. They shook hands and introduced themselves as ISI. 'Please sit,' Jibran said. 'What brings agents of the esteemed ISI to my humble home?' He knew all the social graces when he needed them. He called out to his servant to bring tea and samosas.

'Please no formalities,' the major said. 'We heard there was trouble in this village and came to see if you were OK. An important man such as you... We had to make sure it was not a terrorist attack.' The lie came easily.

Jibran's look of surprise said a lot. It was obvious he had not called the police. He tried to compose himself. 'Yes, dacoits raided the village this morning.'

'I am sorry to hear. I hope there was no loss of life.'

'Tragically, they killed eight of my men. We were caught completely off guard. I was also injured.'

'Did you catch any of them or kill any?' Fazal said respectfully, his voice wavering. A rich and powerful man like Jibran was always intimidating.

'No son. They all got away. They had powerful weapons, and we could not catch them.'

'Did they steal anything?' the major asked.

'What do you mean?'

'You said they were dacoits. Surely, they came to steal something,' the major said.

'Well, as a matter of fact, they stole my Porsche.'

Just then the servant came in pushing a trolley with tea and samosas. Stealing the Porsche was a plausible enough motive, in Pakistan they cost more than the house they were sitting in, but the man was lying. He had interviewed enough people in his life to know.

Jibran waited as the servant poured the tea for them. 'Please help yourselves before you leave,' he said as he slowly stood up. 'You will have to excuse me. I have an important land deal to complete, and my lawyers are waiting on the phone.'

They reversed down the long driveway, turned the car around and picked up Yousaf, who was waiting for them beside the road.

'The villagers told me they were attacked by dacoits. They were many men with powerful weapons. They all described it to me in the exact same way like they were reciting something,' he said as soon as he closed the car door.

'That is perceptive of you, Yousaf. It is what the wadera told us as well.'

'But that is the foreigners' car, and the villagers said the dacoits were men. One of the foreigners is a woman. Why are they lying?'

'Very good question, Fazal. Do something for me quickly. Check on the GPS if any of Mack Hameed's other cars have moved recently.' The foreigners were resourceful and dangerous. Unarmed they had bested two terrorists in Shakar Parian and armed with only two rifles they had attacked one of the most powerful men in the country in his village.

The first attack was ostensibly to help the villagers in Shakar Parian. What was the reason for the raid on Shisha Wal? Was there a link between the terrorists and the wadera? And how were the foreigners involved?

SERGEI

Melbourne, 1 year 11 months ago

Sergei's phone rang. It was Jane. He could tell she was excited even before she spoke.

'It's here,' she said breathlessly, 'they're assembling it now.'

He smiled. He knew what she meant.

'How does it look?'

'In pieces, they've just started.'

They had ordered an ultra-king-size bed. It was too big to fit in the lift or through their front door, so it was being assembled in-situ in their bedroom.

They had realised almost immediately that a normal-sized bed was not made for three people. They each needed room to move, stretch and turn. They needed both space and intimacy and at different times. After two mornings of waking up cranky with scratches from sharp nails and bruises from the odd wayward elbow or knee, they had ordered the bed.

It had taken three weeks to make at the factory. In that time, they still shared the same bed.

Once they had discovered the joy of their togetherness, there was no going back. It was like finding a magic kingdom. Their threesome was the new normal. Naturally, the sleep problems persisted, and by the time the bed finally arrived they were all thoroughly sleep deprived.

Even in his zombie-like state he was still constantly smiling, thankful Razane had come into their lives.

As individuals, they were all different. Jane, warm and

soft, a people person but almost too trusting and giving. He was the complete opposite, logical, often too logical, hard at least on the outside and too blunt. Razane was like a bridge between them. She could be hard and soft, diplomatic, and brusque, logical and emotional.

They also had different sex drives, energy levels, even different interests. But they shared something that overcame it all. They were deeply in love with each other, and all were open and honest and secure and passionately committed to making their threesome work.

Of course, none of them were saints. They were all in a way flawed, damaged souls in search of something and they all helped complete each other. He and Razane loved the outdoors, mountain biking, caving, and rafting. Jane had never been into that. Jane and Razane were both deeply spiritual and enjoyed discussing Sufi poetry and were exploring classical music. Jane loved playing the saxophone, Razane was a great singer. He was not religious and did not have a musical bone in his body. He and Jane loved movies, beer and cooking, Razane hated beer and only liked films based on true events.

Sleeping and sex were not the only issues they had to navigate around, but they were big ones and would become a template for how they'd coexist in love and harmony in all parts of their lives. From the beginning, there was never any question of self in the bedroom. It was always about sharing and caring for the comfort of the other two. No one had a permanent position in bed. They just fluidly moved between the middle or the outer without thought. Whoever got to bed first would choose how and where they slept, and the other two would find the most comfortable way to sleep around them.

If they all felt horny, they'd engage in a threesome. If one of them felt like abstaining they'd move to one end. He found he could enjoy Jane and Razane's hot love making whether he was taking part in it, or not. Even when they were at their most passionate, he could still feel their love for him. If during their lovemaking he wanted to participate they'd welcome him enthusiastically. Jane and Razane were the same. There was simply no jealousy or ego or judgement in their relationship.

In the same way, they alternated between different positions in the car when they all went out. They all naturally shared the housework. Whoever started would dish out tasks to the others. They all came together to handle arguments and disagreements and never took sides.

Razane and Jane saw their love as part of their greater union with God and creation. To them love was God, and God was love. Sergei didn't believe in God but if he ever found someone by that name he would sure remember to thank Him.

THE DISCOVERY

Shisha Wal, Saturday 3 December, 10:35am

A brar checked Google Locations. He was bored and annoyed. Jibran blamed him for the disaster at the hotel. He blamed himself for not having thought of tall buses. The map took a second to refresh. The fat Pakistani was still at the Avari in the same spot. He zoomed out to check on Ben and almost dropped the phone. He had moved to Dubai. He zoomed in. He was at the Marina Yacht Club of all places. What the fuck was he doing there?

Abrar was in the huge sunken-in lounge in Jibran's mansion. He was looking at his phone to avoid talking to the bearded scumbag on the other sofa. He looked like a fucking terrorist with his long beard. He had an ugly scar on his left cheek that seemed to have been made with something long and sharp and then never stitched properly. On his forehead, he had a dark brown prayer mark. His eyes were watchful and hard and his calloused hands restless. This was not your average village mullah.

The man did not look like he wanted to make conversation with him either. He held a string of rosary beads and was praying under his breath.

This was surprising. Ben was obviously linked to Sergei, Razane and Damon. No one shared their location with anyone except close friends and family. If Ben was family, why would he all of a sudden up himself and travel to Dubai and end up at a marina of all places, when his loved ones were in Pakistan, in trouble? Was he planning a cruise? If so why Dubai? Melbourne had cruises. What was so special about cruising in the Middle East? Something odd was up.

The man, with his stupid beads, was still mouthing prayers. Why was Ben at a marina in Dubai? He zoomed out of the map till Dubai became a dot in the United Arab Emirates. The UAE was close to Iran, just the narrow Straits of Hormuz separated them and next to Iran was Pakistan. Shit! He almost stood. Of course! Dubai was so close to Karachi. He Googled the distance. A fast yacht could do it in less than two days. Damn! He wanted to laugh. He knew what they were up to, how they were leaving the country. He got up. He had to tell Jibran, but not in front of this village troll.

He walked to the kitchen. 'Where is Sahib?'

'Still with his guest in the front lounge, Sahib.'

Just then, Jibran came through the glass door from the front part of the house. Abrar motioned him to stop and walked over.

'I've got to show you something super urgent, and not in front of that bearded goat.'

'Come with me. I agree we need to be careful what we say in front of Abdul Zubair,' Jibran said.

He followed Jibran upstairs to his weapons room. The smashed window had just been replaced. A workman standing on the scaffolding outside was spraying some liquid on it and wiping it down. He wouldn't be able to hear them.

'You just might voluntarily present me with the Barrett when you hear what I have to say,' Abrar said.

'The foreigners were hit by a truck and died a very slow and painful death, bleeding out by the side of the road?'

'No, but look here.' He showed him Ben's location then zoomed out as he had done before. 'They're going to escape from Karachi, or somewhere near there, by boat.'

Jibran's eyes lit up, and he snatched the phone from his hands. 'How do you know? Show me.'

You fucking imbecile, you could not see a fly sitting at the end of your nose. 'Ben is at a marina,' Abrar said, with more patience than he felt. 'That's where they sail yachts from.'

'Yes, yes, I know what a marina is,' Jibran said in an offended tone.

'Tell me then why would Ben come from a country like Australia, that's surrounded by water, to travel to Dubai just to go sailing?'

'Unless it is to help our foreigners escape.' Jibran had finally caught up.

TRACKER

Dubai, Saturday 3 December, 10:15am

The phone rang. It was not a number he recognised. He muted the call. The report for his French client had to take priority. The man had been defrauded by one of his debtors who had bought a large consignment of used road construction equipment and had left France. The scoundrel was now living the high life in Dubai. The detailed report included the man's address, his Emirates ID card number, phone numbers, car registration details, photographs, and bank account details.

He checked the information in the report again. It was all correct with no typos or grammatical errors. He attached it to an email along with his final invoice and pressed send.

The phone rang again. It was the same Pakistani number. He wasn't sure he wanted a Pakistani client. The last one had not paid him. Nevertheless, he answered it.

'I hear you solve problems?' the voice said.

'I do, for a fee.'

'Money is not a problem.' He had heard that before. It never was before a job.

'It's cash up front,' he replied.

'I can pay now, but the job needs to be done today.'

'I need to know details before I can make promises.'

'There is an Australian man, Ben. He is going to get on a large yacht soon. I need to be able to track where it goes.'

'What's the name of the yacht?'

'We don't know, but it is heading to Pakistan.'

'You must mean a superyacht?'

'Yes, possibly.'

'Dubai is a big place, with many people, where can I find this Ben?'

'I'll hand the phone to my friend; please talk to him.'

Jibran gave the phone to Abrar.

'Hi, we're tracking him on GPS now and can send screenshots of his position,' Abrar said.

'I need to see his location in real time.'

'We can't do that, but I can keep sending you screenshots, around every ten seconds.'

'If you can help me with his location, I can do the job. I require Bitcoin payment up front.'

'Send the invoice; you shall have it within five minutes. I have sent a screenshot of Ben's location to your WhatsApp. Please accept me as a contact so you can receive it.'

The first screenshot showed Ben at the Dubai Marina a minute ago. Dubai Marina was only eight minutes from his home office in the Al Fahad Towers in Barsha Heights. Well, it was eight minutes the way he drove.

He would postpone gym till the evening. It was a useful sum of money for what seemed like hardly any work, and it needed doing straight away.

As he edged his metallic white Lamborghini Huracan Spyder out of its spot in the basement of his residential tower, he was already thinking of a tracking device for the yacht. It would have to be a satellite tracker with an internal battery. As he waited for the boom gate to open he received another screenshot. Ben was still at the marina but in a different place.

All superyachts had trackers, but their IDs were often not made public. He didn't know and didn't care why his client needed to install a second tracker. He did the job and got paid, end of story.

He blipped the engine as he waited for the boom gate to open. The sound reverberating off the concrete made him smile.

It was one of the best things about the car. The boom gate finally opened, the tyres squealed on the smooth marble of the driveway as the supercar leapt forward. At the end of the little street, he gunned the engine as he turned onto the main road.

Traffic was light, and he was able to maintain a rapid pace as he weaved in and out of lanes. The speed limit was eighty, but there usually was a twenty kilometre per hour leeway before the police took an interest. He had never gotten a ticket in the Lamborghini. These cars were special even in super rich Dubai. If he ever crashed, he would be in serious trouble as a foreigner, but he had never come close to losing control.

He turned off Emaar Drive into Marina Mall car park. It had taken him nine minutes. He walked through the large shopping complex out onto the promenade hoping there were not too many white people. He wondered idly who Ben was and why it was important to track him, not that he cared. It was just a job. Ben was not even the target, the boat was.

The promenade was busier than he had hoped but thankfully they were mostly local couples, men dressed in their white robes and the women in black abayas. Here or there a few groups of foreigners strolled and sat at the outdoor tables of the many restaurants along the waterfront.

The latest screenshot showed Ben on the water which meant he was on a boat, but which one? Something sailing to Pakistan would have to be on the larger side. He started walking towards Ben's last position. Only one vessel, a superyacht, the Shalayla, was berthed at that location. It made it easy. There was no need to guess.

Two white men were talking to an Asian on the deck. One was slender, the other six foot four and heavily muscled. Bingo! He took out his tiny Nikon compact with a zoom lens that extended to an almost impossible length and took a few photographs of the men. Maybe one of them was Ben? He'd find out soon enough. Hopefully, they weren't planning to sail just yet. He transferred the photos to his phone and sent them off.

The reply was almost immediate. 'Very well done. I am impressed. You have found Ben. He is the shorter one. Let's hope the rest goes as smoothly.'

It had been almost too easy to find Ben. Maybe he had just become too good. After all, there came a point in everyone's career where finely honed instinct replaced a lot of the effort.

He walked over to the nearest cafe and ordered a coke. The men came down the gangplank just as the waiter brought him his drink. They were walking away from him. He didn't have to follow. Pleased with himself he asked the waiter for the menu. He needed food to think.

The plan didn't take long to formulate. He called his dry cleaner. I am looking for a DMCA, Dubai Maritime City Authority, uniform for two hours. There are two thousand Dirhams in it for you.

'I have one in your size.'

'Shukran. I will be there in half an hour. No wait, make it an hour,' he said ending the call. He would first pick up the tracker and receiver from the maritime supply store.

It was a rare occasion when Jibran had almost no frown on his face. He certainly sounded pleased even though his bedside manner hadn't improved one bit.

'You are a shit assassin but one clever man. I never thought we could find Ben so fast,' Jibran rubbed his hands together in glee.

'On top of it you got Damon as a bonus,' Abrar said beaming.

Abdul Zubair just sat there stone-faced not listening, a faraway look in his eyes. No doubt he was contemplating Jibran's unexpected generosity.

For his part, Abrar couldn't believe what he had heard. Right there in front of him, Jibran had just offered Abdul Zubair the use of his lands to train on, and it wasn't for the Olympics. For men with beards, training meant only one thing. They were fucking terrorists. Jibran was power-mad, but this was crazy reckless. He was committing a capital offence. Jibran was too full of himself if he thought he would never be caught. Simply associating with such nutjobs was madness. Besides, there was no telling when they would one day turn on him.

'I'll even let you have my Barrett even though you have not killed anyone for me yet,' Jibran laughed heartily as he clapped him hard on his back. The fucker was enormously strong, and Abrar was caught off balance. Thankfully he was able to pivot into the sofa chair, albeit clumsily.

Maybe it was time for him to end this alliance with Jibran, but how?

'Why are they leaving on a boat?' Abdul Zubair said abrubtly. Jibran had not told him about having seen Jane yet. Maybe he wasn't sure how he was going to react.

'We believe the foreigners are escaping on the boat,' Jibran said. 'The ones you were supposed to blow up.'

Abdul Zubair's face changed hues and shades like a chameleon, albeit an ugly one. He looked like his eyes were going to pop out of his head.

'My men killed them all!'

'For dead people, they did a very good job of shooting my village to pieces. Even the blonde blasphemer was here.'

Abdul Zubair sat in stunned silence. 'Have you told the police?' he said eventually.

'No, why do you want to?'

'So, they catch her?'

'Why so they lock her up somewhere out of our reach,' Jibran replied. 'We have all seen you are not very good at killing the right people, Maulana Sahib.'

Abdul Zubair ignored the insult. 'So, we just let her run free?'

'No Maulana Sahib. I know exactly where they will be and you will be by my side when we catch them.'

The DMCA officer was let on board the Shalayla by a crew member. He carried a satchel bag and a clipboard, ticking things off a list as he walked around. He oohed and aahed, mightily impressed by the fit-out of the yacht. The crew were used to such reactions from visitors. They were not overly nervous. The boat was in tip-top shape, but one never knew with officials. They could always find something. They were relieved when the inspection was over, and he left the boat.

Jibran received a text message, 'The tracker is in place on the Shalayla, the following is the link with a passkey that allows you to track it on the Internet. I am sending you a satellite tracking device. It will let you see the boat from anywhere. Send me an address. I will post it overnight.'

'Well done. I do not want to trust the post. Can you have it hand carried? I'll pay extra.'

'No problem.'

'Please send to Jibran Ghaffar, Marriot Hotel, Karachi.'

'OK. Consider it done.'

SOUTH

Jane was the first to wake. Razane and Sergei were still asleep. Razane had her arm over Jane's chest and her head on her shoulder. Sergei still held Jane's other hand.

Jane needed to pee badly but held it in. The mattress was soft and wobbly, and any movement made the whole bed shake. Last night they'd been so exhausted, she didn't have it in her heart to wake them. She also wanted to savour the moment. Her two loves lay on either side of her, warm and peaceful. They were not out of danger, not by a long shot, but finally, there was hope they could escape.

On the way to the house, Sergei and Razane had told Jane how they had planned to break her out of the police station and then smuggle her out of the country. Things made sense all of a sudden. She didn't tell them how simplistic and desperate their plan sounded. How could two unarmed people have taken over a whole squad of armed police? They must have known just how foolhardy it was and were still prepared to risk everything for her. She was the luckiest woman in the world to be in a relationship with these two.

Jane gently touched Sergei's cheek with the back of her hand. Thank goodness his fever was gone. Razane's field medicine had worked wonders.

There was no clock in sight. They had planned to leave Lahore at six in the morning, but from the sunlight filtering through the curtains, it seemed quite a bit later than that.

Maybe she should wake them? Ben and Damon would

reach Karachi around midday on Monday. So they had to reach Karachi in under two days. There wasn't much leeway for things to go wrong.

A part of her felt sad. Despite all the chaos, dirt and poverty, Lahore had gotten under her skin. She was leaving and would never return. The thought made her feel short of breath. Tears welled in her eyes. She'd never see the village again. They'd not be able to get the free electricity she'd promised them. Their children would grow up poor like their parents. Everything she'd planned for, hoped for and worked for had been for nought. A teardrop fell onto the sheets and then more.

'Hey, what is it, sweetheart?' Sergei moved over, his voice thick. His sleep filled eyes full of concern. He stroked her hair. She was crying. She wrapped her free arm around him and burst into tears, huge sobs wracking her body. A moment later Razane, soft and warm, nuzzled behind her, kissing her on the nape of her neck.

'What is it, my love?' Razane said in hoarse voice as she stroked Jane's hair.

'Just everything. How I'm running away, like a criminal, all my work… in ruins.'

'I understand,' Razane said gently. She had spent almost her whole life fighting one enemy or another and all for nothing, the battles, the victories, the sacrifices meaningless.

Jane turned and lay on her back again. Both Sergei and Razane were lying on their sides facing her.

'The fact I can never return makes me feel so down, I can't tell you.'

They could see the pain on her face, and both wished they could take it away, but not all pain could be made better with a kiss.

She wiped her eyes with the back of her hand. 'How's your side, darling?' she asked looking at Sergei.

'A bit sore but manageable, nothing at all like last night. I feel myself again.'

Razane touched his forehead. 'The fever's almost gone.' She sounded relieved.

They lay there for a while longer. Getting out of bed meant facing the world and reality. They still had a country to escape from. Finally, Jane just couldn't hold it in any longer. 'I gotta pee.'

Sergei sat up to let her out. He was still a little dizzy. Hopefully, it would wear off. He looked at his phone. 'Hey, it's 10:55. We're late.'

They were indeed. By the time they showered it was 11:30. They had a quick breakfast. Sergei looked through the house for the weapons Mack had promised, but found none.

Half an hour later they were ready to leave. Sergei put their rucksack in the boot of the Corolla and out of habit checked the wheel well for the spare tyre. Hopefully, the car had one. People always forgot the air in their spare tyres until they were stranded in the middle of nowhere. Two packages wrapped in oily cloth lay under the spare wheel board. One was long and the other rectangular. They were the weapons Mack had promised.

'You haven't let us down, friend,' he whispered. His heart was heavy. He felt a lump in his throat.

Razane wrapped her arms around him from behind. She'd heard. He gently pulled her around to face him and stroked her hair.

She gazed into his eyes. 'We will all miss Mack. He had such a huge heart.' She held him tight. They stood there for a while. Then she remembered. 'What did you find?'

'The weapons Mack promised.' They unwrapped the three packages. The long bundle was an AK74 with a spare magazine.

'Good, I was almost empty,' Razane said.

The square bundle contained four small semi-automatic pistols of an unfamiliar make.

'Oh wow,' she picked one up turned it over and removed the magazine. 'Never thought I'd see one of these again,' she said as she cocked it 'they are a great little 9mm pistol, Bulgarian, Arcus something if I remember correctly.'

'We should keep them in the cabin. Let's put the rifles in the boot.'

'They won't help us in the boot if we need them fast. Can we keep our two AK's in the cabin, maybe under the mats and put the new one back in the boot?'

'OK, I'll try,' Sergei said.

Razane deftly swapped over the nearly empty magazines for the two full ones. Sergei double checked the safety catch was on both rifles then he lifted the front passenger mat and placed them both on the floor. He had to slide the seat fully rearward and position the ends of the barrels under the seat before he was satisfied. He placed the mat back and inspected his handiwork.

'Looks good,' Razane said, as she climbed into the driver's seat, 'let me drive today.'

Jane came out, clad in the burka, and sat in the rear. The car's windows were heavily tinted, but they were still loath to take any chances.

Razane reversed slowly out of the gate. Sergei locked the front door and left the key in the letterbox. He looked at the house as he closed the gate. Mack was not going to be needing it any longer. He pushed the thought from his mind as he climbed into the front passenger seat. He would have all the time to remember and mourn later. Now he had to stay sharp.

Razane turned south on Gulberg Main Boulevard and skilfully merged with the traffic. It was her second time driving in Lahore, and she was coping with the chaos, admirably.

The phone rang, startling them. Sergei answered.

'We got a problem we hadn't thought of before,' Ben said.

They watched as the white Corolla turned onto Main Boulevard and headed south, its path immediately visible on the tracker Fazal held in his hand.

'I wonder, who is the third person?' Fazal said. The Corolla had tinted windows. They were able to make out the faint outlines of someone in the back seat.

'Hmm yes, it's not the big giant man,' Yousaf said.

'You know he flew out yesterday...' Fazal said touching his forehead.

'Yes. That is why I said it.' Yousaf shook his head. There were days he wished he had never met Fazal. Today was one of them.

'Settle in boys; something tells me this is going to be a long drive,' the major interrupted.

'Could that be--' Fazal said.

'Where do you think they are headed?' Yousaf interrupted from the backseat. He no longer had a bandage over his eye. Instead, the doctor had ordered him to wear goggles to keep the dust away.

'So far somewhere south,' the major said dryly.

'You mean Karachi?'

'That is a long shot. I just meant south on the Boulevard. They could be going shopping for all we know.'

'If it is Karachi,' Fazal said turning to Yousaf, 'you are well prepared for swimming in the ocean with your goggles,'

'They are very annoying,' Yousaf said, sourly, 'almost as annoying as you, you chootia.'

'Keep your language civil in my presence,' the major said, in a gruff tone, 'OK?'

'Sorry sir,' Yousaf said, miffed.

'Would it not be safer for us to pick them up now?' Fazal said, 'we have them right in front of--'

'I am wondering that too sir,' Yousaf interrupted, 'what if we lose them?'

'I remember having this conversation before,' the major said. 'What does the I in our name stand for?'

Fazal had heard this one before, many times. He folded his arms and looked out of the window. If they were headed to Karachi, it would be a long and frustrating trip. The major behaved so superior, but he was a pedantic old fart who couldn't see something if it sat on him. Then there was the dummy in goggles in the back. It was enough to drive him mad. Yes, the major was right. Their job was primarily to gather intelligence, but this was a clear-cut situation. These people were dangerous and armed. They had possibly helped a prisoner, charged with blasphemy, escape. They could even be foreign agents maybe from the KGB. The man did have a Russian name.

If it all went bad, he would let their superiors know he had wanted them arrested straightaway. The major had a carefully cultivated reputation for being meticulous and honest. He had never failed, not that he knew, but there was always a first time.

'Look boys. If we arrest them now,' the major was droning on, 'we will never know what they were planning to do and who they were going to meet. My old mentor used to tell me. A good intelligence analyst can construct and rebuild the past, but no one can ever construct a future that hasn't yet come to pass.'

'I understand sir; I don't think Yousaf does. He actually thought it was dacoits who attacked Shisha Wal.'

'I did not,' Yousaf said through clenched teeth.

'Well, it is dangerous to jump to conclusions,' the major said, 'always keep facts and supposition separate.'

He turned to follow the Corolla onto Zahoor Elahi Road. Their target was two cars ahead. The sun had just burnt off the morning fog, and the sky was reasonably clear.

Traffic was light. At that time of the day, it would be housewives doing the shopping or meeting friends for coffee. Ahead of them a truck backed out of a driveway and brought the traffic to a halt.

'Let's try a little exercise, shall we?' the major said. 'Let's see if we can separate facts from conjecture. What's the first known fact in this case?'

'Persons of interest visited Pakistan,' Yousaf said quickly, 'and... they visited Jane Kelly every day.'

'Another is they behaved oddly, going out of their way not to be spotted.' Fazal said sourly.

'Yes, so far you have not jumped to any conclusions, so those are all clear facts.'

'They organised the bombing to release Jane, is a theory,' Fazal said.

'Yes, conjecture.'

'Jane escaped. Is it a conjecture?' Yousaf asked.

'Plausible but still conjecture.'

'The third person in the car in front of us is not the young man. It's a much smaller person, so most likely Jane, so can't we call it a fact?'

'The son flew out yesterday, which is a fact. We have not seen Jane Kelly. It is likely, but still conjecture.'

A car horn tooted behind them. Ahead of them, traffic was moving again.

'Then why can we not stop them immediately?' Fazal said, 'she has committed blasphemy.'

'We'll get the DNA results today, both from the bodies in the police station and the hair sample from Shakar Parian. It will give us some much-needed facts,' the major said.

'Then we arrest them?' Fazal was not letting up.

'All in good time, Fazal. I am not going to remind you what our first purpose is.'

'Intelligence.' Fazal rolled his eyes.

Their quarry turned south onto Canal Bank Road. Major Hamdani accelerated to get through on the yellow light.

'We know they went to Shakar Parian and attacked Shisha Wal,' Yousaf said.

'Yes, that is a fact. We have many independent witnesses, and their car was abandoned there.'

Traffic picked up speed. They were now doing ninety. The phone rang in the car. It was the laboratory.

Major Hamdani put it on speaker. 'Asalam Alaeikum' he said.

'Salam Alaeikum sir, I have the results.'

'Tell me.'

'The DNA in the hair sample did not match any of the bodies.'

'OK thank you. Allah hafiz.'

'You are welcome sir, Allah hafiz.'

'I knew it,' Fazal said excitedly. 'So that is one hundred percent Jane in that car.'

'Yes, most certainly,' he conceded.

'Then why not pick her up?'

The major clenched his fists. He took a deep breath and unclenched them again. Fazal was insisting a bit too much. Maybe he was a radical. The armed forces and the intelligence community were rife with them. They were like a cancer. He would have to keep an eye on him. In any event, it was going to be a long trip with these two. 'To find the answers we need,' he said in a level voice.

There was silence in the car.

Now, what are they?' The major growled. His fists were clenched again. He was losing his temper. There was still no reply. 'For God sake,' he erupted, 'am I training a pair of mules?'

'We don't know why they attacked Shisha Wal,' Yousaf said.

'Good, but there are more unknowns,' he looked at Fazal.

'Why did those Jaamat e Ilahi men attack a village in the middle of nowhere,' Fazal offered, 'and what is Jibran Ghaffar's connection to these foreigners.'

'Yes, that is a very important unknown, especially since he is in a powerful position.'

'Do we have foreign influences in our government?' Fazal countered.

'Sadly, that is almost a certainty, but an even more important question is whether anyone in our government is connected to terrorists.'

'There is another really... seriously important question. I am not going to blame you for not asking it. I myself just got the information yesterday.'

The foreigners' Corolla was five cars ahead of them. He accelerated and overtook a slower moving truck to get closer. Canal Bank Road became Multan Road as they passed Thokar Niaz Baig. Yousaf had been right they seemed to be going to Karachi.

'Yes sir, we are listening,' Yousaf said.

'Oh, sorry… I got distracted,' the major replied, 'we got a preliminary bomb report back.' He paused for effect. Yousaf and Fazal listened with bated breath. Bombs were always fascinating.

'Yes sir,' Fazal could wait no longer.

'It was a sophisticated device designed to be directional, and needed serious expertise. It would have taken many months to plan and make,' the major said.

'So, what does…?' Yousaf began. He always thought and spoke at the same time which sounded most unimpressive.

'They made this bomb before Jane was arrested. So, it was not necessarily connected to Jane at least at the beginning.' Fazal was working it out faster.

'Yes, good, and?'

'They did not know they would need to bomb the police station when they started making it,' Yousaf said.

'Yes, someone diverted it. It could not have been the foreigners. Bombs of this size are not used to break out of jail.'

'So, the question is what was the original target and if this bomb was diverted from its original purpose, are they making a replacement?' Yousaf said.

'Very good, Yousaf.'

'Oh, now I understand. You think the same bombers will try to attack the foreigners again… and when they do we have proof of their crime.' Yousaf said shaking his head in appreciation. The major was quite intelligent. He was glad he was learning from him.

'Thank Allah, you finally have shown me some brains,' the major smiled. 'So now do you understand why we need to wait a bit longer before we pick them up? They are our bait.'

MULTAN

Multan, Saturday 3 December, 4:35pm

They had been on edge when they left Lahore, hyper-vigilant for anything that might represent a threat. However, as they put more distance between themselves and Punjab's capital, they began to relax a little.

Jane even found herself enjoying the scenery, which was mainly green fields and villages punctuated every so often by a larger town.

The road was a nicely surfaced dual carriage highway. Traffic was heavy and chaotic yet flowed well. They shared it with all manners of transport, cars new and old, overloaded Bedford trucks wheezing along at half the speed limit, buses that would stop without warning to pick up or drop off passengers, kamikaze motorcycles, and tractors pulling overloaded trailers.

Poor lane discipline and evidence of drivers putting too much trust in a divine power meant Razane had to stay super alert and was far more exhausted than she would have been driving the same distance in Australia. 'I am never going to complain about traffic back home, ever again,' she said as she braked to avoid a motorcycle cutting across their lane.

By the time they reached the outskirts of Multan, they were in a better frame of mind, but were hungry and exhausted from the long drive.

'I could eat a horse, or that camel there.' Jane pointed to a herd of five camels sitting by the side of the road.

Multan looked and felt like a smaller and less glamorous

Lahore, with wide boulevards and grand old buildings interspersed with modern office blocks and shopping plazas.

Jane checked Google Maps; they had not travelled as far as they had hoped. Multan was only a quarter of the way to Karachi, but it was the largest city for the next many hundreds of kilometres.

'I believe we left Lahore too late,' Jane said.

'How far to Karachi?' Sergei said as he pulled out his phone. 'Google says over thirteen hours.' He answered his own question.

'We should be safer sleeping in a big city with a decent hotel where they're used to seeing foreigners,' Jane said.

'I agree,' Razane said. 'Let's sleep here and get up very early tomorrow.'

A quick Internet search led them to Multan's best-rated accommodation, the Ramada Multan, a western style hotel on Abdali Street just outside the old city centre.

The white Toyota that had been following them since Lahore pulled into the hotel car park behind them.

They hadn't spotted the Toyota, and neither they nor their pursuers noticed the lone motorbike rider stop across the street and make a phone call.

They had no suites, so Sergei asked for a Queen room with an additional bed.

'Welcome to Multan, we hope you have a nice stay,' the receptionist said with a smile as she handed Jane their keys.

The room was surprisingly nice and clean. A hotel employee was busy assembling a single bed alongside the queen-sized bed when they entered.

'They are very efficient,' Razane said in a quiet voice.

'Yes madam, we aim to be very very efficient. Always we please our guests,' he had obviously heard her. They smiled.

As soon as the man left they pushed the beds together and remade them.

The room was small but nicely appointed and clean. Jane

kicked off her shoes and threw off her clothes. 'The first to follow me gets a good time,' she sang as she walked to the bathroom.

She had just turned on the shower when Razane joined her. They were soon giggling and splashing. Sergei poked his head in. Jane was soaping Razane's back, her hand dropping lower and lower. Razane was leaning against the tiled wall, her back arched outwards.

'Oh, that feels good,' she moaned as Jane's fingers expertly played with her body, sending shudders of delight coursing through her.

'Pity the shower isn't large enough for three,' Sergei said sighing. He walked out and put the kettle on for tea. Then he kicked off his shoes and sat on the couch. He loved listening to them making love. It filled him with pure joy. He put his head back, closed his eyes and drifted off to sleep. When awareness returned, the room was silent. How long had he slept? He kept his eyes closed and listened. The kettle had stopped boiling.

The water in the bathroom turned off. He heard their bare feet walking on tiles and then carpet. The scent of soap and shampoo and washed bodies wafted over him before he felt their warmth and sensed their proximity. He was getting aroused. A drop of water fell on his face, then wet hair. Soft, warm lips were kissing him delicately, first on one eyelid then the other. It was Jane; her lips were fuller. Her kiss was a bit more closed. Razane's lips were always slightly more parted. His shirt was being unbuttoned. Hands soft, knowing, loving, gently stroked his chest. Razane's hands were ever so slightly rougher and more calloused. She raked her nails on his chest sending ripples of delight coursing through his being. Jane probed his lips with her tongue. He parted them and met her tongue with his, the contact electric. He opened his eyes and caressed Jane's face. At the same time, he reached out and stroked Razane's wet hair.

'Let me up; I need a quick shower too. I can't be the dirty one.'

Razane gently peeled his shirt away to look at his wound

then inspected the stitches on the side of his head. 'Try not to get these too wet.'

'Yes, doctor.' He showered as fast as he was able to.

Jane and Razane were waiting for him in bed. The next hour was lost in the soft touch of skin on skin, of giving and receiving pleasure, of being elevated to a higher plane as they loved each other first gently, then fiercely and passionately.

They lay there in the afterglow holding one another, their limbs intertwined, feeling one with the universe.

Eventually, hunger made them get up.

'Jane, you were going to eat a camel?' Sergei said.

'OK, find me a nice camel restaurant then.'

'My stomach is growling too.' Razane was looking at a promotional pamphlet. 'These guys are nearby. They don't do camel, but everything else looks tasty.'

'It looks yum,' Sergei said, glancing at the menu, 'let's go.'

It was only seven hundred metres on the same road they were on. They debated walking, then decided they were probably safer in the car.

Sergei drove the short distance. As they left the hotel car park, the same motorbike rider followed them. He was no longer alone. Six others followed behind him.

They parked near the restaurant. Two burly security guards stood to attention outside the restaurant door. Their uniform consisted of long flowing kurtas with matching turbans and ancient .303 rifles affixed with sword bayonets.

'Nice decoration,' Razane remarked.

'The men or their guns.'

'Both,' Razane said smiling.

'Don't be mean; they're just doing their job,' Jane said.

'I was not,' Razane said. 'I meant it. They are quite handsome.'

A waiter showed them to a table next to a giant potted rhododendron.

The bustling restaurant was noisy and warm inside. It only

served slow-roasted chicken using a traditional recipe. About every half a minute the door to the kitchen was flung open as a waiter rushed another serving of the sizzling dish to hungry patrons.

The kitchen was behind a solid pane of glass. It took up an entire wall and served as entertainment. Six chefs were busy cooking, slicing and skewering chickens before placing them on large coal braziers. Every so often they threw cooking oil onto the red-hot coals, causing flames to flare up dramatically.

'I hope they don't burn themselves,' Jane said as they waited for the food.

The reason for the restaurant's popularity soon became apparent. The food was delicious, and the serving sizes were generous. Waiting staff were super attentive and never let a glass empty before rushing to refill it.

'Wow, I am bursting at the seams,' Razane said, sitting back. Jane and Sergei were full too, their plates piled with chicken bones.

'The service here is… amazing,' Sergei said.

'That's Pakistani hospitality for you,' Jane replied.

'I have not eaten anything not delicious since we got here, but this is the best of the lot,' Razane said as she took a sip of water.

'The food is another reason I'm a bit sad to leave,' Jane said as she looked at the chefs through the glass.

Sergei leaned over and stroked her arm, 'never say never, darling.'

Jane squeezed his hand and sighed. Just then another flame front leapt to the kitchen ceiling, eliciting oohs and aahs from the diners

'You never know, we might one day return,' Sergei said.

'I don't think so,' Jane sighed.

They paid the bill and walked slowly to the car. The heavy meal had made them sleepy.

'We should be able to sleep well tonight if you lovely ladies let us,' Sergei said with a grin.

'If the gentleman can keep his hands off us lovely ladies, then maybe,' Razane said as she gave him a quick nudge.

'Before the hotel, can we go see some of the historic buildings? They should be lit at night,' Jane said.

'I'm fine with that. The threat seems to have passed,' Sergei said, 'what do you think Razane, sweetheart?'

'I don't know what to think. Whatever we do, let's not be too long. We must get up early.'

'If someone was going to do something, wouldn't they have done it by now?' Jane said. 'We haven't even been followed or anything; I've been looking.'

'To be honest, we are unsafe until we leave Pakistan, but… OK, let's have a look.' Razane always found it hard to say no to Jane.

It was Sergei's turn to drive. They turned left on Abdali Street and continued past the hotel towards the centre of town. Behind them, the pack of motorcycles followed.

The city centre was beautiful. Floodlights illuminated the old historic clock tower and the tomb of the local saint. They turned towards the similarly lit Fort. Traffic was dense and soon slowed to a walking pace. It seemed everyone else in Multan had the same idea as them. To make matters worse, police armed with assault rifles had placed barricades across the road and were inspecting every passing car.

'They're making me nervous,' Jane said cowering in the back seat in the burka, 'what if they recognise me?'

'They are looking for terrorists not you, my love,' Razane said. She reached back and held Jane's hand. Her poor darling was trembling. 'We will be OK,' she said soothingly.

'Let's go back to the hotel,' Sergei said, 'we shouldn't have taken any more chances than we absolutely had to.'

There was no way for them to turn so they continued with the flow of traffic. All left-hand turns had been blocked off, and they soon found themselves further and further from the hotel.

'This is not good... my Internet is gone,' Razane said in an anxious voice. 'Do you remember the way we came?'

'Shit, not really, I was depending on the sat-nav,' Sergei said. Hopefully, their little joyride wouldn't turn out to be a huge mistake.

Traffic was turning left up ahead. Thank goodness. Now maybe they would find a way out of this mess. As they turned onto Tughlaq Road, traffic began flowing again. Sergei tried to work where they were heading but gave up. Without GPS, they were hopelessly lost.

Behind them, their pursuers followed. As he floored the accelerator, he glanced in the rear-view mirror and noticed seven motorcycles all bunched together. Possibly friends out on a cruise but could they be something else? He accelerated. They did as well. Concerned, Sergei tried everything to shake them off. He changed lanes, sped up and slowed down but the motorcycles mirrored his every move.

Gradually, after many intersections, the old city gave way to the new. The road opened up to a divided dual carriageway. They were now in the midst of rows of low-rise office buildings. Traffic here was quite heavy, but they maintained a steady speed.

Razane and Jane were both checking their phones. Internet coverage was poor. They would get a signal for a brief moment, and then it would vanish. It wasn't enough to get their location on the map.

Behind them, the motorcycles maintained a steady gap.

'Maybe I'm just jumpy,' Sergei said, 'but I'm sure some motorbikes are following us.'

Razane and Jane both turned to look. Traffic was dense. Almost half the vehicles on the road were motorbikes.

'What makes you say that?' Razane said, sounding concerned.

'I noticed a pack keeping in step with us... just my gut feel.'

'Well, I am not taking chances,' Razane pushed the seat back and lifted the floor mat. She slid her Kalashnikov out of its hiding spot and out of habit checked the magazine.

Jane was looking back. 'There are more motorcycles than cars.'

Razane took two pistols out of the glove box and handed one to Sergei who took it and placed it in his door map pocket.

Then she turned to Jane. 'My darling, take this. Hopefully, you will not have to use it, but just in case.' She turned the safety lever on and then off again. 'Turn this lever like this before you need to fire.'

Jane hated guns with a passion, but took it and placed it on the floor between her feet.

'When you fire, hold it firmly. Otherwise, it won't hit anything, and you can hurt your wrist,' Razane said.

'Sure, sweetheart,' Jane said in a nervous voice while glancing back, 'I wish we'd gone straight to the hotel.'

Sergei accelerated, and the Toyota surged forward, picking up speed till it was around five car lengths clear of other vehicles. A group of seven motorcycles, that were till then interspersed with the rest of the traffic, sped up as one.

Razane spotted the breakaway pack. 'Sergei is right. That group seem like they want to catch up to us,' she said. 'My love, try not to stop at any intersection if possible.'

'It was easier said than done.' They were coming up to a large intersection. The lights were still green. A car in front of them accelerated past a slower moving truck and moved left to give way. Sergei pressed his foot down. They picked up speed. The motorcycles sped up as well. 'They are definitely all accelerating as a pack,' he said looking in the rear-view mirror.

The next two intersections were green as well. At the one after that, the light turned amber as they approached. It was too far off for them to make it. By the time they reached it the light had turned red and traffic was already flowing on the crossroad. Sergei braked to a halt.

Three motorcycles stopped behind them. Two riders peeled off to the left and two to the right. Even in the poor lighting, the bulges under their shawls were unmistakeably guns.

With visions of what had happened in front of the Avari, Sergei was not willing to take any chances. He couldn't afford to. They were clearly displaying hostile behaviour. He put the transmission into reverse and slammed his foot on the accelerator. The car lurched back and struck one of the motorbikes with an almighty bang, sending the rider flying. He turned the wheel left, placed the car into first gear and accelerated hard. The Corolla clipped the lead motorcycle on their left as it surged diagonally forward.

A minibus in the cross traffic braked heavily to let them in, probably less out of courtesy than an instinct of self-preservation. Fighting inertial forces, Razane looked back. Five of the motorcycles were still upright. The second one Sergei had hit was straightening his bike and preparing to get back on his machine. She could see one of them sling something that looked like an Uzi back on his shoulder.

One by one, each of the six motorbikes followed. They now had a ten-second lead. Sergei pressed his foot hard on the accelerator. He began weaving in and out of traffic, looking for every opportunity to increase their advantage. Jane looked back, the motorbikes were not gaining, but they were also not losing ground.

The lights were red as they approached the next intersection. Cars ahead of them had already come to a stop. At the last moment, Sergei saw a slip road on the left and took it at speed. The Corolla clipped the apex and bounced uncomfortably over cat's-eyes.

'Give me some directions please; I'm driving blind.' He sounded desperate.

'Wait, I got a bit of a signal,' Jane said, 'it looks like we're somewhere north-west of the city. There are no side roads for a while.'

As she spoke, buildings no longer surrounded them. They were out in the countryside.

'This looks bad,' Jane said. She looked back. One by one the six motorcycles took the same slip road.

'Fuck,' Sergei said. They had managed to achieve the exact opposite of what they should have. They were alone and lost with six armed and hostile people after them.

They passed a large poultry farm on the left. Ahead of them, the road was dark.

THE HOUSING ESTATE

Multan, Saturday 3 December, 8:40pm

He put the phone down. Tufail had found them and had them trapped in a new housing estate outside town. They must be important if the bounty on their heads was five lakhs per person. But what did he care who they were? With any luck, he would be photographing their corpses within the hour, and an hour later he would have the money. The client was reliable and always paid on time. The Internet had made it easy to find work. Demand for murderers and assassins was high. Maybe because anyone with money could effortlessly and anonymously order a kill.

'Hey Wateen, you lazy sack of potatoes,' he said kicking the sleeping form, wrapped from head to toe in a blanket, 'get up we have work to do.'

The man woke with a start. He was holding his rifle in his hand. He had been cradling it all night.

'One day that thing will go bang in the middle of the night and blow your head off.'

Battery and Irfan sauntered in. 'We heard Tufail has found them,' Battery said rubbing his hands together, looking eager.

'If only I had your energy, Battery, I would be a happy man,' he said. 'Tell Guddu to bring the Pajero to the front. We are leaving.'

'Yes, boss. And boss...'

'What?'

'You need to lift weights and drink lots of beef broth like I do.'

'How about I stick some weights up your bunghole?'

'Yes boss, I mean no boss. Sorry boss.'

'And make sure you all bring Kalashnikovs and spare magazines.' He smiled in spite of himself. One could not help being cheerful around Battery. Of course, the promise of easy money always did wonders for his mood as well.

The motorcycles had dropped back. Sergei slowed slightly to take a right-hand bend in the road. Without cat's-eyes or any street lighting to guide him he had to be extra careful. They couldn't afford to crash. Up ahead a large well-lit board advertised "Stage 8 - Riverviews Luxury Housing Society - Next Left". Two hundred metres further, he saw the exit. Razane saw it too.

'See if you can take that turn with your lights off,' she said.

It was going to be hard. He took a careful look at the way the road curved. From what he could tell, the land either side of the road was flat and featureless. If they ran off the road at least, they wouldn't hit anything. It was still a crazy, dangerous thing to do. There could be unseen ditches, and he could lose control. But if he could pull it off maybe they could outwit their pursuers.

The motorcycles were around two hundred and fifty metres behind. Their headlights the only thing punctuating the complete dark behind them. Would the riders be fooled? They didn't have many options left. He decided to go for it.

With a last look at the road, Sergei switched off the lights. Everything became pitch-black, much darker than he'd anticipated. He was effectively blind. He fought the panic clutching at his mind. He followed the curve of the exit as he remembered it. Just when he thought he had managed to stay on the road, the left wheels came off the tarmac. The car began bouncing hard over unseen corrugations. He tried compensating, but it was too little too late. All four wheels were in the dirt. Thick clouds of dust rose on both sides. This was going to give their position away.

Sergei tried swinging harder to the right to get back on the bitumen, but it was no use. He had no idea where he was. The Corolla continued to buck and bounce violently. Still blind and in a panic, he lifted his foot off the accelerator, the car slowed, but not enough. They were still going too fast. He slammed his foot on the brake.

In the inky blackness, their tail lights glowed like a beacon. A nanosecond later he realised his mistake. How dumb! Behind them, the lead motorcycle slowed. They'd been spotted. Unless the housing estate had a second exit, they were trapped.

Sergei turned his headlights back on again. What they saw left them speechless with horror. A small road roller partially blocked the road. They hadn't run off the road, it had ended. This section was under construction. Had he not braked hard when he did they would have smashed into the roller.

'That would have been the end of us.' Razane let out a tuneless whistle.

Sergei was still trembling from the shock of what had almost happened. He put the car into gear and manoeuvred around the construction machinery. The Corolla bounced alarmingly over the bumps and corrugations.

The housing estate had not yet been opened to the public. It appeared empty of any other living soul.

As far as they could see, it was laid out in a square grid, a bit more than half a kilometre on each side. It was bounded by a wide outer road and crisscrossed by narrower streets. They were all paved and well-lit.

The centre of the estate was a large park and next to it were two under-construction multi-storey buildings.

Scattered within the estate, houses were in various stages of construction, many with scaffolding around them.

They crossed the outer road and continued straight towards the park. A signboard advertised the two large buildings as the future Riverviews Shopping Centre. Jane and Razane looked back. All the motorcycles had taken the turn-off and had stopped just before the road roller. They were probably having a conference, planning what to do next. This was going to get hairy.

'Drop me off at those buildings and keep driving,' Razane said holding her rifle, 'try to stay on the outer road.'

'What are you going to do?' Jane asked.

'I'll climb to the top and try to pick them off one by one.'

'Shouldn't we all stay together and defend from here?' Sergei said. He hated the thought of leaving Razane behind.

'Not if you want to end up trapped,' she said, a little too sharply. He was wasting time arguing. 'I'm sorry, please trust me,' she pleaded.

Sergei realised Razane was right. If the motorcycles followed him, she would have a chance to shoot at least some of them. It was better than any plan he had come up with. It had to be because the sum total of all his ideas was zero.

What if any of riders decided to stop chasing them and went for Razane? What if reinforcements came? The time for thinking was over. They were at the building. It was now or never.

He killed the lights and stopped in the car park outside the future shopping centre using just his handbrake. He wasn't going to repeat the same mistake. A board displayed the names of some of the planned shops; many were famous fashion brands. This was going to be an upmarket area. Razane switched off the internal overhead light and got out with her rifle.

'Remember, turn on your phones and use your headsets,' she said, checking she still had hers in her pocket.

As soon as she was clear, Sergei drove off, heading towards the outer road.

Once there, he switched on the lights. Now he wanted them to be seen.

The nearer building was four storeys, one higher than its neighbour. It was the better choice. In the dim light, she barely saw anything. If she couldn't get to the top, her plan would backfire badly.

She put her headset on as she ran up to the building. No doors or windows had been installed yet. The interior was in deep shadow. Street lamps provided the only source of illumination. She could barely make out the shape of the building against the sky. Sturdy towers on each corner held up the floors. As her eyes adjusted to the dark, she began to make out its interior features. She walked inside with slow, careful steps. Her eyes adjusted further. The staircase she was looking for spanned the two back towers. Hoping she would not trip on anything, she sprinted to it and ran up. In the distance, tyres screeched, and a car engine revved. Sergei and Jane must have reached the outer road. A gunshot rang out. Oh God, hurry!

Razane's legs felt leaden, and her lungs burned, but she pushed on. She reached the landing at the top of the staircase. Ahead of her, a metre-tall steel railing spanned the two towers to stop people falling off the edge. She was grateful for it. She didn't like heights much. It was dark enough that she could have easily miscalculated and taken a nasty tumble.

Her view to the outside was blocked by the second building. She needed to get higher. The next flight of stairs continued between the adjacent two towers on her right. She ran towards it, past future shops in various stages of fit-out. Straining to see anything that could trip her over she made her way to the second flight of stairs. She was severely winded even before she got to the top. She had to get to the third floor for the best possible chance of hitting her targets. Another few shots rang out. Again, the next flight of steps was between the adjacent two towers.

Razane's heart beat alarmingly as she paused to get her breath back, and to quell the tremor in her legs. She was not as fit as she wanted to be. The view from the top floor was excellent. Most of the outer road was visible, except in a few places, where under-construction houses blocked her view.

Where was the Corolla? She couldn't see it. More shots rang out in the distance. They came from the opposite side of the estate. She ran across the middle of the floor to the opposite railing. The motorcycles had gotten dangerously close to the speeding Toyota. The car needed longer to brake for each corner, and this gave the motorbikes an advantage. In another ten seconds, the leading rider would be close enough for an unmissable shot. Razane steadied the rifle with her hand resting firmly on the railing, rotated the safety catch off, took careful aim, and fired. The shot reverberating through the building was deafening, but it had no effect on her target. She had missed.

She needed to calm down and breathe, and predict their position. Shoot where they would be when the bullet arrived not where they were now. In the dark, it was almost impossible to see the riders, except when they passed directly beneath a street lamp. All other times only their bikes' headlamps and tail lamps were visible. That made it so much harder to get a good shot. Sergei was now slowing for the corner. The lead rider was catching up fast. She had a two-second window after that they'd be around the bend, and she'd have to run to the next railing.

Once again, she steadied the rifle, aimed, and pressed the trigger. For the briefest interval of time, nothing happened, then the motorcycle began wobbling violently. The corner street-light showed the rider slumped over the handlebars. The-out-of-control bike ran straight through the corner and crashed into an under-construction house. Part of the scaffolding fell in a cloud of dust on top of it. One down.

By now their car had vanished around the corner. None of the other five motorcycles so much as slowed for their fallen comrade. Razane took careful aim at the new leader and missed. She hadn't anticipated him braking sharply. He turned into a side street just before the corner. He was going to try to cut the Corolla off by going through the middle of the estate. One by one the other riders did the same. She took careful aim at the last one. For a brief moment nothing, then the motorcycle began sliding. It hit a boundary wall in a shower of sparks. The rider must have come off and struck the corner street light because it shook violently.

Thank goodness. But it was no time to celebrate. There were still four too many.

'Sergei, they are now coming from the inside streets,' she said into her earpiece. She had almost forgotten it. Hopefully, Sergei had remembered his. 'Look out to your left. Jane, my love, if you can hear me, now is the time for you to use your weapon.'

For a moment, there was no reply.

'We hear you, darling. How many are left?' Jane shouted.

Oh, thank God, they could hear. 'Four.'

Razane ran across the floor to the adjacent railing. The Corolla was in the middle of the next segment of road. One of the motorcycles was riding away from her towards the outer road to intercept it. He had miscalculated and was going to come out behind the Corolla. This was going to be an easy shot. She took careful aim and fired a little above its tail lamp just as it passed under a streetlight. The rider pitched forward onto the handlebars, the motorcycle began wobbling and ran into a ditch. 'I got one more,' she said scanning for the others. They were all hidden by houses. 'Careful, they are now coming from the side streets. They might be coming towards you.'

The clack-clack of a diesel engine alerted Razane to a new threat. She ran towards the railing at the front of the building. A red four-wheel-drive was pulling up outside. She had to crane her neck to see where it stopped. All four doors opened. She waited just long enough to count five shadowy figures as they climbed out. All carried rifles. From her position, she couldn't aim at them. Trying to shoot them would just waste bullets.

'My loves, I have company… five armed men. They'll be on the top floor in minutes.' This was going to be a problem. The staircase was so wide she could not cover it effectively from her position if they all came up at once. If she ran to the landing and tried to fire down, she would be completely exposed. It might become a nice shopping plaza, but it was the worst possible building to defend in a gunfight.

'Fuck!' Sergei said. 'We're coming for you.' He was not

more than a minute from reaching her if he took the next road that ran towards the centre. By then the men might have climbed high enough to see him approach. They would be able to perforate the Corolla with a hail of bullets. He had to take the chance. There was no way he could leave Razane to face the men on her own.

'Stay away from the building it's not safe,' Razane breathed into the mic. The men below would reach her floor in a minute. Still not having worked out how to defend herself, she ran to the railing on her right.

The Corolla was about to turn into the road that led to the rear of her building. Sergei had not heeded her warning, but of all approaches, it was the best. The smaller building blocked off views from all but the top floor. If Sergei had chosen the road because of it, he was smart. Then she noticed. A motorcycle with its lights switched off had stopped just around the corner facing the outer road, waiting for them. She couldn't see the rider clearly, but he would have his weapon ready. Sergei and Jane would see him in two seconds. She had one shot. She flicked the fire selector lever one notch forward. Taking a deep breath, she aimed and fired a burst. Sergei rounded the corner. The rider's gun went off, its flash clearly visible. The motorcycle toppled over.

The Corolla accelerated. 'Are you guys OK?' Razane asked anxiously.

'Yes, we are,' Sergei's voice crackled in her ear, 'stop watching over us and save yourself. It was a great shot though.'

Sergei's mind raced. What should he do? Razane didn't have much time. A shopping plaza would be an open-plan design. It wouldn't have many hiding spots. She'd have a hard time defending herself against a concerted attack. Two riders were still after them, and he'd lost sight of them both.

A headlight illuminated the side of their car as a motorcycle approached them side-on at a frightening speed. Four projectiles hit their vehicle in rapid succession.

Jane shrieked, as the bullets thudded into the car shattering all four side windows. She felt them whizz past her. Her heart raced like mad. Her hands and body went numb with shock. She felt herself all over.

'You OK?' Sergei shouted. His voice sounded far away. He was unhurt. The bullets had passed inches behind his head.

'Yes, what about you?' Her voice was panic-stricken. She could hardly get the words out.

Somehow all the bullets had missed them. The rider swept into view less than thirty metres behind them. He straightened his bike and accelerated hard.

'Get down,' Sergei shouted as he slammed his foot on the brake.

Jane flung herself onto the seat. The motorcycle was under full acceleration. All its weight was on its rear wheel. There was little the rider could do to avoid the collision. The bike hit the back of the Corolla with a deafening bang. The rider catapulted over the handlebars and struck their back window with his knees, shattering it. His body slid forward scraping along the roof and smashed onto the road several metres ahead. Somehow, he was still alive because he sat up immediately, probably a reaction of his nervous system.

Sergei put the car into gear. As it launched forward its front bumper snapped the fallen rider's head back and slammed it onto the road.

Terrible dragging sounds, bumps and thuds came through the floor as the rider's body was mangled beneath the Corolla. Sergei kept his foot on the pedal. With a final sickening thump that lifted the car's back-end, the body folded over itself and was left behind on the road.

It was the most gruesome sound Jane had ever heard in her life.

'We need to get to Razane somehow,' Sergei said, as he braked hard and brought the car to a halt. He had gone pale. His hands shook as he turned off its lights.

The last motorcycle revved its engine somewhere, unseen to the left and ahead of them.

The rear of the shopping centre building was just a hundred metres ahead. From this angle, the double storey building blocked the view to its taller neighbour from all except the top floor.

Only Razane would be able to see them coming, as long as she was still in control of the upper floor. Please let it not be too late. At least he'd not heard any gunfire from the building, which had to be a good thing.

Sergei tried hard not to rev the engine as they drove the last hundred metres to the second building. They coasted to a stop under a large awning. Sergei got out.

Razane focused on the sounds coming up the staircase, trying to judge her assailants' positions. In the distance, she heard the four bullets hitting the Corolla, followed a few seconds later by the loud squealing of tyres and then a loud bang. Her heart stopped for the briefest moment. She feared the worst. Their car had been hit and had crashed into a wall. She was benumbed with fear. Her whole world collapsed around her. She wanted to die. Total paralysing fear and insane grief stopped words forming in her mouth, leaving her incapable of asking if they were OK. Then miraculously the Toyota's engine revved loudly, its tyres squealing as it accelerated. She started to breathe again, but the shock had taken its toll. She was still rooted to the floor.

Downstairs the men were shouting. From the way, their voices were all huffed they sounded like they had climbed a flight of stairs. They were on the second floor. Probably fanning out cautiously, looking for her, checking all open shops and seeking out all viewing angles to the top. Their voices grew louder. It snapped her out of her torpor. They were at the foot of the stairs to her floor.

She lay flat on her stomach. Her arms stretched out ahead of her. Her bony elbows painfully pressing into the unyielding hardness of the floor. All her senses were heightened. This was the moment of truth. At the same time, she felt dizzy. It was an effort for her to focus. Her head felt heavy even though she lay prone on the floor.

Outside, a car neared, its tyres crunching gravel. Had she heard it through her headset? It came to a halt. Was it Sergei and Jane?

She had to focus on what was in front of her. Even if Sergei managed to approach the building without being seen, he would be too late.

Footfalls on the steps corresponded with faint vibrations travelling up her elbows. They were climbing. God, please let them not all pop up together. Should she go single fire or more? How many rounds remained in the magazine? She had hit three riders and missed three. She had also fired a short burst of three or possibly four rounds. If she had counted correctly, there were at least twenty rounds in the magazine.

If she wasted ammo now, it was all over. She turned the selector lever to single fire and waited.

The footsteps grew louder. More than one person was coming up the stairs. Irrational fear overcame her. She was usually icy in such situations. Why was she breaking down now at the crucial moment? She had to stay strong.

There was movement; a head appeared on the extreme left. She was expecting right. She pivoted her arms and swung the rifle silently. Ouch, her elbows dragged on the rough floor and scraped her skin. She fired. The head disappeared. As the echo died, it was replaced by the thuds of the body hitting the steps as it fell.

She had two or three seconds to get out of there and find cover. The next time instead of a head it would be the barrel of a gun. It would strafe the floor. That is what she would do.

Razane tried to leap to her feet, but her legs shook like jelly.

A tension headache made her dizzy with pain. She half crouched and half stumbled towards the far left.

The men were as good as she had expected. They were not suicidal and not in any hurry at all. A few moments passed before someone plucked up the courage to do just what she had predicted. Bullets whizzed across the floor, one ricocheting off the railing with a resonating ping. She cowered behind a half-metre-high wall. From here she no longer saw the landing at the top of the staircase.

She was cornered and unable to defend her floor.

Sergei was on the ground floor when he heard Razane's shot, reverberating through the building, then the sound of a body falling and men cursing. He cautiously climbed halfway up the first flight of stairs. They were most likely on the second floor.

'Sweetheart, I'm on the first flight of stairs. Where are they?' he whispered.

Razane was crying. 'I hear them on the second floor,' she said. 'I'm cornered. Be so careful, please...'

'Hang on. I'll be right there.'

'Please take care, Serge. I love you so, so, so much...' Her voice trailed off into a whispered squeak.

'I love you too. You're my wonder woman. I will get you out of this. I promise!'

He couldn't waste time in contemplation. He heard the loud burst of fire strafing her floor. They were attacking. He ran up the remaining steps. No one was on the first floor. He looked madly for the second flight of stairs and ran towards them. The firing stopped. He slowed his pace. He needed to be as silent as possible. He crept up the second flight of stairs. The last few steps he was on his hands and knees making sure his rifle didn't clang against the concrete.

At the top, he cautiously looked over. Two men stood in the middle of the floor. One was at the foot of the staircase to the top floor looking up. Next to him, a body lay crumpled in a heap. Razane must have gotten that one. The fifth man was most likely at the top of the stairs, out of sight. Sergei checked the safety and flicked the fire selector to fully automatic mode. He lifted himself silently, aimed and fired. The two men in the middle fell forward as bullets ripped through them. The man at the bottom of the steps half turned as he got up and tried running up. Bullets tore into his legs. He was tough. He managed to turn his rifle in Sergei's direction, but it was too late for him. Two more bullets ripped into his chest, and he slumped to the foot of the stairs. Sergei took his finger off the trigger trying to work out how many rounds he'd used. At the same time, where was the last man?

'Sweetheart, I got three of them,' he whispered. She didn't answer. 'I think the last one's trapped somewhere at the top of the stairs.' The sound of Razane sobbing was like a serrated knife in the heart. Was she hurt? 'Sweetheart, are you OK?'

A loud scream echoed through the building, like a war cry. It was the last man. He had reached Razane's floor. Faint footsteps reverberated above him. A loud shot rang out followed by more. The man was firing in all directions. Throwing caution to the wind, Sergei raced up the last flight of stairs. He felt sick. Razane, please be OK.

A shot rang out, followed by a blood-curdling scream that ended in a thud, the sound of a body dropping. The total silence was almost as deafening.

There was no point being cautious any longer. Sergei ran onto the top floor landing. A body, cloaked in shadow lay in the middle of the floor. He ran towards it. Please let it not be Razane. Whoever it was stirred and turned. Razane was sobbing through his earpiece. He got closer. The figure lifted a rifle and pointed it directly at him. It wasn't Razane. A shot rang out.

THE FLING

Dubai, Saturday 3 December, 8:00pm

'I don't like this one bit,' Damon said, 'tomorrow's an important day.' He was fuming. Ben behaved like he didn't give a shit. Their parents and Razane were in danger. Getting them out was the only thing that mattered. Dubai could wait.

'We have to eat man, I don't know what you're getting so worked up about. Look at you; your veins are popping outta your forehead.'

'We have to set off tomorrow, early morning. If anything goes wrong, it can put Mum, Dad and Razane in even more danger.'

'Chill man, we're in Dubai, the safest place on Earth.'

'It doesn't mean you can't be hit by a car or get food poisoning or get in trouble some other way.'

'Yes and this hotel can fall down in an earthquake, or a meteor can strike us,' Ben was getting annoyed. Damon was always so single-minded in everything he did, and it always pissed him off no end. Granted, it explained why Damon was so good at everything while he always struggled. Maybe why Damon had become such an accomplished guitarist while he couldn't even strum a few chords. It was still bloody annoying.

But Damon had never been this much of a ninny and had always loved to party. Pakistan must have had a profound effect on him.

Seeing the bad bruises on his face and arms, he could understand to some extent. Still, life was short. Who knew what would happen once they set sail. Besides they weren't returning to Dubai anytime soon.

Damon wasn't about to give up. 'What's wrong with room service or takeaway or the restaurants in the hotel?'

'It's boring, and I haven't seen anything of Dubai since I got here.'

'Neither have I,' Damon was raising his voice again.

'So, get up and come with me... dick.'

Damon refused to budge. Ben stared at him for a few seconds, shook his head and walked out.

'Damn you! You stupid, stubborn ass.'

Ben responded by showing him his middle finger.

Damon fought the urge to get up and punch him. 'At least don't be late. When will you be back?'

'In time to set sail tomorrow,' Ben said breezily, just before the door slammed.

He took the lift down to the lobby and walked out into the Dubai evening. In the distance the world's tallest building, the Burj Khalifa glowed blue as it dominated the night skyline.

It was cool with a gentle breeze. Different from the lovely warmth, earlier in the day, on board the Shalayla. By the time he got back, the temperature would drop further. Dubai was after all in the desert. Thankfully he'd decided to wear a long-sleeved cotton jumper.

According to Google Maps, it was a reasonably short walk. He glanced right as he stepped off the kerb to cross Burj Khalifa Boulevard. A car's tyres screeched as tortured rubber fought with asphalt. Oh shit! He glanced left at the last minute and realised his mistake. He jumped back on the footpath, his heart thumping like crazy. With a violent rush of wind, a silver Lexus came to a shuddering halt where he had stood less than half a second ago. Its driver put his arm out of his window and shook his fist at him, his other hand planted on the horn.

'Sorry,' Ben mouthed and waved apologetically.

What an idiot he was. Traffic drove on the other side of the road to Australia, and he'd looked the wrong way. Thankfully, Damon hadn't seen him. He'd have never heard the end of it.

Still shaken, Ben put his phone in his pocket. He was going to have to be more careful. Focusing, he looked left and crossed over to the median strip. Then he looked right and crossed over to the footpath on the other side. A short walk later he turned left along Emaar Boulevard. The street furniture in Dubai was amazing. Funky looking lamps dotted the footpath casting their illumination evenly. The lamps were interspersed with tall and slender palms. A clipped, low growing, hedge separated the footpath from the road.

He crossed the busy Sheikh Mohammed bin Rashid Boulevard at a zebra crossing. What a mouthful that name was. Traffic was almost at a standstill. Money, and lots of it, was in evidence everywhere. Some sections of road were surfaced not in asphalt, but a mosaic of tiles. The street clocks were Rolexes. Just about every second car was a Mercedes, Porsche, Lamborghini, Bentley or Ferrari. Drivers blipped their throttles, as they idled, generating a mechanical symphony that would no doubt be music to the ears of any petrol head.

He turned right. After a short stroll along the main road, he turned left and entered the breath-taking Burj park. It was the first time he'd seen the Burj Khalifa from its base to its tip, and the magnificent view took his breath away. Threading his way through the crowd, he walked down the steps and along the lake. It was crowded. Street performers mingled with tourists and locals to create an air of festivity.

He crossed a small dimly lit footbridge. To his right, the lake became wider. Loud music started, spotlights played across the lake, and the famous dancing fountains came to life as water jets spurted into the air to the rhythm of the music. People stood entranced. Dancing in public was frowned upon, but many were swaying gently, caught up in the moment; others were filming.

'What a nice place it would be to dance,' a heavily accented woman's voice said.

'Yes, but you could be in trouble if you do...' He turned around as he spoke. Two young women stood along the railing enjoying the show. The one closer to him had spoken to her companion. Hearing him, she turned and smiled. It was too dark to see all her features, but she had high cheekbones and curly dark brown hair that came to her shoulders.

'We are looking for somewhere to dance,' she explained in a thick Spanish accent motioning to her friend.

'Yup, me too,' he said, 'I heard there is a really rad place at the Armani hotel.' He took out his phone and showed her the location.

Her friend leaned over to look as well. 'Shall we all go then?' she had the same accent.

'My mum told me I am not supposed to go anywhere with strangers,' he said with a note of mischief in his voice. Where had that come from?

'Oh, where is your mother?' The first one looked around.

'Not here,' Ben said.

'Then what she doesn't know won't hurt her,' she said playfully.

'I am Ben,' he put out his hand.

She shook it firmly, 'Well Ben, I am Lorena.' Her hand was soft with long and slender fingers that ended in tapered nails. 'My friend is Maria Luiza.' They shook hands too.

'Where are you ladies from?'

'Can you guess?'

The accent and names suggested Spanish or South American. 'Brazil?'

'Not bad,' Lorena said with a laugh, 'well Ben now that you know our names and where we are from, we are strangers no longer!'

'You're right,' he smiled, 'let's go. By the way, I'm from Australia.'

'Hey, your funny accent could not be from anywhere else.' She smiled, 'Now lead the way, Australian Ben.'

The Armani Prive was an impressive venue. A well-known DJ was playing a down-tempo house beat. Lorena was the most beautiful woman he had ever flirted with, and Maria Luiza was not bad either. They danced and drank and danced some more.

For a while, they both danced with him. For a crazy moment, he had a vision of taking them both back to his hotel room. Drat, he was sharing with Damon. He would have to find another place. But then Maria Luiza started dancing with someone else. In a way, he felt relieved. It was a silly thought anyway. He was not the threesome kind of guy. He wouldn't know what to do.

Eventually, hunger got to him. He hadn't eaten since lunchtime and was starving. 'Let's go and grab a bite to eat,' he had to shout in her ear to make himself heard above the music. She smelt heavenly and was even more alluring close-up. Everything about her was lovely. Hopefully, she was hungry too.

'I thought you'd never ask, Ben.'

'Is Maria Luiza joining us?'

'No. She is a big girl. She can find her own way back. Dubai is a safe place.'

'Yeah, that's what I told my brother.'

They walked around a bit, hand in hand. He couldn't remember who'd initiated that. There was something special about her. Hopefully, he wasn't behaving too infatuated. He couldn't remember the last time a girl made him feel that way. It was almost like he was floating on a gentle breeze in some alternate universe. There had to be magic in the air in Dubai. They walked around the lake past a series of restaurants, most facing the Burj, and found a nice outdoor eatery. A street performer strummed his classical guitar on a small stage. They enjoyed the music while they ate deliciously spiced roasted lamb with dips and Turkish bread. Soon they were talking and laughing like old friends. She was a trainee customer service officer for Emirates and had arrived a week ago. Her family was from Brazil, but they now lived in England. He told her he was going on a cruise in the morning to explore Asian ports for a documentary. She was simply delightful, and there was definitely some chemistry between them. Did she feel it too?

After dinner, they went in search of ice cream and found a delicious caramel and baklava sundae at a little lakeside cafe.

Later they walked some more through an underground souk and found their way back across Sheikh Mohammed bin Rashid Boulevard.

Finally, they stopped in front of a large square sandstone building surrounded by huge date palms. She turned to face him. 'This is my hotel.'

He looked into her eyes. He did not want the evening to end. 'That was awesome; I had so much fun.' His voice ended in a croak. How lame? Was that the best he could do? She was so beautiful; her proximity must have choked the blood supply from his brain. Was it just his imagination or had she moved closer? His mind cast around in a mild panic. What else should he say? He didn't want to leave it at that.

'Would you have sex with me, Australian Ben?'

'Wha- yes- it'd- be- of course.'

She smiled, her eyes locked on his.

Her room was on the top floor. The elevator was the slowest he had ever been in and seemed to go on forever. She stood close, pressed up against him, her warmth more than pleasant. She was shaking ever so imperceptibly. Was she nervous too? Oh shit, did he have a condom? He always kept one in his wallet. It was the same one for at least the last year. Damon had called it an optimistic prophylactic.

He had to let Damon know where he was. 'With a girl,' he texted, 'C U on the boat before 7:30.'

'Dude, I'm gonna kill ya,' came the immediate reply.

'Up yours. C U on the boat.'

'Will call U at 6:00 to remind you.'

Damon was way too intrusive. He should never have

given him his old phone. He switched his own phone off.

Ben woke with a start. His head was full of cotton wool. Where was he? The sun's rays shining through the window were warm on his face. It felt like the afternoon. What time was it? It looked late. His head was heavy like he'd overslept. His watch showed 11:55. Oh, shit! Damon would kill him. They'd be late for Pakistan. He looked for his clothes in a panic.

Lorena walked in whistling. 'Was I that bad last night?' she sounded hurt as she jumped on the bed.

'No, I am sorry, I am late for our cruise,' he mumbled still searching for his shoes. He desperately wanted to stay, forever, but he had to leave.

'You told me it was at 7:30,' Lorena said.

'Yes,' he looked around for his socks, a vein pumping in his head.

'But it's not even six in the morning.'

He stopped. 'What?'

He took out his phone. It was 5:59. Just then the alarm beeped. Of course. He'd forgotten to set his wristwatch to Dubai time.

RED FOUR-WHEEL-DRIVE

Multan, Saturday 3 December, 9:20pm

The staff at the Ramada Multan took the business of being accommodating to their guests most seriously. So when two Pakistani women and an Australian man checked in wanting to share a room they happily acquiesced to their wishes. A few minutes later when three men who claimed they were government servants wanted to share a room, with three single beds, they were more than happy to fulfil that request as well. After all, hotels existed to serve guests and who were they to judge.

Major Hamdani sat in bed reading the Quran; his teeth were in a cup next to him. Yousaf was already fast asleep. After a while, he carefully placed the book on the bedside table and lay down. Thirty seconds later he was snoring.

Fazal yawned. What did the major think he was going to learn by letting these foreigners run free. It was obvious they were going to Karachi. He could think of only one reason why that was the case. Karachi was the favourite route for people-smugglers. If he wanted a publicly known figure to leave the country that is the way he would have chosen as well.

He was no longer following the spy movie on TV. It had become needlessly complicated. Life was rarely ever like that. He switched it off and lay down. He plugged his phone into the charger and set the alarm to wake before the other two. On impulse, he checked the tracker app.

The foreigners' Toyota was not in the hotel car park but

outside Multan in the middle of a field. How bizarre. Why would someone drive a Corolla there?

The major would surely want to know. He had a fleeting impulse to go by himself. Maybe he could observe what they were doing, or who they were meeting before arresting them. But it could also be a career-ending move. Most likely it would be seen as gross insubordination. He chose the safer option.

'Sir, you might like to see this.'

The major woke with a start, his mind foggy with sleep. Fazal was showing him something on the tracker. It could only mean one thing. He leapt out of bed and grabbed it from him. 'Wake Youfaf, we neef ooo geh ouf fhere.' He stopped to put his teeth back in.

Damn, Damn, Damn. How unprofessional was he? He focused on avoiding the rickshaw that veered across his path. One of the two should have kept watch. He needed to be tougher on them. They were grown men, ex-soldiers in the Pakistani Army.

He accelerated up to speed again. Traffic on Ghaus ul Azam Road was light, so he was able to drive at a hundred. Most other people seemed to do the same even though the speed limit was sixty.

He knew Multan well, so he avoided the city centre. That would only get them stuck. This way they should be able to reach the place in around twenty minutes, if they were lucky.

'Are they still there?' he asked Fazal.

'Yes, sir.'

'By the way well done for keeping an eye on them.'

'Yes sir, but I think I should have checked them continuously, sorry about that.'

'You are right, we all should have. Let us hope we are not too late.'

'Too late for what, sir?' Yousaf asked rubbing his eye gingerly with a tissue.

He shrugged. 'If I knew the answer to that do you think I would be chasing them in the middle of the night?'

Sergei stood rooted to the spot for a long moment. The body fell back in a lifeless heap. Where was Razane? She was still crying softly in his earpiece. He ripped it out. 'It's OK, my darling. I'm here'. He heard her better now and walked over to where she sat crouched on the floor, holding her rifle, and slowly swaying. The barrel was pointed down; her finger was still on the trigger.

He stepped around the rifle and crouched down beside her. She didn't look up at him. Her hair covered her face. She was crying silently, tears streaming down her face. He held her rifle by the barrel and carefully slid her finger off the trigger. She put up no resistance. He put his arms around her and held her. She was as limp as a rag-doll and drenched in sweat, shaking and sobbing uncontrollably. The post-traumatic stress disorder was manifesting itself. Her therapist had forbidden her to even watch violent movies.

'My poor baby,' he said holding her, stroking her wet hair. She should never have been in this situation. 'I am so sorry this is happening to you,' he whispered into her hair.

He remembered and put his earpiece back in. 'Jane, can you see the last motorbike?' he said.

'No,' she whispered. She sounded scared. 'Is Razane OK?'

'She's in shock but otherwise unhurt. Can you please come to the building? Bring your gun and be careful. The last rider is still somewhere out there.'

'Sure, sweetie.'

Come to think of it, the housing estate had gone completely silent. Where was the last man? He had to get down to Jane.

He scooped Razane's limp form in his arms and carefully carried her down the three flights of stairs. Jane was crouched behind a pillar, waiting. Seeing them, she opened the Pajero's door.

'The key's in the ignition,' she whispered as he approached, 'I feel we should take this car.'

Sergei gently placed Razane on the back seat. He heard a movement, a footstep. Jane gasped. His head was halfway inside the car, his hands under Razane. A shot rang out. His heart racing, he pulled himself out of the doorway and turned. Jane held her pistol pointed at a body on the ground.

'He came out... suddenly from... he had a gun,' she said with a whimper. The pistol fell from her limp hands. 'Oh my God, I shot him!'

'You did well sweetheart,' he said gently. She was trembling.

'That must've been the last bikie.' Her voice shook.

He pulled her close and glanced at the body. Jane had shot him through his left eye. He was not going to get up again.

'That felt so...' Jane's voice trailed off, muffled by his shoulder. It was an awful feeling to shoot someone. It didn't matter that he deserved it. She had killed someone. A mother just like her would have her life torn apart.

But she couldn't just stand there feeling sorry for herself. Not with Razane in such a state, sitting motionless in the back of the four-wheel-drive. Jane's heart went out to her. How many times would Razane have been in such a situation? It explained why she was traumatised. She climbed in beside her and wrapped her in her arms. Razane's skin was clammy, her breathing ragged and shallow.

Jane kissed Razane on the lips, then on each eye, her hands stroking her damp hair.

'I need something warm around us; I believe there's a shawl in the rucksack.'

Sergei ran to the Corolla. The boot was all mangled from the impact with the motorcycle. It took a lot of force, but he managed to yank it open. He grabbed the rucksack, the rest of the weapons and spare ammunition and ran back to the Pajero.

He gently draped the shawl over the two women. The wind picked up speed. The openings in the building were beginning to howl. The whole estate was littered with dead bodies. Thank goodness, he didn't believe in spirits.

He put his arms around them both. They had to get out of here. Any moment someone else would come along, the police probably, but he just couldn't separate himself away from their embrace. He was starting to tremble. They'd almost been killed, again. When was this madness ever going to end?

'I can't believe how lucky we are.' His voice shook.

'Yes, thank God,' Jane responded, touching his cheek.

'If he's there, he must like us.' He smiled. First spirits and then God. He had to pull himself together.

Seeing Razane in this state was tearing him apart. Every person had a breaking point, and she was at hers. Her breathing was shallow and hurried, and she was as stiff as a board. Ever so gently he kissed her on her cheek then moved to her ear and her neck. Jane massaged her hands and her arms. Gradually her breathing became more even; she relaxed a bit. After a while, she moved a little and gave him a weak squeeze.

'I'll be OK,' she said feebly, 'we need to leave.'

Jane squeezed his arm and looked at him. 'What about you. Are you OK? You are shaking.'

'I'll be fine. It's just the adrenaline.'

'I need a kiss,' Razane said, pulling him in. She smelt of sweat and fear, but he kissed her tenderly on the lips like she was the sweetest smelling rose in the world. He was sure he stank as well. She finally became more responsive and pushed him away gently. 'This time you saved us. You're our hero.'

'We all did something amazing. You're an unbelievable shot, and Jane killed the last rider.' He stroked her hair as she lay back against Jane.'

'Jane's also my hero,' she mumbled weakly, 'now drive, get us out of here.'

'Yes, madam,'

He got in the driver's seat and turned the key. The Mitsubishi's diesel engine sprang into life.

'We need to head straight for Karachi.' He heard no argument from the back.

They entered the partially constructed housing estate. It was dark and eerily silent.

'Are you sure this is the place?' The major asked.

'It has to be,' Fazal said, 'the maps on the tracker don't show these roads, but the car is here somewhere. Stay on this road we are getting closer.'

They approached a large four-storey building. It was under construction and dark. Yousaf shone a flashlight out of his window at the building.

'Sir, stop,' he hissed loudly, his torch illuminated a shape on the ground, 'what is that?'

'A dead body,' Fazal said.

The major slammed on the brakes pushing everyone forward.

It was a heavyset man with long black hair, not one of the foreigners. His heart was racing. Why was he surprised? The foreigners seemed to have a knack for leaving corpses behind wherever they went.

He drove on a few more metres and pulled into the car park, the tyres making crunching sounds on the loose gravel.

Silence descended as he switched off the engine.

'The target is twenty-five metres that way,' Fazal said looking down at his tracker. He got out and began walking towards the rear of the building.

'Fazal come back,' the major said sharply, 'we need to be armed.' He opened the boot and pulled out three Glock semi-automatic 9mm pistols and handed them out. 'Yousaf, you examine the body.'

Yousaf checked his magazine and walked over to the

body, his gun at the ready. Fazal went looking for the Corolla.

Major Hamdani sighed and looked up at the building. Apart from the wind howling through the window openings, it was all silent. They had arrived too late. Whatever had happened here had involved a lot of shooting. The smell of gunpowder was still strong. Something told him they would find more bodies. He pulled out a slender torch from his pocket and looked around.

'These tyre tracks look fresh,' he said. 'A four-wheel-drive was here recently.' It was obvious from the tread pattern.

'The man is dead,' Yousaf said, 'shot through the eye. The killer knew what he was doing.'

'Another conjecture,' Fazal shouted, 'could have been caught in a crossfire.' He couldn't give up the opportunity. 'Major sir, I found the Corolla.'

The major walked over and shone his torch in the dead man's face. He was young, fair skinned and clean-shaven. He looked like an Afghan. He had sunburn on his cheeks, and the tip of his nose was flaking. The skin on his cheeks was burnt. From his appearance, he had spent a long time in the sun at a high altitude. His fingers still clutched an Uzi. A large hole on the inside of his left eye showed where the bullet had entered. A puddle of blood had collected under his head and spread in the gravel.

The major stood, 'Yousaf, check this building and be careful.' He walked to the Corolla with Fazal. The car looked like it had been in a war zone. Most of its glass was shattered. The side was peppered with bullet holes, and the rear was completely caved in. Most of the car was covered in streaks of blood. The metallic blood smell, mixed with gunpowder and melted brake lining, made his stomach turn.

He looked inside without touching anything. It was empty.

Yousaf's urgent shout shook him out of his concentration. 'Sir, sir come quick!'

He walked as briskly as possible back to the building.

Yousaf was on the second floor. He began climbing the steps. He had to pace himself. There was no point getting a heart attack. Fazal followed.

Yousaf shone his torch on the face of one the bodies on the floor, 'do you recognise him?'

He did. Luqman Qayyum was number seven on the list of most wanted terrorists and criminals in the country. He had a long and bloody history having fought first against the Russians then with the Afghani Taliban. Later he had set up a faction of the Pakistani Taliban. He was also a gun for hire and was suspected of having masterminded many bombings and assassinations in Punjab.

Fazal let out a whistle. 'Why would Luqman Qayyum be here, dead?'

'Someone probably offered a lot of money to have our foreigners killed,' the major replied. 'Terrorists need money more than most.'

'I see now why you are letting these people free,' Yousaf said, 'they are taking care of the terrorist problem single-handedly.'

'Don't be a smartarse.' The major snapped.

Yousaf had hit on something that annoyed him, no end. The government had not recognised the existential risk terrorism posed to the country. Destroying terrorist networks and discouraging extremism needed to be their number one priority.

Much of the violent crime was committed by, or with the support of, the many terror networks. It was no longer about religion or politics but had become a business, a notoriety competition to capture the attention of the big financiers. The army was only now beginning to go on the offensive. Truth be told they could use all the help they could get, even from amateurs.

'I know this guy. His name is Battery.' Yousaf's torch shone on another body. 'He is a well-known career criminal in Multan. I heard of him while at cadet college. Back then he used to beat people up for money.'

'And this person is Irfan something...' Fazal said scratching his head.

'OK, now check the rest,' Major Hamdani said as he dialled a number.

'Get me the Brigadier please.'

THE N5

Rahim Yar Khan, Sunday 4 December, 1:00am

Sergei was so tired it was making him fidget. He could no longer find a comfortable position on the seat. He rolled down the window to let in some fresh air. Rather than help, the cold made him shiver and feel even more jittery, less in control.

His neck ached, and his head throbbed with a dull pain. His vision had blurred to the point of seeing double. He rubbed each of his sore eyes, in turn, scared to close them both at once in case he dozed off. In the high-riding, Mitsubishi travelling at a hundred and twenty with no barriers on the side of the road, the tiniest micro sleep would probably mean never waking up again.

He searched for music stations. There were none. The radio had Bluetooth, but in their haste to leave, he hadn't paired his phone.

He moved the rear-view mirror to look at the back seat. Razane was fast asleep in Jane's arms, her head resting on Jane's shoulder. Jane was sleeping too. Her face in Razane's hair. He smiled. They looked so perfect together. The two most beautiful women in the world.

Poor Razane, over the years she'd suffered so much trauma her adrenaline system now malfunctioned and could make her body go spontaneously into shock without the normal fight or flight response.

Over the last few days, they'd all been extremely lucky. It was probably only love that had enabled Razane to function the way she did. Her abilities were almost preternatural. The way she had responded to threats, with countermeasures, almost in the blink of an eye, would have been the envy of the most elite fighting men and women in the world. Ironically, she was also the most gentle and sensitive soul imaginable. It was easy to understand how every person she killed weighed on her.

The pain she'd be in would be unbearable. The stress they'd all been under was enough to make the toughest person crumble. They wouldn't survive another encounter.

They still had no idea who they were dealing with. Who was the maniac with the moustache? Why destroy Jane's work? How had Jane's work threatened him? Was it financial? Or something else? But what could it be? He had destroyed everything she'd built and was still out to get them. At some level, Sergei could understand he would take their attack on his village personally, but he had started it by kidnapping Damon.

Somehow, inadvertently, they'd made the most dangerous enemy, with enormous resources and influence that reached across the country. And from the beginning, they had massively underestimated the threat they'd faced.

It was incredible how they'd been spotted in Multan. The riders must have been on the lookout, waiting at the entrance to the city or maybe near the hotel. In hindsight, foreigners checking into a quality hotel was an amateurish mistake. From now on he'd have to think differently, certainly no more hotels.

After getting a bloody nose the last few times, their enemy's next move would be more deadly and focused.

To survive, they'd have to focus at every step of the way. Like now. He had to focus on the road. His reaction times were starting to suffer. Normally he could react faster than anyone he knew, but now he felt the lag. The vital microseconds between the car in front applying its brakes and him responding had almost tripled.

Thankfully the traffic had thinned out. They were far enough outside any large population centres that the only people on the road were long-distance travellers in semis, cars, and the odd coach.

A sign to Rahim Yar Khan flashed past. It was now only 25km away. They had to stop there for a cup of tea or coffee.

THE ENEMY OF MY ENEMY

Multan, Sunday 4 December, 1:15am

The game of chess depended on guessing the opponent's move many steps in advance, while hiding one's own intentions. Major Hamdani was great at chess, but he was having a hard time guessing what was going to happen next. There was a game afoot he was not part of, and bodies were piling up. He was tired. Age was catching up and even though he exercised daily, late nights no longer suited him.

He looked outside at the dimly lit network of streets and ghostly silhouettes of partially constructed houses and yawned. They sat in their car while the army squad locked down the estate. This was now a joint operation between the military and the police. They often cooperated when terrorism was involved. Two army jeeps blocked the exit ramp off the main road. A police forensics team was poring over every detail, taking photographs, collecting evidence, and bagging bodies.

Two army jawans carried a body bag down the stairs and placed it next to the others on the ground in the car park. So far, the count was eleven, all spread around the estate, and not one foreigner, which beggared belief. Most had been identified except for one. It had been mangled beyond recognition. A DNA test would be needed there. They were all hardened criminals and known terrorists. Many had fought in wars in Afghanistan and Iraq. A few were even linked to Islamic State activities in Syria.

There had been underground whispers the Islamic State were setting up in southern Punjab. What they had found here certainly added credence to that.

Just a few hours ago he had received more detailed information about Razane Silan and Sergei Markoff. They were not average citizens. Razane had achieved almost legendary status among the Peshmerga, but she had become unstable and was discharged. Sergei had been in the Australian military decades ago but never saw any fighting. It still did not explain how they had overcome such odds.

How was Jibran Ghaffar linked to the foreigners and the dead terrorists? On the surface, it looked like a contract killing, a terrorist group augmenting their income. Was Jibran the initiator of the contract? It would provide proof of a disturbing link between some of Pakistan's powerful elite and terrorist cells.

The ISI and the army were trying hard, but it had been incredibly difficult to make any meaningful headway against the terrorist cells. They had tentacles inside the government, the military and big business. They were like a cancer and rooting them out was becoming increasingly dangerous for the patient.

Power hungry people like Jibran Ghaffar were making it much harder still. In their mad quest for power, many were reputedly sponsoring the cells, using them in land grabs and to intimidate competitors.

'Sir,' Yousaf said, shaking him out of his thoughts. 'I received the financial transaction report for Mack Hameed.'

'Huh, and?'

'He made many small payments for fuel, groceries, bills and clothes. He withdrew twenty lakhs in cash seven days ago, which could be normal for a rich person. But this payment is most strange and the biggest...' He took a breath as he paused for dramatic effect. 'A big, very big payment to World Yacht Charter based in Dubai for... over seven hundred thousand dollars.'

The major slid over to look at Yousaf's screen. Thank Allah, this was the break they needed.

'Do a Google search for World Yacht Charter,' he said.

'Here, I have done it,' Fazal said quickly, 'they hire out

superyachts out of the Mediterranean, Dubai and Australia.'

The major craned his head to look at Fazal's laptop. World Yacht Charter provided Yachts for hire. Five were listed in Dubai. Three were available for booking.

'If their site is current, it means Mack hired one of the other two yachts.' Major Hamdani was thinking aloud. 'It means we know how they are leaving Pakistan.'

'Do we?' Yousaf was clearly not on the same wavelength.

'Sir, can I throw something at him?'

'Leave him. His mind works at a different speed.'

'So, at what point do we put an end to this chase?' Yousaf asked ignoring the jibe.

'Based on what you have seen here how would you answer your question?'

'Well if they are leaving by sea,' Yousaf said slowly, 'then, I think, just before they leave Pakistani territory.'

'So Yousaf, you do have a brain. Fazal, I need you to contact our UAE liaison. Find which yacht they hired and get its satellite tracking number, so we can look for it.'

'What if it doesn't have a tracker?'

'These things cost over fifty million American dollars. Their owners will always want to know where they are.'

'OK sir, I will check.'

ANGEL

Rahim Yar Khan, Sunday 4 December, 1:20am

This was not the first time she had frozen during combat. The last time two of her comrades had died, their unit's position almost overrun. It was the final straw. She had been given the option to leave voluntarily or face a court-martial. She chose the former.

It was the lowest point in her life. More than once she had tried to end it by placing the barrel of her rifle in her mouth and willing her fingers to press the trigger. Suicide needed more courage than she had or perhaps some part of her fought back, but she could not go through with it. She had been left with an unpleasant oily metallic taste on her tongue and an even greater feeling of despondency and uselessness. Everything in her life had gone black.

One of her few remaining friends forced her to apply for a job as a translator for a foreign company working in northern Iraq. If he had not driven her to the interview, she would not have gone.

There she met someone as diametrically opposite as was possible for two people to be.

Jane was soft and sweet where she was hard and bitter. Even more important, Jane was whole where she was in pieces, shattered, spent, her life force all but drained.

During the interview, Jane did most of the talking. She tried to convince Razane, rather than the other way around as she explained their plans in Sharanish. Here was someone trying to make and build, rather than break and ravage. But she would be in danger. Iraq was no place for anyone, let alone a white woman on a humanitarian mission.

A part of Razane wanted to run. Surely someone with the darkness she had inside could not associate with someone with so much light. Yet she saw a way to redeem herself. Maybe helping Jane do a good deed could give her own life some meaning.

The calm and warm fire in Jane pulled her in, and before the interview was over, she wanted the job.

Razane became Jane's translator and guide. She accompanied her, wherever work took them, from Sharanish to Zakho and sometimes Mosul.

For all her vision and skills, Jane had an almost otherworldly innocence she had not seen in an adult before. She saw the good in everyone and trusted like a child. She was like an angel.

Jane was deeply compassionate and a great listener with a complete absence of judgement. Razane found herself opening up to her more and more. Soon she was telling her things she had never shared with anyone. They were secrets she had kept bottled up under a shell that became harder and tougher over the years.

She had an idyllic childhood that was brutally interrupted by the Iran-Iraq war. Her father, a colonel in the Republican Guard, was killed when his Jeep drove over a landmine on the border with Iran.

Two years later her mother was among the thousands killed in Halabja when Saddam dropped chemical weapons on his own people. It was the point when Razane's life completely unravelled. She was in an anatomy class in Baghdad University when the news came in. She left the same day to look for her mother and never returned. Her dreams of being a doctor, forgotten in her desire to fight anyone and everyone.

Razane moved to Erbil and joined the PUK – The Patriotic Union of Kurdistan and then its military wing, the famed

Peshmerga. Her first combat was in skirmishes against the weakened Iraqi army. Then she fought in the pointless Kurdish civil war. By the time it was over, she had spent nearly half her life with a gun in her hands. When the civil war started in Syria, she crossed the border to join the Syrian Kurds in their fight against Islamic State and other rebel groups. The battlefield had become her home, her unit, and her family.

There was only so long a person could fight. Everyone had their breaking point. When she broke, her own side disowned her. That was when she realised her whole life had been in vain. She had not achieved anything and had become a burnt-out shell of a woman, hollow, incapable of love or being loved.

Being able to unburden on someone who cared was a cathartic experience. Her emotional outpourings became the opening of a floodgate. Gradually, she began to feel again. One day she became aware she saw in colour. It dawned on her the last twenty years of her life had been a depressing, monotonous scheme of black and grey.

Jane made her feel human, a woman, somebody who mattered.

For the first time since her mother died, Razane went shopping for feminine things with Jane. She bought women's shoes and clothes and got a feminine haircut. They found a little cafe and ordered coffee and shared a cake. She could not remember the last time she had enjoyed eating or drinking.

They began spending more and more time together outside of work. They watched movies, explored restaurants and cafes, and enrolled in a poetry class.

One day Razane woke and realised she had fallen in love with her angel.

At first, she had felt deep shame. It was abominable for a woman to love a woman in that way. She contemplated leaving her employment. She did not want to but could not find a way to reconcile her feelings with her beliefs. In a state of emotional turmoil, she recalled her favourite poet Rumi. Had Rumi not described love as the most sublime and exalted of human emotions? Was it not the way to be one with the divine? It did not matter who the beloved was or even whether it was unrequited or reciprocated. True love was blind and selfless.

She need not have worried. Her life turned out all right, far more than all right. Through Jane and Sergei, she found a happiness that wiped away all the pain in her life, many times over.

Their love was worth fighting for. She had to be strong and not let her past get in the way.

Jane was fast asleep. Her chest rose and fell with a deep and relaxed rhythm. Her breath was warm and soft against her scalp where her face nuzzled into her hair. There was nothing about Jane she did not love. Every moment was special. Jane was simply everything one human could be to another.

Razane was about to fall into a warm, comfortable sleep again when she thought of Sergei. Her poor darling had not slept the whole time, and his injuries had not yet fully healed. His head was bobbing up and down with every small bump. He was no longer fully awake and alert.

'My love, are you OK to drive?'

Sergei sat more upright. 'Actually, I am bloody tired. I was going to stop in the next city and grab a tea or a coffee.'

'Let me drive a bit and you can sleep.'

'No sweetheart, you just went through hell back there.'

'I'm so sorry for melting like that. I feel so bad for it. You could have been killed.'

'You didn't melt. You were super brave.'

'I froze again. I feel like I am... I became unstable--'

'No, you didn't, and you aren't.'

'Will you stop worrying about letting us down.' Jane woke up. She cleared Razane's hair from her face and kissed her gently on her forehead. 'We're all alive... and very much thanks to you, and that's all that matters.'

Deep down inside Razane wanted to believe Jane, but she

could not shake an irrational fear. She had lost control, and it was only luck, Sergei had not been killed. She had looked up just when the man had raised his gun, and somehow, had pulled the trigger. Her fear was irrational because the event had passed but the memory still made her shudder. Maybe it was because she knew, she could no longer trust herself.

'You are right, it is all that matters.' She sighed. 'Nothing makes me whole again like a warm hug from you two.' She squeezed Jane tightly.

'And please don't ever call yourself unstable,' Sergei said, 'I've never seen anyone hold it together like you. You're human! Humans break because... we're human. If you didn't, you'd be a monster. So look on the bright side.'

He was right of course, his reasoning impeccable. She could not help but smile. She loved him so, even his almost computer-like logic. Still, what would happen next time? She was sure there was going to be a next time. Their enemy was not going to give up.

'I just want us to get out of here.' Razane took a deep breath. 'And I never want to see another gun in my life. So, will you pull over and let me drive, please?'

'Serg, I haven't driven yet. Let me. Razane can go next.'

Sergei checked it was safe and pulled into a roadside rest area. Jane swapped places with him.

By the time she merged back on the highway and eased the Pajero back up to speed, he was already fast asleep, his arm around Razane and her head resting on his shoulder.

'You go for two hours then it's my turn.' Razane whispered from the back.

THE SUPER SLEUTH

Karachi, Sunday 4 December, 1:30am

Abrar had to focus hard to stay awake. The drive from Lahore had been long and tiring. The Land Rover was at a panel beater. He'd taken his black Jaguar instead. Even though it guzzled fuel, it was his favourite long-distance cruiser. It had a way of swallowing huge distances and leaving him refreshed at the end of most journeys. But the distance from Lahore to Karachi was a bit much even for the Jaguar's plush interior and magic carpet ride. He was now in serious danger of crashing as a result of fatigue.

He'd done well though, managing the trip in around twelve and a half hours. He had pushed himself, and the Jaguar, to the limits, managing to remain alert for almost the entire trip. But now his eyes burnt, his reaction time had become glacial, and even his hands felt tired from gripping the wheel.

Thankfully, he had entered the outskirts of Karachi. The end of his journey was in sight.

He hated what Karachi had become. It used to be exciting and progressive, a city of lights and tall buildings, wide boulevards, and the beach. But that was a long time ago when he was young. As a child and then a teenager, he used to enjoy visiting with his parents. Karachi always had better concerts, more prestigious art shows and better restaurants than Lahore. It was brash, modern, and fast-paced but still friendly and safe.

Then on its way to becoming a mega city with a population of twenty-seven million it also became one of the most dangerous places on earth. It started eating itself inside out. Politics of sectarianism and religion drove the population into submission as gangs began to dominate in much of the poorer and middle-class parts of the megalopolis. These gangs were sponsored by political parties who used them as their street power.

After countless years of bloody conflict, a single political party became dominant. The party's leader was a megalomaniac so corrupt, ruthless, and single-minded in his pursuit of power that the people and their problems fell by the wayside. He became Karachi's warlord, and the city his personal fiefdom. In many ways, he was like Jibran.

Karachi became a free for all, its development driven by corruption and greed and the ever-consuming hunger for more power. It spread out more and more into miles of miserable shanty towns. The old grand and charming parts still existed, but they became a smaller and smaller part of the metropolis.

Abrar's face hurt from lack of sleep. He was looking forward to his hotel.

The M9 Motorway became the Lyari Expressway. He had to do something to stay awake. He turned on the air conditioner and turned up the music. It was his favourite, Swedish melodic death metal. He had now been driving in Karachi proper for the last hour, and it had been nothing but slums and squalor, poorly constructed houses, no trees or open spaces and utter chaos.

He heaved a sigh of relief when he saw his exit. All bad things must come to an end. He turned right onto Garden Road. His mood lifted.

He was close now. This part of Karachi was how he remembered it, old buildings, mature trees, and wide boulevards. There was no garbage on the side of the road, at least not much, no illegal hoardings, and no gangs hanging around looking for trouble.

Even the traffic had changed. Cars were bigger and classier; people were better dressed. He spotted quite a few police cars, some patrolling, others, parked at intersections with lights flashing, warning would-be evildoers of their presence. No doubt, they contributed to the general sense of calm and well-being. In any event, they were a huge contrast to the armoured police troop carriers he had seen earlier.

Traffic had thinned out, and Abrar was able to drive fast. He turned right into Castle Street and then left into Abdullah Haroon Road. He drove past tall buildings, several of them headquarters of banks and insurance companies. He passed through an expansive roundabout with a strange monument in the middle. The hotel was only a block away. He turned left onto Club Road and followed it around. One last right turn and he was in the hotel driveway. A valet took his car, a porter his suitcase.

Check in was efficient. They knew him by name. The porter saw him to his room. He took a quick shower and dropped into bed. It was a bit after 2:30 in the morning.

It had been a joyless trip and not one he had wanted to make. He had tried talking his way out of it, telling Jibran he could keep his Barrett. At first, Jibran had tried cajoling him, but it didn't take him long to turn nasty and threaten him with the direst of consequences.

Abrar was annoyed with himself. Jibran was flesh and bone. A simple bullet fired from a strategic spot, and he would no longer need to deal with the cunt. Why had he been unable to tell the arrogant dickhead to go fuck himself?

Was it fear? He knew what would happen if he missed. Not that he ever had. What had transpired over the last few days had not been a failure on his part. If they hadn't launched the bomb into the police station or that bus hadn't come in the way, he'd have fulfilled his contract. The miss at Panjo Katla Chowk was also not his lack of skill. He had hit the car in the most extreme conditions. But someone had warned them, at the last moment.

The Australians were smart. In a way, he felt closer to them than to Jibran.

Ordinarily, it would be his professionalism that drove him to complete a job, but now it was fear. Jibran had a remarkable range of resources and contacts, and he knew how to use them. It was like his mental telephone book was full of all the killers and shady characters in Pakistan and the region. It was crazy how he'd been able to contact the man in Dubai within minutes of them finding Ben.

For all his arrogance and apparent thick-headedness, the man was shrewd and cunning and thought in a different way than he did, which made him unpredictable and dangerous.

In the morning somehow, he would have to figure out where their targets were hiding. He was unable to track them any longer on Google Maps. Even Ben was no longer sharing his location. He had to think like them if he was to have any chance.

Jibran had put the word out on the street among his local contacts. A staff member at every major hotel would be on the lookout.

If his calculations were right, Ben and Damon could be in Karachi Harbour as early as the following morning. That didn't give them much time to get their shit together and find them. He knew he wouldn't want to be anywhere near Jibran if the foreigners managed to escape the country. He had to do his best.

How would they think? They had shown themselves to be intelligent and were now aware of the danger they were in. They used the Internet and were resourceful. They would do everything possible to stay out of sight.

Maybe he needed to put himself in their shoes. What would he do? For one, he'd stay away from hotels. He could park his car somewhere and sleep in it, but that was risky. There were no isolated places around Karachi and way too many curious people.

The only place anyone could hide was in a private residence. Chances were his targets didn't know any locals, so unless they made friends quickly or entered someone's house by force, they'd be unable to do that. That only left small hotels, bed and breakfasts and guest houses and they'd use the Internet to search for them.

Abrar's busy mind wasn't letting him sleep. He turned on his phone and searched for small bed and breakfasts. A list of properties appeared along with a link to Airbnb. Oh shit! Airbnb was the answer, he was certain. That was exactly how they'd think. He clicked on the Airbnb website. It showed fifteen properties in Karachi.

THE STRAITS

Dubai, Sunday 4 December, 7:30am

'Have a safe journey.' The immigration official smiled as he gave back their passports. 'Dubai always welcomes visitors of distinction. We look forward to your return.'

'Thank you kindly,' Damon said. He smiled inwardly. This man was almost fawning.

The dour immigration officer at the airport, a day before yesterday, looked like he hadn't ever smiled in his life. Damon hadn't felt like a visitor of distinction then and didn't feel like one now. It wasn't after all his yacht. He hadn't even paid for it. It was Uncle Mack's money.

Sadness overwhelmed him. Uncle Mack had simply stopped existing; he had stopped being a person. The world just kept on turning without so much as a pause, not the slightest acknowledgement that someone had died, someone good and generous and funny.

The immigration officer walked down the gangway. A crew member waited for him to get off and engaged a switch. Electric motors pulled the gangway up towards the deck and folded it against the railing. Ben was already walking to the bridge. They hadn't spoken about the night before and the girl he'd met. Ben was acting strange and distant. The girl had dropped him off at the Marina, but she'd been too far away for him to see what she looked like. Ben had acted irresponsibly but had managed to make it to the boat on time. As far as he was concerned, there was no need for an argument.

Damon climbed the stairs to the upper deck. A slight tremor ran through the boat as the three mighty diesel engines started. A flutter of excitement ran through him. It was finally happening. Ben's simple but brilliant plan was being put into action. Would they pull it off? Everyone always said life wasn't meant to be easy, but this seemed to be just that, easy. What could possibly go wrong? That was the problem. He couldn't think of anything. An uneasy feeling seeped into his mind. They had missed something. It was not possible for them to have thought of everything.

The captain engaged the thrusters. Almost imperceptibly slowly, the Shalayla edged away from the pier. Its speed increased gradually to a walking pace as the captain manoeuvred it out of its berth. The huge boat accelerated as it sailed through the marina and into the channel that would take them out into the bay. Shadows from the tall buildings, lining the waterfront, moved faster across the boat as they picked up speed. They left the marina and turned to port to clear the enormous man-made Palm Island cluster. Sticking to the channels, they were now past the breakers.

Dubai was receding behind them. They were in the Persian Gulf proper. A moderate north-westerly wind cooled the effect of the warming sun on the side of his face as they turned in a north-easterly direction. Soon, Dubai's tall skyscrapers were the size of raisins.

This was his second time on a boat in the ocean. The last was a fishing trawler off the coast of Tasmania. He'd been thrown around in the one-metre waves. In comparison, the Shalayla was almost perfectly stable and level even though the waves appeared to be of similar size. He had expected a difference between a fishing trawler and a superyacht, but not this great.

Damon stood there awhile enjoying the stiff breeze, the fine spray, and the smell of the ocean. The moment didn't last long. This wasn't a pleasure cruise. It wasn't right to stand there, enjoying himself, when his parents and Razane were in Pakistan, possibly in danger.

He had anxiously scanned Pakistani newspapers, Facebook and Twitter for any news of his parents, but had found nothing. The night before he had tried to contact them, but the phone call hadn't gone through. Hopefully, they were just in a bad reception area and not something worse. In the morning he tried again, but to no avail. Finally, he had sent them a message, letting them know they had left Dubai.

Ben was busy chatting with Captain Philipe when Damon entered the bridge. From his accent, the captain seemed French. He looked the archetypal sea captain, a fit sixty-year-old with a shock of white hair, a weather-beaten face, clear blue eyes, and a scruffy white beard. Damon half expected him to pull out a pipe and start puffing on it.

'Captain says we should reach Karachi just after lunch tomorrow unless we are slowed by some unforeseen event,' Ben said.

'What unforeseen events are we talking about?' Damon said.

'If we knew, they wouldn't be unforeseen.' Captain Philipe grinned.

Damon looked at him unsmilingly.

'I s'ppose it could include storms, mechanical trouble, piracy or local authorities delaying us.'

'Thank you, Captain, let's then hope for the best.'

He pulled Ben to the side. 'Can we go over the plan please.'

'Sure, let's go to the entertainment room. I have set up all our gear there.'

They wandered down to the lower deck and opened the large glass door into a rectangular lounge. It was tastefully decorated, with soft white leather armchairs arranged around a square glass coffee table. Beyond, a sliding partition closed off a smaller area designed to be a small theatre. Eight armchairs were arranged to face a large LCD screen.

'This area all opens up at the press of a button,' Ben said.

'Do you want me to show you?'

'Not now, please.' Ben was too much of a geek and lived in a parallel universe, one where his parents were not in danger. 'Maybe later.'

Ben had already connected his laptop to the screen. A website popped up. 'Do you like it?' He said.

'What am I looking at, man?'

'Dude, it's my new site. It's a resource for sailors. Kind of everything they'd need to know about a port, its facilities, regulations, maps, contact details and the like.' He paused to take a breath. Damon did not say anything. 'It's to explain why we're visiting Karachi by boat. It'll have a video showing the channels and any marinas and other info, like a short documentary.'

'OK, well…'

'You need to pay attention here… This website will make it easier to visit and do business.'

'You did all this in how long?'

'Three days.'

Damon nodded and smiled. 'Impressive. I just hope the Pakis buy it.'

'It turns out I might've overkilled it a bit. I got in touch with reps from the Karachi Chamber of Commerce. They almost fell over themselves to welcome us. I never showed them this.'

'Well, if we do need it... at least it looks convincing.'

'It won't be a waste,' Ben said. 'There's nothing out there like this so... I might take it online after we're outta this mess.'

'So, you are planning to sail around the world to all the ports?'

'Maybe...' Ben said defensively.

Damon shook his head. His brother was able to dive in and out of la la land a bit too easily. He shook his head. 'Well it's very impressive even if it's overkill.'

'Thanks.'

'You know, Pakistan is actually a very chilled place,' Damon said stretching out on the chair. 'Most people are super friendly.'

'Yup, just before they shove a bomb up your arse.' Ben grinned.

'C'mon man,' Damon said, 'don't sound so immature. You can't go from coming up with a clever plan to sounding like a ten-year-old... I'm sure we won't have too many problems with immigration or the coast guard.'

'Touch wood,' Ben said.

'Yeah, don't we have a lot of that around.' Damon rapped his knuckles lightly on Ben's head who swept his arm away in annoyance.

'There is only one thing that's making me uneasy,' Damon said.

'What?' Ben frowned.

'We've still no idea who the fuckers are who're after Mum. You know the expression, Know thy enemy.'

'Know thy self, know thy enemy. A thousand battles, a thousand victories,' Ben said. 'It's Sun Tzu, one of Dad's favourite quotes.'

'Well, whatever. The point is we don't know our enemy at all.'

They kept the United Arab Emirates shoreline in sight as they made their way northeast. By early afternoon they reached Omani waters. The sky and the ocean were a similar colour, and the sun was shrouded in wispy cloud. Quite a few oil tankers passed them in the distance further out to sea. Other than that, they saw no other vessels. By mid-afternoon, they were sailing through the Musandam Fjords at the tip of Oman. Sheer cliffs rose almost vertically out of the water. Damon stood on deck and took lots of photographs. Ben was in his cabin throwing up. After a promising start, he'd found sailing didn't agree with him after all. His brother was a wuss, thankfully he hadn't come to Pakistan, or he'd have died just hearing the first gunshot.

Maybe that was a bit mean, but he was still angry with Ben. His stupid fight with his parents was one reason their mother had taken the project in Pakistan, just to get away from the brat.

Captain Philipe walked onto the deck. 'Lovely, isn't it?'

'Yes, it is.'

'If you have time, we could show you Kumzar. It's a small port town through that way.' He pointed south.

'Nah, would love to, but we've a deadline.' He wasn't sure what Ben had told the captain, so he kept it vague.

'Next time then?'

'Yeah sure. Hey, by the way, where's Iran?'

The captain pointed north to the open ocean. 'Those are the Straits of Hormuz and on the other side... that's Iran. I can get you some binoculars.'

'That's OK. Do they ever cause problems?'

'Who... the Iranians?'

'Yeah.'

'Only sometimes to smugglers. They know who to catch.'

'Oh! I suppose the western media loves to scare people.'

The captain laughed. 'Well let me put it this way...If there weren't Iranian Navy Patrol boats, this place would be swarming with pirates.'

Damon swallowed nervously. He hadn't thought of pirates.

REVENGE

On a day when he should feel triumphant, he was feeling anything but. Allah be praised, his Jihad against everything that was not pure Islam was finally growing in strength. He was no longer just a simple lone soldier of Allah. He commanded men and had been offered training grounds by Jibran Ghaffar. He had enough money to build more *madrassas*. His first big bombing had been most successful. The story was headline news in all Pakistani newspapers. Even better, it had made it to Al-Jazeera and all the big American and British news outlets.

Another bomb was being built that would bring death and destruction to unbelievers, *Inshallah*!

It would be followed by many more, of that he was certain. He had been receiving phone calls from people in Saudi Arabia and Qatar who congratulated him and offered him money and support. Success always brought more success. Soon he would receive calls for alliances with other groups.

The money was most useful, but the training grounds were a true blessing from Allah. Their location was perfect. They were in Punjab, Pakistan's heartland, within striking distance of its most decadent and vulgar of cities, Lahore, the city he would bring to its knees.

They would now be protected by a powerful and feared man. No one would touch them or look in their direction.

But Allah who had given so generously, had also taken away. Adil was his eldest son. He had more sons from other wives, but they were younger. It would take longer for them to shoulder his legacy and he might not live to see the day they did.

The woman with dark skin and black hair who had murdered him was, by all accounts, Pakistani and most likely Muslim. Deviant behaviour was to be expected from Christians or Westerners. When it came from a Muslim, it was ten times as concerning. Muslims had to be punished far more severely. He would teach her.

His most dangerous men had joined him to travel with the wadera to hunt them down. Getting revenge for his son would cleanse his soul and purify his mind so he could once again focus on his holy mission.

The voice from the loudspeaker snapped him out of his thoughts. 'Flight Airblue 401 to Karachi is now ready for boarding at gate 2.'

His whole group stood.

CROISSANTS

Karachi, Sunday 4 December, 9:25am

The smell of the ocean filled their nostrils before they saw it. It smelled of freedom and immediately lifted their spirits. As they approached the intersection to turn left into Sea View Road, they saw the water.

'Wow, that's what I've been waiting for,' Sergei said. His tone was bright, but he had butterflies in his stomach. He was on tenterhooks; they were so close but still so far.

Jane concentrated on holding the coffee cups upright as the four-wheel-drive leaned into the corner. 'The ocean always makes me feel free,' she said happily.

Her stomach rumbled at the smell of the gigantic croissants they'd just bought from a bakery along with jumbo cups of coffee. Razane, her head on Jane's shoulder, said something unintelligible. She was dreaming. Hopefully, the sleep was doing her good.

'Touch wood, I believe your idea of using Airbnb instead of a hotel will keep us safe,' Jane said.

'I hope so,' he said with a sigh, pleased he'd thought of it. 'The people after us are psychos.'

They couldn't afford to make any more assumptions about their enemy. A hotel would be the first place they'd look. It wouldn't be hard for them to persuade or bribe the staff to keep an eye out for a trio of foreigners. And they seemed to have no shortage of people to cover all the hotels in Karachi.

The ideal place to hide in a city as large as this was in an ordinary house.

That's why Airbnb made so much sense. It was also far more comfortable than camping in a secluded spot in the Pajero, his other idea. Airbnb only gave out property addresses after a person had booked. That made it extra secure.

Jane had found a nice house. Its rate was more than double that of the next most expensive place, but it was large and clean. It was also close to the ocean and a marina where the Shalayla could moor. Amazingly it had taken her a mere five minutes to find, book and pay for it. They were lucky to find something. Karachi had only fifteen Airbnb listings, and only one had a vacancy.

The Internet was amazing. 'Sergei remind me never to call you a geek again,' Jane said.

'Just send me a text, that way I've something to show you the next time you do.' He smiled. 'Thank goodness Ben realised the flaw in the plan.'

'Oh yeah, imagine realising out in the ocean, we had no means of locating them,' she said with a mirthless laugh. She shivered at the thought.

Thank goodness Ben had realised there was no phone or Internet coverage out at sea. It would have been impossible for them to rendezvous without a means of communicating. Ben had bought two satellite transceivers in Dubai, and the plan was for Damon to find a way to hand it to them at the marina.

They had been tempted to change the plan and board the Shalayla at the marina, but that was super risky. Their enemy could ambush them, or a member of the public could alert the coast guard.

They had to be patient and hold their nerve. There was no way they could risk another confrontation. They'd never survive it.

They turned left onto B Street and right onto 31st Street.

The house was the third from the corner. A guard with a huge handlebar moustache, a long beard, and an old .303 rifle slung over his shoulder, saluted them smartly and opened the gate. He was expecting them.

The house was huge and quite old. Two newer wings, one on each side of the main building, near the back of the property, served as guest accommodation. Each had its own carport.

The owner, a tall and lanky, elderly man dressed in a black *sherwani* rushed out to meet them as they drove in. He ushered them to their parking spot to the right.

'Welcome, welcome, to my home,' he said, pumping Sergei's hand as soon as he stepped out.

Razane woke when she heard him. 'Where are we?' she asked Jane quietly.

'Hopefully a safe place, darling.'

Jane was about to step out and compliment the man on his house when she remembered, just in time. Burka-clad women were supposed to be submissive and not speak to strange men.

Their host, Javed Joseph, unlocked the door and showed them their accommodation. They had the whole right wing to themselves. The Airbnb website hadn't exaggerated its size. It was a small double storey townhouse, with a huge lounge, a dining room and a kitchen on the ground floor and a small lounge and two large bedrooms on the first floor. It was bigger than their city apartment in Melbourne.

'I built these for my two sons,' Mr Joseph said, in a sad voice, 'but they left me and went to Canada.'

For half an hour they sat, slumped wearily, in the plush sofas as they wolfed down the croissants and coffee made more delicious by their hunger. Sergei did a Google search for a boat that could take them out to their rendezvous, while Jane scanned the online newspapers and Razane busied herself with a search for lunch.

'Look at this,' Jane remarked, 'a joint police and Army

Rangers operation destroyed a terrorist cell in Multan last night, killing eleven. That is--'

'These have to be the people who attacked us,' Razane said as she looked at Jane's screen.

Sergei craned his neck to look as well. 'I'm quite happy to give the army the credit,' he said. 'Any mention of us or the red Pajero?'

There was silence while Jane continued reading. 'Nope, nothing.'

THE AIRBNB

Karachi, Sunday 4 December, 9:30am

A brar woke at 9:30, shaved, had a shower, and went down to breakfast. He hadn't eaten since eleven yesterday morning and was famished. He savoured the buffet, taking his time. He enjoyed buffet breakfasts, and he loved the food and service at the Avari. The quality of a buffet breakfast was the main reason he chose one hotel over another.

An article in the Pakistan Times caught his eye. "Army Smashes Terrorist Cell in Multan - 11 Dead". The army was doing well recently. Well done! Pity the number wasn't higher. When was it going to be Jibran's turn? He certainly did not want to be anywhere near his village when the Army decided to raid there. This was definitely going to be the last time he ever took on a job for this moustachioed motherfucker.

He drained his cup of coffee and dabbed his mouth with his napkin. He stood up uncomfortably. He was nearly bursting at the seams. Tucking the newspaper under his arm, he made his way back to his room. It was time to do some work.

He went through the list of Airbnbs. They were all clustered around the south of Karachi, in the more expensive and upmarket areas. He tried putting himself in their shoes. What would they do? How would they choose? If they went for an Airbnb it would be for safety. Which one would make them feel safer? What would he do? If they were going to escape by boat, then proximity to the ocean would be important. For properties at a similar distance to the coast, they would probably go for the nicer one. Nicer properties would invariably be more expensive. He decided he would rank them that way but in the interest of being thorough, and because there were only fifteen, he would still look at them all.

Airbnb only provided an address when someone made a booking, so he booked them all using different dates. Within a few minutes, he began getting responses. Within half an hour he had all the addresses and phone numbers. It was time to make some calls. He would first rule out the ones lower on his list. He rang number fifteen.

'*Asalam Aleikum.*'

'*Wa aleikum asalam.*'

'My name is Saif. I just received a confirmation of booking.'

'Saif *Sahib*, thank you thank you for making a booking. How can I be of assistance to you?'

'I, just have one or two questions.'

'Yes, yes, of course, please.'

'This booking is for some overseas visitors, my friends from Australia.'

'Oh yes, yes, that is OK. We are happy to have overseas visitors.'

'Have you ever had overseas visitors?'

There was a pause, 'no sir, but they are most welcome. People are people; it doesn't matter where they are from, they are most welcome.'

'Thank you. That is good to know. *Allah hafiz!*'

'No problem, sir. *Allah hafiz.*'

He called the next and asked the same set of questions. Fifteen minutes later only two remained. So far it wasn't looking good. None of the Airbnbs had ever had foreigners stay with them. His heart beat faster as he dialled the final two. Both owners were proud to tell him their houses were popular with overseas visitors and they, in fact, had foreigners staying there at present.

Abrar hung up and sat back in the chair, smiling with

satisfaction. That had been almost too easy.

By his calculations, his targets would have reached Karachi by now, so they were almost certainly in one of the two.

What to do next? He would not tell Jibran, at least not until he had narrowed it down further. Jibran and his gorillas would most likely go in, all guns blazing, and kill the occupants in both houses.

No, he would take care of the foreigners the right way, with precision and finesse.

The houses were only two blocks from each other in DHA. Traffic was reasonably light. As he drove, he put the first address into his GPS.

At a whim, he stopped at a cake shop and bought the two largest cakes they had. Each was for at least forty people, or so the storekeeper claimed. He hadn't quite decided how to enter the houses but was confident he'd find a way. The cakes would give him another option. Cakes and flowers always made people lower their guard.

He decided to try the one on 31st Street first. It was closer. He drove south along Abdullah Haroon Road and followed the GPS till he got to Sea View Road. From there he turned onto B Street and then right onto 31st Street. It was just three houses from the intersection. He recognised it from the photos on the Airbnb website. The tall boundary wall hid most of it from view, but it was easy to tell just how large it was. A gardener stood outside the neighbour's house trimming a large English Box hedge with garden shears.

He continued driving past the house. He didn't need witnesses, and he preferred not to kill an innocent gardener. He'd try the second house first. It had an equally good chance of being the right one. He put its address into the GPS as he drove past the gardener. The man was actually butchering the beautiful hedge. Maybe he did deserve to die after all. He continued straight and turned left at the end of the street. He drove on for two blocks and took the second right turn. The house was halfway along the street on the left. Thankfully there was no one about, no street hawkers, servants cleaning or anyone leaving or entering their properties. It was a good sign.

The house had a tall boundary wall and an equally tall steel gate. Both had vicious looking spikes along the top. The owners were security minded. He looked for cameras. There were none. He considered his options. In most cases, a servant would come to the gate. If that happened, entry to the house would be easy. If it were the owner, it would be harder. He might then have to use force. He needed a bit of preparation for this, so he drove on till he found an empty block. He parked in front of it and switched off the engine.

Moving fast, he went to the boot and lifted the carpet to expose his toolkit. It contained his SIG, a .22 Ruger pistol, and a Pneu-Dart X2. The latter was a compact tranquiliser gun that used a small compressed carbon dioxide canister to fire a tranquilliser dart. He had six darts in a small glass case. He had filled them with a small, precisely measured, amount of deer tranquiliser. One of them would give him twenty minutes before his victim woke. He was an assassin, not a butcher. Needlessly killing innocent people was not acceptable collateral damage.

Looking around to make sure no one was watching, he screwed a silencer onto the end of the Ruger and checked its magazine. He was using subsonic hollow point bullets for their quietness. They would fire barely louder than the click of the pistol's firing pin. The magazine was full. He inserted a dart into the tranquilliser gun. He slipped the Ruger, the Pneu-Dart, and the remaining darts into a large leather pouch that he slung over his shoulder. Then he picked up one of the cakes and put it on the front passenger seat. He would first try with the cake.

He turned the car around and drove up to the house. Outside the gate, he horned loudly.

After thirty seconds he horned again. Ten seconds later an old man, a servant from his appearance, slowly opened the gate and peeked out.

Abrar heaved a sigh of relief. Hopefully, this was going to be easy. He motioned to the old man to come to his door.

'*Asalam Aleikum Chacha.*'

'*Wa aleikum asalam,*' the old man peered into the car as he raised his hand to his forehead in greeting. He was appraising Abrar and his long shiny black car.

'I am here to see your overseas guests. They said they would be in today.'

'OK, I'll go and fetch them, *Sahib.*'

'No, no, don't trouble them. I have brought a cake to celebrate with them. It is a surprise.'

'OK,' the man scratched his chin. Abrar could see him trying to process the situation. He would have learnt from childhood to obey important people. On the other hand, he had a responsibility to look after the house.

'Open the gate *Chacha,* this very expensive cake is going to melt,' Abrar said a bit more forcefully, 'your guests will get very annoyed at me and you if it does.'

'OK *Sahib,*' he said finally. He must have decided Abrar was trustworthy. Robbers would not bring cakes. He'd have been right, but assassins were another matter. The old man opened the gate, and Abrar drove in.

The house was large and unassuming. Its Airbnb site had mentioned a separate side entrance for guests. A red arrow on a wooden plaque on the wall pointed to a door. A board with the words "Guest Entrance" was affixed to the door. Not much guesswork needed there.

Abrar took out a chamois from the glove box and handed the man a thousand rupee note.

'*Chacha,* could you please clean the car for me?' He had to stop the old man going back into the house.

The man's eyes lit up at the sight of the easy money. 'Yes, *Sahib.*'

'Do it now before you go back inside. I need to leave in five minutes.'

'Yes, *Sahib*, I will do it first thing.' He took a garden hose and began washing the car.

He had to work fast. If the old man's employers called him back into the house, he would probably tell them of the visitor, and they would come out and investigate. He did not want to kill more people.

Still holding the cake and with the bag over his shoulder, Abrar walked to the guest entrance. He tried the door. It was unlocked. He was in the right place. No Pakistanis would neglect to lock their front doors. Hopefully, they were the right foreigners. Everything had gone smoothly so far. Why should it stop now?

The door opened to a set of stairs. The guest rooms were upstairs. Treading as soundlessly as possible, he walked up. The stairs ended in a small landing and a single door. Please be unlocked. He tried it. The door opened. He was in a large lounge with two yellow leather settees and two armchairs, also yellow, facing a big-screen TV. Five people turned around and looked at him. They were elderly, all with grey hair.

He froze. Fuck! They were the wrong foreigners.

'Hello everyone, Mr Chishti, your host, asked me to give you this cake with his compliments,' he said in a loud voice, recovering from his disappointment. Thank goodness, he remembered the name of the owner, 'I hope I'm not disturbing.'

The expressions on the five faces turned from surprise to mild annoyance and then to friendliness when they saw what he carried. One of the women, in a blue floral print dress, came forward and took it from him.

'Thank you,' she said, 'but this is so big.'

'Maybe you can give some to the servants.'

'OK, thank you so much,' they all spoke together, 'we weren't expecting this.'

'That's fine, all part of Pakistani hospitality. But you can thank Mr Chishti when he returns from the shops,' Abrar said casually. The lies just kept on coming, easily, one after the other. He was enjoying this all a bit too much. It was better he left while he had the chance. The five were crowding around the cake, still looking surprised.

With a wave, Abrar backed out of the door, closed it behind him and almost ran down the stairs. The old servant was still wetting the car with the hose.

'*Chacha*, I need to leave. I forgot something.'

He began reversing the car as the old man opened the gate. He slowed a bit to let a man on a bicycle go by. After all that, the wrong foreigners. Damn! He reversed out onto the road, braked, put the car in drive, waved at the servant and drove off.

As soon as he was out of sight of the house, he stopped by the side of the road and transferred the second cake to the passenger seat. Then he sent Jibran a text message.

'I've found where they are staying; it's an Airbnb here in DHA. I'm going there to finish the job.'

THE BOAT

Karachi, Sunday 4 December, 12:15pm

Sergei thanked the taxi driver and handed him the amount displayed on the meter and a bit more. 'Can you wait for me? I won't be very long.'

The driver pushed the money back. 'No, *Sahib* I trust you. Pay me after… when you come back, and I drop you home. I wait.'

It was always nice to meet a trusting man, someone whom the world has not yet embittered. 'That's nice of you,' Sergei said.

He climbed out of the back seat and closed the door behind him, trying not to extend his arm too fast or too much. The pain in his side was almost gone as long as he didn't push himself. The redness around it had diminished as well. Hopefully, it meant he was on the mend.

They had decided a taxi was the safest option. There was an outside chance their pursuers knew what kind of car they had escaped in. A red Mitsubishi Pajero was far more conspicuous and hence less safe.

He walked through the parking lot. A steel shed with plastic windows stood by the waterside. On its side, the words "Arabian Sea Adventures - Lunch, Dinner Tours, Fishing, Corporate Trips" were emblazoned in large blue letters.

No one was in sight. He tried the door. It was unlocked. He opened it and entered to the sound of a tinkling bell. The inside smelled of damp rope and seaweed. A small grey-haired woman sat behind the counter. She wore thick glasses and was reading an Urdu magazine.

'*Salam Aleikum,*' he said.

'*Wa aleikum, beita.*'

'Do you speak English?'

'Very small, yes,' she said optimistically as she moved her thumb and forefinger together to illustrate.

'I want to rent a boat for fishing. How far do you go?' Sergei spoke slowly. He pantomimed fishing.

The old lady handed him a sheet of laminated paper and stabbed at it. 'These, these, these boats we having, where you want go?' She twisted both hands.

'I want to go fishing in deep water.'

'Ah, fish cruises... forty thousand rupees.'

'Where do you go and how far?'

She shook her head. After a brief pause she pulled out a map of the bay and placed it in front of him. He poked his finger at a few spots and twisted his hand to ask where.

She pointed to a spot out in the ocean. From the scale on the map, it seemed around ten kilometres from the coastline. It'd have to do.

'I need to book for tomorrow after lunch.' He showed her the date on a desk calendar and the time on his watch.

She shook her head, 'only go... early morning. After lunch come back. Dark.'

'I want to fish in the dark.' He showed her the dial on his watch. Hopefully, she could understand.

The woman looked at him as if he was crazy. 'Eighty thousand rupees.'

He had around a hundred thousand left. There was nothing to be gained by arguing. He pulled out twenty thousand. 'Is this OK for a deposit?'

IN FLAGRANTE DELICTO

Karachi, Sunday 4 December, 12:15pm

A brar was back on 31st Street. The neighbour's gardener had trimmed the hedge down to bare twigs and had gone back inside. The whole street was deserted. He drove up to the gate and blew the horn. Hopefully, it would be just as easy to gain entry.

A man with a huge moustache and carrying a rifle approached the gate, opened it slightly, and looked out. He could have been Jibran's better-looking brother. Abrar beckoned him to approach.

'*Asalam aleikum*, I have come to visit your overseas guests.'

The guard shifted the ancient .303 rifle to his other shoulder. He bent and looked inside the car before replying. '*Wa aleikum asalam*.' He was markedly less compliant and enthusiastic than the old man in the last house. This was not going to be as easy.

'What is your name, *Sahib*?'

'I am Abrar, their friend, I've brought them cake to help them celebrate.'

The guard looked at the box on the front passenger seat. 'OK *Sahib*, I will go and tell them.'

'Just open the gate. My cake will spoil, and your guests will be annoyed at both of us.'

'*Sahib*, I have my orders. I cannot open the gate without permission,' the guard said firmly.

'OK, then take the cake with you and bring it to them.' It

was his last option. The guard would be easier to subdue with his hands full.

The man hesitated. It sounded like a reasonable request. Abrar switched off the engine, got out and walked to the passenger side and took out the cake. The guard walked back to the gate and waited for him. Abrar picked up the large box and pretended to struggle with it and the door.

'Let me help you, *Sahib*,' the guard said as he came forward and took the cake from him.

'*Shukria*.' Abrar closed the door and followed him to the gate. Casually folding his arms, he reached into the satchel with his right hand and took hold of the Pneu-Dart. He was ready.

The guard pushed the gate further ajar with his foot as he struggled to hold the cake upright.

It was his moment. 'Careful, careful, here let me help you,' Abrar said and sprang forward. In the same movement, he pulled out the dart gun and fired into the man's buttocks.

The guard was inside the gate and in the process of turning around when he felt the sharp jab. He stumbled. Abrar leapt forward and grabbed the cake. He placed it on the ground and straightened up all in one quick movement.

'What happened?' he said in a concerned voice. The guard mumbled something unintelligible in reply, his eyes already glazed over.

'You look unwell, let me help you to the chair.'

By now the guard was starting to lose coordination. His legs were giving way. Abrar put his shoulder under the man's left arm. Half dragging, half lifting he helped him to a chair in the carport, near the front door of the house. By the time they reached it, the guard was almost a dead weight.

With great effort, Abrar reached behind, pulled out the dart and let it fall to the ground.

He tried to ease the unconscious guard onto the chair, but the man fell hard causing it to tip backwards. His rifle dropped off his shoulder and clattered onto the polished concrete floor.

Abrar reached forward and grabbed hold of the chair just in time. The guard was heavy, and it took all his strength to straighten it.

The .303 had made quite a sound when it fell. Abrar waited to see if anyone would come to the door. No one did. He propped the rifle against the unconscious guard, picked up the fallen dart and placed it in his satchel.

He was breathing heavily. He had to calm down and take stock of the situation. First things first. He picked up the cake.

The guest areas were in the two double-storey wings, either side of the main building towards the back. They were built with a different colour brick, evidently a later addition to the house.

A red Mitsubishi Pajero was parked under a carport in front of the right-hand wing. It had Multan license plates. He recalled the Multan story in the morning paper. Was it even conceivable these people were involved in that? Fuck! Anything was possible. They had, after all, raided Jibran's village. On the other hand, it could be a mere coincidence? Perhaps someone from Multan was visiting Karachi, and the foreigners were in the other wing.

The carport in front of the left wing was empty. On balance, the right wing offered the better prospect. He'd check that first.

Hoping no one was looking out of any windows, he walked along the right-hand side of the main house. As he passed the Mitsubishi, he glanced inside. It was empty. What did he expect? Guns, or a body or two. He approached the door to the guest accommodation and tried the handle. It was locked. The foreigners in the last house hadn't bothered. His targets were running scared. If anyone had a reason to lock up, it would be them. So, it was either normal locals or paranoid foreigners behind that door.

How to get in? The ground floor had two large bay windows to the right of the door. Both were heavily shrouded in a single bougainvillea that stretched almost the full width from the door to the neighbour's boundary wall. It also covered much of the windows on the top floor.

A row of three magnolia trees, bare of leaves, stood in front of the creeper.

Squeezing sideways, he approached the first of the windows. He put his face against its left edge and tried looking in. The foliage was too thick. He had to move a few branches out of the way to see anything. It was a large lounge, comfortably appointed with sumptuous brown leather sofas arranged around a timber coffee table. A TV screen hung on the far wall. The room was unoccupied.

He moved to the next window. It revealed a dining room with a wooden table and six chairs; behind it was a small modern kitchenette. It was also empty. If anyone were home, as the red SUV suggested, they'd be upstairs. He went to the front door again and put his ear to it. There was no sound. With a last quick look back, he pulled out his picks and manipulated the lock open.

He carefully opened the door, listening for sounds inside. Thankfully the hinges were well oiled.

The door opened into a small entrance. Abrar walked in. A timber screen partially blocked his view to the lounge he'd just seen from outside. To his left, a staircase wound hundred and eighty degrees as it climbed. He closed the door softly behind him and listened. It was silent. Gradually, he became aware of muffled voices, coming from the top floor.

He walked upstairs carefully, stepping on the outside of the treads, hoping to avoid them creaking. The landing opened into a small lounge containing a divan and two armchairs. Bookshelves lined the walls. The host liked to read. The two closed doors on the far wall had to be the bedrooms. The Airbnb website had mentioned two in each wing.

He walked to the one towards the front of the house. The sounds became louder. He quickly checked the second bedroom just to be sure. It was empty, and so was its attached bathroom.

One could never be too careful. He walked back to the first bedroom and put his ear to the door.

The sounds were not of conversation but sex. If they were having sex, where was the second woman?

He pulled the Ruger from his satchel and silently eased off the safety catch. Placing his hand softly on the handle he first pulled the door to take the weight off the striker. Then he turned the handle ever so slowly until it came to the end of its travel. His moment had arrived. He took a deep breath and pushed the door gently forward till he was able to see inside.

A large bed took up nearly half the room. Two people lay on it, crossways, on their side, in a sixty-nine position. They were partly covered in sheets. Razane faced the door, her eyes were closed. Her head was between the other person's legs; her hands squeezed and caressed her partner's hips. Her nails left crimson trails on the soft white skin as her fingers danced all over.

They were both moaning and rocking in the throes of passion. Abrar could have walked in and stood there, and they wouldn't have noticed him. The door to the bathroom was open, and it too appeared empty. There was no sign of any third person.

His kinky side had hoped to see them engaged in a threesome. It would have made them a bit more human. He had never killed anyone while they were having sex. Assassinating three people in a ménage à trois would be a story worth telling. Not that he had anyone to tell such stories to.

He stood there transfixed. There was something about people making love that gave him the tingles, in a pleasant way. He watched them wistfully. They were totally lost in the moment, not hurrying nor slowing down, not consciously calculating. They looked completely comfortable with each other and so in love.

He had never had much luck finding a long-term sexual partner himself, someone on his wavelength. He was a control freak and needed moments where he could hand over control. But all the men he'd been attracted to were either too domineering, rough and disrespectful or too effeminate and oversensitive. He lived in the hope of finding the right man, someone balanced and flexible, with whom he could have a meaningful relationship. Maybe then he'd experience sex like these two.

As he stood there, it dawned on him things were not what they seemed. The second person did not have a man's legs. He looked again, not sure he could trust his eyes. This was crazy, were they both women? Their moans were unmistakably two distinct female voices. Holy fuck! He opened the door a bit more and poked his head through. The second person was Jane Kelly.

They were now both writhing and bucking, synchronous, spiralling towards the inevitable orgasm. They were gay! What a pity he had to kill them. He realised he wasn't breathing and vaguely remembered he still held the Ruger, his finger on the trigger. Shit! Thankfully he hadn't absentmindedly squeezed it.

Carefully, making sure he did not bump it against the door he aimed it at Razane's head. Damn Jibran.

THE SHOWDOWN

Karachi, Sunday 4 December, 12:50pm

The taxi turned onto 31st Street. Sergei's heart skipped a beat. An ambulance stood in front of the house. Its back doors were open. He jumped out of the cab and ran inside, forgetting to pay the driver. The guard was being stretchered into the back of the ambulance.

'What happened?' he asked Mr Joseph who stood there with a worried look on his face.

'He says he had a sudden stabbing pain in his lower back and collapsed, I am no doctor, but it may be a stroke.'

'Oh, that's bad,' Sergei said, trying to calm his breathing. 'I hope he's going to be OK.'

'Yes, I hope so too. I have organised a replacement from the security company, so you don't have to feel worried.'

'Oh, thanks. Great. Please excuse me!' Sergei said and ran to their guest rooms. What if the guard's condition was not medical? What if he had been attacked and incapacitated somehow? He put his trembling hand on the door handle to steady himself. The handle turned, and the door opened. His blood froze. Bloody hell, he clearly remembered locking it. The place was silent.

Abrar parked at the Marriott and took the elevator to the top floor. He knocked on the door. A large beefy man in a black *shalwar kameez* and a dark brown waistcoat answered the door.

He looked like an angry gorilla. 'What is it?' he said brusquely.

'Move out of my way, you big oaf,' Abrar said and tried to push his way through.

The gorilla man did not budge. Abrar stepped back and put his hand in his satchel to pull out the Ruger. He was in no mood for games.

Just then Jibran's voice sounded from inside, 'if it is Abrar *Sahib*, let him in.' He sounded in a cheerful mood.

The man stepped aside to let him pass. Abrar took a deep breath and let the Ruger drop back into the satchel.

'Who's the big ape?' He said as he entered the large and tastefully decorated lounge. The big man had followed him and was standing so close he could hear him breathing. Jibran stood near the window at a desk.

'Jamal, go wait outside,' he said without turning around.

The door opened and slammed shut. Jamal had left.

Jibran turned around holding a dagger. He was cleaning the dirt under his fingernails. '*Yaar* you have exceeded even yourself. I am impressed and grateful you found them.'

'It was not that hard,' Abrar said curtly.

'So, do you have a photograph?'

'A photo? Of what?'

'Of their bodies, *yaar*... surely any successful contract requires a receipt or some evidence.'

'Here is evidence.' Abrar pulled out the Ruger.

'I want hard--' Jibran froze when he saw the gun pointed at him. His pupils contracted. 'What are you--?'

'What I should have done a long time ago, put a mad dog down.'

'You are calling me a mad dog?' Jibran growled.

'Yes, you are dirty cock-sucking pig, making me go around killing decent, innocent people.'

'Hey, sisterfucker did you get a little hard-on for those women or rather the man before you killed them?'

'Fuck you!' Abrar fired two shots straight into his chest.

Jibran staggered back onto the desk. As he fell he knocked a chair over.

Sergei ran up the stairs in a mad panic. He flung open the door. Razane and Jane were in bed; the room smelled of them and sex. 'Come join us,' Jane said dreamily, her arms stretched lazily above her head, 'did you find a boat?'

'You almost gave me a heart attack!' He was breathing heavily.

'What is it?' Razane hurriedly got out of bed, naked. Her silky black hair draped over one of her shapely breasts. Sit down. 'You look pale.'

Sergei sat. His erection happened instantaneously. The shock was receding fast. 'The guard is being taken to hospital, he collapsed. I thought he was attacked and someone had...'

Razane put her arms around his neck. Jane came over and joined him. The sensation of their naked bodies next to his fully clothed form was exciting.

He turned and put an arm around them each. His fingers stroked and played on their bare skin. They both responded almost identically, arching their backs forward. They loved how he touched them. He knew just how to.

'Someone had what?' Jane said.

'I have completely forgotten.' He smiled. He was kissing them. Razane pulled his top off and pushed him back on the bed in one movement. Jane pulled off his pants. Razane sat astride his face. She was dripping. He explored her tender heavenly softness with his tongue, while Jane's warm mouth enveloped the whole length of him. Her warm breath adding yet another dimension of pleasure.

'You never said. Did you find the boat?' Jane paused and asked.

Don't stop now. He was on the verge of coming. 'Yup all done,' he mumbled, his voice completely muffled by Razane. He was drinking her in, his mind barely even thinking.

'I didn't hear that,' Razane said with a giggle.

He put his left hand up and stuck his thumb out.

'Good boy, now work that tongue,' she purred.

He went over to Jibran's prone form. 'You rotten savage. They never deserved to die,' he spat out the words. Now that he had pulled the trigger on Jibran all his emotions rushed out. 'Just so you know, I didn't fucking kill them. It's you who deserved to die.'

He was about to bend down to check Jibran's pulse when the suite door opened and Jamal rushed in. The falling chair must have alerted him. Abrar spun around and pointed the Ruger at him. Jamal stopped, frozen in his tracks. He still held his revolver, pointed sideways, his eyes popping out of his head.

'Stay where you are and put the gun down,' Abrar growled.

The big man bent his knees and slowly lowered his gun.

'Drop it now,' Abrar's voice was steely. The man bent his knees further. The revolver was on the ground, but he still held onto it. He wasn't in any hurry to let go.

'Last chance, drop it, or I'll shoot you in the head.'

He felt a sickening blow to his lower back. Paralysing pain and what felt like massive electrical shock overwhelmed him. What had just happened? He could not comprehend. He looked down, horrified. Something was sticking out of his stomach. Something red and pointed. It couldn't be.

Jamal, meanwhile, straightened and pointed the revolver at him. Abrar tried to shoot, but his arms refused to obey and fell to his side as if made of stone. Another severe blow and a piercing pain went through his rib cage. He felt a presence near his ear and heard a voice, whispering. 'No one crosses Jibran Ghaffar. Fucking no one!'

THE DIRTY RAT

Karachi, Sunday 4 December, 1:30pm

Jibran pulled off his kameez and fingered his new bulletproof vest. It was ultra-thin which made it unobtrusive. He had been trying it on when Abrar had walked in. He smiled. It had done what it's makers had claimed. The bullets had felt like two punches Mumtaz would have thrown. It was not force nor pain but the shock that had unbalanced him. The vest did not, of course, stop the two holes in his kameez.

What a dirty fucking rat Abrar had turned out to be? How disloyal and untrustworthy?

'*Sahib*, let me get you another kameez.' Jamal ran into the next room and returned with a replacement.

'OK, good. Clean up this mess. And get me a towel for the blood.'

'Yes, *Sahib*. It's lucky he stood right on the plastic sheet where you wanted him to.'

'Yes,' Jibran said laughing. Jamal had placed two large plastic sheets on the floor so they would not get Abrar's blood on the floor when they killed him. It would have been such a nuisance to explain the blood to the hotel people. He liked the Marriott and didn't want to be banned.

But he was planning to kill Abrar only after he got proof of the foreigners' deaths, not before. He was a loose end. Besides the cocksucker had always taunted him with his superior intelligence and his high-class airs.

But why did Abrar not kill the foreigners? He had sent him

the text message saying he was going to the house. Something had gone wrong after that. Were they not home? Did they bribe him? How was that even possible? Abrar was not a poor man. He didn't need money. What then?

If only he had not let his anger get the better of him.

He wiped the blood off his hands with the folded hand towel that Jamal had wetted for him. How did Abrar find the place? He had mentioned Airbnb in his text message. What was Airbnb? He bent down and fished in Abrar's pocket for his phone. He had seen Abrar use an A to unlock his phone. He found Google Maps and tried to make sense of it.

'Does this mean anything to you, Jamal?' He asked.

'Yes *Sahib*,' Jamal said brightly as he took the phone from him. 'This is an address. It is where this man went last, 'and...' he scrolled on, 'here on 31st street is where he went before that.'

'That is very clever. OK, write them down on a piece of paper for me. You can keep the phone as a gift.'

Finally, he had the address. The second last address was definitely a mistake or Abrar would not have gone to the last address.

Who should he send to finish the job? Abdul Zubair and his crew could do it but could he trust them not to mess it up? On the other hand, how hard was it to raid a house? They were all killers, most had fought with the Taliban.

Abdul Zubair and his gang could kill, but not without bringing the whole police and army down on them. If even one of them were caught, they would be identified as terrorists and Karachi would be in lockdown faster than one could blink an eye.

As Abrar would have put it, they lacked finesse. Abrar's finesse had also not served him. That was the problem with intelligent people; they were never able to stay loyal.

There were, of course, many ways open to him. Karachi's underworld was teeming with hitmen and killers. Home invasions were an industry in Karachi.

He pulled out his phone and dialled a number.

THE BAD NEWS

Karachi, Sunday 4 December, 6:01pm

Jane switched on the television and looked for an English station. They had spent a beautiful afternoon making love, and they all felt pleasantly worn out and hungry for food. The pizza delivery guy had just dropped off a family-sized Super Supreme and a bottle of Coke.

The breaking news story was a home invasion that ended in a triple murder. One victim was an elderly American woman, a member of a Christian group visiting Pakistan to set up a charity. The other two were the homeowner and his servant. Had her companions not been out for lunch the casualties would have been higher. The hapless victim had been feeling unwell and had decided to stay home and rest.

'How terrible,' Jane said. 'Shows why houses here have such walls and tall gates.'

'Walls and gates never keep people out,' Razane said absentmindedly as she watched the broadcast.

'Well it's good then,' Sergei said, 'that we've got guns and also a guard.'

'All walls and guns do is create more of a need for them,' Razane muttered. 'Take away the huge gap between rich and poor and everyone will be safer.' She poured herself some Coke and grabbed another slice of pizza.

Sergei and Jane did not reply. Their eyes were frozen on the TV screen. The reporter was talking about Airbnb and how they were emerging as a popular alternative to hotels.

Razane dropped the pizza slice back in the box, 'did he say… Airbnb?'

'Yup,' Jane said not moving her eyes from the screen. 'The house was an Airbnb. What a strange--?'

'Are you both thinking what I am?' Razane coughed. Something had lodged in her throat.

'Holy shit, that house wasn't the target?' Sergei said, his expression had become solemn.

'Oh no,' Jane said, 'they know we're in… an Airbnb?'

'Yes… it could be,' Sergei said shrugging his shoulders. 'With these bastards, we best be over cautious.'

Razane stood up. 'I agree. I am not sitting here unarmed,' she said as she ran to the door.

Sergei followed.

'No, no, no, it was the wrong house,' Jibran shouted into the phone.'

'But *Saeen* it was the right address, the one you gave us.' The voice on the other end protested.

'Then I need you to go the second address.' He knew the man on the other end of the phone was not to blame. He had killed everyone at the address he had given him. He could not explain how the two houses had gotten mixed up, but the reason did not matter.

'*Saeen*, whatever are your wishes, just give us the address.' Jibran read it out to him.

'The price will now be double,' the voice said after a pause.

'Double?' Jibran bellowed.

'Yes *Saeen*, this address is very close to the first house. There is more police around; we run a higher risk.'

'Just do it. I am sending the money now.'

'In Bitcoins, please.'

'Yes, Bitcoins.' The bloody criminals were more sophisticated than him. He needed to better understand how the modern world worked. It wasn't right for those lower than him to be smarter.

'How fast can you do it?'

'We are always ready, and we are everywhere. I'll send the men now.'

Razane checked the magazine in the Kalashnikov. She had eighteen rounds left. Sergei checked his; it was almost full. Jane came out to join them.

'Razane, sweetheart, what do you think?' he said.

'We have enough ammo, but the problem is the police. They'll be here in minutes if anyone starts shooting.'

'We can't let the police come,' Jane said, 'we have to leave.'

'You're right, sweetheart,' Sergei said.

'OK let's get our things and go,' Razane slung the Kalashnikov over her shoulder and ran back inside. Jane followed. Sergei stowed his rifle in the passenger seat footwell, started the engine and reversed out of the carport and turned the Pajero around to face the front gate. He let the engine idle. In the rearview mirror, Razane and Jane were closing the door.

The guard, seeing them preparing to leave, unlocked the gate and pulled it open. As he did a car drove inside at high speed. The unfortunate guard had nowhere to run. The car struck him and threw him several metres in Sergei's direction and came to a screeching halt in the main carport. Sergei half expected it to collide with the house, but it didn't. Only its rear bumper and taillights were now visible.

The guard lay on the ground, motionless. His rifle was beneath him. Sergei looked back. Razane and Jane were nowhere to be seen.

His heart beating fast, senses on high alert, Sergei switched off the Pajero's internal light and turned off the engine. He stepped out and closed the door without latching it. Up ahead the car's brake lights turned off. All four doors opened and then slammed closed. That meant at least four or possibly five assailants. Better to assume five until he saw them. The guard was now moving, trying to get up. He groaned and lifted his arm. Two men carrying rifles ran and closed the gate. A shot rang out from the direction of the carport, and the guard was still.

Sergei lay on the ground beside the Pajero's front wheel, trying to think through the haze of fury that had enveloped his mind. How dare these bastards keep on after them!

He trained his rifle in the direction of the front carport. They all had around five minutes at the most, before the police came. Had the attackers bitten off more than they could chew. This house was built on land almost three times the size of most others in the area. They would have to enter and exit three separate dwellings. There wasn't much time.

What would he do in such a situation? Probably send two and two to each of the side wings and leave one person to guard the front of the house. But under pressure, people didn't always behave rationally. What would these men do? He didn't have to wait long to find out.

Two men came around the side at a fast pace. He fired at the one nearer the front of the house. Almost simultaneously, another shot rang out. Both men fell. Where was Razane? She was unbelievable. How had she worked who to shoot?

Now what? Would the other men charge or try to leave?

There was silence. The men in the carport were arguing in loud voices. They couldn't agree what to do. Something behind him rustled. Razane dropped down beside him.

'Good shot, sweetheart.' Feeling her next to him was reassuring.

'You too, my love.' She was breathing hard from the exertion.

'Any thoughts?'

'The men might enter the house and attack through those doors or windows.' She pointed at them. 'If they do. We are completely exposed. Even worse if they turn on those lights.'

As if on cue, they heard a loud bang. The front door had been kicked in. Loud male voices came from inside the house.

'Where's Jane?'

'Back inside.'

'OK you go back too, we can defend from there more easily, I'll cover you.'

Razane didn't argue and ran off. He was grateful. Tense situations were no time for debates. He heard a soft whistle and looked back. She was crouching inside the open doorway, her rifle trained in his direction. It was his turn. Keeping close to the main building he ran towards her. The main house reverberated with a gunshot. Poor Mr Joseph.

The outside lights came on. With a final leap, Sergei was through the door. As Razane slammed it shut, police sirens sounded in the distance. They were trapped. Razane used the butt of her rifle to smash the smoked glass panel beside the door. The sirens got louder.

THE GRILLE

Karachi, Sunday 4 December, 6:15pm

M ajor Hamdani sighed and shook his head. The elderly woman's body lay on the floor beside a yellow settee. A bullet hole in the middle of her forehead showed what had killed her. She had come to Pakistan to do good, at least her interpretation of good. Little had she known she would never leave. Maybe she should not have tried to spread Christianity under the guise of a charity. Sometimes God punishes us for impure motives.

He walked over to her companions. A man was consoling a dark-haired woman. A grey-haired woman wearing a crumpled blue floral print dress sat on her other side. She was holding her hand and stroking it.

'Hush Suzette, Abigail is with the Lord now and at peace,' she said soothingly.

'We should have been here as well,' the man said looking up at the major, 'maybe we could have saved her.'

'You would have been killed as well.' The major's voice was impassive.

The man did not reply. The woman called Suzette blew her nose loudly.

'Did you have any enemies in Pakistan or did you receive any death threats?'

'No sir, we already told the police two hours ago we've been well received here by so many groups. Today, someone even brought us a big cake, completely out of the blue.'

'Cake?'

'Yes, a big chocolate cake in the box over there.'

'Can you describe the man?'

'Yes, he was slim, young, well dressed. He spoke very good English.'

'Almost with an English accent,' the other man said.

The major walked over to the cake on the coffee table. A few slices had been eaten, but it was otherwise intact. It was huge and would have been enough to feed his whole department.

'Fazal, come over here and take a photograph of this, and of the box.'

He had seen enough. When he had heard the news that a foreign woman, staying at a local Airbnb, had been killed in a home invasion, he had jumped to the wrong conclusion. The TV news had not shown the woman's image. He had called his contact in the Karachi Crime Bureau for the address. The forensics team was still combing through the property, and the bodies had not been removed, so yes, he was welcome to check it out.

Was there a connection to his foreigners? Did their pursuers believe they were staying at an Airbnb?

He was tired. He couldn't think anymore. They would stop by the cake shop and see if the shopkeeper could tell them anything about the person who bought the cake.

They were about to sit in the car when a gunshot rang out in the distance.

'It is very close by,' Yousaf said.

Even though it was illegal, people still discharged their weapons, to celebrate at weddings or even for target practice. Something told him this was for more sinister reasons.

Two more shots rang out almost simultaneously. Was it a gunfight?

'Those were Kalashnikovs,' Yousaf said, 'I am sure of it.'

'All rifles sound the same,' Fazal said. 'Anyone who thinks they hear a difference is imagining it.'

'No, a Kalashnikov sounds angry, almost like a bark.' Yousaf was adamant.

'Get in the car, both of you,' the major said sharply. Their incessant bickering had really started to get on his nerves.

They drove in the direction of the gunshots. Another shot rang out, this time muffled. Somewhere, sirens blared. 'Turn on the police radio,' Yousaf said from the back seat.

'Serge, I think I found a way out,' Jane said from the top of the stairs. 'Can I show you?'

Hoping she was right, Sergei ran up.

'Yup, how?'

'The window to the second bedroom. It looks out onto the neighbour's property.'

'Wow, you're amazing!' He kissed her on the forehead. He had forgotten. The top rear bedroom had the only rear facing window in the whole dwelling, and it was almost at the rear boundary line.

They looked through the window, it was dark outside.

'I remembered this looks into the neighbour's backyard,' Jane said. 'It's a messy jungle.'

'We need some way to climb down.'

'I'll get some sheets.' Jane ran off. Sheets were used in almost every book where someone had to escape through a window. She'd find out if it really worked.

'And I'll try removing this grille.' The window was barred with an ornate steel grille and a fly screen. Sergei examined it closely. It had a catch on both sides with holes for padlocks. Thankfully no one had bothered to lock them. He tried to undo the catches by hand, but they were stuck solid.

Behind him, Jane had made a pile of sheets. She began by folding the first one diagonally, twisting it and then tying knots along its length.

Sergei repeatedly struck the catches with the butt of his

rifle before they loosened enough so he could open them. He finished removing the grille and the fly screen and looked out. The boundary wall was, at the most, a metre away from the house. They could manage that.

Jane was working feverishly and had tied the knotted sheets end to end. Sergei looked around for something solid to tie their improvised rope to. The bedpost looked solid. He tied one end of their sheet rope to it and pulled on it with all his might. It would do. Jane was in the process of tying the last sheet to lengthen their rope.

'You finish up, and I'll fetch Razane,' Sergei said.

'OK, I'll start climbing down. Turn off the light, please.'

'Be careful!' He flicked off the switch as he ran out into the lounge. He did the same there. The whole upstairs was plunged into darkness. He ran to the front window. The courtyard was empty. He smashed the glass with the butt of his rifle and poked the barrel through.

'Razane, I've got you covered. Come upstairs, he whispered loudly.'

'OK.'

She ran up the stairs. The courtyard outside was still empty. No one had come out. The police sirens were loud, and their red and blue lights were reflecting off neighbouring houses. They were less than thirty seconds away. 'We're climbing out the back window. Go!'

Razane ran towards the back room, her rifle banging on the door jamb.

'I am climbing out now,' Razane whispered from the back room.

The police car was now at the front gate. The men in the house had either run off or were trapped. In any event, they were no longer coming for them.

He left the window and ran to the rear bedroom. Razane had already climbed out and was halfway down. Jane was sitting astride the boundary wall. He watched as Razane kicked against the house wall and swung outwards. She caught the top of the wall and hooked her arm over it. The sheet rope swung free as she let go and hoisted herself up next to Jane.

It was his turn. He hated heights, even small ones. He slung the rifle over his back and grabbed the rope. It was nice and thick, and the knots were large. It was easier than he had thought and before he knew it, he was sitting on the wall next to them.

The neighbouring property was dark. The rear of the garden was planted quite heavily with tall bamboo to form a thicket and an effective privacy screen. Thank goodness, they didn't appear to have dogs.

'I'll go first,' he whispered.

Major Hamdani climbed out of his car. It was another home invasion. The police had just arrived and were standing in the carport next to a small white Suzuki hatchback, sizing up the situation. All external lights were on, the front door of the main house was ajar, and all lights inside were on as well. A body lay on the right-hand driveway. A red Mitsubishi four-wheel-drive blocked his view to a wing of the house set further back. A similar wing was built on the left side of the house. This was likely an Airbnb as well. If it were, Karachiites would shy away from Airbnbs for a while.

He bent down to examine two large patches of darkened blood on the ground. Someone here did not walk away; they were carried.

More police appeared. They fanned out. Some cautiously entered the main building. Others headed towards the right hand guest-house.

'It looks like this side is where all the action happened.' He took his Glock out of its holster. 'Follow me, boys.'

The front door of the extension was unlocked, the adjacent glass panel, smashed. The inside was in darkness.

'Someone broke this glass from inside,' Yousaf said

bending down.

'Most likely to defend themselves,' Fazal said.

'Very good, your observation and deduction skills are improving. Now if only you could stop always stating the obvious.'

A police officer knocked loudly on the door. 'We are the police. Put down your weapons. We are entering. Anyone with a gun will be shot with no warning!'

There was no reply. A policeman carefully pushed open the door. Two constables with torches mounted on their rifles entered. The downstairs was clear. They proceeded upstairs. Someone found a light switch.

The whole place was empty. They spread out.

'They have escaped,' a voice from the rear bedroom said.

The rear bedroom window was ajar. A rope made out of bedsheets dangled out of it.

The phone rang, it was the courier. Jibran looked at his watch. It was 8:30 in the evening.

'I'm downstairs sir, in the lobby.'

'OK, I'll send my man down.'

Jamal came back five minutes later carrying a package. It was about time. He had paid for the transceiver to be hand delivered from Dubai. It should have arrived the night before, but the courier had made some stupid excuse about a sick mother.

Jibran opened the box. It came with a card with simple instructions. The Shalayla's code had already been entered. He turned it on. The map of the ocean appeared on the large colour screen. The Shalayla was around one hundred nautical miles south of the Iranian port of Bandar-e-Jask and heading almost due east. For a moment he had a sickening thought they might be meeting up in Gwadar, Pakistan's other port.

Abrar had found them just after midday. If they had left Karachi straight after, they would be there in another hour. If that was the case, all was lost. He would never intercept them in time. They would win.

He had not heard from the men he had paid to raid the second Airbnb.

He called his contact.

'Did you raid the second house?'

'Yes, *Saeen*. We only found a guard and a Pakistani. There was no one else.'

The motherfuckers had slipped away again. There was a good chance they were on the outskirts of Gwadar. Did he know anyone there?

He sat, head in his hands, watching the screen.

Jamal ordered five kilos of chicken *karahi* and ten naans. Jibran watched the screen as he ate. The *karahi* was delicious, the chicken tender and moist but he was not hungry. He gave up after a few bites.

'You finish it, *yaar*,' he said to Jamal.

An hour later the boat was still heading east. It had not turned north towards Gwadar. His spirits rose. He got up and poured himself a whisky.

It was near eleven o'clock when he was certain the boat was heading to Karachi. It had gone well past Gwadar. He breathed a sigh of relief. It meant the foreigners were still in Karachi. He was going to get his revenge after all.

DONZI CUSTOM

Jibran looked lovingly at his boat. It was a Donzi Custom he had bought from a friend a few years ago. It was easily the fastest and most beautiful speedboat in Karachi. His mechanic had given it a full-service yesterday, and it was ready to go. Its four Mercury 400 outboard motors throbbed menacingly as they idled. He blipped the throttle, and the burble changed to a subdued roar, a cacophony of mechanical engine noise, the violent in-rush of air into the induction and the exhausts churning the water violently. He smiled as a flock of seagulls, startled out of their insouciance, flew off in a flurry of flapping wings.

The boat had a top speed of sixty-knots and a range of ninety nautical miles. It could seat six on the deck, and he found he could stuff another four in the cabin below. For today that would be plenty. Abdul Zubair had wanted to bring all his men, but it was better to leave two behind than lose top speed and manoeuvrability.

He left Jamal behind. He liked the man-mountain so he could not let him be part of this operation. He did not want him to be a loose end. Besides, he weighed almost as much as two men.

Jibran blipped the throttle one last time and switched off the motors. No need to waste petrol. He might need the full range from his tanks today.

From where the boat was moored he could look out through Baba Channel into the bay. He lifted his binoculars to his eyes. The sky was overcast and the sea a dull grey-green. Traffic on the water was heavy. It was busier than when he was here last with Mumtaz. In the last half-hour, four container ships, two oil tankers and a live cattle ship had entered the channel, and three container ships and an oil-tanker had left.

He had chosen the Manora Marina because it was central. From here he could quickly reach any of the other marinas in Karachi in half an hour. The Shalayla's advertised cruising speed was twenty-five knots. It was slow and clumsy compared to his Donzi. He would catch them effortlessly. There was no need to panic or do anything rash. This time he was going to be patient and methodical.

Abdul Zubair had confirmed what he had suspected. The army operation in Multan was just a cover-up. An armed outfit had responded to the contract he had put out. Something had gone wrong, and the three foreigners had managed to get the better of eleven. They must have been eleven complete amateurs.

Sergei had been nervous and unsure of himself at their last encounter; it was hardly how a capable killer would act. Razane was another matter. She was an excellent shot. By all accounts, she had killed most of his men. It was not going to help her on a boat.

After a heated debate, he and Abdul Zubair had agreed to wait till the Shalayla was out at sea, away from prying eyes, where no one would step in to help them. Eventually, when the Shalayla was found, the loss of its crew and passengers would be attributed to pirates.

He could finally close this chapter, his honour restored. In five years, maybe less, Shakar Parian would be a fully-operational gold mine with him the only shareholder.

He looked forward to the kills. It would be sweet revenge for how they had violated his sanctuary. Killing Razane would be especially satisfying. She had shot him twice, and the pain of that was much more than just a physical hurt. It was emasculating. Women needed to be kept in their place otherwise all hell would break loose. He knew it was impractical, but he would love to drag her back to his village and keep her prisoner for a month or so while he took his time with her. It was how things were done in the olden days. He felt an erection coming on just thinking of it.

Abdul Zubair was in the front passenger seat of his hired van, in the marina parking lot. He was talking to his men about something. Quite possibly it was a prayer before jihad. Little did the bearded fool know what he had in store for him.

His plan was sound. He would wait till the Shalayla passed outside the contiguous zone, twenty-four nautical miles from land. It was as far as the coast guard patrolled and way beyond where fishermen or tourists ventured.

The transceiver showed the Shalayla had entered Hawke's Bay. They were finally in Karachi.

Ben stood unsteadily on the middle deck. His sea sickness had not abated. He had not eaten since last night, but he still wanted to throw up. Boats and the sea were just not his thing. He looked at the flotilla of vessels on the water, mostly smaller pleasure craft, speedboats, and a few launches, that had come out to meet them. Going by the number of curious onlookers superyachts like the Shalayla were a rare occurrence in Karachi.

A coast guard speedboat came alongside. Over the radio, Captain Philipe informed them of their plans to moor at the DHA Marina and requested immigration formalities be conducted there. The coast guard captain happily agreed and offered to escort them.

Damon came out on deck and stood beside Ben. The day was overcast, not too cold but cooler than Dubai. Karachi was smellier, which was not unexpected. It was older and more densely populated. Overhead black headed seagulls rode the currents, diving down to the water level every so often.

Damon waved to several onlookers on the many boats.

'Wow, we're celebrities,' he said as he noticed several photographers with ultra-long zoom lenses.

'Hey dude, if your ugly face gets on social media it'll get to those fuckers,' Ben said angrily, 'You better get back outta sight.'

'Oh shit!' Damon pulled the peak of his cap lower and turned his face away from the railing. He hadn't thought of that. 'I just came to tell you your phone has a signal.'

Ben turned, 'well what are you waiting for dude?'

'Your password, you spud.'

Ben entered his password and Damon walked back to his cabin dialling.

Sergei responded after three rings. 'Hey, it's great to hear you! Are you boys in Karachi?'

Damon heaved a sigh of relief. 'Hi, Dad, yes... thank goodness you guys made it.'

'Yes, all good. You found the transceiver?'

'Yup, it's got a great range too.'

'Good, you boys have done well.'

'Thanks, Dad. Do you have your boat lined up?'

'Yes, we'll head there straight after the marina. Should take us around forty minutes to get to the boat and then goodness knows how long to get out to sea. I don't know which one we get but all theirs looked slow and clunky.'

'That's fine. We'll be able to keep an eye on you…and you us.'

'I can't wait.'

'Hey, what are the plans at the marina? How do I hand you the transceiver?'

'Just walk into the car park. When I see you, we'll drive in. Just hand it to us and walk back to the boat and head out to sea. Don't say hello or talk or anything. We'll check out the area beforehand to make sure no one's watching the place.'

'OK, got it.' Damon replied was starting to get butterflies in his stomach.

'By the way, we'll be in a taxi. And please be alert. Any sign of trouble, head straight back into the building, get on the boat and head out to the bay. We'll then have to come up with a plan B.'

'OK see you soon, fingers crossed.'

Major Hamdani answered his phone. 'Commander Iqbal, *Asalam Aleikum*...'

'*Wa aleikum* sir, nice talking to you again. We are waiting for you at the dockyards at the very end of West Wharf Road. It's where the road curves around...'

'We are already on our way. We will be there in ten minutes, *Inshallah*.'

'Good we are in the hovercraft already, waiting to go.'

'Hovercraft *zabardast*,' he was glad he had been assigned one of them. At over thirty-five knots they were fast and had a long range. They were also manoeuvrable and stable.

He had worked with Commander Iqbal and his men of the Special Operations Force two years before. They had cooperated to stop a weapon smuggling operation.

He was happy to be working with them again. Last time they had lived up to their fearsome reputation as the toughest and most professional marines in the world.

Commander Iqbal's directions were easy to follow.

The hovercraft sat menacingly on a concrete pad separated from the water by a thin strip of sand. With its machine gun turret in the back, it looked like an oversized and flattened armoured personnel carrier made for the water.

The way, they sucked in their breaths when they saw it, Fazal and Yousaf were equally impressed.

Commander Iqbal walked up to them as they exited their vehicle. 'Welcome gentlemen,' he said saluting, 'we are ready.'

'Nice hovercraft, sir,' Fazal said. 'I have always wanted to be in one of these.'

'Thank you. We are very proud of our machine and hope

to show you why.'

They climbed aboard and greeted the rest of the squadron of ten tough looking marines.

The pilot started the engine with the turn of a key. The skirt around the base of the hovercraft filled with air as the craft rose slowly to its full height. The single large fan behind them started spinning faster and faster. Slowly the pilot eased the craft into China Creek.

'We are following the Shalayla; it is a forty-metre yacht. Here is the MMSI number,' he gave the pilot a piece of paper.

'Thank you! I already have it, sir.'

Major Hamdani made his way to the empty space on the bench next to Fazal and Yousaf and took the safety vest the commander handed him.

He couldn't help feeling a thrill as the hovercraft made its way through the shipping channel past Salehabad and Manora and into the Baba Channel. He loved the ocean. Soon they were out in the bay.

He looked at his watch. It was 2:05pm.

HAWKES BAY

Karachi Docks, Monday 5 December, 2:20pm

Jane trembled as Razane helped her out of the taxi. She was tired, cold, and hungry. She hadn't slept a wink the night before. After escaping from the Airbnb, they'd flagged down a passing taxi. A few blocks away they'd found an under-construction house and had huddled in a corner till the morning. Only Sergei managed to catch some sleep. They walked to a nearby shopping centre and whiled away the time in a succession of coffee shops. They were walking through a shopping centre looking for another eating establishment when Damon called from the Shalayla.

That lifted their spirits no end. They caught a taxi and stopped at the marina where Damon handed over the transceiver. Thankfully there was no trouble of any sort. It was a good sign. It showed their enemy was not all-powerful.

A scarf covered Jane's hair and part of her face. She was falling apart from the stress. Freedom was achingly close, but it could still be brutally snatched away. They had been so violently attacked so many times; she didn't think any of them could withstand another encounter.

The jetty was around thirty metres away. The launch to take them to freedom beckoned. Its hull was painted a bold aquamarine blue, and everything from the deck upwards was bright white. An orange flag fluttered on a mast on its stern. She looked like a happy boat. Hopefully, that was another good sign.

After ten crazy days, they were finally going home. It

seemed almost too good to be true.

'My legs feel like jelly, completely wobbly,' Jane said, her voice was shaking.

'It's the feeling of relief after all the madness you have been through.' Razane hooked her arm into hers. 'Come, my love, my sweet love,' she crooned soothingly, different words but a familiar melody, as they walked towards the boat.

Sergei paid the taxi driver and walked to the booking office to pay. He looked along the jetty at their boat. He knew next to nothing about them. Hopefully, it was seaworthy.

Jane and Razane had reached the water's edge. 'I've got this uneasy feeling we'll suddenly hear sirens and see police cars rushing us,' Jane said. 'She tried in vain to stop her voice quavering. 'Where's Sergei?' She looked back. He was entering the steel hut.

'There is nothing my love.' Indeed, the only sounds were the lapping of the waves, the clatter of the launch's diesel engine and the squawking of seagulls. In the background was the ever-present noise of traffic and people going about their daily lives. There were no signs of anything untoward. Yet even for Razane, every step got heavier. Was this how all escapees felt?

The jetty timbers were soft underfoot and looked long overdue for replacement. That would be the ultimate irony, their escape foiled by a rotten board on a jetty. Jane looked back again. Sergei had just left the hut and was stuffing his wallet back in his jeans as he strode towards them.

He walked fast to catch up. Jane and Razane were already at the boat when he reached the start of the jetty. The boat captain held the mooring ropes tight so Jane and Razane could climb in. A young boy of fifteen stood on the boat with a pile of life-jackets. Razane went first then turned to help Jane.

The dread that had enveloped Jane's mind was dissipating rapidly. Her legs felt better. They were really going to make it. She took a deep breath and reached for Razane's hand. Just then a gust of wind blew her scarf away. The captain tried to grab it as it fluttered past him into the water. He almost let go of the ropes. The boat bobbed sideways. A small gap opened between it and the jetty. Jane gave a little scream. Razane lunged forward and grabbed one hand firmly and held on tight. 'I've got you, babe.'

'And I've got you, babe,' Jane smiled and sang it back to her as she clambered into the boat and landed in her arms. She was elated and squeezed Razane tightly. The captain gave her a look of surprise. Was it because of the blonde hair? If he recognised her, he did not make it obvious.

The captain waited on the jetty till Sergei was onboard before climbing in himself.

The launch was around fifteen metres long with a flat deck surrounded by a three-foot-high railing. A canvas shade covered two wooden benches in the middle.

They sat as the captain walked forward to the enormous steering wheel.

He looked back at them. 'We go?'

Sergei waved back at him. 'Yes, we go. *Fatafat.*'

'*Fatafat,* yes sir,' the captain said giving him a mock salute. He was smiling.

His young assistant pulled in both mooring ropes and used a long pole to push the boat clear.

The throbbing diesel engine became louder as the launch moved forward smoothly. Jane looked back. No one was rushing onto the jetty with guns drawn. They were finally away, free.

Damon stood on the upper deck, the satellite transceiver in his hand. The dot on the screen was moving slowly away from the coastline. Thank goodness Ben had remembered the transceiver.

The windows in the houses along the shoreline, reflected the sun as the Shalayla navigated through the narrow channel between DHA and Bundle Island. They were finally leaving Pakistan behind. It was a pity, it wasn't in better circumstances. He did not like running away from any place. Pakistan was an interesting country for sure, and its people were nice and friendly. Even the immigration officers who came on board when they docked in the marina had been polite and courteous. He had expected they'd want to search the boat and inspect everything, but they had stamped his and Ben's passports with an instant visa and welcomed them to Pakistan. He had anticipated lots of probing questions for which they had rehearsed carefully on the journey from Dubai. The silly story about doing a documentary and Ben's website had been a waste of time. If only they'd known. He walked down to the control room.

Ben, was busy looking at the navigation screens. He could lose himself in something that took his fancy, even in stressful situations like the one they were in now. How different two brothers could be. His own favourite part of the yacht was the spa, the beautiful sun lounge and in the evenings the marine aquarium.

He smiled at Ben, 'douchebag.'

'What...?'

Damon showed Captain Philipe the transceiver. 'Do you think you can follow that boat?'

'Of course, easy but may I ask why?'

'They are friends of ours. We would like to pick them up.' A gull shrieked as it swooped their yacht.

The captain said nothing as he moved the little joystick a few millimetres to the right.

'Don't worry it's legit. They're Aussie citizens with passports and all.'

Captain Phillipe grunted. 'Well, you're the client.'

The bay was still crowded and chaotic even though most of the watchers had left. Pleasure craft of all types mixed with commercial vessels and fishing boats, all heading in different directions. In the distance, a ship horn sounded. One of the large tankers was warning a small sailboat. It was a minor miracle there were no collisions. The transceiver showed the Shalayla was less than half a kilometre away. Damon picked up a pair of binoculars and looked, but it was an impossible task. He should have asked his Dad for a description of their boat.

'Please follow their heading for a while,' he said to the captain.

Jibran watched the GPS signal. The Shalayla had stopped for half an hour at the marina, plenty of time for it to pick up its passengers. It had come out of the narrow channel and was sailing in a westerly direction retracing its earlier route. After a few minutes, it started arcing southward. He was itching to go and attack straight away but doing now would be too risky even for him. He needed to stick to the plan.

If it were left to Abdul Zubair he would attack in the middle of the harbour, most likely with an RPG, a rocket-propelled grenade, fired amidships. It would block the shipping channels and cause havoc. Abdul Zubair would happily sacrifice his men for such an outcome. That would not happen today. They were going to follow his plan and wait and do it properly and discreetly.

He looked at the screen again. The superyacht was heading in a south-westerly direction. He could take his time and enjoy the hunt and then the kill.

He waved at Abdul Zubair to come over and watched as the old jihadi and his men piled out of the van and began walking towards him, all identically dressed, with beards and skull caps. He had khaki pants, vests, and helmets in the hold for them. They would look like soldiers rather than a bunch of religious zealots. Hopefully, they would also fight like soldiers. Their arsenal of older AK47s and more modern AK74s and the RPG launcher along with coils of rope with grappling hooks were already in the hold. He smiled at the thought of all the violence that was to come.

'That is a beautiful boat, sir,' Yousaf said. They had caught sight of the Shalayla in the distance. 'I hope we don't have to damage it.'

'We are only interested in its passengers,' Fazal interjected.

'Commander, can we drop back so the Shalayla cannot observe us?' the major asked.

'We can stay just beyond the horizon. At maximum speed, it puts us about fifteen minutes behind them if they also travel at their full speed.'

'No, too far. I need us to be closer, where we don't seem a threat but can respond fast if needed. What do you suggest?'

'In that case, let's stay around seven to eight minutes behind. We have a very low profile and are hard to spot among the waves and even on radar.'

THE RENDEZVOUS

The Arabian Sea, Monday 5 December, 3:30pm

They were now well out to sea. Their last sighting of land was well over an hour ago. Sergei had been tracking the Shalayla since they had set off, but she was not yet in sight.

The sky had turned from hazy and overcast to brooding and unsettled. Dark storm clouds had seemingly come out of nowhere and covered the sky. The wind was still moderate, and waves were about a metre high. The launch was coping well and had settled into a steady rhythm as it rose and fell on the waves.

The captain had offered them fishing rods and bait and had been surprised when they had all declined.

A pod of dolphins swam near them for a while. They played a game, popping up alternately on their port and starboard sides. Sergei and Jane had tried counting them. Sergei thought he could see eleven; Jane was sure there were only nine.

They were now the only craft on the water as far as the eye could see. The dolphins had abandoned them. The occasional seagull swooped for fish, but their numbers had dwindled dramatically. It suddenly all seemed lonely and forbidding.

Razane fidgeted nervously with her hair. It kept on coming loose. They were still within Pakistani waters. Jane was still a fugitive. By now someone might have sifted through the rubble and worked out her DNA was missing. They were close enough to shore to get a nasty surprise like Multan. Hopefully, nothing would eventuate. She would only breathe easy when they were onboard the Shalayla and a few hundred nautical miles out to sea.

Sergei kept glancing at the transceiver, he held in his hand, and back at the horizon. Razane walked over.

'How far away are they, my love?' Her teeth chattered, the spray had made her clothes damp, and the freshening breeze was making her cold.

Sergei put his arm around her and gave her a squeeze. 'According to this they're very close.' He turned to face her. She was shivering; her forehead was creased with worry. He pulled her close and kissed her. 'Don't worry we'll find them.'

'I hope it will not be much longer,' Razane said. 'I can see our captain… he is getting restless.'

'Yup, I've noticed too. Don't worry I'm sure the Shalayla will show any minute. They can see us as well.' It was a damn shame they had to leave the Kalashnikovs behind. What if they needed them in international waters against pirates? It was too late to think of that now.

Jane came over. 'What is it?' She also looked worried. It was contagious.

Razane was the first to spot the yacht. They had been looking in the wrong direction. The Shalayla was behind them, close enough to see Damon and Ben standing on the deck, waving.

They were a welcome sight. Jane couldn't help herself. Tears began rolling down her face. After ten mad days, it was finally happening. They were going home. She had to sit down, or she would fall.

'Hold me,' Jane said unsteadily to Sergei who put his arm around her and helped her to the bench.

Razane walked over to the captain. 'Slow down,' she said, reinforcing her words with a movement of her arm.

The man looked noticeably relieved. The launch did not have any navigation gear, and he had been nervously looking at his watch and the sky for the last ten minutes. He glanced at Sergei as if to seek his permission. Sergei nodded, and he pushed the lever to the left of the steering wheel forward. The high-pitched thrum of the diesel engine quieted down as the launch slowed. They were now bobbing up and down noticeably.

The Shalayla closed the gap. Within minutes they were alongside. Damon and Ben were on the superyacht's lower deck waving at them. The crew threw down ropes which the captain used to tie the launch. Then they rolled down a chain ladder coated in grippy rubber.

One by one Damon and Ben helped Jane, Razane and Sergei on board. The Shalayla was a lovely vessel, but at that moment they did not appreciate its beauty. They were finally together. Relief swept over them. What had seemed impossible when they had first discussed it in Lahore had become real.

Jane hugged her boys while Sergei helped the crew members roll up the ropes. He waved back at the Captain who was all smiles after Sergei had given him the last remaining cash in his pocket.

The two vessels slowly separated. Sergei watched the launch turn around as their yacht gradually picked up speed.

'Welcome to the Shalayla. I am Captain Philipe.'

Sergei turned around, smiled at him, and shook his hand. 'Thank you, Captain, it's good to be on board. You have a lovely yacht.'

The captain was clearly attached to his boat and beamed widely.

He bowed to the two women as he shook their hands. 'Welcome, welcome, madame and madame.'

'Thank you, Captain,' Jane said.

'This is a rather unorthodox way of picking up passengers, but Damon assures me you have passports.'

'Oh yes, we do.' Sergei handed him his. Jane and Razane did the same.

'Thank you. This all seems in order. Once again welcome to my boat. I hope your cruise is enjoyable. Would you care for a brief tour?'

None of them had ever been on a superyacht before, and

they gladly accepted his offer. For the next fifteen minutes, they were entertained and delighted in turns by the sheer extravagance of its layout and appointments.

They started on the lower deck which led into a lounge and an entertainment area. Forward of that was an impressive dining room with a massive table for twelve.

'I would have thought things were smaller on a yacht,' Sergei said.

'Not on a luxury superyacht, no monsieur.'

The dining room afforded expansive views to both sides of the yacht. A staircase in the dining room led down into a pantry containing three commercial fridges and a freezer.

'All the food here is at your disposal whenever you are hungry or thirsty. You can grab it yourself or call one of the staff to serve you… And don't hold back there's more in the cargo hold freezers.'

The pantry opened into an industrial style kitchen all lined in stainless steel. A chef was busy cooking something on a large commercial stove.

'Meet the chef, Mr Prakash. He can prepare most cuisines. He even does French very well, for an Indian,' Captain Philipe said with a wink.

They walked through the kitchen back up to the dining room via a second staircase. From here the captain led them to the bridge.

'This is where I control the Shalayla from.'

The control room was dominated by a captain's chair behind a four-spoke steering wheel made of wood. Arrayed ahead of the steering wheel, monitors and dials displayed everything from the state of the engines and hydraulics to the position of its rudders. Other screens were devoted to navigation, radar, and the weather. A huge monitor showed a bird's eye view of the whole boat and the water beside it. 'I can even look underwater with my reverse periscope,' he said, 'and…' he pointed behind him at the row of couches behind the captain's chair, 'my guests can sit here and view everything I do in complete comfort.'

He pointed to doors on either side of the control room.

'They lead to walkways along the port and starboard sides of the boat.'

He led them through the door on the starboard side. An internal staircase led to the upper levels.

They stopped on the middle deck. 'Here are three bedrooms and the middle sun deck and jacuzzi. The first two are taken by your sons. I understand now why they did not take the master bedroom.' He opened the third room. 'This is for the lady,' he motioned to Razane.

'No, we are all together, we are three,' Sergei said. He noticed the slightly bemused expression on the captain's face. 'I hope the bed in the master bedroom is large.'

'Aah, oh I see, of course,' Captain Philipe said recovering his composure. 'The bed is huge and comfortable.' He had a twinkle in his eyes. 'Follow me please.'

They followed him to the top deck.

This was the most luxurious part of the yacht. A mezzanine lounge opened into a huge bedroom. A walkway to the side led to an outside deck with an array of four lounge chairs.

The master bedroom was tastefully appointed. The bed was huge as promised and looked comfortable. Consistent with the rest of the yacht the walls and ceiling were lined in a light mahogany interspersed with stainless steel strips. The bedroom opened into a black marble bathroom with a large spa bath.

'That's amazing,' Jane said when they were finally alone, 'We've escaped from hell and landed in heaven.'

'From a frying pan into a bed of roses,' Razane said with a smile.

'It's beautiful,' Sergei said sadly, 'what a pity the person who paid for it isn't--'

He was cut off by the sound of rapid gunfire.

'So, sir when do we finally intercept them?' Fazal said leaning over to speak into the major's ear, 'we have just passed out of Pakistani waters.'

'Don't rush me Fazal,' the major said in a flat voice, 'even the coast guard has the right to intercept boats until the contiguous line.' Fazal's incessant questioning was grating on the nerves. 'And since we are on a navy vessel we can go well beyond there into international waters.'

They had dropped a bit further behind the Shalayla than where he had wanted them to be. He was beginning to think his gambit, to use the foreigners as bait, might not pay off, after all.

'Sir, they have just picked up passengers. I saw three people transfer over.'

'Show me.' the major grabbed the binoculars. 'That is them,' he muttered to no one in particular. 'I thought they had boarded at the marina.'

He handed the binoculars to Yousaf. A launch emerged from behind the Shalayla and began to head back towards them.

'Shall we intercept the launch,' Commander Iqbal said.

'No, there is no need. Just note the registration number for reference.'

Sergei's heart beat like mad. His temple throbbed. 'Bloody hell,' he growled as he grabbed the rucksack off the bed and fished for a pistol and a spare magazine, 'I knew we should have brought the fucking AKs. Damn!' He ran out of the master bedroom and down the stairs.

Jane sat on the bed. All the strength left her body, her face contorted with worry.

'Stay here my love.' Razane said as she too grabbed a pistol and raced after Sergei.

'Take care, you both,' Jane shouted. Her mind was in turmoil. She had to do something. There were more pistols in the bag. She fished in the rucksack and pulled one out and looked at it. How did the safety catch work again? She switched it off and on.

She couldn't let the mind-numbing fear and the overwhelming disappointment defeat her. There was no going back to prison. Not after being a few kilometres from freedom. She'd also not sit there while her family was in danger. If this was going to be the end, she'd find the strength to face it as well.

Ben and Damon were sitting with Captain Philipe looking at the monitors when Sergei rushed into the control room.

A speedboat full of armed uniformed men was ten boat lengths away on their port side.

'Is that the coast guard or navy?' Sergei asked.

'No idea,' Captain Philipe said scratching his beard, 'but we must stop. If we don't, and they are navy, we'll be arrested.'

'Please don't stop. What if they're pirates?' Sergei said frantically. How could he explain to the captain that they were fucked, either way?

'Look I have sent out a mayday, saying we are being boarded by pirates, just in case.'

'Please just try to outrun them.' Sergei's voice was frantic. He tried to think, but panic had fogged his mind. Nothing came to him.

'Mr Markoff, that is a serious boat with some real horsepower. My guess, they are easily twice as fast as us but look carefully.' He pointed at the screen. 'There see that. We can never outrun that RPG.'

Sergei looked closely at the monitor. His blood froze. One of the men in the boat had an RPG launcher on his shoulder. He hadn't aimed it at them yet.

A gruff voice came over the radio. 'Come in Shalayla.'

'This is the Captain. Please identify yourself.'

'This is the coast guard patrol. We need to do a routine search. Stop the boat and bring all your crew and passengers on the deck. We are coming on board.'

The captain took his finger off the radio button.

'I am sorry, but I am stopping. I cannot risk the boat. If they use the RPG against us, we sink like a stone. It's as simple as that.'

'How could the coast guard shoot a civilian vessel?'

'Do you want to find out?' the captain said in an angry tone.

Sergei knew he was right. They were out of options. He watched in frustration as the captain pulled back the throttle. The Shalayla began slowing down. The other boat came closer. The captain pressed a button and lowered the ladder.

'I should have known you three were trouble,' he said with a frown. 'You stay here. I'll try to talk my way out of it.'

'Can you think of anything sweetheart?' Sergei whispered to Razane.

'There is not really any place to hide on this boat,' she said in a low voice. 'The only option we have is to surprise them when we're amongst them.'

'If we can even the odds quickly we have a chance,' Sergei said. 'It's all or nothing.'

'I don't like our chances,' Damon said, 'but count me in.'

'OK but let's wait till we know their intentions. If for any reason they want to take any of us back to Pakistani territory we fight.'

They were interrupted by three men, armed with Kalashnikovs, who stormed onto the bridge.

Surreptitiously, Sergei let his pistol drop into the gap on the side of the seat cushion. Hopefully, Razane would do the same. Bravado against such odds would only get them shot even sooner.

'Out,' one of the men barked menacingly, waving his rifle.

Razane went pale. Something about them was wrong. These men held AK47s. The last year they were officially sold to government agencies was in the 70s. Nowadays only small militia groups still used them.

Jibran climbed up the gangway barely holding on to the side rails. He sucked in the sea air. It was invigorating. He felt more alive than he had in a long time. Moments like this were made to be savoured. He leapt onto the deck. The captain, a bearded white fucker, came down the outer walkway on the starboard side, the dumb cunt.

Jibran pulled the Heckler and Koch off his shoulder and walked up to him. This rifle was one of his favourites. He had never shot a human with it, but he was sure going to use it today.

'What can I do for you officer?' the captain said calmly, as he showed him the yacht's registration papers and his passport. 'We have already gone through immigration, here are the clearance papers.'

'Sit down...on the floor,' Jibran ordered, 'and shut up!'

'You and you, search the boat from top to bottom,' he said waving to two of Abdul Zubair's men.

'Go fast,' Abdul Zubair chimed in.

Just then the people he had come for were herded out through the glass doorway, at gunpoint. Jibran smiled with satisfaction. Only Jane Kelly was missing. Burnt Saleem, shoved Ben hard as he stepped onto the deck.

Ben just managed to stay upright. He turned his head around and looked angrily at his aggressor, 'what the fuck?'

Burnt Saleem responded by placing the barrel of his Kalashnikov against his neck. Ben put his arms up; his face had gone ashen.

'Hah, look at the white motherfuckers,' Jibran said smiling broadly at the shocked recognition on their faces, 'you didn't think I meant it... No one fucks with Jibran Ghaffar,' he said. His smile changed to a snarl. 'No one. Now, where is the blonde whore?'

Sergei's mind reeled in shock. Fuck, if only he'd killed the man as Damon had suggested.

Without warning, Abdul Zubair advanced towards

Razane brandishing a knife. There wasn't time to think. Sergei intercepted him with a sharp punch to his side below his ribs. His knuckles made painful contact with the stock of the old man's rifle. At the same time, he kicked down onto his left shin causing Abdul Zubair to collapse into a semi-prone position and drop his knife. His Kalashnikov slid off his shoulder onto the deck.

Jibran swung the butt of his rifle and caught Sergei on his chin. With a painful grunt, he staggered and fell backwards hitting his head on the deck. As if on cue the men behind Damon and Ben swung their rifle butts at their heads. Ben caught the full force. His head rang, and he saw black. He toppled over slowly. Damon managed to see the blow coming and instinctively raised his right elbow. The rifle hit his funny bone and sent a jarring pain into his arm. He turned around, but his arm was paralysed. The man backed away and lifted the rifle threateningly.

Sergei tried standing, but Jibran kicked him in the abdomen. Sergei saw it coming and tensed himself. The kick still winded him badly, and he doubled up in pain. Jibran was about to kick him again when Razane leapt at him. 'Leave him,' she screamed.

Jibran swung around and pushed Razane hard. He was uncommonly strong, and she was unprepared. Completely off balance she almost flew towards the railing. She struck it hard and fell overboard.

Razane tried desperately to hold on to something, anything, but her hands found only air. She hit the water at a painful angle. All her breath was knocked out of her, and she went under.

Jane descended the stairs trying to remain as quiet as possible. She turned her pistol's safety off and held it ahead of her. What would Sergei or Razane do? She listened. A struggle was taking place on the deck below. Men were shouting in Urdu, Ben was yelling. Razane screamed loudly; seconds later there was a loud splash. Someone had fallen in the water. Please let it not be Razane. She couldn't swim. Jane looked over the side. There was a faint shadow in the water. Someone had fallen in.

Jane ran down the rest of the stairs almost stumbling in her haste. Her only thought to jump in after her.

Strong arms held her from behind. A bearded man in uniform grabbed her arm and wrenched the pistol from her hand like he was taking candy from a baby. The man's face was vaguely familiar. She tried to struggle, but it had no effect. The first man pinned her arms painfully behind her back. Tears ran down her face in anger and frustration. She screamed at the man restraining her. Unmoved, he roughly pushed her forward to join the rest of the captives.

Sergei and Ben were on the deck. Sergei was holding his stomach, coughing and trying to catch his breath. Ben was holding his head, trying to sit, his hands red with blood. Damon was rubbing his elbow and crouching next to him. Razane was nowhere to be seen. Jane almost burst with anger. She tried kicking backwards, but the man holding her blocked her leg with his.

Jibran lifted his rifle and aimed it at Sergei. 'I will start with you.' He was interrupted as Mr Prakash, and two other crew members were unceremoniously pushed in front of him by Abdul Zubair's men.

'*Aqa*, I have checked the whole boat. There is no one else,' Burnt Saleem said coming through the glass doors. He ignored Jibran who was glaring at him.

He saw Abdul Zubair trying to get up and rushed over to help him, '*Aqa* please let me.'

Jibran lifted his rifle again. Maybe he would make Sergei suffer and first kill one of his sons.

The wind picked up speed and began howling. Rain started pelting down.

The hovercraft pilot killed the engine and let the vessel glide the rest of the way using its momentum. Commander Iqbal was looking through his binoculars and saw a woman fall overboard. She disappeared under water and popped up a few seconds later only to go under again. She was clearly in difficulty and was drifting away from the yacht.

'You and you, pull her out,' he ordered two of his men.

'To your positions,' he called out to the rest. The two men assigned to rescue Razane jumped into the water as their craft glided past her. Four men clambered out and onto the roof. They stood in a single file prepared to run forward. The other four took up positions on the hovercraft's flanks, two on either side. Their precise movements, a choreography seemingly practised to perfection.

Razane was in trouble. She had never been able to swim. She tried to stay calm and kick with her legs but the water stung her eyes and her nostrils, and she was severely fatigued. She flailed her arms around in a desperate attempt to get her head above the surface, but she had already swallowed too much and was coughing and spluttering and taking in more and more of the salty water. Her breathing became impossible; darkness enveloped her.

A hand reached out to her and then another. She felt herself being lifted, her head held above the water.

The hovercraft completed its powerless glide and bumped softly into the Shalayla's stern. As if on cue, rain started pelting down. As the two vessels made contact first two and then two more marines ran forward, jumped and landed on the yacht's lower deck with the well-oiled precision of dancers. Almost simultaneously the four marines on the flanks jumped onto the hovercraft's roof and pointed their weapons at the Shalayla, covering their comrades.

Inside the hovercraft, one of the men wrapped a khaki blanket around Razane's shivering form. She was blue in the face and repeatedly gurgled up water. Her rescuers rolled her over. She was vaguely aware of the marines as their footsteps drummed against the roof of the hovercraft. They were assaulting the yacht. Convulsions wracked her body as more water came rushing out. She was still unable to breathe. She badly needed to throw up. She managed to push past her rescuers and crawled to the door.

The bump from the hovercraft knocked Jibran sideways before he was able to press the trigger. Motherfuckers! He staggered but righted himself. He turned around with a snarl but froze when the marines landed on the deck. He wisely kept his rifle pointing down.

Abdul Zubair was trying to stand with Burnt Saleem's help. Sergei's kick had almost broken his shin. He had also twisted his bad left foot, and it was throbbing painfully. He gingerly felt his shin bone. It was intact but swelling rapidly. If it hadn't been for Burnt Saleem, he would have toppled over again.

The sight of Jane inflamed his anger. Here was the *farangi* bitch who had evaded his men, but no longer. He barely registered the sound of the marines running onto the deck behind him.

Abdul Zubair's men responded to the assault by raising their rifles. Shots rang out. The five who had raised their weapons fell where they stood. All of them shot in the forehead. In shock, Abdul Zubair looked down at their bodies sprawled on the deck. Blood was pooling around their heads and running through the small gaps in the oiled teak.

Sergei sat up feeling dazed and groggy. The sounds of the gunshots rang in his ears. He was unable to fully comprehend what was happening but he registered the men swarming onto the Shalayla were different from Abdul Zubair's men. They were the real deal. Their uniforms were different, and their guns were modern. They looked tough and hard and moved with precision and purpose. The last time he'd been in the company of men this hard was when he was one of them, training for the Australian Special Forces.

One walked to the port side and fired a single shot. The man in the speedboat screamed and was silent.

Sergei looked around with an effort; his head was spinning. Jane had tears running down her face. One of the fucking terrorists still held her arms pinned painfully behind her back, his mouth agape in shock at the turn of events. Abdul Zubair and Jibran had the same expressions of disbelief.

Ignoring the pain in his head, Sergei stood, his mind ablaze with fury. The bastard holding Jane was going to die. Sergei landed a vicious straight punch to his throat, with all his weight behind him and using all his Taekwondo training, condensed into that one moment.

The man never saw it coming. His head first snapped back then bobbed forward. He let go of Jane as he staggered back. He opened his mouth to try to breathe but couldn't. His eyes went up in his head. Clutching frantically at his throat, gasping for air, he fell to the deck in a heap.

Jane was like a spring released. Without looking back, she ran to the railing and looked over. There was nothing. 'Razane!' Her shrill scream was painful to hear.

Commander Iqbal stepped off the hovercraft and walked up to her. Still in a daze, Sergei realised what had happened and rushed over too.

'We have the woman, madam. She is in the boat.'

'Is she...?'

'Yes, she will be OK.'

More marines boarded the Shalayla. Three civilians accompanied them, one of them an older man with a beard.

Jibran's mind was still reeling with shock, but he recognised Major Hamdani. That was a lucky break. He knew the man. He was a devout Muslim and didn't drink or smoke and apparently prayed five times a day. His swagger returned. He realised he still held onto his rifle. No one dared take that away from him.

'Major *Sahib*, you have come just in time.'

'Yes, Mr Ghaffar, I can see that.'

'We have found your fugitive and were about to bring her justice, I mean to justice. Now you can take her in.' He ignored Abdul Zubair's furious expression.

One of the marines recognised Jane and looked at their commander expectantly.

'Which justice do you mean exactly,' the major said curtly. 'Commander Iqbal please do the needful.'

Abdul Zubair could see they no longer held the upper hand. Only two of his men were still standing, and only Jibran still had his weapon. The tables had completely turned against them. His rifle and knife were on the deck, dropped when he fell. There was not going to be a martyr's last charge to glory. 'The blaspheming woman needs to be punished,' he yelled.

'Arrest the woman as well,' Fazal said to the marines. Sergei stepped in front of Jane shielding her with his body.

On the hovercraft, the two marines watched as Razane put her head over the side of the hovercraft. With a rush, the contents of her stomach and the remaining water in her lungs emptied into the sea. Her nasal passages burnt from the acid and salt water. The pressure on her lungs eased, and her head cleared almost instantly. One of the marines handed her a water bottle. She rinsed her mouth, spat, and stood up shakily. 'Thank you,' she said gratefully as she used the railing to steady herself.

'No, leave the lady to me,' Major Hamdani retorted and raised his hand to stop them. 'Arrest those men.' The marines stepped forward and pulled the rifle from Jibran's hand. They forced Abdul Zubair and Burnt Saleem to kneel on the deck with their hands over their heads. Cable ties were produced and used to secure their wrists.

A shot rang out. The major stumbled and fell forward. Fazal fired again. He pointed his Glock at Sergei. 'Step out from behind him, woman, or I shoot him too.'

WHAT HAPPENED NEXT

The Arabian Sea, Monday 5 December, 4:15pm

Razane was in a daze and trying to breathe without coughing, her mind close to melt-down. How was she going to turn this around? They could not go back. She heard the shots ring out as the marines took control. Someone was shouting, ordering the arrest of the men. She had to see. She stood. Two shots rang out.

Someone was telling Jane to come out. They were going to execute her. An overwhelming need to protect Jane energised her. She leapt onto the hovercraft's roof. A young man in civilian clothes was pointing a gun at Sergei and Jane. Razane was too far away to charge at him.

She looked around wildly. One of the marines who had helped her was climbing up beside her, his rifle in one hand. 'Sorry about this,' she said as she snatched it from him. In one sweeping motion, she lifted it to her shoulder and fired. The man with the revolver fell.

Razane dropped the rifle and with a running jump landed on the Shalayla. Jane and Sergei rushed over to her.

Yousaf ran to the major. He was kneeling on the deck his face contorted in pain. Two bullet holes in his safety vest showed where he had been hit. There was no blood, though. He groaned. 'Help me up.'

'Sir you are wearing a bulletproof vest? Thank God--'

'I think you are too.' The major grunted in pain. He had landed painfully on his knees. 'These safety vests are not just for the water.'

Fazal had not been so lucky. Razane's bullet had hit him in the neck and had exited from the bridge of his nose. He was dead.

'I'm very disappointed in him,' Yousaf said.

'You are? I was training him.'

Jibran Ghaffar, Abdul Zubair and Burnt Saleem were safely in the back of the hovercraft. Jibran had protested furiously when they tried to arrest him. One of the marines went up to him and slapped him hard in the face. He went quietly after that. Photographs were taken and the bodies, including Fazal's, were zipped up into body bags. One of the marines tended to a nasty looking cut on the back of Ben's head.

Sergei, Razane, and Jane were comforting him.

'So, what now?' Jane said to the major.

'We take these terrorists and this traitor in and make them face justice for their crimes,' the major said.

'I mean what about me?'

'What about you?'

'Am I, are we free to go?' Jane was almost afraid of the answer.

'Of course,' the major said. 'I was never after you. You three were helping me uncover these villains.'

After all the ups and downs she had experienced recently it sounded too good to be true. 'The charges against me?'

'It will probably be a mistrial. The word of a criminal will have no weight in court. But it will be wise you do not return for a few years, just for your own safety.'

'Thank you so much!' Jane almost wept with relief. 'You are a most reasonable man. Can I shake your hand?'

'Of course, you may. I know the work you did in the village and would like to thank you on behalf of all the good people of Pakistan. Also, my sincerest apologies for how some of my countrymen treated you.' He offered his hand for her to shake.

Tears poured out of Jane's eyes, as she hugged him instead.

'Sir and madam,' he said to Sergei and Razane, 'I would like to commend you for your bravery and apologise for taking my eyes off you in Multan. I am most gratified you were not hurt in that incident.'

'No hard feelings on my part, mate,' Sergei said. Razane nodded.

'Your son needs stitches. I don't think he should travel for too long at sea without it,' the marine who was tending to Ben said. 'We can treat him in Karachi.'

'I'll go with him,' Damon said. 'We can catch a flight back to Melbourne. I wasn't really looking forward to the voyage. Not with you three crazy people onboard.' He smiled.

'I've decided, I'll take my stitched-up head to Dubai for a while,' Ben said. 'I don't think I'll be able to manage the long flight to Australia in this condition.'

Damon shook his head as he smiled. So, there was more to the girl than a simple one-night stand. He turned to the major. 'Do you guarantee us safe passage?'

'Of course, son.'

'One more thing,' the major said, 'I have arranged a naval escort till you are clear of the pirate zone. It's the least the Government of Pakistan can do to repay you.'

They watched as Ben and Damon were helped into the hovercraft.

The rain had become a torrent, each drop the size of a grape. The trio stood there till the two vessels vanished into the distance and Sergei and Jane were as soaked as Razane. The crew were back at their stations. The Shalayla slowly picked up speed. The wind howled louder.

'I'm cold. Let's go inside and warm up.' He put his arms around them both as they walked into the main lounge.

Behind them, the rain had almost washed the blood away.

EPILOGUE

Yarra Valley, Melbourne, 1 year later

Jane flicked the tablecloth onto the large hardwood table. The sun was an hour from setting. It was no longer hot, but the timber deck was still pleasantly warm under her bare feet. A balmy breeze carried the sweet perfume of their Madagascar jasmine creeper and gently curled the edge of her summer dress.

She lay on the divan, stretched languorously, and closed her eyes. Above her, the leaves in the red flowering gum tree rustled. In the distance, a cicada droned.

The kitchen door creaked open then closed with a twang. Razane's bare feet padded across the deck. She carried two large bowls of salad which she placed in the middle of the table. She grabbed two beers from the cooler and gave one to Jane. Then she lay on the opposite end of the divan and intertwined her legs with Jane's.

'Where's our meat?' Jane called out. She smiled blissfully as Razane's toes found their way under her dress. Their cool touch delicious on her warm thighs.

Sergei placed the last steak on the serving dish and turned off the barbeque burner. He removed his apron and walked over.

'Here it is, my ladies.'

'Put that meat on the table and bring your meat here,' Razane said with a smile. Both her feet were under Jane's skirt.

They made love, as the sun set, to the music of the cicada and the crickets.

Later they ate cold steak with warm salad and washed it

down with beer from a local brewery.

'It's poetry time,' Jane said.

The night was well and truly dark. Constellations of stars shone brightly in the cloudless sky. Outdoor lamps had turned on and were casting a soft light, just enough to read by.

Razane picked up a writing pad and read aloud in a soft voice,

'Your sun thawed my frozen heart,
And melted my ice, to a torrent,
that flowed like a river into your sea,'

'That is sublime,' Sergei said smiling. He kissed Razane tenderly on the lips. Jane did too.

'Sweetheart that is so beautiful. Now my turn,' Jane said in eager tone,

'Even as I imbibe from the cup of your love,
I am forever dying of thirst,'

'Wow, now that is deep,' Razane said, 'I am so impressed, my darling.' She hugged Jane.

'We have obviously two world-class and very sexy Sufi poets here,' Sergei said. He smiled as they both looked at him expectantly. 'OK, don't say I didn't warn you.' He took a sip of water and cleared his throat dramatically,

'There are no walls between us, no bounds,
nothing separates our hearts,
You are both my lovers,
I am your reckless worshipper,'

'Or the keeper of the harem.' Jane giggled as Sergei began tickling her. Razane joined in.

POST EPILOGUE

Lahore, One year later

The mason led him to the grave site. 'I hope, *Sahib*, the workmanship will please you,' he said with a slight bow. 'Like I promised I have used the best white marble for your brother. May his soul rest in heaven.'

Amjad handed him the money he owed and then some more. 'Yes, it is most beautiful, thank you.'

The mason counted the notes and pocketed them gratefully. 'Thank you, *Sahib*! May Allah, watch over you and your family. I could see, from the date, it is your brother's *barsi* today. I have said a prayer for him.'

'Thank you.'

When the mason left, he spread some rose petals over Fazal's grave then he did the same to the two older graves on its left.

Their mother and father were buried there. Thank God, they had not lived to see the day their son was murdered.

He sat and prayed for their souls, for their place in heaven and for the strength to carry out his plan for revenge.

GLOSSARY

Allah Hafiz: May God keep you in his protection. A form of goodbye.
Angrezi: English.
Aqa: Lord.
Asalam Aleikum: Muslim greeting in Arabic, means peace be unto you.
Barsi: Death anniversary.
Begum: Wife. Begum Sahib is a term of respect for a married woman.
Beita: Son.
Chacha: Paternal uncle.
Chai: Tea.
Charas: Cannabis resin.
Charpoy: Woven jute-rope bed.
Chimta: Long slender solid steel tongs used for music.
Chootia: Derogatory term. Dumb. The literal meaning is "from the vagina".
Chowk: Intersection.
Dhol: Punjabi drum.
Dost: Friend.
Farangi: Foreigner.
Fatafat: Quickly.
Haramzadi: Bastard.
Haveli: Mansion.
Inna lillahi wa inna ilaihi raji'un: We surely belong to Allah, and to Him we shall return. Uttered on news of a death.
Inshallah: God willing.
Jamaat: Group.
Janaat al Firdous: Heaven.
Jawan: Soldier. The literal meaning is a young person.
Karahi: Wok. A karahi refers to a meat dish cooked in a wok.
Lassi: Watery yoghurt drink often with added salt.
Madrassa: Religious school.
Maghreb: Two meanings, sunset and also west. Prayers held at sunset are Maghreb prayers.
Makkah: Mecca.
Masha'Allah: God has willed. An expression of thanks.
Maulana: More respectful term of address for a priest. The title for Abdul Zubair.
Mem Sahib: Respectful term for a non-Pakistani woman.
Mubarak Ho: Congratulations.

Mullah: Derogatory term for a Muslim priest.
Oey: Hey.
Patwari: A land record official.
Pulao: Rice with meat, usually mutton. Related to pilaf.
Pulis: Police.
Purdah: Separation between unrelated men and women.
Saeen (Sindhi): Lord.
Sahib: Mister. Term of respect for a person in authority.
Salam: Informal greeting. Shortening of Asalam Aleikum.
Shabash: Well done.
Shaheed: Martyr.
Shaitan: Devil.
Shalwar Kameez or Kurta: A loose traditional dress. Shalwar are baggy pants. Kameez is a long shirt. Kurta is a regional variation.
Sherwani: Collarless jacket.
Shukran (Arabic): Thank you.
Shukria: Thank you.
Wada: Big in Punjabi.
Wa aleikum asalam: Reply to *Asalam A Leikum.* It means: and peace unto you.
Yaar: Friend, or lover depending on context.
Zabardast: Fantastic.